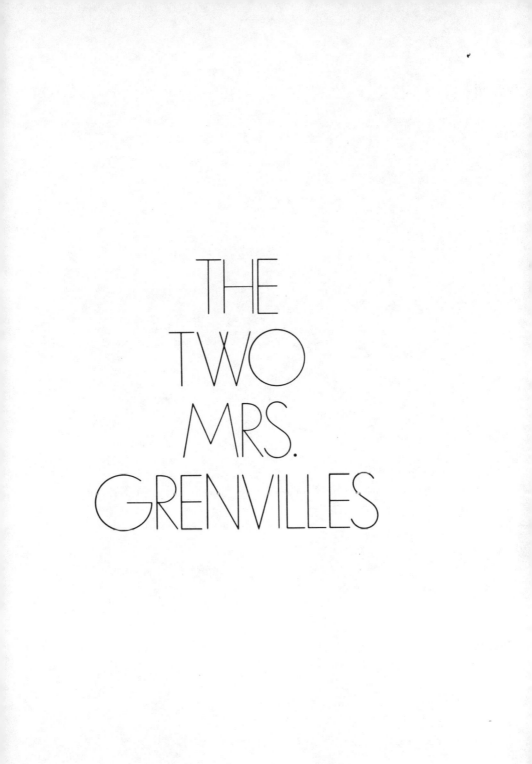

THE
TWO
MRS.
GRENVILLES

ALSO BY DOMINICK DUNNE

The Winners

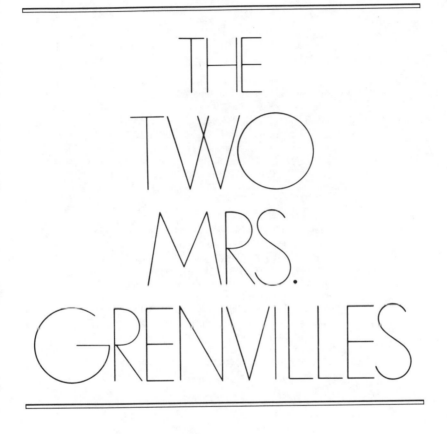

THE TWO MRS. GRENVILLES

A NOVEL BY
DOMINICK DUNNE

Crown Publishers, Inc. New York

Grateful acknowledgment is made for the
following:
ZING: WENT THE STRINGS OF MY HEART
© 1935 (Renewed) Warner Bros. Inc. All Rights
Reserved. Used by permission.
JUST ONE OF THOSE THINGS © 1935
(Renewed) Warner Bros. Inc. All Rights Reserved.
Used by permission.

Published by Crown Publishers, Inc., One Park
Avenue, New York, New York 10016, and
simultaneously in Canada by General Publishing
Company Limited.
CROWN is a trademark of Crown Publishers, Inc.
Manufactured in the United States of America.

Library of Congress Cataloging in Publication Data
Dunne, Dominick.
    The two Mrs. Grenvilles.
    I. Title.
PS3554.U492T8   1985   813'.54   85-445
ISBN 0-517-55713-4
Design by Dana Sloan
10 9 8

For my son
Alexander Dunne

PART
ONE

The room was filled with the heady scent of roses past their prime. Pink petals fell from swollen blossoms in a Chinese bowl onto the polished surface of an ormolu escritoire. Although it was day, rose-shaded lamps were lit, and curtains of the same hue, drawn for the night in voluminous folds, remained closed. The bed had been rested upon, but not slept in, its rose-colored linens still pristine and uncreased. A vermeil clock, unwound too long, had ceased to tick; a radio, left on too long, had lost its tonal focus.

Lying on the floor, face down on the rose border of an Aubusson rug, was a golden-haired woman in a satin-and-lace nightgown. She was dead. More than a day dead. Perhaps even two.

Had she been alive, she would have told you, whether you asked her or not, that the Chinese bowl had once belonged to Magda Lupescu; that the escritoire had once belonged to Marie Antoinette; that the vermeil clock had been given to the Empress Elizabeth of Austria by the mad King Ludwig of Bavaria; that the Aubusson rug was a gift of the Belgian court to the Empress Carlotta of Mexico. That they were ill-fated women was of less consequence to the deceased than the sense of luster she acquired when repeating the history of her possessions.

The dead woman's name was Ann Grenville. Leaning against a wall of her bedroom was the infamous portrait by Salvador Dali that had so deeply offended her on its completion years before. Long gone from sight, surprisingly present now, it stared out from its canvas at the rose-hued tableau, its knife-slash repaired, its prophecy fulfilled. Carnage had it promised. Carnage had it delivered.

HER OBITUARY, when it appeared, was not impressive. If you had not been reading about the defeat of the German Chancellor on page one of Section A of the *New York Times* that continued over on the next-to-last page of Section D, after the business news and stock market quotations, you might have missed it, for that was where it appeared. There was her name, Ann Grenville, with the word "Dead" after it, and then a few paragraphs, all easily missable.

On second thought, of course, the placement of Ann Grenville's obituary was probably exactly where Old Alice Grenville wanted it to be, and if she had called whatever Sulzberger was in charge of the *Times* and requested exactly that remote a placement in the paper for her daughter-in-law's obituary, no one who knew her would have been surprised. It would not have been her first call asking for considerations from the newspaper on behalf of her family. Exceedingly old, in her nineties, Alice Grenville, born one of the Pleydell triplets, was still running things in her family, and one thing she felt, and felt strongly about, was that her family had been far, far too much in the news.

The obituary said Ann Grenville had been found dead in her apartment on Fifth Avenue. It said she was the widow of sportsman William Grenville, Junior, the mother of Diantha Grenville, the daughter-in-law of Alice Grenville, the philanthropist and social figure. It said she had a history of heart ailments. It said she was fifty-seven years old. It said she had been cleared in 1955 of slaying her husband.

She wasn't fifty-seven at all, and hadn't been for three

years, but her lie, if lie it could be called, was closer by far to the truth than the age she had given twenty years earlier, at the peak of her notoriety, when, at forty, she had claimed to be thirty-two.

"MRS. GRENVILLE. Mrs. Ann Grenville," called out a ship's steward, hitting the gong that he was carrying as he walked along the decks and through the public rooms. "Telephone for Mrs. Ann Grenville." Not a head turned at her paged name. Too many years had gone by. Not a soul on the ship remembered what *Life* magazine had called the shooting of the century.

A few years before her death I encountered her, for the first time in many years, aboard a steamship heading to Alaska. Long vanished from the social scene, she was, even on shipboard, a reclusive voyager. Unlike the Ann Grenville of yore, she was no longer the life of the party; rather she had resigned herself to the sidelines, not just of the party, but of life. I was transfixed. Her once beautiful face was ravaged a bit, perhaps by drink, and had acquired the similarity of surgically treated faces of women after middle age. Her slender splendid figure had widened some. Her golden hair semed less lustrous.

And yet there was magic still. Perhaps it was magic for the memory of her, for the weeks of my youth when she had held center stage. Her clothes were expensive and simple. Her perfume filled the air around her. Her jewelry was mostly gold, except for a sapphire-and-diamond ring of a size and cut that looked as if it had been handed down for several generations in the same family. She read. She did needlepoint. She looked for hours at the coastline of Oregon and Washington, smoking cigarettes, inhaling deeply, dropping the butts into the sea. She spoke to no one.

"Not bad news, I hope," I said later, passing her deck chair.

"What's that?" she asked, as if she were being intruded upon.

Of course, I knew who she was, right from the beginning, even though I only said that she looked familiar, nothing more, when the man in the next deck chair, a Mr. Shortell from Tacoma, asked me if I knew anything about her. It is one of my traits that I least care for that I am very often a bundle of pertinent information about people I don't know, especially important people I don't know. But Ann Grenville I did know, although not as a friend. In the years when she was riding high as Mrs. William Grenville, Junior, and her name constantly appeared in Fydor Cassati's column in the *New York Journal American* and her pictures, photographed by Louise Dahl-Wolf and Horst, appeared in all the glossy magazines, our paths sometimes crossed in the dining rooms of New York. She resisted me. In fact, she never trusted me. I felt she thought I could see right through the performance that her life was, in the same way that Salvador Dali had seen right through her when he painted her picture.

"Your telephone call. I hope it wasn't bad news," I said.

She had developed a way of looking at you without connecting with you, the way film stars sometimes do to protect themselves from the curious, as if deciding whether to get into a conversation or not. It took the tragedy to give Ann and Billy Grenville the prominence accorded them in the social history of New York. During that time, the autumn of 1955, all of New York, and much of the country, and world, rocked with horrified impatience at each day's revelations in the Grenville case. What is so enticing as the rich and powerful in a criminal circumstance? Even the stately *New York Times* and the conservative *Herald Tribune* read like lurid scandal sheets. Except for it, Ann and Billy Grenville would have been nothing more than a rich and fashionable couple, both endowed with great good looks, who dazzled for a time in the society of New York.

"It was, rather," she said finally. "Bad news, that is." Her voice was deep and rich and matched the look of her.

"I'm sorry," I said.

"My dog died in New York. That probably doesn't seem a bit serious to you, but I was incredibly devoted to her."

"I'm sorry."

She smiled faintly and went back to her book, indicating that the conversation was at an end. I returned to my deck chair.

Please do not think that I stalked her through the years, gathering information on her. I did not. But I did, even then, before it happened, occasionally make entries about her, and Billy too, in my journal.

From the festivities elsewhere aboard the ship, dance music was heard in our lonely corner of the deck. I noticed that her elegantly shod foot tapped to the beat. In that instant it was still possible to conceive of this middle-aged woman as young and beautiful, a show girl in headdress and feathers slithering across a nightclub stage, the mistress of rich men, the wife of a handsome American aristocrat, the hostess and social figure of an earlier decade, and, alas, the killer.

"Good legs," I said admiringly, omitting the word "still" that occurred to me.

She laughed a low throaty chuckle and raised her leg in the air to look at it, turning her foot one way and then the other. "Not bad," she agreed, admiring her limb, "for the golden years."

"The golden years," I repeated, laughing.

"Fuck the golden years," she said, bursting into laughter, letting me know in her tone that the highly praised charm of the golden years had escaped her completely.

It was how we started to talk. She didn't register surprise that I was there. She didn't mention the last time we had met, in St. Moritz, when I had affixed the nickname Bang-Bang to her, a nickname that stuck as a permanent appellation. She just accepted the situation. She hadn't talked to anyone for the whole trip and was ready to talk, and I hadn't talked to anyone for the whole trip, except Mr. Shortell from Tacoma, and I was ready to listen. We talked about books we were reading, plays we had seen, places we had been. We talked about people on the ship.

"What do you suppose he does, in the yellow T-shirt, pretending he's reading Proust?" she asked.

"How do you know he's pretending?"

"It's the sort of thing I used to do," she replied and laughed. She had beautiful teeth and a lovely mouth. "When I first married my husband, during the war, my mother-in-law tried to groom me into being a Grenville and gave me a list of fifty books to read, but I could never read Proust then, so I pretended to."

"The man in the yellow T-shirt is a Mr. Shortell from Tacoma. Not bad. He finds you fascinating. Would you like to meet him?"

"Oh, no. I tend to avoid new people."

"Why?"

"Everything works out well at first, and then, somehow, they find out my story. 'She's the woman who killed her husband,' someone tells them. And then they look at me differently and wonder about me. Alone is better." Then she changed the subject. "What's at the movies?"

"An oldie."

"Which one?"

"*Le Rouge et le Noir.*"

"Gérard Philipe. I never saw that," she said.

"Neither did I," I replied.

"Let's go."

It is a fact of my life that coincidences happen to me or things with thousand-to-one odds against happening happen. I didn't know, never having seen it before, that there was a scene in *Le Rouge et le Noir* in which a husband enters his wife's bedroom in the middle of the night, and the wife, mistaking him for someone else, shoots him. Imagine, with the devious plan I had up my sleeve, that I should be sitting with Ann Grenville in the ship's theater watching this scene.

Ann, with a hand on each arm of the theater seat, raised

herself to almost standing height and, mesmerized, watched the scene. Then she lowered herself back into her seat when the scene was over. I did not know what to say, and said nothing, continuing to look straight ahead at the screen.

On the way back to our staterooms after the film, neither of us said anything for a bit, but I could not let the moment that had been provided for me pass without speaking.

"Would you ever talk about it, Ann?" I asked.

"Never," she replied.

"It might help if—"

"Never."

"But no one has ever heard your side."

"My husband's death was an accident, but no one believed me except for the grand jury. I know that people refer to me as 'the murderess.' I know that my children suffered."

"Sit here," I said, leading her to a bench on the deck.

"I made a deal with my mother-in-law that I would never discuss it, ever, ever. And I lived by that deal. Several times a year I was trotted out by the family, my sisters-in-law and my mother-in-law, and shown off at their parties. It beatified them in the eyes of New York for being so blessed to the tart who had married their brother and son and then killed him. There are people, I know, who say I was a hooker. I wasn't a hooker. Oh, yes, I took the occasional lizard bag from one of those dress manufacturers I used to go out with before I married Billy Grenville, with the implicit understanding, never stated, that there would be a hundred-dollar bill inside, way back in the forties when a hundred dollars was still a lot of money, but that was part of life in those days. What's so goddam wrong about wanting to do better for yourself in life? Would you want to live on that farm where I was born?"

"Do you want a drink?" I asked.

"Listen, Basil," she said, standing up and walking to the rail. "It's a mistake to try to get friendly with me."

"Oh?"

"I seem to have acquired the capacity to drive everyone

away from me. Even my children." She made the motions of retreat, looking about for her bag and scarf and book. Those things found, she gave me her hand. "Well," she said, "so ends our night."

I didn't want her to go, but I didn't know how to keep her, other than not to release her hand. "You're a different person, Ann, from the Ann Grenville who—"

"—who necked with a Kraut in the bar of the Palace Hotel in St. Moritz a year after I killed my husband?" she asked, finishing my sentence for me in a way I had not intended to finish it. In the darkness I blushed and let go of her hand.

"You can't spend as much time alone as I have in the last few years and not arrive at some conclusions about yourself," she said, turning to leave, terminating our intimacy.

IT IS A FACT that even today, years after it happened, there are people you meet at New York dinner parties who can tell you, in vivid detail, the whole story of that October night in 1955, or at least the whole story as far as they know it, because no one knew the whole story except the two principal players, and one of those was shot dead and the other went to her grave without ever, not once, talking about it. Except to me.

Yes, I know that people say I killed Ann Grenville. Oh, not literally kill, as in "Bang Bang you're dead," but that I am responsible for the twenty-two Seconals and the pint and a half of vodka that she gulped them down with after reading a chapter from my novel that appeared in the magazine *Monsieur*. But I feel absolutely no responsibility whatsoever. I didn't call her Ann Grenville in my story. I called her Ann Hapgood. If she chose to think I was writing about her, that was her problem.

In the years when I was as famed in the media for my

intimate, if platonic, friendships with some of the great ladies
of New York, like Jeanne Twombley and Petal Wilson, neither of whom speak to me now, as I was for my exquisite little
books, they told me things about Ann and Billy and the
Grenville family that I would have had no way of knowing.
Jeanne Twombley was the only one of the whole North Shore
crowd who made any attempt to see Ann after it happened.
She feels now that I betrayed her, but what did those ladies
think when they whispered into my ear all the secrets of their
world? After all, they knew I was a writer. You see, I have
this ability to get people to talk to me. I don't even have to
maneuver, very much, to make it happen. I listen beautifully.
I laugh appreciatively. I never register shock or dismay at
shocking or dismaying revelations, for that will invariably
inhibit the teller of the tale.

On that damn ship, where I wish now I'd never seen her
again, my own life was in a precarious state. It could even be
said that I feared for it. Not that my life was in danger. It
wasn't. At least not from criminal elements or terminal illness. What I feared was that the totality of it amounted to
naught. Oh, the blazing moment here, the blazing moment
there, of course, but too many wrong turns and different tacks
along the way for it to be seriously considered by those concerned with such matters, and serious consideration was what
I had always aspired to.

It was whispered more and more about me that drink and
drugs and debauchery were interfering with my work, that I
was throwing away my talent in drawing rooms playing the
court jester, and in discotheques. The people who said these
things let it be known that I was unable to complete what I
had immodestly referred to as my masterwork when I appeared
on television talk shows. Sometimes I called it a mosaic.
Other times a collage. Or even a pastiche. In fiction, of
course, depicting the thousand facets of my life that, when
placed together, would present the whole of myself—mind,
body, heart, and soul.

I was stung by their criticism. Trying to pick up the pieces of my wrecked life, I took to the sea to rethink my unfinished work. Ideas did not come. And then I saw her, Ann Grenville. A name from the past trying to pick up the pieces of *her* wrecked life. The idea began to form. So much had been written about her all those years ago. Was now not the time to tell her side of the story, to set the record straight? She, so much maligned, had never spoken in her own defense. We were there, on the same ship, and conversation would have to take place if a situation was manipulated. Yes, yes, yes, I admit that what I did was wrong, but I was helpless to resist the opportunity. I knew, I simply knew, that with time she would tell me, Basil Plant, what she had never told a living soul. I am the kind of person to whom people confess their secrets. It has always been so with me.

I, who can remember the commas in people's sentences, began to think back on Ann Grenville's story as I had heard it and read about it.

WHEN YOU LOOK at old photographs of Ann Grenville, at the yearling sales in Saratoga, for instance, sitting between the Ali Khan, with whom she was said to be having an affair, and Mrs. Whitney, of racing fame, or on safari in India, wearing huntress array from London, or at the de Cuevas ball in Biarritz, jeweled and haute-coutured, what you see is a woman at one with her world. Her world, however, was her husband's world. When she married Billy Grenville, during the war, she forsook any prior existence of her own and stepped, with sure foot, into her husband's exquisite existence.

Look for yourself at Mr. Malcolm Forbes's list of the richest people in America, and you will see how the wealth in our country has changed hands over the last thirty years. There isn't a Vanderbilt on the list. Even Babette Van Degan is not, nor are any of the people who appear in this tale. While those still alive continue to linger in the Social Register, except for poor Esme Bland in the loony bin, and Neddie Pavenstedt, who left Petal, and the bank, to run off with a television actor whom he later adopted, they are no longer considered rich by the rich today. But at the time of which I write, the Grenvilles were considered to be among the richest families in the land.

William Grenville, Junior, was used to many things, not the least of which was adoration. From his father. From his mother. And from the four sisters who preceded him into this world. It was never a spoken thing, but had he arrived earlier in the lineup of children, it is safe to say that there would have been fewer daughters. In a family like the Grenvilles, sons were the thing.

When he was born, he received a note from President Wilson welcoming him to the world, and, framed, it hung over all the beds of his life. The Grenvilles lived in a Stanford White French Renaissance mansion just off Fifth Avenue, across the street from old Mrs. Vanderbilt, next door to the Stuyvesant family home. Weekends were spent on a five-hundred-acre estate in Brookville, Long Island, summers in a cottage in Newport, following the annual sojourn to Europe.

It was a splendid life, and he emerged from it splendidly. His nanny, Templeton, and his tutor, Simon Fleet, and his dancing teacher, Mr. Dodsworth, were all enchanted with his sweetness, his shyness, and his exceedingly good manners. It was through Templeton, who had been nanny to his four sisters before him, that he acquired the precise manner of speaking that would distinguish his voice, for the rest of his life, from the voices of nearly everyone he encountered, except the few who were brought up in the exact manner that he was.

In time his father began to feel that he was too much adored and that the constant companionship of four sisters who could not get enough of holding him and passing him about among themselves might lead to a softness of character.

He was sent to the same early school that his father had attended before him, expensive and spartan, in preparation for the great life and responsibilities that were to be passed on to him in time.

Indeed, there was a melancholy streak. He was fascinated reading about the two English princes who were beheaded in the Tower of London. It was a moment of history that he read over and over, and was always moved, often to tears. On an early trip to England, he was taken to the Tower on a guided tour, and a chill ran through him when he saw the room where they were held captive. He told his sister Cordelia, closest to him in age and spirit, that he felt he would die young.

In later years his most vivid memory of the New York house, where the family spent most of its time, was of the vast chandelier in the main hall. He was always to pass beneath it with trepidation and repeat the story to newcomers about what had happened on the eve of Rosamond's coming-out ball. Rosamond was his eldest sister, already fourteen when he was born, a distant and glamorous figure of his childhood who married an English lord at nineteen, a year after her ball, and moved away to London. The chandelier, quite inexplicably, crashed to the floor, killing the man who was cleaning it. Funeral expenses and generous recompense were provided rapidly and quietly, and it was agreed, among the household, that it be unmentioned so as not to cast a pall on the ball. It was his first experience of death; it was also his first experience of closing ranks. Much was to be expected of him. There was the bank, the Cambridge Bank of New York, founded by his grandfather, of which his father was president. There were the directorships of half a dozen big corporations. There were the Grenville racing stables, and the Grenville stud farm, twenty-five hundred acres in Kentucky, a vastly successful commercial enterprise, having produced three Kentucky Derby winners. It was for all these things, and more, that the young boy was being groomed.

At some point doubt began to stir within him. There was a quality beneath his elegant shyness that eluded happiness, a consciousness of his own limitations. When he thought about such things, which was not often, the fear was deep that he would have been a failure in the world if he were not an inheritor of such magnitude.

His father sensed his secret fears and dealt with them contemptuously so as to shame weakness out of him. At one point his father said about him, in front of him, and his sisters, and his mother, that he should have been a girl. It was not a thing his father meant. It was said, like a lot of things he said, in careless dismissal without thought of the psychic consequences. The wound to the young boy was devastating, made worse when his mother, whom he worshiped, failed to swoop him up, comfort him, and defend his gender. Nor did his sisters. None of them dared to contradict the head of the family.

"I don't like my father," said Junior one day.

"It's not so. It's not so," cried Alice. "You don't mean that."

"But I do," persisted the boy.

"No, you don't," insisted his mother.

He was never sure what he felt, because he was taught by the person he loved most, his mother, that what he felt wasn't so, that what she told him he felt or didn't feel was so. Her interpretation of his feelings conformed to the proprieties of their way of life.

Only Cordelia, the fourth daughter, the one closest in age to Junior, understood. And Bratsie; he understood.

IT IS OF NO significance to this story but of great significance to his character that Jellico Bleeker, or Bratsie, as he was known to one and all, except his mother, the partygiver Edith

Bleeker, who loathed the nickname, that he had only four fingers on his right hand. He lost his index finger during a Fourth of July accident, when he was ten years old, holding on too long to a lit cherry bomb that he had been expressly forbidden to play with. On another occasion, a year or so later, he took one of the family sailboats from the house on Long Island, without supervision, or any real knowledge of sailing, and set sail for he knew not where. He was not missed until after darkness, and it was twelve hours before the Coast Guard, having nearly given up hope, spotted the small craft bobbing about aimlessly in Long Island Sound with the nearly frozen Bratsie safe and totally unconcerned about the drama he had caused. His smiling photographs in all the newspapers made him somewhat of a hero to his contemporaries, among them Junior Grenville, whose best friend he was.

The incident further confirmed Edith Bleeker's strong feeling that her untamed colt needed to be tamed, and she was going to do it. Life thereafter became for him a game of getting even with her. He accompanied his mother to a relation's society wedding and escorted her down the aisle wearing, unbeknownst to her, a yarmulke atop his head. He swung from a chandelier at Mr. Dodsworth's dancing class and was asked to leave and not return. He listed his mother's Pekinese, Rose, in the New York Social Register as Miss Rose Bleeker. He could imitate any limp or speech impediment with unerring accuracy, and did. He memorized the ritual of confession, although he was not a Catholic, and confessed elaborate sins to a shocked priest. He was the first of the boys in the group to smoke cigarettes, to sneak drinks, to masturbate, to get kicked out of school, to have sex with a prostitute, and to wreck the family car.

Bratsie Bleeker's accounts of his escapades kept the less adventuresome Junior Grenville rolling on the floor in uncontrolled laughter. Junior Grenville adored his friend. They were chauffeured back and forth between the Grenville house and the Bleeker house in the city and the Grenville estate in

Brookville and the Bleeker estate in Glen Cove in the country.

In contrast to the tall and handsome Junior Grenville, Bratsie Bleeker was small and compact, fair-haired and always tanned. Five generations of Long Island Bleekers gave him a natural look of haughtiness and superiority, which he interrupted repeatedly with the beguiling and mischievous smile that was his own contribution to his looks. He contradicted his upper-class accent with lower-class words, and he had a way of snapping Junior Grenville out of his melancholy moods as no one else could do.

"You didn't have to explain that the fart on the elevator wasn't yours," said Bratsie one day after school. "No one said it was."

"I felt guilty," said Junior.

"Sometimes I think you don't know who you are," replied Bratsie.

"I don't," said Junior.

EXCEPT FOR BRATSIE, with whom he was at ease, the boys at Buckley found Junior Grenville aloof and uncommunicative and often joshed him for the elegant ways his family's life-style was manifested through him. It embarrassed Junior that he was driven the thirteen blocks to and from school each day in the family's Packard limousine, but it was a thing his father insisted upon. Junior would have preferred to be left on the corner of Seventy-third Street and Park Avenue and to walk to the entrance of the school, because he dreaded the razzing of the other boys, many of whom were allowed to walk, or even take the bus. He appealed to his mother in heartfelt tones to decrease the grandeur of his arrivals and departures, and the compromise that was reached was that his nanny, Templeton, not ride in the car with him, and that the chauffeur, Gibbs, not open the door for him so that he could scoot in and out of the limousine by himself.

On a Friday afternoon, when he was being picked up to go to the country for the weekend, he bade farewell to Bratsie Bleeker and hopped into the Packard. A man wearing a wide-brimmed hat that partially concealed his face appeared out of nowhere in the crowd of boys mingling on the street and followed Junior into the backseat of the car. For a moment the boy thought the man was a friend of the chauffeur's, and the chauffeur thought the man was a friend of the boy's. It was a well-planned maneuver.

The man pulled a gun and took hold of the terrified boy and directed the equally terrified Gibbs, whose name he knew, to proceed across Seventy-third Street to First Avenue and turn uptown, where, at a given point, there would be a rendezvous with the car of an accomplice. So expertly was it carried off that no one standing outside the school realized what had happened, even Bratsie, who had been standing there with Junior, and who would be jealous for years that the kidnapping had not happened to him.

At the corner of Seventy-fifth Street and First Avenue, Gibbs, old and nervous, ran a red light while reaching for the already-prepared ransom note that the kidnapper handed him, missing by inches a Gristede's truck crossing First Avenue. Amid shrieking brakes and angry horns, a police car took off in hot pursuit, red lights flashing and siren screaming, and flagged the limousine to the side of the avenue.

Maintaining his calm, the kidnapper stepped out of the limousine as unobtrusively as he had entered it, hailed a passing cab, stepped into it, and was gone, never to be seen again, before the police officer arrived at the chauffeur's door to deal with the privileged occupant who felt, the officer assumed, above the law in traffic matters. The only evidence of the six-minute drama, other than the weeping boy and frightened chauffeur, was the dropped ransom note.

"I hated it most when he touched me," said Junior.

"Touched you? How did he touch you?" asked his father.

"He held me by grabbing my blazer in the back."

"How did you feel?"

"I wanted to kill him."

A call was made by Alice Grenville to Mrs. Sulzberger, whose family owned the *New York Times,* asking that the newsworthy story not be used, and it was not. Bars were put on the windows of all the bedrooms in the Grenville house. For the rest of the school year, Junior was driven to school in the Chevrolet that was otherwise used for family shopping and transporting the servants to the country on weekends. The following fall he was sent off to Groton.

As a precautionary measure, so as not to waste time in a future emergency, packets of money, thousands and thousands of dollars in hundred-dollar bills, were placed in manila envelopes beneath the leather jewel cases in a wall safe behind a Constable painting of Salisbury Cathedral in Alice Grenville's bedroom. The money would sit there, untouched, for twenty-three years.

JUNIOR GRADUATED from Groton in 1938. All the family attended. His sisters thought he was the handsomest boy in his class, and he was. He would have graduated from Groton even if his father had not donated the new dormitory called Grenville House, but it did assure the certainty, as well as entrance to Harvard. Knowing that so much was expected of him, sometimes he froze in examinations, even when he knew the answers. His masters, which was what his teachers were called, and even Endicott Peabody, the headmaster, praised the young man's beautiful manners. He won no prizes, either academic or athletic, but he sang in the chapel choir, which pleased his mother, and acquired a passion for guns, which pleased his father. He said that in time he would like to shoot big game, tigers in India, and the exoticism of the desire appealed to the entire family's perception of son, brother, and heir to the name Grenville.

Europe was on the verge of war. A cross-country trip in Bratsie Bleeker's new car, a Cadillac convertible, planned with meticulous care by the two friends, was deemed inappropriate by William Grenville for his son. It was decided instead that Junior would spend the summer in New York with his father, training at the Cambridge Bank, and in Saratoga, attending the yearling sales. He complied, as he always complied. He confessed to Bratsie and to Cordelia that he was not seriously interested in banking, but he applied himself diligently to the work that was expected of him. Unlike his sister Grace, who could quote the pedigrees of a thousand horses off the top of her head and who knew the stallion register backward, he was not much interested in the business of racing either.

"Every time I look at my father, all that I ever see in his eyes is his disappointment with me," said Junior to Bratsie.

"That's the problem with being an only son," answered Bratsie. "Your life was mapped out for you the minute you were born. Buckley. Groton. Harvard. The bank. The horses. Marriage to a friend of one of your sisters in St. James' Church with ten ushers in morning coats. An apartment on the Upper East Side. A house on the North Shore. And then another little Grenville for you to send to the same schools you went to, and it starts all over again."

"You too," said Junior.

"Oh, no, not me," said Bratsie. "They'll never get me."

"Me either," said Junior, but he didn't mean it.

"Balls, my friend," retorted Bratsie. "In a very few years every mother in New York with a marriageable daughter will be out to trap you."

What William Grenville wanted to do was to avoid for his son the inevitable pitfalls of a young man pampered from birth who would one day inherit a great fortune. For his daughters he would say, "Learn golf and learn bridge, or you'll have a very lonely old age," and leave the rest of their upbringing to Alice, but for his son his counsel was more exacting.

"Out there in this world," he told Junior, as Gibbs drove them uptown from Wall Street, "no one is going to feel sorry for your problems. They will say about you, no matter what befalls you, 'I wish I had his problems.' They will think that because you are rich the kind of problems you have are of little consequence."

"Do you remember Brenda Frazier?"

It was what Ann Grenville asked me, when finally we spoke, aboard the ship on the way to Alaska. Do I remember Brenda Frazier indeed! Who could forget Brenda Frazier? Poor sad Brenda. She had been, Ann told me, Billy Grenville's first girl friend, but I already knew that. At Edith Bleeker's party, on the night of the shooting, when Jeanne Twombley brought me along at the last minute when Alfred couldn't go, I was seated next to Brenda Frazier at dinner, and Billy Grenville was on her other side, so I heard about it straight from the horse's mouth.

In 1938 there probably wasn't a more famous woman in America than Brenda Frazier, and she was only seventeen years old and had accomplished absolutely nothing except being the most beautiful debutante of her time. Her picture appeared on the cover of *Life* magazine and people read more about her than any movie star in Hollywood. Her every step was chronicled in the society columns, and even the news pages, of every paper in the city.

In those days Billy Grenville was still called Junior. It was Ann who changed his name to Billy when she said she didn't want to be married to a man called Junior. Well, Junior met

Brenda going through the receiving line at her coming-out party in the old Ritz-Carlton Hotel on Madison Avenue, which has long since been demolished. She was a beauty, and he was a knockout, and when he asked her to dance, people stepped back to watch, and all the photographers took their picture, and Maury Paul, the society columnist then called Cholly Knickerbocker, wrote that Brenda Frazier and Junior Grenville were the most beautiful young couple in New York.

Needless to say, Alice Grenville was not pleased. She had those four daughters, but Junior was the apple of her eye, and she had big marital plans for him when that time came. She felt that Brenda Frazier got much too much publicity and not nearly enough parental supervision. Alice Grenville was of the old school who believed that a lady's name appeared in the papers only three times—when she was born, when she married, and when she died—and Brenda Frazier, at least in New York, was a household word.

One day Brenda went to tea at that big gray pile of stone the Grenvilles used to live in, in the Eighties just off Fifth Avenue. It was Junior who asked his mother to invite her. All the sisters came too, just to stare at her. The sisters all had had their coming-out parties at home, in the family ballroom, with no press invited, and no outsiders on the list. They were all prepared to dislike her, but they couldn't. She was too nice, and they found her absolutely charming. Even Alice, who called her Miss Frazier throughout, liked her and could see the possibilities of her.

They saw each other for a while, but Junior was starting Harvard and not ready to think about anything serious. Along came a football player called Shipwreck Kelly and swept Brenda off her feet and into Catholic marriage in the Lady Chapel of St. Patrick's cathedral. Alice breathed a sigh of relief.

The thing about Brenda was, she and Billy stayed friends right up until the last day of his life. She was probably the last person he spoke to that night at Edith Bleeker's before he got into the fight with Ann.

"DO YOU REMEMBER Kay Kay Somerset?"

Ann Grenville asked me that too on the ship. She was Billy's second crush. Her life didn't turn out well, but in those days, she was pretty hot stuff, before all those marriages and the drink and the drugs took their toll. I once read in the columns about Kay Kay Somerset that she played tennis in white gloves so as not to coarsen her lovely hands, and she never played until after five when the rays of the sun ceased to burn. That was also about the time she was getting up.

Kay Kay was a very different cup of tea from Brenda and the Grenville sisters. She was very very rich; even rich people called her rich. The money came from spark plugs on her mother's side and a hydraulic drill used in the production of oil on her father's. Her kind of out-of-town money, no matter how much of it there was, never seemed the same to people like the Grenvilles as their kind of New York money. Remember, too, in those days, people were still concerned about family, as in bloodlines.

Kay Kay went to the very best schools, and came out at a party even more lavish than the lavish party of Brenda Frazier, under a tent lined with ice-blue satin at an estate in Southampton, marred only by Bratsie Bleeker's swinging from a chandelier while drinking champagne out of a bottle.

Kay Kay was not asked to join the Junior Assembly, as all the Grenville sisters were, and the flaw of it heightened her glamour in the eyes of Junior Grenville, on whom she had cast her eyes. "It would be a wonderful first marriage for you," said her mother, the spark-plug heiress, a remark unheard by Alice Grenville but nonetheless sensed by her.

William Grenville was disinclined to interfere in Junior's

affairs of the heart, being secretly pleased that his early fears of other inclinations were unfounded. However, when Junior announced to his astonished family that he would leave the day after Christmas for a cruise in Caribbean waters on a hundred-and-eighty-foot yacht made available to Kay Kay by her indulgent father, it was felt that the time was at hand to break off the incipient romance.

His father forbade him to go. Junior, accommodating always, did not accommodate. Suppressed wrath surfaced instead; a litany of remembered disappointments poured out. Shocked by the unexpected outburst, William Grenville remained implacable. Bratsie Bleeker, in a similar outburst with his mother, ran off and joined the Royal Canadian Air Force. Junior Grenville threatened to do the same. On the day following Christmas, he left for Palm Beach, where he joined Kay Kay Somerset and her party on the yacht called *Kay Kay*. He did not feel triumphant in his victory.

Shortly thereafter, certainly unrelatedly, William Grenville suffered an aneurism of the aorta, a bursting of the main blood vessel to the heart. The Packard, with Gibbs at the wheel, awaited him at the front of the house to drive him downtown and to the business day. When he had not appeared at nine minutes after eight, Gibbs went to the front door and informed Cahill, the butler. He was found by Cahill in his bathroom, to which he had repaired, as was his habit, with the *Times* and the *Wall Street Journal*, after his breakfast.

Alice Grenville, who would achieve personal fulfillment in widowhood, telephoned the home of the Somersets in Palm Beach and asked Arthur Somerset to contact the yacht, wherever it was, and have Junior call his home in New York. Within several hours a call came from Junior in Barbados. "He is dying," said his mother. "You must come right away, to speak to him." She understood the never-reconciled chasm between son and father.

But it was not to happen. He stood in the hospital room of Bleeker Pavilion at New York Hospital, with his weeping mother and weeping sisters, and watched the expiration of a man who did not want to expire. When he felt nothing but relief that his days of disappointing were over, he simulated grief, for appearance's sake, for grief was the order of the day.

The casket was open and set up in the reception room off the main hall. Over the mantelpiece was a large portrait of three young ladies in long white dresses poised in elegant comfort among the cushions of an immense green sofa. They were the Pleydell triplets, painted by John Singer Sargent nearly forty years before. Alice Pleydell was on the right. The legend was that William Grenville had fallen in love with the face in the picture, pursued her, and won her.

Alice, and Junior, and the four sisters stood in front of the mantelpiece and received the hundreds of mourners who passed through their house: the banking world, the racing world, the membership of his nine clubs, the part of New York society in which they moved, and the friends of Alice, and Rosamond, and Felicity, and Grace, and Cordelia, and Junior. The smell of flowers was oppressive. Outside it was raining.

And then Bratsie Bleeker arrived, unexpectedly, in his Royal Canadian Air Force uniform, waiting his turn in line, behind Archie Suydem, the family doctor, ahead of Edith Bleeker, his own mother. "Let's get out of here," he said to Junior after making his amenities to the family. "Where?" asked Junior. "Wherever," said Bratsie.

Outside was Bratsie's Cadillac convertible, its bright-yellow color glaringly inappropriate for the circumstance, between limousines with umbrella-carrying chauffeurs helping elderly people in and out of the huge Grenville house. They entered Central Park at Seventy-second Street and sped across in silence. Junior was lost in thought, believing, even in death, that the disapproving eyes of his father were upon him.

At a red light on Central Park West, three toughs eyeing the young swells raised their thumbs in the hitchhiking position. "We're only kids and we have a Cadillac," screamed

Bratsie at them, gunning the car and speeding off, breaking the gloom within. As always, Junior was Bratsie's best audience and screamed with shocked laughter.

"Let me ask you something, Junior," said Bratsie.

"What's that?" asked Junior.

"The truth," stipulated Bratsie.

"The truth," agreed Junior.

"Have you ever been laid?"

"Bratsie!"

"The truth."

"No."

"That's what I thought."

"What's this all about?"

"I am about to introduce you to the establishment of Miss Winifred Plegg, also known as Bootsie, on West End Avenue and Ninety-first Street."

"Tonight?"

"It's the perfect time."

THE GRENVILLES were not the kind of people who cried at funerals. To remain stoic in adversity was, like honesty, a trait learned early. At William Grenville's funeral at St. James' Church and the burial in the family plot at Woodlawn Cemetery, with Dr. Kinsolving in attendance, William Grenville, Junior, stood, stalwart, by his mother's side, his long elegant hands holding her arm, guiding her through the rituals of the long day with nothing in his demeanor to divulge the debauchery of the night before at the establishment of Miss Winifred Plegg on West End Avenue.

Junior Grenville was much admired, and it was whispered from pew to pew that he would be, after Harvard and the war, a worthy successor to the positions and responsibilities of his father. When, at the graveside, his eyes fell on the Caribbean-tanned Kay Kay Somerset, he felt a deep disinclination toward her, as if his single act of disobedience, over her, might have caused the burst blood vessel that ended his father's life.

William Grenville left his large estate in perfect order, so there would be no lessening of grandeur in scale of living for any of his descendants during their lifetimes. His daughters, already married rich, became independently rich. His widow, Alice, received all the houses outright to do with as she wanted, with the fervent hope expressed that the vast structure off Fifth Avenue, which he had built, would continue to be lived in by her for her lifetime and then, dynastically, be passed on to Junior so that he could raise his own family, when that time came, in the house in which he had been raised. Alice, who understood money, got the main bulk of the fortune, with it, in turn, to be passed on to Junior when she died. Junior himself received ten million dollars, a vast sum in that preinflationary decade, making him one of the wealthiest young men in the country.

Life resumed, after the mourning period, in the Grenville houses in New York and Long Island and Newport. Alice's children would have been surprised to know that their mother felt released by her widowhood. Slowly the strictures imposed on all their lives by William Grenville abated, and, despite the impending war, laughter was heard again in the huge houses where they lived. Alice, freed from the constant entertaining of bankers and horse breeders that had made up her husband's life, enjoyed more and more the companionship of her children and her friends, and parties and concerts filled the houses.

It was inevitable that when the war actually came Bratsie Bleeker would be the first to enlist, transferring from the Royal Canadian Air Force, and the first to distinguish himself in combat, where his natural bent for recklessness was often mistaken for bravery.

Junior Grenville could not wait to follow suit, but he promised his mother that he would finish Harvard first. He did, spending most weekends in New York enjoying the renewed adoration of his four sisters. Immediately upon graduation he enlisted in the Navy and entered Officers Training School, from which he graduated as an ensign.

On February 19, 1943, Ann Grenville, who was then called Ann Arden, and before that had been called Urse Mertens, walked into the life of Ensign William Grenville, Junior.

"Glamorous" was more the word than "beautiful" that applied to her. She had a bright glow about her, and there was an interplay between her lovely blue eyes and glossy red mouth that captured you with its seductiveness. From the age of twelve she knew, even before she really knew, that she could wrap men around her little finger, an expression her mother was fond of using.

She was at this time a show girl by night and a radio actress by day. Although she was voted the most beautiful girl in radio, it was as a show girl that she was magnificent. Elaborately costumed in sequins and feathers and giant headdress, she held her arms aloft and beautifully presented her beautiful body as she glided across the stage of a Broadway musical behind the star, Miss Ethel Merman. Her most ardent admirer would not have called her talented, as either a singer or a dancer, but she possessed something that called attention to herself—there was amusement in her eyes and a private smile on her lips—and men followed her every movement across the stage, ignoring the other girls in the line. And of all the girls in the line, she was the most sought-after, and her nights, after the show, were spent with the kind of men who took chorus girls to nightclubs, and whose names occasionally appeared in Broadway columns. There was always the hope of being discovered by a talent scout from Hollywood, and the possibility of movie stardom was a dream that she cherished.

Sometimes it terrified her that her life was advancing, had advanced, in fact, and she had not achieved her potential. Young still, she had already begun to lie about her age to make herself younger. It was when she was looking into a mirror, applying powder and colors to her face, that she confronted herself. She was not a star; she was not going to be a star. Adele Jurgins, with whom she had danced in the line at Fefe's Monte Carlo, had gone on to Hollywood and was starring in films at Republic, and Babette Lesniak, with whom she had danced in the line at the Copacabana, well, everyone knew what had happened to Babette, or, at least, everyone who read the tabloids knew what wonders had come to Babette. Perhaps, she thought, this is not what I am supposed to be doing. Perhaps this is not it, after all.

Overdrawn at the bank again, rent looming, fighting off feelings of despair, she dressed and went to El Morocco. You never know what's going to happen, she thought to herself. Tonight I might meet the man who is going to change my life.

She was with the Argentinian playboy Arturo de Castro She thought he was the best dancer in New York, and she told her best friend, Babette Van Degan, that the Latin beat was in his blood. She loved to dance and knew that people looked at her when she and Arturo took to the floor, but she realized, before he told her, that he was about to kiss her off. She had read in Cholly Knickerbocker's column that he was seeing a Standard Oil heiress, and she knew that the affair would be winding down and that her days were numbered. She fought down the rage of rejection that was within her, determined that she would not make a scene at El Morocco. She concentrated instead on a white fox jacket he had seen her admire in the window of Saks and hoped he would at least give her that when the end came.

She loved El Morocco, with its white palm trees and blue-

and-white zebra-striped banquettes, and could never stop looking around her at the other tables and the other people on the dance floor.

She had a habit of singing into the ear of the man she was dancing with in her deep throaty voice:

> "Dear, when you smiled at me,
>   I heard a melody
>   that haunted me from the start.
> Something inside of me
>   started a symphony.
> Zing went the strings of my heart!"

At that instant zing went the strings of her heart.

"Who's that?" asked Ann.

"Who's who?" asked Arturo back.

She had spotted him over Arturo's shoulder when he entered. She didn't know who he was, but she knew right away that he was more than just a handsome naval officer on leave. Johnny Perona himself was on the door that night, and Johnny Perona greeted Junior Grenville with the deference he usually reserved for Alfred Vanderbilt and Gary Cooper and the Rockefeller brothers.

"That ensign saying hello to Brenda Frazier," answered Ann, refraining from saying the one with the beautiful teeth and the beautiful smile.

"Where's Brenda? I don't see Brenda," answered Arturo.

She had an instinct for quality. It went beyond looks and clothes; she could spot it even in nakedness. When she squeezed past the ensign on her way to the ladies' room and said, "Excuse me," in a teasing but somehow intimate tone, he noticed her for the first time. She was wearing a black satin dress cut low. Her looks brought pleasure to his eyes, and he feasted on them for the moment of passage. The thing that he noticed about her, that he would always notice about her, even when he was long used to her, was her breasts. He was alone, having come from one of his mother's parties, having slipped out during Madam Novotna's musicale. He was standing in the same place when she came back from the ladies' room.

"We have to stop meeting like this," she said to him as she squeezed past him the second time. She laughed at her own joke, and he joined in the laughter, and the contact was made.

"I'm Junior Grenville," he said.

"I'm Ann Arden," she replied.

"Hello, Ann."

"Hi, Junior."

There was a moment of stillness amid the racket of the packed nightclub as they looked at each other.

"Junior, are you going to join us?" called out Brenda Frazier.

"In a minute, Brenda," he called back.

Ann's heart was beating very fast. It astonished her that anyone would not leap at the chance to sit at the table of the beautiful Brenda Frazier.

"I should be getting back," said Ann.

Later, when she was dancing with Arturo again, not singing into his ear this time, Ensign Grenville cut in on the dance floor, tapping Arturo heavily on the shoulder. Arturo turned around to the tapper.

"May I?" asked Junior, holding out his hands.

"See here, Lieutenant," said Arturo, annoyed.

"Ensign," corrected Junior.

"This sort of thing is just not done here at El Morocco. Save it for the proms back at the base." He turned back to Ann to resume his fox-trot.

"Oh," said Ann, gleeful at the possibility of a scene. "Get into a fight over me, why don't you? Let's have pictures in all the papers! Finally I'll get a screen test."

Arturo, furious, walked off the dance floor. "I'll be at the table," he said, not pleasantly, over his shoulder.

Ann and Junior stood on the dance floor looking at each other for a moment, and smiled.

"It was just one of those things," she started to sing. She held her arms out and he stepped in to dance with her.

> "Just one of those fabulous things,
> A trip to the moon on gossamer wings,
> Just one of those things."

He told her he liked her voice more than Libby Holman's, and Libby Holman had been his favorite singer. She moved in closer to him.

"I suppose it would be impossible for you to extricate yourself from whoever that is you're with?" he stated as a question.

"And do what?" she asked.

"Leave here with me," he answered.

She liked his precise manner of speaking. It was a voice peculiar to a tiny portion of the Upper East Side of New York City and the North Shore of Long Island.

"No," she replied. "That wouldn't be impossible at all. Meet me at the front door."

HER BEDROOM was in morning disarray. Her fastidiousness did not begin until later in the day. Stockings and underwear were strewn where they fell, and chairs were smothered with clothes and towels. From the bathroom came the sound of the shower stopping; it awakened her, although she was not used to awakening until noon.

Through mostly closed eyes she watched him dress. She liked the look of him in undershorts and shirtsleeves— shaved, bathed, combed—tying his tie in front of her mirror, completely concentrated. She wished she hadn't sat on his face on the first date, but she always got carried away with the rich boys, the old-money boys, not the new-rich ones you met around the stage door, but the ones who had that look that comes from generations of breeding, and that speaking voice that identified them all to each other. On top of that, Ensign Grenville was without doubt the handsomest boy she had ever seen. She longed to know who he was.

All of a sudden Arturo de Castro, who she had thought was so divine for so long, looked like a greaseball to her, even if he was, as Babette Van Degan had told her, from one of the oldest families in Argentina. She felt, suddenly, patriotic that the good old U.S.A. had produced a specimen of aristocracy that was right up there with the best that England had to offer with all their dukes and earls, and, of course, their king, or, rather, their ex-king. Her mother, lately departed, always called him the catch of catches, and the lady who landed him, Mrs. Simpson, now the Duchess of Windsor, was the women she, and her mother, admired more than any woman alive.

She supposed she shouldn't pray for such things, but she prayed that Ensign Grenville wouldn't think that she sat on the face of every man she went out with, especially the first time. It was just that he was so beautiful, and young, and well-built, but also so totally inexperienced that she had inadvertently assumed the role of teacher, and her passions, which were abundant, had simply run away with her. Even at the moment of climax, he had retained his wonderful accent, and that, more than anything else, brought her to new heights of desire.

She stared at his profile as he finished his tie and went looking for his shoes. She surprised herself as she heard herself say, in her first words of the day, "I like to see a man's shoes in my closet."

She saw his shirttail stand out in excitement at what she had said. He blushed; she liked his shyness. Watching him, she lit a Camel. She lipsticked the tip, inhaled deeply, and held it, and when she exhaled allowed some of the smoke to escape up her nose.

"Come over here," she said, "and let me get a good look at that in the daylight." She remembered from last night that her rough talk thrilled him. He walked over to her, and she reached into the opening of his shorts. "It's really lovely," she said. "I could be awfully happy with this for a while. How long's your leave?"

She didn't wait for an answer. Her mind was on other things. As he lunged for her hungrily, she said, "No. No, stand back. This one's on me." She pulled his shorts down his legs and knelt on the floor in front of him. She didn't know if she should let him see how good at it she really was.

Looking down, he was mesmerized watching her, still holding her Camel. He thought he had never seen such a beautiful woman. He knew he had never seen such beautiful breasts.

"You're much too quick, you know," she said afterward. "Speed is *not* of the essence. I'm going to enjoy teaching you. How long did you say your leave was?"

ENSIGN GRENVILLE could not get enough of Ann Arden. Everything about her fascinated him. The ashtrays in her apartment were from the Stork Club, and her refrigerator was filled with splits of champagne, wilted gardenias, and doggie bags from El Morocco. V-letters from captains and lieutenants in far-off places vanished from her desk top after his first night with her, and 8-by-10 glossy pictures taken in nightclubs with a variety of men disappeared from the walls of her bathroom. She had records of all the show tunes and knew every lyric to every song.

Each noon he met her in the lobby of the Plaza Hotel, or the St. Regis Hotel, or the old Ritz-Carlton Hotel, and they ordered martinis, and ate lobster salad, and stared into each other's eyes. Each night, to the consternation of his mother and sisters, who wanted to show him off so splendidly uniformed, he sat, transfixed, in the Music Box Theater and watched Ann descend a silver stairway and sidle across the stage, as if there were not another person on it. He was consumed with curiosity about her radio career and listened avidly to each daily episode of "Marge Minturn, Girl Intern," in which she played Marge's best friend, thrilling him with the sound of her deep actressy voice. She talked of Chet Marx, her agent, and her hopes of a screen test, and the possibility of a meeting with Humphrey Bogart.

He did not withhold information about himself, but he did not thrust his suitability at her either. Of the two of them, he found her to be the stellar attraction; everything about her was new to him. Once aware of the possibilities of him, beyond his good looks and beautiful manners, she asked the pertinent questions impertinently, and bits and pieces of his story came out.

"Where did you go to school?" she asked him.

"Just the usual places," he answered, and when she looked at him, he went on, "Buckley, Groton, and Harvard."

"Oh," she answered over her rush of pleasure.

"Not exactly expanded horizons, is that what you mean?" he asked, fearing she thought it was too conventional.

"No, that wasn't what I meant at all," she replied.

She knew he was someone very swell, but as with all very swell people, there were no hints forthcoming. Finding out would be up to her. It was after he told her about the near kidnapping that she decided to pay a visit to her old friend Babette Van Degan, and check out, as Babette would say, the lay of the land. She took a Madison Avenue bus from Murray Hill, where she lived in a tiny penthouse, to Sixty-seventh Street, and walked over to the Park Avenue apartment where Babette lived. Babette was everything that Ann wanted to be.

She had started out life as Barbara, then Baby, then Babette Lesniak, somewhere in the middle of a large Lithuanian family in Willimantic, Connecticut, where her father was a milkman. She left home early and made for New York, where she somehow ended up as a show girl at the Copacabana nightclub. She had no theatrical ambitions whatsoever and no real aim; she simply waited for life to happen to her and rolled with whatever did, all with life-of-the-party good humor. Her luck was astonishing. Dickie Van Degan, the stupidest of the very rich Van Degan brothers, swooped her up in a whirlwind romance and eloped with her to Elkton, Maryland, a marriage that captivated readers of the tabloid press for its Cinderella theme. With no guile on her part, simply forgetfulness, she became instantly pregnant. By the time the marriage ended a year and a half after it began, to the intense relief of all the Van Degans, she was the possessor of not only the first Van Degan heir but the largest divorce settlement in the history of New York. Since her great good fortune, she became a meticulous reader of all things financial and read the stock market quotations with the same enthusiasm that she had once read the gossip columns. In time her divorce settlement would double, treble, and, perhaps, quadruple under her uncanny ministrations.

Babette claimed that she knew Ann before anyone else in New York knew Ann, and she was very nearly correct. She was one of the very few in Ann's life who overlapped from one phase to another, and she was probably the only one in New York who ever knew Ann's mother. Unlike Ann, who never looked back, or remembered back, Babette was a great one for reminiscence. "There was a guy around New York in those days called Chet Marx," she once said. "He called me up one day and said, 'Babette, I need a black dress and a pair of size six shoes,' and I said, 'Chet, what the hell do you need with a black dress and a pair of size six shoes? You're not going nelly on me, are you?' And Chet says, 'You of all people ought to know me better than that, Babette.' We had a good laugh over that one. He told me there was a new girl in town, and he got her an audition for the Copa, and she didn't have a thing to wear. So I took the dress and shoes over to Chet's place, where she was staying, and that's how I met Ann."

Babette's Park Avenue apartment was big and sloppy; the few pieces of Van Degan furniture were lost amid the more florid examples of her own imperfect taste, and the rooms were littered with her son's toys. Her poodle, Phydeaux, had untidy habits, and her maids sometimes didn't wear uniforms, but there was about the place a pleasant and relaxed atmosphere.

When Ann entered Babette's bedroom, she found her friend sitting up in bed, breakfast tray in front of her, grumbling over the *Wall Street Journal.* "Ann," she said, looking up, "what brings you out at this hour of the morning?"

"Are those sheets yellow satin?" asked Ann.

"Yes," said Babette, caressing the satin against her. "I bet you don't know who said yellow satin can console one for all the miseries of life." She buttered her corn muffin, using her index finger as a knife and then licking the finger.

"Some queen," asked Ann, not interested in literary talk, impatient to get on with the business at hand.

"It was Oscar Wilde," said Babette grandly.

"That's what I said, some queen," replied Ann. Their conversations were bawdy and their language blue, and they always laughed at each other's vulgarities. "Now listen, Babette. I'm here on important business. I need some information on somebody I've met."

"What do you want to know?"

"If he's the real turtle soup, or merely the mock."

"Look him up in the Social Register."

"Do you have one?"

"My husband got kicked out of the Social Register when he married me and was promptly reinstated when he divorced me, so it's not a book I happen to have lying around."

"How, then?"

"Who is it?"

"His name is Junior Grenville."

"William Grenville?"

"Junior."

"Oh, my God! Millions."

"What?"

"You heard me. Millions."

"Do you know him?"

"No, but the Grenvilles are right up there with the Van Degans. The old boy was quite dashing. I saw him at the track once. He cut quite a figure in racing circles, flower-in-the-buttonhole, that kind of look. Courtly manners, but only with his own crowd. Terrible snob otherwise. Mrs. Grenville has the same table at the Colony every day for lunch. What's he like, this Junior? Is he good-looking?"

"Very."

"Are you in love?" asked Babette.

"I'm in physical attraction," replied Ann.

"What is it you notice first about a man?" asked Babette. It was the sort of conversation she liked best, and she settled in for a long chat with her friend. Babette was several years senior to Ann, but they were not women who discussed their age, even with each other; they simply allowed the older woman/younger woman relationship to occur.

"His hands," replied Ann.

"Hands!" exclaimed Babette. "What an odd thing to notice first."

"I can't *bear* small hands on a man."

"Why even think about them?" asked Babette.

"You know what they say, don't you?"

"What do they say?"

"Small hands, small dick."

"I never heard that," said Babette, screaming with laughter.

"And by the same token, large hands, large, uh, need I go on?"

"Dickie Van Degan had small hands," said Babette, captivated by the conversation. "As a matter of fact, Dickie Van Degan had a small dick too, now that I think about it. What kind of hands does Junior Grenville have?"

"Large, darling," replied Ann, stretching luxuriously.

"Have you, uh—"

"Yes."

"Is he a good lover, then?"

"Not yet."

"Those swell families, you know. Prep-school sex. Slam, bam, thank you, ma'am."

"When I kissed him the first time, he held his lips together, and I could feel his teeth pressing against my mouth."

"Not one of the great feelings."

"No. But you know, he's just waiting to be taught."

"Knowing you, you probably sat on his face on the first date, and he probably thought he'd died and gone to heaven." They screamed with laughter again. "Am I right?"

"Something like that," conceded Ann.

Babette told her to look up the Grenvilles in the Social Register at the Rhinelander Florist on the corner of Madison Avenue and Seventy-second Street. She saw that Junior's mother's name was Alice Pleydell Grenville, and that he had four sisters named Rosamond, and Felicity, and Grace, and Cordelia. There were other abbreviated things that she could not understand, and the addresses and telephone numbers of the house in New York, and the house on Long Island, and the summer residence in Newport. Her heart began to beat faster. She felt that the florist was watching her, which he was not, and ordered flowers, a half-dozen roses, to be sent to Mrs. Babette Van Degan.

She walked fourteen blocks up Madison Avenue until she came to the street where the address was that she had memorized and turned left toward Fifth Avenue until she came abreast of number 9. It was a châteaulike gray stone mansion. In front of it was parked a Packard limousine. From inside the house a butler opened an iron-grilled door, and a tall woman past middle age, beautifully attired, emerged from it and entered the rear of the limousine, helped and then covered with a blanket by a chauffeur, to whom she spoke warmly.

Standing opposite, Ann watched. She did not know if she

felt elated or depressed. She retraced her steps back to Madison Avenue deep in thought. When people asked her when it was that she fell in love with Junior Grenville, she did not tell them that it was then.

He called her later in the afternoon to make arrangements for meeting that night after her show. Already she had given him keys to her apartment, and she asked him to meet her there, as he had to dine with his family.

"And Junior?" she said in closing.

"Yes?"

"When you open the door to let me in?"

"Yes?"

"Be naked."

If, indeed, a man could swoon, she knew, over the telephone, that William Grenville, Junior, had just swooned.

He was astonished by the magnitude of her passion for him. "Hold it!" she had ordered him the night before as she felt his excitement building to a too early conclusion. "Not yet, for God sake! We're just getting started." It thrilled him when she barked out her sexual orders to him.

He slipped away from his mother's dinner when Horowitz began to play and let himself into her tiny penthouse in Murray Hill. It worried him that there was not a doorman or an elevator man in the building where she lived. Since his near kidnapping ten years before, he was always conscious of personal safety for himself and his friends. Throughout dinner at his mother's, he had talked to plain and pretty Esme Bland about the importance of having a gun for her own protection. He did not notice her stricken look when he told her he was going to slip out.

He lit Ann's rooms by candlelight. He moved the two dozen long-stemmed roses to a more pictorial spot. He arranged champagne and ice and glasses. When he heard the gentle and excited taps of her gloved hand on the doorway of her own apartment, he undid the belt of his silk foulard dressing gown and let it slide off his shoulders and drop to the floor. He walked naked toward the door in his loose casual stride, elongating in front as he moved, in anticipation. He opened the door.

There she stood, looking more ravishing than ever: that smile, that look in her eye. Her eyes traveled down his splendid body.

"Oh, my darling," she said, entering the room, closing the door behind her, reaching out for him. It excited Billy that she liked to have her throat kissed before her mouth. She, in turn, found areas of his body to explore that he had not known were part of the sexual experience. It was not, she explained to him, with the patience of a teacher to her favorite pupil, an act simply to be gotten through. It was an experience to be savored and prolonged. There would be plenty of time for champagne and conversation later.

JUNIOR WAS bewildered by the contents of her dressing table; it could have been a makeup counter at Saks. He was further bewildered by the enormous amount of time she spent there, and he watched her, fascinated by her expertise and concentration.

"I want you to meet my friend Jellico Bleeker," he said.

"How could anyone name a child Jellico Bleeker?" asked Ann, continuing to do her face.

"Mrs. Jellico Bleeker could," answered Junior.

"His mother?"

"His mother."

"Don't any of you guys have names like Joe or Jim?" Junior laughed.

"I hope you don't call him Jelly," said Ann.

"No, he hates that. We call him Bratsie."

"And he likes that?"

Junior laughed again. "It suits him," he answered. "You'll see."

"When will I see?"

"I'm bringing him to the show tonight," answered Junior.

There was a silence. "To look me over, I suppose," said Ann. "Check me out. Case me."

Junior Grenville was not in the habit of having to clarify his reasons. "He's my best friend," he said. "He always has been. I want you to know him and I want him to know you. That's all. No big deal."

"Okay," she said, turning from her dressing table, her beautiful face perfectly attended to, and smiling at him in the chair where he sat watching her.

Miss Ethel Merman, performing rambunctiously, did not exist for the two young officers that night. Their eyes were riveted on the near-nude show girl gliding magnificently behind the star. Ensign Grenville looked proprietary. Captain Bleeker looked dazzled. Their applause was fervent, exceeding by far the extent of the show girl's accomplishment.

Amid a great deal of laughter the trio had supper in the Cub Room of the Stork Club, and Sherman Billingsley greeted the two young officers affectionately and sent them champagne. Ann, thrilled to be there, gazed at the two old friends, fascinated by their lifelong friendship, and listened to stories of Bratsie's antics at bygone deb parties. Their faces shared the look of easy living and freedom from financial stress; it was a look she liked. Her bare shoulders moved to the Latin beat from the orchestra in the main room.

"Junior, I want to dance with this beautiful lady," said Bratsie, rising to do an elaborate mime of the rumba.

"He may be little, Ann, but he's some dancer," said Junior about his friend.

"Did you know the only part of your body that shouldn't move when you do the rumba is your bowels?" asked Bratsie.

"Bratsie!" shouted Junior, screaming with laughter. "You'll have to excuse him, Ann. He's just back from the front."

Ann was delirious when, dancing with Bratsie and following his dips, she caught a lucky balloon and was rewarded with a giant bottle of perfume. It seemed to her that life had never been so lovely, and she wanted to prolong the night with these young men for whom favors happened for no other reason than that they were who they were.

"Bratsie's a bona fide war hero," explained Junior, building him up. "He's downed all kinds of planes. Tell Ann, Brats. Explain your decorations to her. He's the bravest man I know."

The merry young man, drunk now, looked sad suddenly. "It doesn't have a damn thing to do with bravery," he said. "I just don't care, Junior. I never did."

They sat silent as more wine was poured.

"I care, Bratsie," said Junior finally. "I need you in my life."

"You'll be a hero pretty soon yourself," said Bratsie. "It's swell, but it doesn't change what's wrong. We still have our father's banks to come back to after the war and those proper marriages. My mother would die happy if I married Junior's sister and Junior's mother would die happy if he married one of the English princesses."

Junior, embarrassed, blushed. "That's only a family joke, Bratsie."

"A thick fog of gloom is surrounding this table all of a sudden," said Ann. "I think we should dance again or go to El Morocco and sit at John Perona's Round Table or think up something festive to do."

"Right you are," cried Bratsie. "Let's hit the road. You lucked out with this lady, Junior."

"It means more to me than anything that you two like each other," said Junior.

They got into Bratsie's Cadillac convertible and began touring the nightclubs of the city. Bratsie, buoyant again, regaled them with tales of mad adventures and drunken behavior.

"You ought to write a book, Bratsie," said Ann.

"What would I call it?" asked Bratsie.

"*Remembrance of Things Pissed*," she volunteered.

"Ah, a rare literary allusion from Miss Arden," said Junior, delighted with her, and the three screamed with laughter, and the festivities continued, finally winding down at an all-night diner on Second Avenue with the implicit but unspoken understanding between them that Ann had passed the test of Bratsie's approval with flying colors.

"My mother would like you to come to tea," said Junior abruptly, catching Ann unaware.

"How does your mother know about me?" asked Ann.

"I've told her. She knows I've been seeing someone every night of my leave."

Bratsie watched the interchange.

"Did your mother ask to meet me or did you ask her to?"

"Somewhere in between, I suppose," answered Junior. He smiled at her.

"This I'd like to see," said Bratsie.

"You come too, Brats," said Junior.

"I'll be gone the day after tomorrow," said Bratsie.

The waitress, tired, pounced on them with orders of scrambled eggs on thick chipped plates and noisily distributed them. Pouring coffee, she slopped it over into the saucers, an irritation for Ann, for whom it had associations. She did not allow herself to remember that she had once, briefly, been a waitress in a coffee shop herself. Now she concentrated on applying paper napkins to the soaked saucers as Bratsie, who took advantage of every situation, loudly slurped his coffee directly from the saucer, to Junior's delight. Ann's heart was beating rapidly. She did not understand what her feelings were exactly, somewhere between triumph and fear, and she did not wish either emotion to register on her face.

"Will you come with me?" she asked finally, her chore completed, bringing the conversation back to where it had been before the interruption.

"I'll be there already. It's where I live."

"Will there be others?"

"Perhaps a sister or two. They usually drop in at that time to see Mère."

"Is that what you call your mother? Mère?"

"We always have, yes."

The French word seemed to make him more remote from her, another thing to accentuate their differences. "What will I wear?" she asked.

"I think this white fox jacket you have on and an orchid corsage," said Bratsie, holding up the fur that Arturo de Castro had given her. It was not lost on Ann that it was her wrongness that made her so eminently suitable in Bratsie's eyes as a companion for his rigid friend.

"And high-heeled shoes and socks," he went on.

Junior put his hand over Ann's and leaned over and kissed her gently. "You'll be fine," he said, and she felt reassured by his tone and his protectiveness, and the tension in her body abated. He enjoyed holding her hand and calming her in moments of nervousness. Protected always himself, he felt strong in his role of protector. She understood his kiss and his role. By now, she loved him, but what she understood was that he loved her even more.

AFTER SENDING little Dickie and his nanny off to Central Park for the afternoon, Babette Van Degan lay on her sofa in a relaxed manner hearing the latest developments in her friend's story. On Ann's finger was Babette's nearly flawless emerald-cut pink diamond, a Van Degan treasure, over which Ann never did not exclaim and which she often tried on.

"I want all the colors someday," said Ann matter-of-factly, handing back the ring. "Red and green and blue."

"And the pastels, too," added Babette. "Some of the pastels are nice."

"No, no, I don't care about the pastels," said Ann. "Just the ems and the saffs and the rubes, thank you very much."

"Has Junior given you anything yet?" asked Babette.

"No," answered Ann. "Except roses and champagne and

lunch at the Plaza and supper at the Stork Club, first cabin all the way, that sort of thing, but no gifts, no."

"Even that tango dancer gave you a white fox jacket," said Babette.

"But Arturo's so ugly. He's the only man I ever met that I'd rather go down on than kiss." They laughed. "Wait until you see Junior. He's beautiful."

"They're all tight, though, those rich kids," said Babette. "Mama probably controls the purse strings."

"Mère," corrected Ann.

"What?"

"They call her Mère, not Mama."

"Jesus." They laughed again. Babette helped herself to another chocolate from the huge box on her faux-malachite coffee table.

"You're going to get fat, Babette, if you keep eating that candy all the time," said Ann.

"No, I've got some great diet pills," she answered, shrugging off the suggestion of fat. "Have I told you about Dr. Skinner?"

"I don't know what to wear. I was thinking of that green suit I got at Bergdorf's, and white gloves, and a hat. I thought I might buy a new hat at Hattie Carnegie, and I thought maybe you'd lend me your lizard bag."

"Sure thing."

"I feel like Kitty Foyle," said Ann nervously.

"Kitty Foyle was a typist, honey. You're a show girl," answered Babette.

"Which is better? Or worse?"

"Neither one is what Alice Grenville has in mind for Junior. Let's put it that way," said Babette, reaching for another chocolate.

♣   ♣   ♣

As she took a five-dollar bill from the lizard bag she had borrowed from Babette Van Degan, Ann looked up at the Grenville house from the interior of the cab. A six-storied limestone château with balconies, it appeared larger than she remembered from her previous expedition.

"That's some mansion," said the driver, leaning over to look up himself. "That must be one of the Vanderbilts' houses, I think."

"Grenville," Ann corrected him.

"Who?"

"It's the William Grenville house," she repeated, while making the transaction for change and tip.

"Probably related to the Vanderbilts," insisted the driver. "I wonder what it's like to live in a pile like that."

She wondered if he was talking to her as if he assumed that she didn't know any more about it than he did, and she terminated the momentary cordiality. For reassurance she opened her compact and appraised herself favorably. She got out of the taxi, breathed deeply the February air, and walked across the street to the iron-grated front doors that opened into the entranceway. Up a half-dozen stone stairs were the glossy black double doors that opened into the front hall Almost immediately after her ring, the door was opened by a butler. They eyed each other. He was almost elderly, and there was a quiet elegance about the dark uniform he wore, less formal, she noticed, than those of stage or screen butlers.

"I'm expected," she said, acting expected. She thought Junior would be there to greet her. "I'm Miss Arden."

"Good afternoon, Miss Arden," the butler said, widening the opening as she passed into the hallway. Where was he? She saw, while experiencing his absence, that the floor was black-and-white marble in a geometric pattern, that the hall-way was circular, that a stairway of vast proportions ascended upward flight after flight. Above her was an enormous chandelier with hundreds of prisms tinkling from the momentary blast of cold air. Her heart beat with excitement for being where she was and concurrently beat with fear at the possibility of abandonment. Unexpectedly self-conscious, she felt suddenly stiff and clumsy.

"What?" she replied, aware of having been asked something.

"Your coat," repeated the butler.

"Yes," she said, allowing herself to be helped in its removal. At least she was not being turned away. Where was he? She needed, she knew, a mirror to look into to check the extent of her flush. She would know in an instant if it reflected high color or panic.

"I wanted to be here when you arrived!" came his blessed voice from above. She looked up. Dressed in his uniform, he ran down the stairway several steps at a time to greet her. "You look"—he paused before completing his sentence, taking her in—"ravishing." She liked the word at once.

He could tell by the look on her face that she was nervous. Except for Bratsie and a few others like Bratsie, it was a look he had seen on the face of everyone he had ever brought into this vast house for the first time.

"Did you meet Cahill?" he asked, turning to include the butler in the conversation. "This is Miss Arden, Cahill."

"Miss Arden," acknowledged Cahill.

"Cahill knows all the family secrets," said Junior charmingly. "At least all mine."

"I've known Mister William since he was this high," said Cahill, holding his hand to a very low level over the marble squares. Ann smiled.

"Let me put your coat in here," said Junior, leading Ann to a sitting room off the hall that looked out on the street.

"Is this the living room?" she asked, looking around.

"They call it the reception room," said Junior. "The living room's upstairs. That's where Mère is."

"What is this room used for?"

"It's where people wait before they go upstairs, or sometimes Mère meets people here who come on business."

"I see."

"It's where my father's casket was. I suppose it will be where mine is as well."

"What a curious thing to say."

"I don't know what made me say it."

She looked up at the portrait of the three young ladies in long white dresses.

"That's by Sargent," he said.

"My word," she answered. "Is one of them your mother?"

"On the right."

"And the other two are her sisters?"

"My mother was a triplet. Did I tell you that?"

"No."

Suddenly she felt unprepared for the event at hand. "Junior," she said in an uncertain voice.

"Yes?"

"I've never been in a mansion like this before."

"Listen."

"What?"

"Just say 'house.' Don't say 'mansion.' It's a silly thing, I know, but it's just not a word we use."

"You don't say 'mansion'? It's one of my favorite words."

"Not in this mansion," he answered, and they both laughed. He pressed up against her, kissing her on the cheek. "I hope you don't mind my correcting you."

"Not at all," replied Ann quickly. "I don't want to make mistakes. You'll find I'm a quick learn. You won't ever have to tell me twice."

He smiled. "I like you better and better."

They moved back out into the hall, and she looked around her again.

"How many servants does it take to run a place like this?" she asked, lowering her voice.

"Fourteen, I think it is," answered Junior.

"Imagine."

"Used to be twenty-one when my father was still alive."

"Cutting corners, huh?"

"The war."

"Oh, yes, the war."

She knew she was delaying going up.

"Where do they all sleep?" she asked.

"The top floor. There's seven or ten rooms up there. The chauffeur, Gibbs, sleeps in his own apartment over where the cars are kept a few blocks away in the old carriage house."

"My." They looked at each other.

"We'd better go up," he said. "The elevator's over here." He started leading the way.

"Oh, no, no," she replied. "I want to walk up those stairs."

"This house had the first private elevator in New York," he said, as if that way up were preferable.

"I still want to walk up those stairs," she said, heading for them. As he always did when passing beneath it, Junior glanced up at the great chandelier, remembering.

"What a beautiful chandelier," said Ann, looking up at it as she ascended the stairs, a hand on the banister. She could imagine Marie Antoinette having danced beneath it.

"It fell once when I was a little boy, and a man was killed," said Junior. "Did I tell you that?"

"No," she answered.

On the landing they stood outside the glossy white panels of the drawing-room doors and looked at each other.

"What a lot you have to tell me," she said, and he heard a whole future in her sentence.

"You're swell," he said, turning to open the door. As he did so, voices from behind were heard in relaxed conversation.

"Guess who's getting married?"

"Who?"

"Cheever Chadwick. It's in the *Times.*"

"To whom?"

"A Miss Green. Rhoda Green. From Brooklyn."

"Oh, dear."

"His poor mother."

"Jewish, do you suppose?"

"Only on her mother's and father's sides."

"Felicity! Really!"

"When I was growing up, we all knew each other."

Ann was always to remember that room as she first saw it in the fading winter sunlight with her own senses heightened by the impression she hoped to make and the conversation that came to her in snatches from the group seated far distant in front of a fire. The pale-green drawing room was dominated by white-and-gilt furniture, great gold consoles, and a chinoiserie mirror. The upholstery picked up the colors of the Aubusson rug. Everywhere was a profusion of books, paintings, and flowers massed in Meissen bowls. She tried not to let it show that she was speechless.

Alice Grenville was an exceedingly observant woman. What she saw, in the moments it took for Junior and the beautiful woman who accompanied him to enter the room and walk the considerable distance to the fireplace where she was seated with her daughters and where the tea table had been set, was that her son was madly in love for the first time in his life. She knew that the other girls who had come before this woman were no more than crushes. She sensed instantly that her son and this woman were involved in an already consummated love affair. She felt a pang of distress that she had too quickly dismissed the lovely Brenda Frazier as a publicity-mad adventuress. This, coming toward her, was the adventuress.

Alice set aside her needlework on a bench overflowing with magazines and rose from her chair to extend her hand to Ann, peering at her through the dark glasses she always wore as if she recognized a person with whom she was meant to interact in life. Elegantly, but not modishly, dressed in plain black silk, with pearls and a small diamond brooch, her reddish-brown hair simply arranged, Alice looked just as she had looked for a number of years and would continue to look for a number of years more.

"Mère, this is Ann Arden," said Junior proudly. He looked

absurdly handsome to his mother in his smartly cut naval uniform, his eyes barely leaving the face of the woman, as if he could not get enough of looking at her.

"I am so pleased you could come, Miss Arden," said Alice. Her smile was warm. Her handshake was firm. "We are all alone, you see. Just family. We have asked no one else," she continued, as if Ann might be expecting a cocktail party. She introduced her daughters: Rosamond, Felicity, Grace, and Cordelia. Felicity, still reading the *Times*, gave Ann her hand without looking at her. Ann seated herself carefully so that her skirt would fall gracefully about her. She pulled at the fingers of her gloves, removing them.

Alice asked if people wanted India tea or China and went about the business of pouring, with assistance from Cordelia, whom the sisters called Cookie. She said there were cucumber sandwiches, and also watercress. She said she had been to the new production of *La Bohème* at the Metropolitan Opera the night before and that Jarmila Novotna was glorious. She said she had lunched across the street at Grace Vanderbilt's and a general had told her the invasion would be in April. She said she adored the new musical *Oklahoma,* and had Ann seen it? She said she was in the midst of a new novel by John P. Marquand and was enthralled. She said she never missed Edward R. Murrow's broadcasts from London, no matter what. She said her English grandchildren were coming to the country for the weekend.

If Ann thought she would be quizzed about herself, she was wrong. Not a single personal question was asked. Alice Grenville was extremely friendly, as was Cordelia, but the conversation was of the general sort.

"I'm off, Mère," said Felicity, putting down her cup and gathering up her things. "I have a million things to do still. I'm going to the Soldiers and Sailors Ball tonight, and I have to get my hair done. Goodbye, dear Mère. Kiss kiss. Goodbye, Miss Eden."

"Arden," corrected Junior.

"*Arden*. Excuse me. Walk out with me, Junior." When they got to the door of the room, she whispered to him, "I liked your blonde."

"Her name is Ann."

"Marvelous figure." She was off.

"Would you like another cup of tea, Miss Arden?" asked Alice. "This cake, by the way, is the cook's specialty."

"No, thank you," replied Ann, handing her empty cup to Junior to replace on the tea table.

"Perhaps a sherry, or a drink even?"

"No, thank you, but I would like to use your ladies' room," said Ann.

Cordelia and Junior both leaped to their feet to show her in which direction to go.

"I'll take Miss Arden up to my room," said Alice. "Stay here and talk to your sister. You never see enough of her."

As THEY ASCENDED the stairs, Ann looked up at the topmost floor, where twelve male heads were painted, friezelike, into the wall just below the ceiling, looking down on the house.

"One, two, three, four . . ." she started to count.

"There're twelve," said Alice.

"The twelve apostles?" asked Ann.

"The twelve Caesars," replied Alice. "My husband was a student of Roman history when he was a young man, and he had them designed into the plans of the house when he built it in 1918. I've become quite fond of them over the years."

"This is a very beautiful house, Mrs. Grenville."

"It's not beautiful really. It's just big."

"It could be a palace."

"One day I'm sure it will be an embassy, or a school, but I like it and I'm going to stay here until the end of my life.

Junior was born in this house, and one day I would love to see him take it over."

The two women looked at each other. Ann wondered if the remark was meant to exclude the possibility of her in their lives. She had smiled sweetly in the face of Felicity's rudeness, and she would continue to smile sweetly, no matter what.

"This is my room," said Alice when they reached the third landing. "Those are guest rooms over there, and all the children's rooms are on the next flight up. Junior still has the same room he always had, except he has his own sitting room as well, and the other rooms that used to belong to the girls are always filled with Junior's friends. I expect you've met Bratsie."

"Yes, I have. How lovely this room is," Ann said, walking to the bed with its great pale-green canopy cascading down from the ceiling. "Green again."

"What?"

"You like green, I said."

"Yes, I do. You notice things, don't you?"

"Is that wrong?"

"No, no, it's not wrong. I was a triplet. Did you know that?"

"Junior told me."

"We were identical. No one could tell us apart, sometimes not even our parents, so we wore different color ribbons always. Amelia wore red, and Antoinette blue, and I wore green, and it stayed my favorite color. The bathroom's over there."

Ann wondered why she had been brought up here rather than sent downstairs to the bathroom off the reception room. In the lavender-scented dressing room she leaned to look at the dozens of framed family photographs: childhood pictures on the decks of ocean liners and foreign beaches, the sisters in coming-out dresses and wedding gowns, Junior on a football team, Junior an usher in a wedding, Junior in a nightclub picture with Brenda Frazier. She realized how little she knew about his life, or his family. Apart from the others was a photograph of Junior's father taken at a racetrack, a forbidding figure, but dashing: a cigar in his mouth, held arrogantly; a carnation in his buttonhole; a hard glint in his eyes behind glasses; an expression of how-dare-you-take-my-picture on his face. She felt instinctively that they had all feared him in the family; she would rather have had him to contend with than the mother and the four sisters. Men she understood.

She made up her mouth with scarlet lipstick, combed her hair, appraised herself favorably. She had, she felt, behaved demurely. Around here were the personal effects of Alice Grenville—her swansdown powder puff, her Floris soap, her gold-backed brushes and mirrors. She noticed her clothes had been laid out for the evening ahead: a black evening dress on a cushioned hanger, shoes, stockings, purse, gloves, and an ermine coat. She wondered what kind of party or ball Alice was going to. She ran her hands in a backward motion down the pelts of the ermine coat and longed to try it on. She thrilled at the kind of arranged and prepared life it was that this woman led.

In the bedroom Alice sat back on her chaise. Behind her was a large marquetry table covered with expensive photographs of elegant people in silver frames. A photograph of Queen Mary was signed simply "Mary," with the letter R following.

"Tell me about yourself, Miss Arden," she said in her distinctive manner of speaking.

Alice Grenville was a woman to be reckoned with, and Ann recognized her instantly for the adversary she was going to be. She decided that truth, or at least proximity to truth, in her own background story was the route to take.

"Is that Queen Mary?" asked Ann, pointing to the photograph while sorting out her tale in her mind.

"Yes," answered Alice simply, not turning to look at the picture, understanding the diversionary tactic, waiting for an answer to her question.

"I was born in Kansas," began Ann.

"Ah, yes, Kansas," said Alice. "Mr. Grenville and I were there some years ago, for a wedding. Lottie Holmes of Kansas City married my husband's second cousin, Eustice Coffin. Do you know the Holmeses? They live in that area, what do you call it, just outside Kansas City, like Greenwich, or Grosse Point, what do you call that part?"

"We were from Pittsburg, Kansas, in the southwest corner of the state, about a hundred and twenty miles from Kansas City," said Ann rapidly, almost all as one word. All her life she had hated the name of the town she was from; always she had to explain she was not from the Pittsburgh in Pennsylvania but the Pittsburg in Kansas that no one had ever heard of, and inevitably a joke was made.

"What do your people do?" asked Alice.

"I'm an orphan, Mrs. Grenville," she said. She felt a momentary pang of guilt that she was glad her mother was no longer alive so that she would not have to explain her to this tall and formidable woman. Early the previous spring her mother had died, and she had taken her back to the place where she was from and about which she never spoke, buried her in the Mertens plot, contacted no one, and returned to New York—contacted no one, that is, except her father's cousin, who owned the pharmacy, and that had been by accident.

"You're not staying on?" he had asked.

"No, no, I'm up for a part in Hollywood," she had answered, dazzling him. She hadn't told him that she was no longer called Urse, or Mertens, or that this was the last time she would ever be there.

"Sad," said Alice Grenville.

"Sad?"

"Being an orphan." She rose. The interview was over. "I'm tired, Miss Arden. I think I shall rest before this evening. Will you send whichever of my daughters are left up? I've so enjoyed meeting you. If you're dining with Junior, tell him not to stay out late. We're leaving for the country early to-morrow. His nephews are coming, and I have a large party on Saturday who particularly want to see him before he leaves."

Ann felt dismissed, as if her visit were a onetime thing with no follow-up to be expected. It was a feeling she remembered from an earlier time. Rarely did she think back—her life seemed always to begin at the period in which she was living —but an old rejection consumed her as, dispirited, she de-scended the stairs of the house that one day Alice Grenville hoped her son would take over. She fought down feelings of rage at having been asked to give an account of herself, and having inadequately accounted.

Below, the sisters' verdict, after the departure of their brother and his blonde, was unanimous, but not favorable.

"The cheapest woman I ever saw."

"Reeks of scent."

"Eye shadow in the afternoon, my dear."

"Those blood-red nails."

"Poor Mère."

"You go up, Cordelia. You're the favorite."

Above, Alice Grenville lay back on the chaise longue by her fireplace. The point of the afternoon had been to accom-modate a sailor's crush, but she felt a sense of unease about the power of the woman who had walked into her home. As a mother, she had seen to it that her children were exposed only to the eligible from the world in which her family played a dominant role. Her daughters, well married into the kind of families of high social standing that she and her late husband approved of, used to tease their mother that no one would be good enough for Junior but one or the other of the English princesses. She had watched every moment of the meeting while she poured tea and carried on the middle-of-the-road conversation that had ensued. She saw that Junior was solic- itous of including Ann in the conversation and listened avidly to the few remarks she had made, as if they were more clever than they were. "It's this damn war," she said to herself. If it weren't for the war, he wouldn't have met a girl like that.

Cordelia entered the room. She handed her mother the needlework that she had discarded below. She picked up a magazine and turned the pages.

"Have they gone?"

"Yes. To the theater. She's an actress. Did you know that?"

"No."

"Well?" asked Cordelia finally.

"The look on my face is disappointment, in case you need to have it translated," said her mother.

"All of a sudden Brenda Frazier's looking awfully good," said Cordelia.

"I wish you hadn't felt it necessary to say that, but, yes, I would welcome Brenda to my bosom at this moment," said Alice.

"But she has become Mrs. Kelly," said Cordelia.

"Alas."

"Did you think Miss Arden was beautiful?"

"Yes, but too conspicuous," replied Alice. "She is a con- spicuous character."

"I thought that was a good-looking bag."

"I hate lizard."

"Actually, so do I. Are you interested in the consensus of the sisters?"

"Tell me."

"Rosamond says gold digger. Grace says trash. You saw Felicity's performance—"

"I wasn't proud of Felicity."

"Junior said Felicity was a bitch and why hadn't he ever noticed it before."

"And you, Cordelia? What did you think?"

"I say, 'Poor Junior.' On top of which he wants me to take her to lunch. He's mad about her."

"Besotted."

"Do you suppose they're having an affair?" asked Cordelia.

"Absolutely," said Alice. "That's her secret weapon."

"The thing is, Mère, I've never seen Junior so happy."

"If only your father were alive. He would put the fear of God into him. He loathed stage people."

"It would be absurd for him to even consider marrying anyone so far beneath him."

"If you want to *make* him marry the girl, tell him that."

"Of course, you're right."

"She conceals her past. She gave me vague answers."

They sat together in silence. Cordelia switched on a rose-shaded lamp. On the table were Ann's gloves.

"Look, Mère, she's left her gloves."

"I saw them."

"Shouldn't we have the chauffeur deliver them to her doorman? That way she won't have to come back."

"Women like her don't have doormen," answered Alice Grenville. Her meaning was clear to her daughter. "Junior hasn't told us anything at all about Miss Ann Arden," she continued, placing a scornful stress on each syllable. "For all we know, that's not even her name. How old do you think she is?"

"Older than he is."

"I think so too. Why is it I don't like her?"

Alice's question was a statement and didn't demand an answer. There was another long silence in the room. They listened to the logs crackling in the fireplace. Alice took pains that the shudder that ran through her body not be evident to Cordelia.

"Are you all right?" asked Cordelia.

"Yes, of course. Just thinking," replied her mother.

"About her?"

"It's odd, isn't it, how someone like that waltzes into your house one day, from out of nowhere, and some deep inner instinct tells you to beware."

"YOU CAME ALONG from out of nowhere" went the lyrics to the song. She was wearing his ensign's hat, cocked on one side of her head, her lovely blonde hair cascading from under it. There were strands of hair in her mouth and a dark-brown Scotch in her hand. She sat on the floor of her tiny living room with her back against the sofa, moodily crooning the words to the song.

"You get mean when you're drunk," said Junior.

"Your sister gets mean over tea," answered Ann.

"I've apologized for Felicity," he said helplessly.

"One of my least attractive traits is that I always get even," she said. "It's the outsider in me reacting. It may take a long time, but the moment will present itself, it always does, and I will take advantage of that moment."

"You're scaring me," he said, alternately meaning it and feeling aroused by her emotion. The Grenvilles did not show emotion.

His leave was drawing to a close. He did not wish it to end on a discordant note. Neither had declared love for the other, only passion and mutual admiration of bodies. ("I'm mad for this hair below your belly button," she would say, kissing his stomach. "I adore the color of your nipples," he would say, his face buried.) She waited for him to declare his love for her before she declared her love for him. She never rushed it. Like sex, it was a thing she understood. She never talked marriage, or even a permanent liaison, and when the subject came up, obliquely, she not only did not leap on it, she let it pass by. Every debutante he had ever known would have leaped at the oblique suggestion.

"I have a present for you," he said quietly.

"You do?" she asked, her mood brightening, her heart beginning to beat fast.

He disappeared into the kitchen and reappeared with a white cardboard box, which he handed her. It was not the kind of box she had in mind.

"Ah, orchids!" she exclaimed delightedly, as though they were what she most longed for. She wondered why she couldn't act onstage the way she could in life, concealing her disappointment with delight, as she was doing. She stared at them, white with yellow centers, and brushed her face against the scentless blossoms, collecting herself for the next moment.

"You like them then?" he asked.

"So much," she said. She was reminded of what Babette had said about rich boys being tight.

"Good," he replied, settling himself in a chair contentedly; for an instant she thought of Percy V. Jordan, the way he sat, contentedly, with pipe and slippers. She shuddered. Since her interview with Alice Grenville, images of her long-ago past kept recurring to her.

"Aren't you going to put them in something?" he asked.

"Oh, yes," she said, remaining sitting where she was on the floor. "I will in a bit."

"There's more," he said.

"What?"

"You heard me." They looked at each other. "Dig deeper."

She lifted the bouquet from the heavy cardboard box. There, hidden among the flowers, was a small red leather box from Cartier's. Junior was to discover in that moment that her joy in receiving gifts was wondrous to behold, sweeping away any dark moments that preceded it, restarting the evening in rapturous mood. The memory of Christmases past, giftless, entered and exited her mind.

It was a pin, a circle of diamonds, such as his sisters wore on the collars of their suits, a gift for a lady, not a gift for a show girl, and she felt tenderness for him, and love. That

mother, those sisters, she thought. She understood him better, having met them. Although they had pointed out to her,
in their own secretive ways, the vastness of the chasm between them, she was not deterred.

Later—sated, satisfied—she said to him, "Do you never
discuss your feelings?"

"What have we been doing for the last hour?" he asked.

"Worshiping bodies. It's not the same."

"But I told you."

"When you were coming. I don't count that. It doesn't
commit you, you know. It's a love affair, and you're leaving
soon, and who knows what will happen then? Let's go to the
moon for however long we have. Are you waiting for me to
go first, is that it?"

Enraptured, he stared at her but said nothing.

"I love you," she said.

He felt unleashed. Torrents of blocked feelings flowed from
him, a lifetime of withheld emotion. "I love you," he whispered to her, and repeated and repeated and repeated the
words. He could not stop saying them.

When he asked her to fly with him out to Tacoma, Washington, where he was to be stationed, she refused. She had to
earn her living, she said. She had been voted the most beautiful girl in radio, and she thought there might be interest in
her at the movie studios. At least that was what Chet Marx
told her, she told him. Chet Marx wanted her to dine with
Humphrey Bogart; he thought she ought to get to know some
of the Hollywood crowd. There was talk of a screen test, she
told him.

WHEN JUNIOR'S favorite sister, Cordelia, called and asked
her to lunch, Ann knew it was only as a favor to her soon
departing brother, but, of course, she went, wearing her new

diamond circle pin. When she walked into the Colony Restaurant, ten minutes past the appointed time, to make sure
Cordelia was there ahead of her, even Gene Cavallero, who
owned the fashionable restaurant and snubbed impostors at
the door, could not tell that she had never been there before,
so assured was her gait.

When Cordelia admired her pin, she did not say it was
from her brother. She did not call Cordelia Cookie. She did
not talk excessively about Junior. Nor did she ask questions
about the family. She did talk about her radio career and her
hoped-for film career. She asked who various people were who
waved at Cordelia and was delighted that she could wave at
her friend Babette Van Degan across the room.

She watched as people she read about in society columns
passed by on their way to their tables. She studied the look of
them. Catching sight of herself in the mirror, she realized her
look was wrong, more show business than social, and that the
time had come to do something about it.

At two o'clock she looked at her watch and said that she
had an appointment with her agent about a screen test and
must depart. She shook hands charmingly in farewell and did
not attempt to make a return lunch date.

Cordelia reported to her mother that she definitely did not
think that Miss Arden had marital designs on Junior. "She
seems very keen on her career. Didn't even stay for coffee.
Rushed off about a screen test or something. She's not at
all designing, Mère. She's terribly amusing, as a matter of
fact. She told me the funniest story about that Lithuanian
girl Dickie Van Degan was married to for about ten minutes."

"You relieve my mind," said Alice Grenville.

"It's Junior sowing his wild oats, Mère, nothing more. She's
the wild oats. It's probably a very good arrangement. He'd
never marry her."

"How can you be so sure?"

"She pronounces the 't' in 'often.' "

*   *   *

HE WAS possessed with love. He didn't want her to know how much for fear it would not be returned; at the same time he wanted her to know the full and total extent of it. His moods were up; his moods were down. His skin was sallow, and there were dark circles from sleeplessness under his eyes; he was more handsome than he had ever been.

"Will you marry me?" he asked. Less than a week was left of his leave. He could not bear to think of being apart from her.

"You must let me think it over," she replied. "It's such a big step. It would be mad to hurry. I don't believe in divorce, you see. I've seen firsthand what it does."

"Nor do I!" he agreed. "There's never been a divorce in our family. Except my Aunt Amelia, one of the triplets, and that's only because Uncle Binkie was a fairy, something he neglected to tell poor Aunt Amelia."

"Let's not talk about Aunt Amelia and Uncle Binkie now," said Ann. "Let's talk about us."

"I want to marry you, Ann," he said again. The hesitancy of the first offer was gone. Having said it, he knew it was the thing he desired most.

"I need a little time."

"For what?"

"To make sure it's the right thing."

He felt deflated. He had thought she would jump at the chance. Like Brenda Frazier, or Kay Kay Somerset, or Esme Bland, or any of a dozen ladies in society who had their eye on him.

"I thought you loved me," he stated.

"I do," she replied.

"When will you let me know? My leave is up on Friday."

"I'll let you know before then."

"When?"

"Please, Junior."

"When?"

"I'll let you know this Thursday."

"For sure?"

"For sure."

"It will be a wonderful life, I promise you that. After the war, I mean."

"Thursday."

There was never any doubt as to what her answer would be, except to Junior, and he shared with no one, not even Cordelia, that the very thread of his life was in abeyance, waiting for Thursday to arrive. He had moments of elation; he had moments of despair. He was bad-tempered and spoiled; he was loving and generous. The eyes of his mother and sisters would meet as his moods fluctuated. Except for her immediate present, he did not know a single thing about Ann, other than that she was an orphan from the Midwest. She never discussed her origins, and there was not a single picture in her small penthouse that suggested a past life.

They were at tea, just the family, and Beth Leary, his mother's closest friend, who was practically family, never having married, when the letter arrived. They had all heard the doorbell, and thought it must be one of the husbands come to join one of the sisters, but no one appeared, and they resumed their conversation about the war, which was all anybody talked about.

Cahill entered, too early to clear away the tea things, but bearing a letter on a silver tray.

"Yes, Cahill?" asked Alice.

"It's a letter, madam, for Mr. William, delivered by messenger," said Cahill.

Junior leaped to his feet, aroused from his lethargy, and his Scotch and soda, which he had preferred to tea, went flying all over his mother's half-finished needlepoint rug. If he had not been in uniform, and with but a few days left of his leave, she might have expressed annoyance, but she merely lifted the rug to her lap and wiped off the liquid with a tea napkin, all the time watching her son as he reached out to take the letter off the tray proffered by Cahill.

Junior's heart sank. There, in Palmer penmanship, round and right-leaning, the i's dotted with circles, was written "Ensign William Grenville, Junior, U.S.N." Lower, on the left side of the envelope, was written "By Hand." He felt with certainty that she had deserted him; why else would she have written to him instead of waiting to see him that evening? He could not bear to open the letter in front of his family, knowing all eyes were on him. He put the envelope in his pocket as if it were of no importance and returned to his place.

"I'm sorry, Mère, about spilling my drink on your needlework. It was awfully clumsy of me," said Junior.

"Doesn't matter," she answered. "Lyd will know how to take out the stain."

"Soda water, I think, is how you do it," said Beth Leary. "Simply soak it in soda water, and when it dries, the stain will have gone."

"Lyd will know," said Alice, who wasn't interested in that kind of conversation.

"What's in the letter?" asked Felicity.

"I haven't read it," answered Junior.

"Why not?"

"None of your business."

"You've gotten so secretive, Junior."

"You've gotten so nosy, Felicity."

"I bet it's from your blonde."

"You don't have to call her that all the time in that bitchy way. Her name is Ann. You're a real bitch, Felicity. I never knew that before."

"Junior!" cried Alice.

He wanted the conversation to move off him onto other things: the opera, the theater, the war, he didn't care which. His heart was beating ferociously, and he was trying not to let the feeling of loss that was lurking around him move in and envelop him. When Beth Leary started to tell a story about Grace Vanderbilt across the street, whom they all loved to discuss, Junior walked out of the room.

Up two flights of stairs he charged and down the long thickly carpeted corridor paneled with bedroom doors to his own door. He entered his room and closed the door behind him, escaping into the white-tiled refuge of his bathroom, where he watered his face with cold water and dried it while looking at himself in the mirror and recognizing the fear in his eyes.

He reentered his bedroom. It was the room that he had grown up in and was now in its fourth stage of decoration. Gone was the memorabilia of childhood, of teen-age, of college. Now it was decorated for a young man, tailored and dark-blue, with horse paintings by John Frederick Herring that had belonged to his father and drawings of prize horses from the Grenville racing stables. The handsome desk had also belonged to his father, and the wingback chairs. He stood there surveying it, as if for the first time, undecided which place to gravitate to that was not dominated by his father. He moved to the window seat in the large dormer window overlooking the park and the street five stories below. It was where he had sat most often as a child and seemed the least-changed part of the room. He peered out the window for several minutes and then reached into his pocket and took out the letter, which seemed to heat against his body. He looked at the envelope again, filled with trepidation, sat down and tore it open.

It read:

> Miss Ann Arden
> accepts with pleasure
> the kind invitation of
> Ensign William Grenville, Junior, U.S.N.
> to become his lawful wedded wife.

War whoops, cheers, screams of joy, and stamping of feet altered the mood of the room.

✹   ✹   ✹

WHEN ANN ARDEN was eight years old, and her name was Ursula Mertens, and she was called Urse, her father, whose name was Claud, and whom she adored, took her for supper, just the two of them, to the counter at Crowell's Pharmacy on Broadway in Pittsburg, Kansas. They exchanged pleasantries with Paul Crowell, her father's first cousin, who owned the pharmacy. Paul told Urse she was the prettiest young thing who'd been into his store all that day. Urse looked up at him, startled into a brilliant flush by the compliment, and beamed with pleasure.

"You're going to turn her head," said Claud to Paul, looking affectionately at his daughter, although his mind seemed to be occupied by other matters.

"What are you going to be when you grow up?" asked Paul.

"I'm going to be an actress in the movies," answered the lovely child without a moment's hesitation. Paul chuckled, and her father, preoccupied, looked off into space.

They ordered cheese delights, which Paul said were the specialité de la maison, melted cheese and bacon sandwiches served open-faced and eaten with a knife and fork, and chocolate milkshakes so thick and plentiful that each canister filled up the milkshake glass nearly twice. It was a rare treat in the young life of Urse Mertens, and she rose to the occasion by keeping her taciturn father entertained with an endless stream of chatter about the dancing lessons and music lessons she wanted to take, and the birthday present she was making for Grandma Smiley.

Her social vivacity deflected totally the purpose of the meal. Claud Mertens had things to tell Urse, important things, about leaving Pittsburg, which was growing into such a big town, nearly fifteen thousand people now, not a place for farming anymore, and moving on to Hugoton to homestead. He was losing his farm on the outskirts of Pittsburg.

"What's 'homestead' mean?" she asked finally.

"It means you live on the land for a year, make improvements on it, you know, fences and barns, like that, and then it becomes yours," answered Claud, more at home in that kind of conversation than about dancing and music lessons that he could not afford to give her.

Urse could feel her lovely evening on the town with her father beginning to crumble in front of her. "Is that where you were when you were out of town last month?" she asked.

"That's right, Urse," answered Claud. "Beautiful country, good soil, you'll love it."

She sat silently, absorbed completely in wiping up spilled milkshake from the marble counter with a paper napkin, frightened by the portent of the conversation.

"Say something, Urse," said her father.

"Mama said there was a big black snake on the front porch up there in Hugoton. Mama said you have to go to the bathroom in a little house outside. Mama said there's only a one-room schoolhouse, and the kids there don't even speak good English. Oh, Daddy, please, please, don't make me leave here and move to Hugoton," pleaded Urse.

"You're your mother's daughter, honey," said Claud, nodding his head slowly and looking at her, holding back his tears. Ethel Mertens had come to Hugoton to look at the new life her husband envisioned for his family there, stayed one night, and returned to Pittsburg, vowing that she would never move there. When they were young and in love a dozen years before, it hadn't mattered that he was just a farm boy with an eighth-grade education and that Ethel had attended normal school and was qualified to teach. But that was before Urse, and Ethel had great plans for Urse.

Claud couldn't bear to tell Urse what he had planned to tell her if his last-ditch hope of interesting her in a life that her mother had rejected failed. He was leaving her mother, allowing her mother to divorce him, moving out of her life.

"I better get you home," he said. "It's almost nine o'clock. If you weren't such a big girl, I'd carry you out to the truck."

He wanted to hold her and hug her and tell her that he loved her and always would, but he couldn't.

The next day her mother told her that her father had moved away. Ethel Mertens consoled the weeping child.

"Does a divorce mean he'll never come back?" sobbed Urse.

"Sure, he'll come back and visit you, honey," soothed her mother.

"But why didn't he even say goodbye, Mama?"

"You know how hard it is for your daddy to say things. I know he wanted to, Urse, but he probably couldn't find the words. Even when he gets mad it's hard for him to say what it is he's mad about."

"Is that why he took me out to Crowell's Pharmacy for supper last night, to tell me he was going to leave us?" She wondered if Paul Crowell knew. She remembered herself prattling on about dancing and music lessons. She felt betrayed.

"He wanted to tell you by himself, Urse, and explain to you what he wanted out of life, and that it wasn't here in Pittsburg anymore."

"He did start to tell me that."

"You see?"

"About homesteading in Hugoton and making improvements on the land."

"All that."

"But I didn't know he was going to move out there and leave us if we didn't want to go."

"It's not the kind of life out there I want for you, Urse," said Ethel Mertens.

"What's going to happen to us, Mama?" She shivered in fear as she looked around her at the holes in the linoleum floor of the kitchen and the broken steps out the kitchen door that you had to jump over. Their little frame house had not been painted in years, and tar paper covered holes in the shingled roof.

"We're going to be all right. Don't you worry about that,"

answered her mother, but neither of them knew whether to believe that.

"When I grow up, Mama . . ."

"Yes, honey?"

"I'm never going to get a divorce, *never*, no matter what."

URSE MERTENS always looked ahead to the time when her life would start. Her childhood and adolescence were years to be gotten through, in preparation for the time ahead when her life would really begin. She longed to be center stage in life, to have her world focused on her. When her celebrity finally came, in a manner radically different from her youthful dreams, reporters sought out her roots for early clues. It astonished them that so few people remembered her. She left no mark; she erased all traces of her deprived youth by remaining unmemorable.

"Now hold still, Urse, or one of these pins is going to stick in you," said Ethel Mertens, intent on her work.

"I can't understand you when you talk with pins in your mouth, Mama," said the little girl, straining around to look at the fitting in the mirror over the bureau.

"Turn around to the mirror and let me look at the length of this skirt."

"I love this color blue, Mama. It's my favorite color."

"Do you know what people are going to say about you?" asked her mother, satisfied with her nearly completed chore.

"They're going to say, 'Urse Mertens has the prettiest dresses of any girl in Pittsburg, Kansas,' " said Urse, and they both laughed, knowing people wouldn't say that at all, but it was a line they often used.

"I've been thinking, Urse," said her mother.

"Oh-oh," said Urse.

"What's that supposed to mean?"

"When you say 'I've-been-thinking-Urse,' that means changes."

"Well, just listen to me. With your daddy gone, there's no reason for the two of us to stay way out here on the outside of town. How about if we sold this farm and moved into Pittsburg?"

"Who would buy it, Mama? It's all falling down."

"Well, somebody would. The other day I saw a real nice house on West Quincy Street that Mr. and Mrs. Cremer want to sell. It'd be perfect, Urse. You'd be able to walk to Lakeside School and have friends right on the street. That Fredda Cunningham lives only two houses away, and you said yourself she's the most popular girl in the school."

"But she's so stuck-up, Mama. She never says hello."

"She will, honey. You'll be best friends in no time."

"Won't you miss the farm, Mama?"

"I don't think either of us is the farm-girl type, Urse. Do you?"

"No, but I thought maybe Daddy might decide to come back if things didn't work out in Hugoton." She pulled the new dress over her head so that she wouldn't have to meet her mother's eyes in the mirror and avoid a finality she was still not ready to accept.

"It'll be easier for us to figure out a way for you to take your music lessons," said Ethel, helping her out of the dress.

"We don't have enough money for music lessons."

"Well, there's something else I've been thinking."

"Oh-oh. More changes."

"I've been thinking of going back to teaching. I went to normal school before I married your father, and I was always planning to teach, but when we got married we moved out here, and I never got around to it."

"What would you teach?"

"Social studies."

"A lot of changes, Mama."

"But exciting, huh?"

"And we'll be able to afford the lessons?"

"That's the whole point. Wouldn't you like that?"

"Oh, yes, Mama," she said, hugging her mother. "I always said I wanted to be an actress in the movies."

HURT, SHE WAILED, "Sometimes I wish my father was dead!" It was Christmas.

"Ursula Mertens!" cried her mother, in the tone of voice she used to let her daughter know she didn't mean what she was saying.

"I mean it, Mama," persisted Urse, not allowing herself to give in to the tears that were welling in her sad eyes.

"No, you don't," her mother insisted.

"Every birthday, every Christmas, is a disappointment. If he was dead, you wouldn't wonder if he was going to remember or not."

"Now listen, you," said Ethel, putting her arm around her daughter. "We didn't have such a bad Christmas, did we? Look at all those nice things you got under the tree. Grandma Smiley knitted you that scarf herself, and Aunt Edna and Aunt Lucy are going to pay for your dancing lessons for a whole year, and Paul Crowell sent you that bath powder from his drugstore, and don't forget the five dollars."

"But I didn't hear from my daddy, not even a Christmas card, and not on my birthday either. It's like he forgot me already, and I know that he loved me."

"You know, there's still one special thing I haven't even told you about yet," said Ethel, her voice filled with enticement, a sound that Urse could never resist.

"What's that?" asked Urse slowly.

"It's from Mr. Percy V. Jordan."

"Who's Mr. Percy V. Jordan, Mama?"

"He's the manager of the telephone company, Urse, not

just for Pittsburg, but for the whole region," said Ethel expansively.

"Why would, uh, what's his name again?"

"Percy V. Jordan."

"Why would Mr. Percy V. Jordan give me a Christmas present when I don't even know him?"

"He's coming over after Christmas dinner, and you will get a chance to know him."

"Is he your boyfriend or something?"

"Oh, Urse, I only just met him, over at the high school when they put in the new phone system."

"What's the present?"

"He wants to drive you and me over to Kansas City next week—"

"Kansas City!"

"—*and* we're going to have lunch in a hotel, and go to the pictures, and, more to come—"

"More?" cried Urse.

"He's going to have your picture taken at Swanson's Department Store. Three poses."

"I'm going to have my picture taken? At Swanson's Department Store? Three poses?"

"That's right!"

"Wait until that stuck-up Fredda Cunningham hears about this," said Urse, delighted with the way the day had turned out after all.

"MRS. PERCY V. JORDAN. How do you think it sounds, Urse?" asked Ethel Mertens.

"Kind of ritzy," said Urse.

"That's what I think, too. I like the sound of it."

"Is it going to change things, Mama?"

"Only for the better, honey. There'll be more money, and

we'll be able to do more things, and I'm sure we'll start getting
invited to some of the nice houses. Some of the ladies in this
town don't take kindly to a divorced woman. You know that."

"Mrs. Cunningham, for instance," said Urse.

"Mrs. Cunningham, for instance," agreed her mother, and
they both laughed.

"You don't love him, do you, Mama?"

"I think he's a very good man. A nice man."

"That's not an answer to my question."

"I'm thirty-one years old. It's different now than when I
was married the first time. I'm looking for different things out
of life. I want to be able to educate you and give you all the
lessons and things you want, and have a nice house, and
parties on your birthday, and friends for you, and when it
comes time for you to get married, the nicest boys in town to
come and call on you, and maybe even some of the swells
from Kansas City."

"Is the manager of the telephone company such a good job
as all that? He only has two suits as far as I can see, and he
doesn't even live in as good a house as this one. Paul Crowell
says he rents the apartment over his drugstore on Broadway."

"Don't you listen to that Paul Crowell, what he has to
say," said Ethel, sensitive to the implied criticism from her
former husband's cousin. "If that's the way Paul Crowell talks,
I don't want you stopping in his drugstore on your way home
from school anymore."

"Mama, Paul's my friend. He charges Fredda Cunningham
for her sarsaparilla, but he always says that mine's on the
house, and anyway, if you want to marry Percy V. Jordan,
that's all right with me," said Urse, her eyes filling with tears.

"Oh, Urse," said Ethel, pulling her child toward her, hugging her, no longer holding back her own tears. "It's going to
work out fine. I know it. You'll see."

"And at least we'll have our own telephone, not a party
line anymore," said Urse.

"If I decide to say yes, he's going to paint the house all

white, with green shutters, just like the Cunninghams', and he said he'd put up new wallpaper in the front room and in the two bedrooms, and he wants to buy us a Frigidaire, and maybe even a new range. And he has a *car!*"

"He has funny hair," said Urse.

"I think it's a wig," said Ethel.

"DON'T TALK TO Ma until after she's had her coffee," Urse warned Percy V. Jordan, as if that were the explanation for her mother's peculiar behavior. Ethel's behavior in her new marriage was difficult for even her daughter to understand. When the excitement of acquisition had diminished—the newly papered rooms; the telephone; the Frigidaire; and the automobile, a Diana Moon—there was the man himself to contend with. Ethel was as sickened when his soft-boiled eggs dripped on his mustache as she was revolted by his bathroom smells. She could not bear to bathe in the tub when his pubic hairs were caught in the drain and refused to wash it herself.

She continuously nagged and found fault with him, and used scurrilous and defamatory language toward him. She accused him of killing his first wife; accused him of being infected with a venereal disease; and accused him of associating with women of questionable character. One quarrel was so violent that Urse Mertens called the police.

For her birthday Percy V. Jordan had promised Urse to take her to Kansas City to see the touring Marilyn Miller in *Sunny*. It was the thing she wanted to do more than anything else. She knew the words to all the songs, and, for once, Fredda Cunningham was jealous of her when she bragged about her forthcoming birthday trip.

On the birthday morning Percy V. Jordan announced that he had had enough annoyance and abusive treatment from his new wife, that the trip to Kansas City was off, and that he was leaving the premises permanently. Urse Mertens was disconsolate and embarrassed by what she expected Fredda's reaction would be. When Ethel realized that Percy was in fact leaving her, she flew into a rage and followed him for blocks through the streets of Pittsburg, screaming abuse at him and attempting to tear his clothes.

Ethel Mertens was hauled into the police station, fired from the faculty of the high school, and divorced by Percy V. Jordan, whereupon her peculiar behavior ceased.

Urse, shamed, remained more and more a solitary figure. She knew that the marriage of her mother and Percy was over almost before it started, and that it was only a matter of time before readjustments in their lives and life-styles were to occur again, that another starting-over was to take place.

She hated the feelings of uncertainty about how they would live, where they would live, if they would be able to manage. She wondered if ever there would be security in her life. She thought of Fredda Cunningham and her seventy-five cents allowance every week, come rain or shine, who always had money to go to the pictures on Saturday afternoons, or buy *Photoplay,* or even a cheese delight, if she wanted one, at Crowell's Pharmacy, and she directed the anger she felt over her own lot in life into jealousies toward Fredda.

The following September she entered high school, and her mother got a new job as the dispatcher at the local taxi service. With the defection of Percy from the scene, both were determined that Urse not give up her dancing and music lessons. She got herself after-school jobs to pay for them herself, first as a check-out girl at the Cash and Carry and then as a counter waitress at Crowell's Pharmacy, serving milkshakes and cheese delights and pouring coffee into thick white chipped cups. Most of all she hated serving Fredda Cunningham.

One night, just before closing, in walked Billy Bob Veblen, the captain of the football team, the handsomest boy at Pittsburg High. Up to that time Billy Bob Veblen, whom all the girls were mad for, had never even noticed Urse Mertens.

Her hand was shaking when she poured him his cup of coffee, but not a drop of it slopped over into the saucer. She was experiencing feelings inside of her that she had never experienced before.

"Where have you been all my life, beautiful?" he asked her, and she felt like she was in a scene in the movies.

MOROSE, THE TWO old friends sat in the dining room of the Brook Club, safe from the world, out of uniform.

"She won't do, you know," said Bratsie. "She won't do at all, as far as they're concerned. Here, let me pour you some more of this wine. It's the most expensive on the menu."

Junior stared at the glass as Bratsie poured the burgundy too close to the top of the glass. Cahill would have frowned, thought Junior, trying to assimilate what his friend was saying, trying not to feel let down.

"Mind you, that's not how I feel. I'm simply doing what you're not doing, which is anticipating what Alice and the sisters are going to have to say on the matter."

"But they adored her," protested Junior. "Except Felicity."

"You're in uniform, home on leave, and in a few days you go off, possibly never to return; they are humoring you until this little affair is over. They think you are sowing your wild oats. Talk marriage to them, and you will see their attitudes change very quickly."

"I love her," said Junior hopelessly.

"I know you do."

"I have never had sex like this before, Bratsie. It's not like at Miss Winifred Plegg's on West End Avenue. I didn't know what sex was all about," confided Junior in a rare moment of intimacy. "What am I going to do?"

"Mistress her for now. And when the war's over, see how you feel then."

He drank some of the burgundy. "I'm not sure I'm going to come back from the war," he said quietly.

"You've always thought that, haven't you?"

"Thought what?"

"That you were going to die young."

"Why do you say that?"

"You've said things like that before."

"I don't remember."

"Would you care?"

"I would now that I've met Ann."

"She'll wait for you."

"That's where you're wrong, Brats. She won't."

"You're pissed off at me, aren't you?" asked Bratsie.

"I thought you would have supported me more, Brats, you of all people. None of all this," he said, looking around the paneled dining room, indicating with his hand the world it represented and the men at nearby tables who had been friends of their fathers', "ever meant anything to you."

"You know, Junior, people always joke and say that Alice wants you to marry Princess Margaret. You see, I think she's serious, only I think she wants you to marry Princess Elizabeth and become the next King of England, or whatever her husband will become."

"That's a nice shirt, Brats," said Junior, not wanting to talk about it anymore, now that his exuberance was spent.

"Had it made," answered Bratsie, glad for a reprieve, looking down at the maroon-and-white-striped monogrammed shirt with white collar and cuffs.

"Expensive?"

"Not for us."

They laughed. They were talking about a shirt, but they were thinking about other things. As Bratsie went on talking, he removed his cuff links, then his tie, then his jacket. Then he unbuttoned the buttons, pulled out the tails, and took the shirt off in the crowded quiet dining room. For a moment he sat there, bare-chested, as men at every table turned to gape at the spectacle of the half-naked man continuing his conversation with great enthusiasm.

"For God's sake, Bratsie, what are you doing?" gasped Junior.

"I'd give you the shirt off my back," said Bratsie, rising, hairy-chested, hairy-armpitted, and handing the shirt across the table to his friend.

"Bratsie!" cried Junior, trying not to look at the other tables and the horrified look of the captain bearing down on them. Bratsie sat down again, oblivious completely to the scene he was causing, and put the jacket of his suit on over his nudity.

"Mr. Bleeker," said the captain. "I'm afraid, sir, I must ask you to—"

"Ah, Casper," said Bratsie. "My mother asked that I send you her best regards. She said my father was fonder of you than almost anyone he knew. What we'd like to order is a marvelous bottle of your best champagne. My friend, Ensign Grenville, and I are celebrating his forthcoming marriage—"

"Bratsie!"

"But it's a great secret, Casper, and you must tell *no* one."

HE TAPPED on the glossy white paneled door of his mother's bedroom the way he used to when he was sixteen years old to tell her he was home from a dance.

"Come in," she said, and he entered. She was sitting up in her enormous canopied bed, reading.

"Mère, I have the most wonderful news," said Junior.

She looked at her son's love-besotted face. "No," she said, lifting her hand and waving it negatively between them, answering his news before he could tell it to her.

"Mère, please."

"No, no, no, no, no, no, no, no. That's all there is to it. Go to bed, Junior."

"Try to remember what it was like when you first met Father, all those stories you have always told us."

"What I felt for your father does not apply to this situation," she answered him, angrily dismissing the comparison of his lust-filled love with her marriage. Her marriage was so totally appropriate. A more perfect match could not have been imagined, from either family, and out of its appropriateness had grown respect, harmony, understanding, and love. Passion had never played a part. At that moment she missed her husband, because he would have known how to deal with this out-of-hand situation.

Angered, he turned about and left his mother's room, slamming the door behind him.

The room was hot. Candles dripped wax on the table, but Madame Sophia did not seem to notice. The card table between them was wobbly, and the leatherette on the seat of his chair was ripped and felt uncomfortable against his leg. Yellow and red wax roses were covered with dust, and a statuette of the Virgin Mary had been broken and pasted together again. Junior noticed that Madame Sophia's fingernail polish was chipped. Her eyes were heavily made up, and her hair was hidden beneath a magenta chiffon scarf; he felt she might not be sufficiently bathed. A small girl with pierced ears slept on a sofa. He wondered why, if she knew all the answers to the future, she lived in such squalor.

The sign in her window said two dollars for the reading, but she suggested that for five her work would be more detailed, and he agreed. He was confused and lonely in Tacoma, Washington; the strenuous routine of his training at the naval station did not erase from his mind his unpleasant departure from New York, estranged from both Ann and his mother. When, to soothe his troubled mother, he asked Ann to wait for him until after the war, she refused. It pained him to hear that the very next night she was dancing at El Morocco with Arturo de Castro. For the first time in his life he fought bitterly with his mother when she pointed out to him that Miss Arden's instant defection to a former beau showed, more than any words of hers ever could, exactly what kind of person Miss Arden was. Except for Cahill and Gibbs, only Cordelia saw him off.

"There is beautiful lady I see," said Madame Sophia, laying out her soiled cards on the table.

"Yes, yes," cried Junior eagerly.

"Her hair yellow."

"Golden," said Junior only the briefest second before Madame Sophia said "yellow."

"Blue eyes," she went on as if there in her shabby card she had conjured up his glorious lady and feasted on her beauty in agreement with him. From his attitudes she read his story. From his despair she told him they had fought and parted (Yes, yes.) From his longing she told him that the beautiful lady longed for him also. (Are you sure?) From his worry she told him that the obstacles in their way (Were there not obstacles? Yes, yes) were only there as a test to prove their love. From his ecstasy at her revelations she told him that happiness was his.

"Is there anything else you would like to ask me?" she asked, warming to him for his enthusiasm for her powers, noticing in his transformation from despair to ecstasy how extraordinarily handsome he was.

"Yes," he answered. "There is."

She looked at him and waited for him to ask.

"This will seem awfully stupid to you. . . ."

"Just ask," she said, shaking her head.

"Will I be killed in the war?"

She laughed, quite kindly, and shook her head again, and a feeling of relief began to flood his body.

"No," she said, moving her cards.

"When?" he asked quietly.

"When what?" She looked at him.

"You see, I've always had this feeling that I would die young."

"Not in the war," she repeated.

"But when?" he persisted. Their eyes met. From his pocket he took a twenty-dollar bill and placed it on the table. She looked down at the cards in front of her. Then, unexpectedly, she pushed the twenty-dollar bill back at him across the table.

"Please," he said, pushing it back toward her. "It's very important that I know."

"Five, five, five, five," she said finally, wanting to be done with what she was doing.

"I don't understand," he said.

"The fifth day, the fifth month, 1955," she said.

The date she gave him, twelve years in his future, seemed, at that moment of his youth, so far distant that he was filled with exuberance over the postponement of the inevitability of his early demise. It was a date to be filed away for years to come. Then, there, in that shabby room in Tacoma, Washington, the vise of anxiety that the war would finish him was unwound.

BABETTE VAN DEGAN, her hands behind her head, lay back against the leopard-skin pillows on the sofa of her mirrored living room and commiserated with the miserable Ann.

"That mother. Those sisters," she said, acknowledging the root of the problem. They, daughters of adversity, had been through the story over and over.

For Ann, her sense of loss over the departed Junior Grenville was overwhelming. She had gone from the heights of ecstasy to the depths of despair in a twenty-four-hour period and remained in the latter. There was a perception of missed opportunity that might not ever come her way again, at least in the elegant packaging that Junior Grenville presented. She was sure she would have loved him if he were less affluent, she thought, but the sight of his life had aroused in her a passion for him that she had not expected in herself.

Even with her natural acceptance of hard facts, the thing she most feared in life was poverty; she had experienced it. She knew, nearly always, that she had within her the means to go beyond, by far, the life into which she had been born, and she merely passed through the first eighteen years of it in anticipation of moving out of it, leaving no traces. Although it was Fredda Cunningham as Cecily Cardew and not Urse Mertens as Gwendolen Fairfax who was remembered in the Pittsburg High School senior class production of *The Importance of Being Earnest,* it was then she had decided for sure that the stage, when she got to it, would be the means for her to experience the kind of life she knew was waiting. In the meantime, after high school, she and her mother had moved to Kansas City where, in due time, she had modeled for several years at Swanson's Department Store. She enjoyed being looked at and had a natural ability for walking down a runway, turning this way, turning that, removing gloves, removing coats and jackets, with what Miss Rose, in Couture, called real class. In no time, half the eligible men in Kansas City, and a few ineligible married ones, had heard about and were in pursuit of Miss Urse Mertens. Ethel Mertens was delighted with her daughter's popularity, and she and Urse, always close, spent many an hour discussing the relative merits of Mr. Barney, or Mr. Hasseltine, or Mr. Stackpole. The only bad fight the two ever had was when Billy Bob Veblen, from Pittsburg, appeared on the scene, and Billy Bob Veblen (Ethel Mertens was the first one to say), was headed exactly nowhere in life. His finest moment, she claimed, had already been played four years earlier in his celebrated eighty-yard run against Hugoton. So Urse continued to see Mr. Barney, and Mr. Hasseltine, and Mr. Stackpole, to please her mother, but, in secret, she sometimes saw Billy Bob Veblen too when he drove up to Kansas City.

After five years in New York, Ann—renamed by Chet Marx, who told her the name Urse Mertens had to go, honey —knew that she had striking good looks, but that her talents as a dancer and an actress were modest. The stage was for her a means to an end. She danced away the nights of her life in the nightclubs of the city with rich South Americans, dress manufacturers, and some second-string producers from Hollywood. She bestowed and received, waiting for fame or marriage, whichever came first, but all previous perceptions of her unfocused dream paled when Junior Grenville came into her life.

"Did I ever tell you what my father, the milkman, used to say?" asked Babette of her grieving friend.

"No," replied Ann.

" 'If he's got the cow's milk, why buy the cow?' " quoted Babette.

"That sounds like Willimantic, Connecticut," said Ann.

"That's probably what Alice Grenville said to Junior. Some Social Register version of that," said Babette.

Ann wondered if she had given too much.

WHEN HIS ORDERS came to be shipped out, Junior called Ann in New York and pleaded with her to fly out to Tacoma and marry him. Joyously she agreed. She knew for sure that she loved him and wanted to be his wife. The contract for the film with Humphrey Bogart had come to naught—a couple of evenings at El Morocco, one of them culminating in a drunken fight over a stuffed panda bear; her name narrowly escaped being mentioned in Walter Winchell's column, a thing she had once craved.

"Yes, yes, yes, yes, yes, yes, yes," she cried.

"I am so happy, my darling," he said.

"When do you want me?"

"As soon as you can get here."

"Listen, Junior," she said.

"I'm listening," he answered.

"I don't want to be married to a man called Junior."

"But I've always been called Junior."

"That doesn't mean you always have to be."

"What's wrong with Junior?"

"It's a boy's name. I want to marry a man."

"They called my father William."

"I don't want to call you William either."

"Bill?" he asked.

"Billy," she answered.

She suspected she might be pregnant, although she did not go to see a doctor about it, once she agreed to marry Billy, because, if it was true, she wanted to get the news at the same time he got the news so that it would not be a condition of the marriage.

"No one is ever going to claim I trapped him with the old pregnancy routine," said Ann to Babette when she related the news to her.

"I think you really love this guy," said Babette.

Ann did not call, or call on, Alice Grenville before she left New York to tell her of the plans, leaving that for Billy to do.

Somehow he was able to book a suite in the finest hotel in the city for an indefinite period of time, and it was there that she lived during the week before the marriage. He left all the wedding plans to her, as he was mostly confined to the base, and was delighted that she chose to be married in a religious ceremony in the Episcopal church instead of by a justice of the peace. Each, independently, was thinking of Alice and her beloved St. James'. "North, East, South, West," thought Ann, "Episcopalian is the best."

She went to St. Andrew's Church rectory and asked to speak to the minister. As always, she was carefully dressed, wearing the same green suit meant to impress Alice Grenville, and gloves, and hat. The ancient housekeeper informed her that the Reverend Dr. Tiffany was in the church. She was invited to wait in the rectory but decided instead to go into the church so as to see what it looked like. The minister stood on the altar performing a service for himself alone. Ann slipped into a pew to wait. After a few minutes the minister became aware that there was someone in the church and turned and saw her in the front pew watching him.

"May I help you?" he asked.

"I would like to speak with you, Reverend Tiffany," replied Ann.

"Can't you see that I am in the middle of a service?"

"I meant when you have finished," said Ann.

"What is it concerning?"

"A marriage."

"Are you a member of this church?"

"No."

"Is it a military marriage?"

"Naval. My fiancé is stationed at the base."

"There are chaplains at the base," he answered and turned back to the altar to complete his service. He was unobliging and ungracious, but she was determined not to be dismissed by him as if she were a gob's girl friend. She continued to sit there, fingering her pearls, as if they were real, in the manner she had seen Alice Grenville finger hers when she was vexed, until Dr. Tiffany completed the service.

"Are you still here?" he asked when he had finished and was about to go around and turn out the few lights that were on.

"The family of my husband-to-be are long-standing members of St. James' Episcopal Church in New York City, and Dr. Kinsolving of that church suggested to us that we come here to this church to marry," said Ann, having prepared her sentence and her exact tone of voice, firm but courteous, to achieve the utmost effect.

"Come along, come along," he said, his manner changing. "Let's go back to the rectory and talk a bit. Tell me, how is Dr. Kinsolving? I'm sorry if I appeared brusque before, but there are so many people from the bases who come here wanting a church wedding when they have no interest whatsoever in the church, do you see what I mean? What is the name of your fiancé's family?"

The fluttery white curtains in the rectory reminded her of Fredda Cunningham's living room in Pittsburg, Kansas. He asked her if she would like a glass of sherry. She declined, but he took one and then another. He talked on and on. She realized that he was considerably older than she had at first thought him to be in the darkened church. He asked her questions and then did not wait for answers, although he seemed considerably impressed with Dr. Kinsolving and the grand church on Madison Avenue that he oversaw.

Ann discussed flowers and talked over music that she wanted played, asking specifically for a hymn that Billy had told her had been his favorite hymn at Groton. The service was set for eleven o'clock the following Saturday at the side altar. He took another sherry, and she wondered if he was getting senile or perhaps drank a bit, but decided that it was the war. He was long past retirement age and all the younger ministers were away being chaplains. He had a confused look in his eyes; she was not sure if he had the plans straight and thought she would call him again the next day and double-check them. To ensure that nothing would go awry, she opened her purse and took from it several large bills, which she handed him as a contribution to the church, telling him that her husband-to-be would be making a further contribution to the church at the time of the wedding. She asked him if he would join them later at their wedding celebration at the hotel where she was staying. When she departed, he called her Miss Grenville instead of Miss Arden.

IN ANOTHER PART of the city, in the area known as the country-club district, a murder occurred. A young girl of good family had been strangled by a former suitor, a soldier, with whom she had broken off a romance. For several days the story remained on the front pages of the Tacoma newspapers while the soldier was apprehended and arraigned. Pictures of the lovely-looking girl appeared in the papers with accounts of her family background, her education, her accomplishments.

Ann, with little else to do during the days, became avidly interested in the story, shuddering at the thought of a young life ending in so violent a manner. She took a taxi out to the address given in the papers to look at the home of the parents of the victim and felt even sorrier for her when she saw the impressive house and grounds where the girl had lived.

When Ann returned to the hotel, she saw that Billy's bags for their three-day honeymoon and a case of liquor from the PX for the wedding reception had been dropped off at the suite by a friend of Billy's from the naval base. She could not bear to have things out of place, and the sight of the bags and case in the center of her sitting room disturbed her sense of symmetry. When she moved the bags into a closet, she noticed for the first time that there was a manila envelope containing unopened mail that the friend had dropped off as well.

She was drawn to one particular letter like a moth to a flame. Although she had never seen Alice Grenville's handwriting, she would have known it was hers—tall, slender, strong, privileged—even if the address of the house in New York had not been thickly engraved on the rear of the pale-blue envelope. She felt snubbed by it, just as she knew its contents concerned her. Long before she did what she did, she knew what she was going to do. She stared at it as if it were an enemy. She wished that the suite had a kitchenette so that she could boil water and steam open the envelope. Instead, she bolted the door of her room and locked the door of her bathroom. Breathing heavily, standing in front of the mirror, she ripped open the envelope and read Alice Grenville's letter to her son. She read slowly. Had she been observed, her slowness would have been exasperating, but it was dread that slowed her.

"My darling son," the letter read. "I am heartsick that we have parted on such dreadful terms. I cannot bear that you go off to war like this, and I beg you to call me once you have received this letter. I know you think you are in love with Miss Arden, but it is an infatuation. I beg you not to marry her. If your father were alive, he could explain things to you that it is difficult for me to say. Yes, yes, she is lovely, vivacious, witty, all the things you say she is, but she has a past, Junior, other men, older men, many men, all rich. Perhaps she is what you need for this moment in your life. Perhaps your life, as we have brought you up, has stifled you a bit, and you need to flap your wings. Flap them, my darling, but do not marry her! Through Mr. Mendenhall at the bank, I have engaged a private detective. She is older than you think, and Ann Arden is not her real name. There was a party several years ago given by Earl Jones and Freddie Strawbridge, at the Waldorf, in a private suite, for Teddy Mander's bachelor dinner, and Miss Arden was drunken and disorderly and nude—"

The telephone rang in the outer room. She realized it might have rung before she became aware of its ringing. The sound startled her from her furtive work. She felt it must be Billy. Her armpits felt moist. Her face looked bloodless. In an instant, without finishing reading, she savagely tore the pale-blue pages into small pieces and flushed them down the toilet.

By the time she got to the telephone, it had rung four more times. By the next ring the person on the other end would have hung up.

"Hello?" She was out of breath.

"Miss Arden," the voice said with relief. "I was afraid you were not there."

"Who is it?"

"Dr. Tiffany." A pause. "From St. Andrew's Church."

"Yes, yes, Reverend Tiffany. Forgive me. I have been distracted. So much to do still, before tomorrow."

"I have made a terrible error, Miss Arden."

"Error?"

"I have booked a funeral at the same time that I booked your wedding, and I must ask you to postpone your wedding for an hour or two."

"No, no, no, no," she cried. "Eleven o'clock. That is when my wedding is going to be. I will not change it."

"But you see, it is the funeral of the unfortunate young Wentworth girl."

"It doesn't matter."

"She is the girl who was murdered by the soldier. Her family are regular members of my church. The error is mine. I ask you to bear with me. It is to be an enormous funeral, and the hour has been sent to the papers and cannot be changed."

"It would be bad luck for me to change. I will not," said Ann. "They must change."

She could not, would not, back down. Her vehemence astonished the befuddled minister. She knew that if Billy had read his mother's letter, he would not have married her. She felt if her wedding was postponed, even for an hour, it would not take place.

For propriety's sake, Ann insisted that Billy spend the night before the wedding at his barracks at the base; they were not to meet until they saw each other at the altar of St. Andrew's. This maidenly retreat pleased the sensibilities of Ann, who wanted to be sure that any word of her wedding that made its way back to New York would be well received.

Eruptions of thunder preceded daylight on the morning of the wedding, and rain beat angrily on the windows of Ann's room. Alone, she refused to acknowledge the gloom she felt. She thought of her mother, who would have cherished this day, marrying as she was beyond the wildest dreams of either of them in the days back in Kansas, when they planned ahead what her wedding would be like. Her mother would have said about Billy Grenville that he was a gentleman to his finger-tips, a favorite expression of hers that she had once applied to Mr. Percy V. Jordan. She wondered what Billy would have thought of her mother, whether the indications of snobbery she occasionally glimpsed in him would have surfaced. She felt twinges of guilt about her mother whenever she thought about her in relation to the Grenville family.

As she arranged flowers in the sitting room of the suite for the small reception that was to follow the ceremony, she regretted the furtive aspects of this day and wished she had someone from her own life to witness the occasion. She could only think of Fredda Cunningham from Pittsburg, but that friendship was long abandoned, and Babette Van Degan. She missed Babette terribly and wished that Billy had not dis-suaded her from asking Babette to come out to be her matron of honor. She knew that the matron of honor she was to have, Gail Bumpers, the wife of an officer from the base, would never overlap to the new life she envisioned for herself and Billy after the war.

Late morning brought an uneasy dark-skied truce with the weather. When Bratsie Bleeker arrived, magically, the day seemed not to be lost. Ann's delight in the unexpected arrival of Billy's best friend was boundless, and the cheerless day brightened.

She dressed in white, bridelike, her face covered with vir-ginal veils. Carrying a bouquet of stephanotis, she walked up the aisle of the nearly empty church on the arm of an officer, in the role of father, whom she had met only the night before, to be delivered to her groom. He, nervous as she, for the secretiveness of their act, lit up with pleasure when his bride appeared. He could not imagine a time when the sight of her would not erase whatever misgivings there were. He seemed not to notice the coldness of the minister, Dr. Tiffany, who performed the ceremony, or the noise of crowds of people outside the church waiting for the funeral to start.

It was too late for the press to print the change of time for the funeral of the slain Wentworth girl, and hundreds of people showed up only to be told they had to wait until the wedding inside was over. As the bridal party emerged from the church, for pictures to be taken and confetti and rice to be thrown, the mourners for the funeral lined up and somberly watched them.

By the curb in front of the church the flower-filled hearse and limousines carrying members of the heartbroken family waited until the wedding party had moved on its way. As the chauffeur opened the door of the car bearing the parents and two brothers of the dead girl, a gust of wind blew multicolored confetti into their car.

Bratsie, when not being irrepressible, observed his old friend's new wife, and wondered. It had all happened so quickly from the night of their boisterous romp through the nightclubs of New York to this subdued wedding reception in a flower-filled but dour hotel suite in Tacoma, Washington, without family on either side. What sort of ambition was it, he wondered, that brought about this conclusion—and conclusion it was—against so many odds?

He wondered if, behind Ann's squeals of delight, he did not sense disappointment in the proportions of her just-arrived engagement ring, from Cartier's, impressive but no match for Babette Van Degan's. He wondered if the matron of honor, Gail Bumpers, officiating in a fairy-tale performance, sensed she was being condescended to by the Cinderella of the piece. He wondered why, hours later, the Reverend Dr. Tiffany of St. Andrew's Episcopal Church had not made his obligatory minister's appearance, his church hundreds of dollars richer through the bridegroom's largess. He wondered about that funeral and those mourners waiting their turn to mourn while eyeing the bold wedding festivities, and shuddered.

"Surely this glum figure is not the infamous Bratsie Bleeker?" It was the bride speaking. A nascent hostess, she felt her party dragging and wanted the playboy to be a playboy and breathe life into it.

"But you haven't provided me with a chandelier to swing from," he replied, adjusting his mood to the role expected of him. Champagne was poured. Livelier music was suggested to the piano player. The rug was rolled back. Dancing began. With more officers than ladies present, the bride was cut in on incessantly, and the appropriate mood of mirth restored to the room.

"Where is the groom?" asked Bratsie, during one of his turns.

"Calling Mère," answered Ann. She moved her cheek against his to avoid eye contact.

"To break the news," he said as both a question and a statement. They dipped elaborately, and amusingly, he shorter than she, and would-be dancing partners held back from cutting in.

"Your career?" he asked.

"My career will be to be Mrs. William Grenville, Junior," she replied.

"Theatrical aspirations abandoned, then?" he asked.

"What is it you are saying to me, Bratsie? You led me to believe you approved of me for Billy." He liked her directness, and told her that, as he turned her, fox-trotting all the while.

"What I'm saying is, don't try to become one of them, like Alice or the sisters, or any of the girls like that he might have married. Be your own self among them, and stay special," said Bratsie.

"The unknown serious side of Bratsie," said Ann, matching his steps expertly: Mr. Dodsworth's classes and Broadway melding on the dance floor.

"Hark," he said. It was a favorite word of his.

"Hark?" she asked. "Isn't that what the herald angels sing?"

"It means, listen to what I'm saying," said Bratsie.

The moment was ended by Billy, about whom Bratsie was speaking all the time.

"It's Mère on the telephone," said Billy. "She wants to talk to you."

"Have you told her?"

"Yes."

"And?"

"Well, more surprised than anything else, I suppose," he said, obviously relieved that the dreaded task was over.

In the bedroom, the door closed against the music, Ann answered the telephone.

"Hello, my dear," said Alice Grenville. Her voice, aristocratic in tone, had resignation added to it, and disappointment. It was a voice that Ann would always fear. "This is, of course, a surprise, but I assure you I will have recovered from it by the time you return to New York. I look forward to getting to know you."

"And I you," answered Ann.

"Have you telephoned your parents?" asked Alice.

"What?" asked Ann.

"Your parents, my dear—have you telephoned them with the news?" persisted Alice.

"I don't have a family," said Ann.

"Oh, yes, yes. You told me that, didn't you?"

"SHE'S BAD NEWS, that one," said Alice Grenville to her daughters. She had minutes before hung up the telephone and presented her family with the disheartening news.

"But your letter, Mère," said Cordelia.

"My letter was never mentioned," replied Alice.

"Did he ignore it, do you suppose, or not get it?" asked Grace.

"My God!" said Felicity.

"What?"

"Suppose it comes now, when he's married to her, about all those men."

"We must act now as if it never happened," said Alice.

"Will you announce it to the papers, Mère?" asked Cordelia.

"I must."

"What about the Copacabana? Will you mention that?"

"What about the Copacabana?" asked Felicity.

"She danced there," said Cordelia.

"Growing up, I accepted the fact that no stage person would ever be asked to our house as a friend. And now look. We have a show girl in our midst," said Alice.

They sat in the late twilight, each in private thoughts of explaining Junior's extraordinary marriage to their relations, friends, and the press.

"In my day people like us knew who everyone's parents were and where they came from," Alice continued. "We were insulated from people outside of us. There was never any question of disobedience. If one of my parents said, 'This is not a suitable person,' that was it; there was nothing more to discuss."

"What about her parents?" asked Felicity.

"She said she's an orphan," replied her mother. "No family whatever."

"That could be a blessing, Mère," said Grace. "At least you won't have to invite her mother and father here or to the country."

"It's this damn war," said Alice. "He would never have met her if it weren't for the war. Going overseas, maybe not coming back. All those things are what she banked on, and she won. I knew the first time she walked into this house what was on her mind."

"What will we do about her?" asked Cordelia.

"I won't speak to her," said Felicity.

"Nor will I," said Grace.

"She is now Mrs. William Grenville, Junior," said Alice quietly, reminding them of whom they were speaking. "We must make the best of this bargain."

"SHE'S NOT THE kind of girl a person like Billy Grenville marries. She's the kind of girl you set up in an apartment on the West Side for however long it lasts, and when it's over, as it certainly will be, you pay her ten thousand dollars and buy her something nice. And marry someone we've all heard of. Like Esme Bland."

Jeanne Twombley, who heard it from Alfred, of course, told me that was the kind of thing that was said at the time at all those clubs where Billy Grenville belonged and where his father belonged before him. What they meant was that that sort of marriage, to a show girl with a dubious reputation, was all right for someone like Tommy Manville, but not for Billy Grenville. They felt, those members, mostly friends of his late father's, that Billy had let them down, and that he had certainly let his mother down.

"What's she look like?" asked Alfred Twombley.

"Bratsie says she has great tits," said Piggy French.

IT WAS NOT thought ill-mannered in the Grenvilles' circle to ask, about a bride, "Who is she?" or "Who was she?" The new Mrs. Grenville fit into none of the categories of identification to which families like theirs surrendered their heirs: schools, summer resorts, clubs, and Social Register. It could not be said about Ann Grenville that she was a relation of someone they knew, or that she had been at Foxcroft with one of the sisters, or that Billy had met her when she visited with friends in Newport or Southampton. The name of the town she was from in Kansas required explanations—"No, no, it's not Pittsburgh, Pennsylvania, it's Pittsburg, *Kansas*" —and her career as a show girl onstage and in nightclubs was an embarrassment. As was her reputation.

The brief announcement of the marriage in the *New York Times*, strategically placed, without a bridal picture, made by Mrs. William Grenville, Senior, said that the wedding of her son, Ensign William Grenville, Junior, to Miss Ann Arden had taken place at St. Andrew's Episcopal Church in Tacoma, Washington. It said that Miss Arden was from Kansas City and had attended schools in that city as well as Kansas City Junior College. It said that Ensign Grenville had attended Groton and Harvard and was the son of the late William Grenville, former president of the Cambridge Bank in New York and owner of the Grenville racing stables and breeding farm in Kentucky. It listed Ensign Grenville's homes as being in New York, Newport, and Upper Brookville, Long Island.

Only Walter Winchell, the Broadway columnist, reported that the new Mrs. Grenville, of, as he put it, "the veddy social Grenvilles," had "showgirled" behind Ethel Merman in *Anything Goes* and, before that, in the line at the Copacabana nightclub. If any of Alice Grenville's friends read Walter Winchell's column, they did not mention it to her. It was whispered, among themselves, that she was heartbroken over the match, although both she and her daughters professed to be delighted with the originality of her son's choice.

Shortly after the wedding, when Billy was shipped to the Pacific, Ann returned to New York. Tacoma, as a waiting place, was not for her. Pregnant now, for sure, she kept her discovery a secret. She wanted her marriage to be dealt with before her motherhood. She lived, until other arrangements could be made, in her own apartment in Murray Hill. It occurred to her that she might be asked to stay in the huge Grenville house, even to occupy the same rooms in which Billy had lived all his life.

The first interview between the two Mrs. Grenvilles was not auspicious. When she arrived at her mother-in-law's house, a lunch party was still in progress. Afterward she remembered maids in aprons and caps and the sound of heels on marble and parquet floors as she waited in the hallway beneath the giant chandelier. Cahill, in greeting her, assumed the attitude of the house in which he had been employed for so many years. Madam would be delayed due to the lateness of an admiral who was, at that moment, delivering a toast to his gracious hostess. Affectionate laughter and applause were heard from the dining room as Cahill led the new Mrs. Grenville across the marble hall to the elevator and up to the third floor, where she was taken to her mother-in-law's sitting room off her bedroom to wait.

It was the first small room Ann had seen in the house, and she found it warm and cozy. Chairs were slipcovered in glazed chintz, and a biography of Lady Asquith had been left open on one of them. A portrait of a handsome young Alice Pleydell, sisterless here, by Boldini, looked down on the room. A needlepoint bell cord, for maids to be summoned, struck Ann's eye, the first one she had ever seen, and she longed to pull it and issue commands. Engraved invitations, piled one upon the other, were propped against the mantelpiece. She wanted to look at them, but did not. The writing desk was littered with sheets of paper, the same pale-blue stationery Ann knew so well, as if Alice had been disturbed in her writing to greet her luncheon guests. Ann shuddered with the remembrance of the purloined and destroyed letter meant to expose her shabby history to her husband. Suddenly she saw that a Pekinese dog, nestled into a chair, followed her every movement. Their eyes met. She was glad she had not looked at the invitations.

She wondered if she would always feel like an outsider in this house. She had not been welcomed as a bride by Cahill, nor had she been asked to meet the luncheon guests downstairs, nor did the Pekinese staring haughtily at her seem to recognize her right to be there. She began to worry about her reception. Uncomfortable, undecided where to sit, she lit a Camel cigarette and inhaled deeply while walking around the small room. Looking for somewhere to drop her match, she saw there were no ashtrays in the room and placed the match beneath the luxuriant leaves of a cyclamen plant in full bloom. She cupped her hand and deposited, nervously, an ash in it. How, then, could she shake hands, she wondered, with ashes in her palm, when Mrs. Grenville came in? Finally, she took a Chinese plate from a teakwood stand on the mantelpiece, placed it on a table, and put out her cigarette on it.

It was the first thing Alice Grenville noticed when she entered the room fifteen minutes later, her luncheon guests having finally departed. Her nostrils flared as though offended by the disagreeable odor. Without comment, she emptied the cigarette butt and ashes into a wastebasket, wiped off the Chinese plate with a piece of her pale-blue stationery, and replaced it on the teakwood stand.

"I cannot bear cigarette smoke in this room" were her first words to her new daughter-in-law. "It is where I tend to my affairs."

"I'm sorry," said Ann simply. She was determined not to be thrown. It was, after all, only a cigarette.

"But you had no way of knowing," said Alice, relenting, willing to let the moment pass. It had made any sort of greeting—a handshake, an embrace—unnecessary.

It was said of Alice Grenville, by her triplet sisters, and her friends of old, that as a young girl she was superbly handsome, and the various paintings of her, particularly the Boldini, in her presentation dress and feathers, attested to this. As a young girl she would rather have been thought beautiful than handsome, but the beauties of her youth, whom she had envied, had not, for the most part, weathered the storm of the years in the way her handsomeness had. Ann was struck by her looks in a way she had not been at their first meeting.

"Have you met Winston?" asked Alice, displacing the Pekinese from her chair and sitting down. "We think he looks so much like Mr. Churchill. Here, Winston, I've brought you something lovely from the table." The Pekinese went mad with delight at the attention he was receiving. Alice broke a cookie in two and threw first one and then the other half of it in the air, and watched in complete concentration as the dog scurried for his favors, yipping and yapping. Ann, forgotten, stared at the interplay between dog and mistress.

"What a good doggie you are, yes, yes, what a good doggie you are, and how your mummy loves you, yes she does, yes she does," cried Alice, swooping the Pekinese up in her arms and holding him aloft. She pulled the needlepoint bell cord, and when her maid, Lyd, appeared, kissed her dog between his eyes and handed him to her maid. Lyd, in the family for years, took in the scene, understood, and departed wordlessly. That accomplished, Alice turned back to the business at hand. The two Mrs. Grenvilles looked at each other once again.

"You must tell me about your wedding," said Alice. "Edith Bleeker, who heard from Bratsie, tells me you wore white. This was your first marriage?"

"Yes."

"Have you brought pictures? I hope so. The girls will want copies. Their only brother, you know. Ah, your ring, do let me look at it."

Ann, barraged, moved forward and held out her hand. For the first time she was glad her pear-shaped diamond was not as big as Babette Van Degan's.

"Lovely," said Alice, looking at it but not taking her daughter-in-law's hand. "Mr. Glaenzer, I suppose."

"No, Cartier's," corrected Ann.

"Mr. Glaenzer is our man at Cartier's," said Alice.

"Oh." She felt she could say nothing right. She turned toward the mantelpiece. "Is that what you do with invitations?" she asked, grasping.

"What?"

"Pile them up like that on the mantelpiece?" It did not seem to demand an answer, and none was given, but she continued to pursue an inane topic. "It looks very smart. You get invited to an enormous number of things."

"I've noticed this about you before," said Alice.

"What?" asked Ann.

"You talk about props to avoid talking about issues," answered Alice.

"Props?"

"But you are theatrical, Ann. Surely you know what that means. The last time we met you talked about my ermine coat and a photograph of Queen Mary. Today you talk about the placement of invitations on a mantelpiece. Then you had designs on my son. Now you are married to him. Shall we begin this conversation?"

Ann Grenville tried to look straight into Alice Grenville's eyes, but she found them impenetrable and unwelcoming.

"I know you don't think I'm good enough for your son, Mrs. Grenville," she said. Alice Grenville did not deny the allegation. She simply did not answer.

"Your parents are dead?" she asked instead.

"Yes."

"They were what?"

Unsure what she meant, Ann answered, "Poor."

"I meant what occupation."

"My father was a farmer. My mother was sometimes a teacher."

"Were they divorced?"

"Yes. When I was eight. My mother married again and divorced again."

"Good heavens."

"Why is it you don't like me?"

Alice, taken aback by Ann's directness, replied, "You are ambitious."

"I *am* ambitious," conceded Ann. "I didn't know it was a bad thing to be."

"*Too* ambitious, which is very different."

"Teach me how to be." She said it simply, without guile. "I love your son. I have never loved a man as I love him. I intend to be an excellent wife. My career on the stage is behind me. Are these the issues you wish to deal with?"

"You needn't be belligerent, Ann," chastised Alice. Her brown velvet eyes assessed anew the woman in front of her. "After all, you are already Mrs. William Grenville, Junior."

"I know I am," said Ann. "I only feel tolerated by you because I am married to Billy Grenville. I feel you are waiting for my marriage to be over, as if it were a wartime thing. It isn't, you know. Till death do us part."

For a while Alice did not answer. She reached out and twisted off a brown leaf from the cyclamen plant. "You call my son Billy?" she asked finally.

"Yes. I didn't want to marry a man called Junior."

"You're right. I suppose he has outgrown that name. Where will you live?"

It was a conversation full of starts, stops, and stumbles. Each, in her different way, was used to controlling, but each knew she had met her match. Until Billy Grenville returned from the war, a state of unspoken truce would be observed.

THE SISTERS, with the exception of Billy's favorite, Cordelia, remained aloof. What they thought of their sister-in-law, that she had trapped their brother, was never expressed, except among themselves, since their code would permit no outside criticism of their brother's wife. But what they felt was sufficiently plain for their friends to form an opinion.

Esme Bland, for one, rolling bandages one afternoon in the Grenville library for the war effort, watched Billy Grenville's glamorous new wife, fascinated. Poor plain Esme Bland had always nurtured the secret hope that one day she would become Billy's wife. She watched the sisters talk about people Ann did not know and parties she had not been to, using nicknames and private allusions, familiar to them, incomprehensible to her.

Ann began appearing at family lunches and dinners without being accepted by the family itself. It soon became apparent that Alice, resigned, had taken her daughter-in-law in hand to show her the ropes of the life she had married into. She suggested books for her to read, which Ann read, and made subtle suggestions about the way her hair was done and the kind of clothes she wore, and Ann listened and acted upon the suggestions.

"I very much hope you won't mind if I make a suggestion," said Alice, determined to make the suggestion whether it was minded or not.

"No," replied Ann, who said about herself that she never had to be told a thing twice.

"When you're in conversation, Ann, your eyes should not dart around the room to see who else is there. Give your undivided attention to the person with whom you are talking."

"Right," said Ann.

"And just pass your hand over the top of your wineglass before the butler pours if you don't want any wine. Never turn your glass upside down."

"All right."

"Don't cut your roll with a knife. Break it always."

"Yes."

And on and on.

Ann sat among them, a stranger in their midst. When she realized that no amount of friendliness would change their impression of her, she stopped extending herself. She watched, listened, and learned, improving herself in small ways not at first apparent to them. Although she was aware of the importance of her new position almost immediately, from the attitude of salespeople in shops she began to frequent, she was content to wait before she began to make her presence felt in her new family.

WHEN LIVING accommodations at the Grenville house were not offered Ann, Babette Van Degan found her a sunny apartment on Park Avenue that she moved into and began to fix up. Babette remained in her life, but she did not try to bring Babette into her new family, not wanting Babette to see her cold-shouldered by Billy's sisters, nor wanting Billy's sisters to size them up as a pair of Cinderellas. In a very short time she began to see her old friend through Grenville eyes.

"With freesia, you know, if you crush the end of the stem, they live longer," said Cordelia when she and Felicity came to see Ann's new apartment. Ann, who did not see the point of crushing stems to make blossoms last longer when you could simply buy fresh blossoms, wondered how they knew all the things they knew, these people, that had so little to do with survival. She wondered if she would ever settle into their kind of life.

"I think you're using the wrong brocade," said Felicity. She will never get it right, Felicity thought: candles at lunch, chrysanthemums in summer, gold brocade.

"You don't like it?" asked Ann, crestfallen.

"Gold, you know, it's not quite the thing. It's so . . ." She stopped before she said "Babette Van Degan," of whom they all made fun.

" 'Show girl'?" asked Ann, bristling. "Is that what you were going to say?" One day, she thought, she would get even with Felicity.

"*Pas avant les domestiques,*" said Felicity to Ann, knowing the Irish maids did not understand, knowing Ann didn't either.

She changed the brocade. She softened the color of her

hair. Even her handwriting changed: the round letters of the Palmer method taught in the Pittsburg, Kansas, school system gave way to the fashionable backhand printing of the Farmington–Foxcroft–St. Timothy's school system. In everything the sisters were her models. She had an eye for the aristocratic gesture, and she acquired that. She had an ear for the aristocratic voice, and she acquired that, with the help of a teacher, found for her by Count Rasponi, whom she paid handsomely for social guidance.

"But you are Mrs. Grenville," he said to her the first time they met, reassuring her.

"They sense that I am different," said Ann.

"But that's what makes you special," he insisted.

"I want to talk like them, dress like them, handwrite like them, think like them. *Then* I'll add my special thing on top of that."

Count Rasponi laughed with delight.

ONE MORNING, in the seconds before awakening, Ann saw Billy's face clearly, brightly. Awake, she was sure he was dead. She examined her feelings. She missed terribly the handsome young man she barely knew, who had defied his family for her, and realized how deeply she needed him. She wondered what would become of her. She knew she would be dropped by the family that had only tolerated her. She knew that even in so brief a time she was beyond returning to the chorus line. The stage had been no more than the means to an end, and the end was where she now was. Later, to her joy, she discovered that Billy Grenville was not dead at all. Rather he had distinguished himself in battle in the Pacific.

The news of Billy's heroism in the Pacific, saving the life of an enlisted man, for which he was awarded a Silver Star, coincided with Ann's announcement to the family that she was going to have his baby. Providence, again, was on her side. It was a miracle of timing, and even Felicity rose to the occasion.

"SHE DON'T get up until noon," Ann heard her maid say on the telephone to whoever was calling. Certainly it was true what the woman said, she didn't get up until noon, but the sound of it, at least in Mary's brogue, was wrong to her ear, and she began her day by firing Mary for insubordination, although it might have been for bad grammar. Later, she told Babette Van Degan, who called to remind her of their lunch date, that she couldn't possibly have lunch because the baby was kicking and her goddam maid had walked out on her, leaving her high and dry.

"Hello, is that you, Ann?" said the voice on the other end of the telephone, in a gravelly kind of way that Ann recognized immediately as the voice of Kay Kay Somerset.

"Yes, it is," she answered brightly.

"It's Kay Kay Somerset." No matter who Kay Kay Somerset married, and she married quite often, three times before she was thirty, she was always called Kay Kay Somerset. Ann read every word about her in the society columns, where her name constantly appeared, and listened avidly to the stories Cordelia told her about Kay Kay's early pursuit of Billy. "She came out, of course, but she wasn't taken into the Junior Assembly," explained Cordelia. "Pots of money, though."

"Oh, hello," said Ann, hoping the thrill she felt at being called by Kay Kay Somerset was not too apparent in her voice.

"I thought you looked so pretty at the Eburys' last night."

"Thank you." She hadn't known she had been noticed. "I feel so enormous these days."

"When will it be?"

"Not for three more months."

"I wondered if you'd like to have lunch today."

"Well, I'm, uh . . ." She thought of Babette, just abandoned.

"I'm driving back to the country at three, but I thought it would be fun to get together. You know, we've never talked."

"I think that sounds marvelous."

"I'll meet you at the Colony at one. In the bar. Away from all the old ladies."

Ann was ecstatic. She bounded from her bed, ran her tub, picked out her most becoming maternity outfit, and wished she had not fired her maid. She walked into the Colony at fifteen minutes past one in splendid good looks and high good humor and was escorted by Mr. Cavallero himself to Kay Kay Somerset's table. It was the beginning of her first friendship in her new life.

"Weren't you on the stage?" asked Kay Kay.

"Oh, only very briefly," answered Ann quickly. "My family really didn't approve at all. And then I met Billy."

"Oh," said Kay Kay. It seemed quite a disappointing answer to Kay Kay, who would have preferred her new friend to flaunt her theatrical past, especially as it was well known that the Grenville family considered her a totally unsuitable choice for Billy to have made. Ann, on the other hand, thought she had answered Kay Kay's inquiry marvelously. She felt no qualms in the least about letting go of any of her past story before becoming Mrs. Grenville. She was more interested in hearing about Kay Kay's life than in revealing to Kay Kay anything about her own life, and she drew out Kay Kay, who loved talking about herself, into hilarious stories of her marital failures.

"It was our usual conversation," she said about her most recent ex-husband. " 'Where's the check?' 'It's in the mail.' 'Fuck you.' Slam."

The happy occasion was marred somewhat by the appearance in the same restaurant of Babette Van Degan and her luncheon replacement for Ann, another former show girl.

Babette, through indignant looks, made no secret of the fact that she was offended by her friend's defection. Ann realized that the time had come to lessen her attachment to Babette, whose loyalty to her former show-girl friends now seemed excessive to Ann.

Kay Kay fascinated Ann, and she treasured her new friendship as she once had treasured her friendship with Babette. She began going places on her own, away from the grudging sponsorship of her Grenville relations.

"Who painted that?" asked Ann, pointing to a large pastoral scene hung over a console table in Kay Kay's apartment. She was ever alert in the learning process.

"I don't know, some Italian," answered Kay Kay, not even bothering to turn around to look at it. She was constantly moving, a new apartment to begin a marriage, a new apartment when the marriage ended. Wherever she was was in the process of being done up or dismantled. Disarray prevailed; she entertained in restaurants, arriving late to her own dinners, face flushed, eyes glazed, *placement* left behind. "Oh dear, you go there, and you go there, by Binkie," she would say, trying to remember her seating plan. Beneath the madcap air, Ann began to sense the deep insecurities of the very rich heirs and heiresses of this group she was beginning to meet.

After several meetings, Ann's awe of Kay Kay began to diminish, and she started to take charge of the friendship, using Kay Kay to meet people she read about in the papers. "I sat between Vere Cecil and Bluey Chisholm," she would say to her sisters-in-law, hoping to impress them with the excellence of her *placement*. More often than not, they did not reply, and she went on, recounting the guest list, at least the illustrious names.

"Let me look them up in the old S.R. here," said Felicity, picking up the Social Register. The Grenvilles thought of themselves as old New York, and therefore superior to Kay Kay's flashy friends. "Surprise, surprise, here they are." She was disappointed to find them.

*   *   *

ANN HOPED and prayed that the child she carried would be a son. Pregnancy was for her a long and tiring period that impeded the progress of the great new life that awaited her. Even Billy, in his letters from the Pacific, referred to the unborn child as "he" and "him." It was, however, more for Alice Grenville than her husband that she wished to deliver the Grenville heir, as if by preserving the name and continuing the tradition she would cement her place in the family and win the affection she yearned for from this woman rather than merely the politeness she received.

All the Grenvilles went to Archie Suydem, and, it seemed, had forever. He'd been in attendance when all the Grenville children were born, and he'd been at the girls' weddings. Archie Suydem was the best doctor in New York, everyone knew that, they told Ann, and furthermore he belonged to the Union Club and the New York Yacht Club, and that said a lot.

Ann, who longed to do the right thing, to conform to all things Grenville, at least until she was sufficiently established in their midst to develop into the self she foresaw, could not bear the thought of such an old man as Dr. Archie Suydem placing his brown-spotted hands on and in her body, Union Club or no Union Club. As there was no one in the family to whom she could speak of her revulsion, she was determined, as her mother would have said, had she been alive, to grin and bear it.

"I have such trouble sleeping, Dr. Suydem," she said during an examination in her final weeks.

"Hot milk and honey before bedtime," replied Dr. Suydem.

"You suggested that last time, doctor, and it hasn't worked. I would like a prescription for some sleeping pills."

"No, no, that's not a good thing," he said, shaking his head. "In all my years of practice, forty-odd, I've never heard of anyone dying from lack of sleep." He chuckled his old doctor's chuckle. "Hot milk and honey and walks in the afternoon. Exercise is very important."

From Babette Van Degan and Kay Kay Somerset, Ann heard about Dr. Skinner. Sidney Silkwood Skinner was fifty, with luxuriant hair, gray turning white, and wavy. Both his hair, of which he was inordinately proud, and his pencil-line mustache appeared always to have been freshly trimmed, and his nails were manicured and polished to a sheen. He was not a member of the Union Club or the New York Yacht Club, and people like the Grenvilles referred to him, snobbishly, as a Park Avenue doctor. He was thrilled when the beautiful Mrs. William Grenville, Junior, forsook the doctors recommended by her husband's family and sought out his services. He was putty in her hands, made house calls day or night, and prescribed a potpourri of refillable prescriptions for the tensions and stress of New York life.

From Dr. Skinner, she heard about Dr. Virgil Stewart, then very much in fashion with the young matrons of New York, and, much to the disapproval of the Grenville family, switched from Dr. Suydem to Dr. Stewart to deliver her baby. When her time was at hand, she picked the fashionable Doctors Hospital, overlooking the East River, with Dr. Skinner's and Dr. Stewart's blessing, rather than Columbia Presbyterian Hospital, where all the Grenvilles were born, and ordered her meals to be sent in from the Colony Restaurant.

Following an easy birth at an inconvenient hour, Dr. Stewart, who arrived at the hospital in evening clothes to deliver the Grenville heir, informed Ann that she was the mother of a bouncing baby girl. Her disappointment in the sex of her child was apparent to both the doctor and the nurses present in the room, and she tried not to let show the resentment she felt toward the baby when it was placed in her arms. While she was reflecting that she would have to go through the nine-month ordeal again, the thought of Alice Grenville's four daughters before the son flashed through her mind, not for the first time. Rather than dwell on a subject so disagreeable to her, she inquired of Dr. Stewart what party her inconveniently timed birth-giving had dragged him away from.

In secrecy Ann would have liked to name her daughter Wallis, after the Duchess of Windsor, or Brenda, after Brenda Frazier, who were the kind of women she admired, as had her mother before her, but she knew better than to risk the derision of her sisters-in-law at these suggestions. She rejected all the names of the Grenville women. She didn't want an Alice, she said to Babette, or a Rosamond, nor a Grace, nor a Cordelia, and most certainly not a Felicity. She decided on Diantha, a name she had read in a novel, and agreed to call her Dolly when Alice said she thought Billy would find the name contrived and theatrical. Dolly Grenville. She began to like the sound of it. It was a name that would read well in social columns, she thought, when that time came.

The Reverend Dr. Kinsolving performed the baptismal service of Diantha Grenville in the chapel of St. James' Church on a cold afternoon in March. Observing every family tradition, she wore the Pleydell christening dress that had been worn by Alice and all of her four daughters. Cordelia was the godmother. Bratsie, in absentia, fighting in North Africa, was the godfather.

A small party followed at Alice's great house off Fifth Avenue. Ann, looking exceedingly smart in dark blue, sat on a sofa in an elegant and relaxed pose, made loving references to Billy, and allowed herself to remain a sideline figure. Outside, the St. Patrick's Day parade passed by—marching bands, baton twirlers, waving politicians, Irish songs, and a cheering populace. Inside, where the christening party assembled for cocktails, only the maids, passing canapés, bothered to look out, and their glances were stolen.

Finished with the photographs and a lengthy discourse on the heirloom baptismal dress, Alice Grenville did not linger in grandmotherly attitudes. "Find the nanny, will you?" she said to her butler, handing him the baby.

PART
TWO

like it when you whisper all the filth in my ear," Billy confessed to Ann, holding her tightly, his face in her hair. Jealous by nature, she liked to drain him of desire before leaving in the evenings for the constant round of dinner parties that had begun to make up their life. They were in their bed, where they were good together; there they satisfied and understood each other. Elsewhere it was not always so.

For all her years it seemed to Ann she had been waiting for her life to begin. When Billy returned home from the war, she felt that finally that beginning had come. The apartment, finished, was not satisfactory. Billy, used to large houses, felt constricted by the proximity of the child's nurse and nursery sounds that began too early in the morning. It was felt, by Billy and his mother, that a house would better serve their needs, and a house was found in the East Seventies between Park Avenue and Lexington Avenue, less grand by far than the grand Grenville house but grander by far than the abodes of nearly every other young couple in the city.

Ann was attracted to her young husband's spoiledness. She realized how little she knew him out of uniform. She realized also that the battle of winning him having been won, the heightened and heady drama of their courtship and wedding had now settled into real life. She was anxious for him to see and approve of her advancements in the years that he had been gone, but she found instead that she merely bewildered him.

"Sometimes I don't recognize you anymore," said Billy. "You're like a different person."

"I thought you'd be proud of me," said Ann.

"If that was what I wanted, I could have married the real thing," he answered. Her eyelids flickered, and her eyes, moistening slightly, widened. She had been hurt. He had not meant the remark to sting her, but it did.

Billy suggested a sojourn to his mother's country house in Brookville, Long Island, as a kind of honeymoon to reacquaint themselves with each other and to introduce Ann to the friends of his childhood with whom he had grown up. The house, called Fairfields, was to be theirs for the several weeks they stayed, without Alice, without the sisters, without Diantha and the nurse. It was Ann's first encounter with the North Shore. Days were filled with sport, at which Ann proved herself to be surprisingly proficient. Nights were filled with parties at neighboring estates.

That night Ann observed the group at Alfred and Jeanne Twombley's: the Chesters; the Dudleys; the Webbs; the Chisholms; Teddy Plum; Bratsie Bleeker; the McBeans; Sass Buffington; Tucky Bainbridge; the Eburys; Petal Wilson. No stray noblemen here, no late-blooming millionaires. This was the core: friends from childhood they were, and their parents before them. Sixty percent of the land of the North Shore of Long Island could be traced to the ownership of those present. In advance she knew their histories: past stories of suicided parents; kidnapped brothers; institutionalized children; divorce; depravity; drink; depression; death in crashed planes, on sunken yachts, off fallen horses. But how elegantly they behaved. She was transfixed by the aristocracy of them.

She noticed how very alike the young women all were. They talked the same way, in the same accent, as if they had shared the same nanny. Their hair was done in the same pageboy style, held back with gold bar pins, and their long skirts, blouses, and cashmere cardigan sweaters over their shoulders were interchangeable. She realized that for country life she was overdressed, overcoiffeured, overjeweled, a mistake she would not make again.

Ann, entering Jeanne Twombley's bedroom after dinner, knew instinctively the women were talking about her. She shrank back against the yellow-distempered wall, undetected by the others, as if to lose herself in it, and heard her background or lack of it discussed.

"She's the cheapest thing I've ever seen," said Sass Buffington, combing her hair.

"Felicity said you must go to one of her parties before she finds out it's the wrong way to do it," said Tucky Bainbridge, and the other ladies laughed.

"Piggy said she went through two polo teams on Gardiners Island before the war," said Petal Wilson.

"N.O.C.D., darling."

Smarting, she turned and left the room, walking down the curved stairway to rejoin the men left behind in the dining room with cigars and brandy. On her entrance, the men rose as one to greet her into their womanless turf. She was pleased to see that Billy felt a glow of proprietorship over her, and she smiled charmingly at him as she sidled next to him.

Later, when the party reassembled in the chintz-slipcovered drawing room, Ann asked Billy, "What's N.O.C.D. mean?"

" 'Not our class, darling.' Why?" he replied.

"No reason."

To herself she vowed that someday these ladies would eat their words, and, silently, she dedicated herself to achieving the social acceptance her husband's family and friends denied her. Ignored by the women, she ignored being ignored, and plunged herself amid them, wanting to be accepted by people who did not want to accept her, prepared to play the waiting game. She looked over at the handsome, rich, socially impeccable young man who had married her and would enable her to open any door, and smiled at him affectionately.

"Bratsie likes you," said Billy, back home.

"But not for the right reasons," replied Ann.

"What does that mean?"
"He likes me because I'm wrong."
"Wrong?"
"Wrong side of the tracks."
"He didn't say that."
"He didn't have to. I can read the look."

It filled Ann with inordinate pleasure when her name appeared for the first time in the New York Social Register. "Grenville, Mr. and Mrs. William, Jr. (Ann Arden)," it read, and then a list of incomprehensible abbreviations that turned out to be the many clubs that Billy belonged to. When she arranged her sitting room, she liked having the black-and-terra-cotta book in a prominent place on her desk, visible to the eyes of visitors and readily available to her touch. She remembered the time when she had looked up the address of the Grenville family in the same pages of an earlier edition in a florist shop. Now, listed herself, it provided proof positive of who she was.

Ann did not understand Bratsie Bleeker's early admonition to her not to try to become one of them but to remain her own self among them and therefore be special. What she wanted most *was* to become one of them, and on the occasions when she was asked, by a new acquaintance, if she had gone to Farmington or if she had been there on the night Bratsie Bleeker swung on the chandelier at Kay Kay Somerset's coming-out party, she felt that she was succeeding in her performance.

She bought her books at Wakefield's, was photographed by Dorothy Wilding, had Dr. Stewart as her gynecologist, and ordered her flowers at Constance Spry. She worshiped at St. James', when she worshiped, which was not often, and lunched at the Colony, which was very often. Caruso did her hair, Blanchette her nails, and she was massaged by Gerd. Hattie Carnegie dressed her for day, and Mainbocher for evening. Jules Glaenzer jeweled her. She was attended to by a cook, two maids, a chauffeur, and a nanny for her daughter. It did not appear that she was unused to this way of life.

As time went on, Ann feared sometimes that there was less to Billy than had at first appeared. He seemed like a second son in a first-son role. When he arrived late at his office, after a night of parties and nightclubs, Ann knew that it did not matter. There was no one to chastise him for unseriousness of purpose. He spent a number of hours there each day, involving himself in unimportant business, reading newspapers and magazines, checking with his stockbroker on conservative investments, making dates for squash or backgammon. He lunched at one of his clubs with friends and stopped for a drink at another on the way home, and his men friends would say about him, after he was gone, what a perfectly lovely fellow he was. Sometimes it surprised Ann that he had seen films that she had not seen, and she discovered that he often went alone, or with Bratsie, during the afternoons. He did not think much about advancing in life, because where he already was, financially and socially, was where most ambitious men he knew wanted to be.

Billy's feelings for Ann were ambivalent. He loved her. She gratified his sexual desires. She made him laugh. She stood up to his sisters. For a long time she even made him happy.

At the same time he disapproved of her. It was an ongoing fact of her life that she could not keep help. Servants, in their various capacities, came and went in varying degrees of haste, stung by her suspicions and imperious tones. Mostly, her social ambition was too apparent for him. She did not give parties to enjoy herself but to advance herself.

"Tell her she doesn't have to climb so hard. Tell her she's already there," Bratsie said to him one night, observing her work the room, as Bratsie called it, at one of Edith Bleeker's parties, collecting future invitations, and Billy, though honor-bound to support his wife, agreed with his friend.

He accepted, without curiosity, the minimal facts of her history that she gave him. References to her past were sparse. If pressed, she presented the life of Fredda Cunningham as her own. When she showed no longing to return to Kansas to present him to relations or friends, he felt relieved of that obligation. When he discovered, applying for a passport, that she was a different age than she had told him, he wondered about other things.

Having provided her with so much that she had never had before, he expected that her gratitude would continue and become the basis of their relationship. Instead, he watched her not only settle into her role too quickly but become the dominant member of their match. Where once he had ruled the relationship, because the world into which he had brought her was his and he had acted as her interpreter and guide, she was now overtaking the reins. He felt anger, and the anger that he felt persisted, but he did nothing to rid himself of it.

As IF SENSING the rumblings of his disaffection, Ann invariably would accomplish something that would make Billy proud, and harmony would be restored. Preferring men's pastimes to women's, she took up backgammon and then skeet shooting, and became proficient in both, winning skeet tournaments at Piping Rock. She loved the feel of a gun in her arms and longed, as Billy longed, for big game. But it was the son she produced and the home she created that cemented her marriage in seeming permanence.

Loathing pregnancy, for the time it took away from her life, and the distention of her lovely body and breasts, she undertook it and the doing of her new home concurrently. She knew her bridal apartment had not been a success, but she found herself unable to get along with the series of fashionable decorators suggested by her mother-in-law to help her: Rose Cummings came and went, as did Mrs. Brown, Mrs. McMillan, and Mrs. Parrish. To a lady they pronounced the young Mrs. Grenville impossible. Then, at a party of Babette Van Degan's, Ann met Bertie Lightfoot. Bertie Lightfoot was the director for her life she had been longing for without realizing it. Under his tutelage she began to give the performance she had been waiting all her life to play.

Ann never firmly committed herself to one of Babette Van Degan's invitations in case something more social should turn up. She said she thought she might have to dine that evening at "the family's," as she referred to evenings at Alice's, or that Billy might be working that night. Babette had become the kind of woman greatly admired by men who would never marry. Decorators and designers filled her rooms, and merriment prevailed. Junior said No, Absolutely Not, he would *never* go there again. Uninterested herself in that kind of appreciation, Ann, on the occasions she did attend, took to dropping in briefly, on her way to somewhere else, where she would be meeting Billy. On what she vowed would be her last time ever at a Babette Van Degan party, she met Bertie Lightfoot. He was at the time helpless with laughter at one of Babette's stories of her chorus-line days. His eyes, vividly Alice-blue, matched his shirt exactly and looked, to Ann, sad beneath his merriment.

"You're not leaving, darling?" asked Babette, breaking in on her own story. "You just got here."

"I must," answered Ann. "I'm meeting Billy." She was evening-dressed, carrying a fur, refastening a bracelet.

"What smart place are you off to tonight?" asked Babette. Bertie Lightfoot watched the exchange with fascination. So *this* was Mrs. Grenville of the society columns.

"Kay Kay Somerset's having a dinner for Lady Starborough," answered Ann. She had learned to neither flaunt grand names, as she once did, nor minimize them.

"She's gone swell on us," explained Babette to Bertie and turned away to take several cheese puffs from a tray passed by her young son, Dickie Junior, and to yell out a request to Edie and Rack, who were playing at twin pianos, to play "Spring Will Be a Little Late This Year."

"*Printemps* is in the air," said Bertie.

Ann nodded farewell to Blue Eyes.

"Linger awhile, so fair thou art," he said.

"Gallantry in Mrs. Van Degan's drawing room," replied Ann. She liked him instantly. He made her laugh.

Not one to let an opportune moment pass, Bertie admired Ann extravagantly: praised her clothes, her hair, her style. Unused to compliments, other than sexual, from her husband, Ann responded to Bertie's flow.

"Tell me again what your name is," she said.

"Lightfoot. Bertie Lightfoot."

"And what do you do?"

"Decorate."

"Decorate what?"

"Whatever."

She hesitated leaving.

"Cigarette?" he asked, snapping open a smart leather cigarette case.

"Leather? In town?" she asked, in mock social horror.

Again he collapsed with laughter. She enjoyed having her humor appreciated.

"I have a new house I'd like to show you," she said.

The house which Billy Grenville had purchased for his family was on a quiet street lined with leafy trees in the East Seventies between Park Avenue and Lexington Avenue. On each side of the street were elegant brick and brownstone houses in which still lived, in those days, but one family apiece and the servants who administered to their needs. The stucco exterior of the Grenville house, at number 113, was freshly painted a cream color, and its doors and shutters were lacquered black, as were its geranium-filled window boxes.

Exceedingly smart, like its new occupants, it was a house meant to be noticed and commented upon.

Within, Bertie Lightfoot, making his name in New York, decorated the rooms in muted luxury. The furniture Billy's family handed over to Ann, in English and French shapes, she realized they did not value highly, assuming that she would not know the difference. It was Bertie Lightfoot, turning the pieces upside down, who, contemptuously, pronounced them reproductions. They were discarded or put aside for country-house guest rooms, when a country house of her own became a reality, which, she knew, it would, and fine furniture was sought in its stead. With Bertie she began to attend auctions, and visit collections, and develop an eye for only the best.

"You have a faggot's eye," he said to her admiringly, "for being able to spot exactly what's right." Bertie was good at intimacy with women but devoid of passion for them.

"I think I'll refrain from repeating that compliment to my mother-in-law," she answered. They enjoyed being together and maintaining absolute secrecy about the interior of the house until it was completed and could be presented as her creation.

Bertie of the light blue eyes was a merry man with a fund of camp wit, a knowledge of eighteenth-century French furniture, and a passion for rough trade. After his evenings in society, or at the opera, especially if he had been drinking, Bertie often changed from black tie and patent-leather pumps into less distinctive gear and took to the streets.

On his way out again after a dinner with Billy and Ann, a young man spoke to him on the street in an easy friendly way. "Hi," he said. "How's it going?" When he smiled, he had a dimple and good teeth, and there was a directness in his eyes. Bertie, who was more than a little drunk, thought for a moment that perhaps he knew him, from a party, or somewhere, and said, "Hi," back, in a matching easy friendly way, and asked him back to his apartment, blessing his luck for the easiness of the conquest.

Bertie had another drink, and a marijuana cigarette that the young man offered him, and a line or two of cocaine, all of which Bertie took without noticing that the young man took none.

The first punch was to the Adam's apple, rendering Bertie speechless. It was a full minute more before he realized what was happening to him: the sound of the switchblade knife opening, its cold blade being pulled across his cheek and neck, its point scratching the skin of his chest and stomach; the thirty-foot telephone wire tying his hands behind his back and attaching his feet and his hands; the pleasant young man of the street turning into a schizophrenic monster, destroying the antique-filled apartment, kicking the inert body, taunting, snarling, hating. He put a brown grocer's bag over Bertie's head and dropped lit kitchen matches on the paper.

Death was in the air. The end of his life was at hand, but his thoughts were not yet with God. Instead they were on the tabloid papers, and what they would say, after he was dead. He heard another match being struck and knew that his face would burn if that match dropped on the bag.

"God, help this man who is killing me," whispered Bertie. "God, help this man who is killing me." Again and again he whispered it, as in a litany. For a long time there was silence, and then he heard the click of a closing door. Amid the carnage of smashed antiques he lay there in shame long after his near-murderer had departed. The most he could do to extricate himself was to shake the brown grocer's bag off his head. There was no way he could untie the cord that bound his hands and feet behind him.

In time he crawled parameciumlike across the floor to the telephone and removed the receiver by knocking it off with his head. It did not surprise him that the telephone was out of commission; his night caller had removed the diaphragm from the earpiece to ensure that it would not be used after his departure.

He struggled more with the cord but did no more than tighten the knots. Had he been able to see his hands and feet behind him, he would have seen that they were turning white from blocked circulation.

He thought of the morning, and the maid coming and finding him in the deplorable state that he was in. Gerta, the maid, a German woman, came to him several mornings a week. The shame of being so discovered by Gerta was overwhelming, naked and bound as he was, and the subsequent story from maid to other clients, including Basil Plant, the writer, to whom she went on Fridays, was a kind of hell that further paralyzed him in its contemplation.

There was another telephone, hidden away in a linen closet, with a different number entirely, for his business calls. Again he crawled across the floor, proceeding by inches, down the hall, across the bedroom, and into the bathroom where the linen closet was.

Again he removed the receiver by knocking it off with his head, and the dial tone to a world outside sounded precious to him. Holding a pencil stub in his teeth, he slowly began to dial

The number he dialed rang, and rang, and rang again, and then it was answered.

"Hello?"

"Oh, thank God, I thought your telephone was off."

"It is, but I could hear it ringing downstairs. Who is this?"

"Bertie."

"Are you crying?"

"I need help, Ann."

"Where are you?"

"My apartment."

"What's the matter?"

"I'm in a jam."

"Isn't there anyone else you can call?"

"No."

"I'll leave right away."

Ann Grenville rose from her bed and dressed quietly while her husband slept. Arriving at his apartment after three, she let herself in with a key he had given her. She untied him, covered him, poured him a brandy, massaged circulation into his whitened wrists, picked up broken things, and helped him into bed.

"Do you want to talk about it?" she asked.

"I was on my way out to meet some friends from California at the Westbury, but I forgot my money, so I came back here to the apartment, and I must have interrupted the guy in the middle of a robbery, and he . . ."

"Save that story for the maid, Bertie," said Ann quietly, as she picked up the vial of cocaine and the plastic bag of marijuana. "Where do you want me to put this stuff?"

"I don't care."

"Talk about it, Bertie."

"Every year in the *Daily Mirror* I read about some decorator on the Upper East Side they find garroted and murdered, and that's all I could think of, how it was going to look in the papers," he said, crying.

"Why did he stop?" she asked him.

"I suppose I gave up."

"Bertie?"

"Yes?"

"While you thought you were dying . . ."

"Yes?"

"Is that all you thought about? The papers? What people would say about you after you were gone?"

"Yes."

"Not about God, and all that?" She waved her hand vaguely heavenward.

He looked away from her. Tears filled his eyes again.

"I'm not criticizing you, Bertie. I'm afraid that's how I'd be thinking, too, how it would look, if something terrible ever happened to me." She breathed deeply. There was a long silence. "I'd better go. My husband will think I'm at Doctors Hospital having the baby."

"Ann, I want to explain to you how it happened."

"Oh, Bertie, it's not necessary for you to explain the particulars to me. I get the overall picture."

"I'll never forget this, Ann."

WHEN HER CHILD was born three weeks later, it was the much-needed son. Amid family joy for the name preserved and the tradition of Grenvilles carried on into a new generation of New York, Ann vowed, privately, that her childbearing days were over. *Now* was the time for her much-postponed life to begin. They named the child, of course, William Grenville III, and when Alice and the sisters began cooing the name Willy to him in his Grenville family cradle, Ann said she wanted her son called Third, and Billy was delighted with her inventiveness and agreed.

SHE WAS, FRANKLY, disappointed with the size of the sapphire in the ring he gave her when the baby was born. She placed it on her finger, looked and looked at it, and looked again, holding her hand at one angle and then another.

"It's just not me," she said, taking it off.

He was crestfallen, she could see that, and she sought quickly to make up. "But the flowers, my darling, the orchids are so lovely, and we have our wonderful son."

"Yes," he said. "There was another sapphire there that I could exchange this for, perhaps."

"Billy."

"Yes?"

"I'd like to go with you when you buy me jewelry."

♣   ♣   ♣

"LOOK AT THIS, isn't it marvelous, what Billy bought me when Third was born," said Ann, showing her sapphire ring at the christening party in her splendid new house, finished finally. Over the mantelpiece in the living room was a Monet of irises, which Bertie said was the final touch in the beautiful and greatly admired room. In the thrill of acquisition, there was a resumption of warm feelings between Billy and Ann, and their guests, including his mother and sisters, were struck by the appearance of harmony between them.

So AS NOT TO seem completely without antecedents, Ann began to mention her mother, although the mother she mentioned bore little resemblance to the mother that had been. Her mother was the one person who had understood her completely. She had been the first to perceive her inner longings and help to mold them into ambitions which she encouraged her to pursue. "Things happen to you, and they always will," said her mother. That she had become who she had become surpassed even her mother's wildest dreams for her, and she sometimes wished for that look of admiration she had grown to expect in her mother's eyes when she began to make her ascensions.

Ethel Mertens had not minded that she was left alone each night when Ann was at the Copacabana performing; nor did she expect her back after the final show, knowing and glowing in the fact that her daughter regularly attended the nightclubs of the city with eligible men who sent her gifts, one of whom might, she hoped, marry her one day. Ethel was quite content with her tabloid papers and gossip columns, over which she pored in the hopes of finding Ann's name; she became as well versed as Elsa Maxwell or Maury Paul in the comings and goings of such prominent social figures as Wallis Simpson and Barbara Hutton and Brenda Frazier.

Sad as it was, Ann knew that her mother's death the spring before she met Billy had been timely. It was not a thought she cared to formulate, but her ascent into the Grenville family, difficult as it was, would have been more difficult, perhaps impossible, with Ethel Mertens to explain. It was a threshold her mother would not have dared to cross. Once uprooted from the Kansas plain she had longed to flee, she invariably did the wrong thing in social situations, knew it, and suffered remorse when she embarrassed her daughter. Eventually she was content to stay behind, root for her daughter, and listen to her stories of life in the great world. Ann, to assuage her guilt from the unformed but lurking thoughts about her mother, began to bring her into conversations, referring to her not as Ma, but as Mother, the way Kay Kay Somerset talked about her mother, as if she were some elegant creature, now gone, whose silver it was, or whose tureen, that was being admired. "Oh, that was Mother's," Ann would say.

Then there appeared the portrait, not prominently placed, to call too much attention to it, but in the hallway of the second-floor landing, over a Regency bamboo settee that was never sat upon. It was Bertie Lightfoot who pointed out the picture to her in the back room of an antiques shop they were scouring through. It was turned against the wall because the frame was broken and the glass cracked, a forgotten lady of gentle birth painted in pastels in a style favored by society painters in the years preceding the First World War.

"She looks like you, Ann," said Bertie in great excitement. "I think maybe it's a Brocklehurst."

Later, when Bertie had gone to see about other matters, Ann returned to the antiques shop and purchased the picture, which did indeed resemble her. "That was Mother," she would say sometimes about the picture, in passing, to new friends not familiar with her history, and she came to believe it was so.

The picture, however, nearly ruptured the remnants of her friendship with Babette Van Degan, who came to call to see the celebrated house. Ann greeted her and led the way back for a tour room by room of the five-story house.

"Look," she said, at the door of her splendid drawing room, looking at it herself, yet again, with a pride of ownership. She moved a needlepoint pillow imperceptibly to the left and surveyed its symmetry with its matching pillow. Each day she secretly reexperienced the beauty of her home. Babette, always enthusiastic at her friend's progress in the world, responded accordingly to each fashionable room.

"Oh, how swank this all is," she said.

Upstairs, on the second-floor landing, on the way to Ann's bedroom, Ann said, in the offhand manner she had acquired about the portrait, waving her hand at it in passing, "You remember Mother, don't you?"

"Of course I remember your mother," replied Babette, "but who's the broad in the picture?"

"How was Babette?" asked Billy later.

"Oh, fine," answered Ann listlessly.

"Not much conviction in your voice."

"She's so cheap, Babette."

"But rich."

"And getting richer by the minute."

"Is Hyman Wunch still in the picture?"

"On and off."

"Think she'll marry him?"

"Darling, you don't change your name from Van Degan to Wunch," said Ann. "I mean, you just don't. A name like

Van Degan makes life easier. That's all there is to it. It's a name people like to say, like Vanderbilt, or Rockefeller, or Astor. All over the world it's a name people recognize."

"Is that what Babette said?"

"That's what I said, but it's what she feels."

"You two have a falling-out?"

"Oh, let's not talk about Babette. I'm not going to see her for a while. You'd better get dressed. We're due at Eve Soby's."

SHE WORKED as hard as an office girl on the daily advancements of her insatiable ambition. Next it mattered exceedingly to her that she be named as one of the best-dressed women in New York. When she achieved that distinction, she pretended to consider it an inconsequential thing.

Bratsie Bleeker, her early champion, began to dislike her. Sensing this, she withdrew from him, not wanting to be what he wanted her to be, the single act of defiance in Billy's life. Neither spoke of their disenchantment to Billy; he would have had to side with one, and neither wanted to risk banishment.

Reluctantly in some quarters, it had to be acknowledged that Ann Grenville had made it. She was not the only maiden of modest social and financial pretensions to marry into a fine old family of wealth and position, but she was the first of the Cinderella girls, as Babette Van Degan called them, to conquer the highest brackets of New York.

Wherever one went, one heard her name. As a new word, once learned, suddenly appears constantly in conversation and print, so her name was spoken in every social gathering. Everyone seemed to know her, or to have heard of her, and to have opinions about her. People who had not intended to take her up took her up. She was seen in the best seat at the best table at the best parties. Men liked her exceedingly; she danced every dance, sang lyrics in their ear, and her conversation was ribald and spicy. Women liked her less but could not deny she was an asset at their parties and on their committees for their charities. Her husband's family, once so reluctant to accept her completely, in hopes the alliance would be brief, were astonished that she so rapidly penetrated an impenetrable world. An intruder in the family, she had become its most highly visible member, eclipsing her husband's sisters in social life.

There was no doubt in anyone's mind that she intended to make a go of her marriage and avoid becoming a former wife with a great last name, like Babette Van Degan, relegated to the sidelines of the social world. She understood that her power lay in remaining Mrs. William Grenville, Junior, no matter what. Despite the mismatch that they may have been as a couple, she knew that she still exercised a fascination over her husband that was stronger than the doubts he sometimes felt about their union.

Fydor Cassati, the society columnist, wrote constantly about the young Grenvilles in his column, far too often for Billy's taste, not often enough for Ann's, whose thirst for prominence was unquenchable. He said they were one of the most glamorous couples in New York and that no party was complete without them. Ann purred in silent pleasure at the superiority she now felt as she read every word about herself, and clipped the clippings, and pasted them in scrapbooks, along with photographs and telegrams and invitations, as if to prove that what was happening to her was, in fact, happening, but also, as if she knew, at some deep level of herself she was not in contact with, that it could not possibly last and should be recorded. If she created in her scrapbooks a perfect picture of a perfect life, then that was how it was.

Their pace of living became more and more frantic. Be

here. Be there. Be everywhere. Know this person. Know that person. She could take in a room at a glance with a skilled and rapid eye and understand perfectly the circles within circles of the overlapping groups that composed the fashionable life of New York. Alice Grenville, always sensible, knew that a young couple who went out every night of the week were a couple who didn't have much to say to each other at home. The times of being alone together, just them, became less and less frequent, and their conversational moments, about family, about children, and nannies and nursery school, occurred only at parties, giving them the appearance of togetherness.

Her dinners were noted as much for the careful selection and placement of those invited as for the style shown in the decoration of her tables with their marvelous arrangements of exotic flowers, and embroidered clothes, and antique porcelain, which she had begun to collect with a passion. The very latest novels, which you were going to read the reviews of in next Sunday's *New York Times*, were already on her tables, artfully arranged. People came on time and stayed late. Billy, standoffish all his life, found himself, not unwillingly, at the center of a pleasure-bent society.

"I don't see Felicity," said Billy to Ann, looking around their crowded living room.

"The point of the party," answered Ann. Her eyes wandered around the room as her husband talked to her, looking over shoulders, glancing sideways, in case there might be a more interesting conversation in progress.

"You mean you didn't invite her?" asked Billy about his sister.

"That's exactly what I mean."

"There'll be hell to pay for this."

"Worth it. Go talk to Wallis. Bertie's hogging her."

♣   ♣   ♣

BY THE TIME Bratsie Bleeker eloped with a Mexican movie star, several inches taller than himself, who spoke no English, his friends, with the exception of Billy Grenville, had become less tolerant of his antics. They were raising children and beginning careers in banks and brokerage houses and settling down in small houses on their parents' estates on Long Island. It was Billy, rather than Ann, who went to Cartier's and ordered from Jules Glaenzer the silver box on which was engraved, in Billy's handwriting, "To Bratsie and Maria Theresa with love from Billy and Ann," because Ann said it seemed ridiculous to spend four hundred dollars on a gift for a marriage that wouldn't last six months.

It didn't last six months, but that was not the point as far as Billy was concerned. Bratsie was his friend, and not to have honored his marriage would have been an affront to the friendship. Billy remembered, even if Ann didn't, that Bratsie had made his way to Tacoma, in wartime, to attend their shunned wedding ceremony, and it troubled him that Ann had put a distance between him and Bratsie, without any conflict ever having taken place.

There were stories in the gossip columns about Bratsie from time to time, chumming around with Errol Flynn and Bruce Cabot in Hollywood, or sailing with Freddy McEvoy in the South of France, always in the company of starlets and playgirls. Very often he was drunk, and in time he was prevailed upon to enter a sanitarium in South Carolina near his mother's plantation for the purpose of drying out.

He invited Billy and Ann to the plantation for a shooting weekend of quail and turkey after he left the sanitarium, but Ann chose not to go when she heard from Edith Bleeker who the other guests would be—"Jellico's cast of characters," Edith called them, in that tone of voice that told, without a single word of reproach being spoken, that the cast of characters were *not*, by any stretch of the imagination, the right sort.

Ann prevailed upon Billy to go on safari in India instead,

a longtime dream that appealed to Billy as well as herself, and they were there, with a maharaja and a maharanee, shooting tigers, when they heard, days after he had been buried, that Bratsie was dead, shot mysteriously while racing his jeep at two o'clock in the morning on the grounds of his mother's plantation.

Ann was quite unprepared for the depths of Billy's grief, and she suspected again, as she had before, that there was something in the rigidity of Billy's character that cried out for the devil-may-care attitude that Bratsie had always expressed toward their upbringing, as if he knew there was more to him than what he was getting out of himself, but he didn't know what it was or how to seek it.

When they returned to New York, Billy and Ann paid a condolence call on Edith Bleeker at her red brick townhouse on upper Park Avenue. They were shown into the library by her butler, Dudley.

"Oh, Edith," cried Billy, embracing his best friend's mother.

"Sit here by me, Billy," she said, patting a place next to her on the red damask sofa. For half an hour they talked and reminisced and laughed about Bratsie. Edith Bleeker had always wished that her son were more like Billy Grenville, with his unfailing good manners and obedience to his family, except in the matter of his marriage, and without the wild streak that had always been a part of Bratsie's makeup.

"I'm glad he had you for a friend, Billy," said Edith.

"I hope they hang the guy who did it," said Billy.

For a moment there was a silence in the room, and Ann, who saw nothing wrong in what Billy had said, felt that an awkward moment was in progress.

"The case has been closed," said Edith Bleeker. She changed her position on the sofa and reached over to push a button to summon Dudley to bring fresh drinks.

"Closed?" asked Billy, shocked.

"Yes," she said quickly, rising, wanting an end to the conversation.

"How could that be?" persisted Billy, and Ann watched the interchange between them.

"It was an accident," said Edith, and added, "an unexplained accident."

"But surely you're not satisfied with that?" asked Billy, wanting to see his friend's death avenged. "What they have is nothing but inconclusive evidence."

"Oh, Dudley," said Edith to her butler, who had entered the room. "Will you bring the drink tray in here."

Later, at dinner at Alice Grenville's house a few blocks away, Billy related the conversation to his mother. "So much better this way," answered his mother, serving herself asparagus from the tray that Cahill held out for her.

"Why?" asked Ann from her end of the table.

"Poor Edith doesn't need all that dirty laundry brought out," answered Alice, and, like her friend Edith Bleeker ordering the drink tray, signaled an end to the conversation.

Later still, at El Morocco, where they stopped for drinks on the way home, Ann related the story to Babette Van Degan, whom she encountered in the ladies' room. "It was odd, Babette," she said, adjusting her makeup and combing her hair. "It was as if Edith Bleeker didn't want to know how Bratsie was killed."

"You understand that, don't you?" asked Babette.

"No, I don't," answered Ann, wanting to know.

"It's those old families. They don't want outsiders getting near them. They'd rather let whoever did it get away with it than have their family secrets all over the newspapers. Their theory is, it's not going to bring him back."

"My word," said Ann, evening her lipstick with her little finger.

"You can be sure Bratsie was up to something unsavory," Babette continued, "like screwing the foreman's wife."

"That's what he was doing, apparently," said Ann. "Edith's maid told that to my mother-in-law's maid."

"You see?"

＊   ＊   ＊

ANN NEEDED constant proof that she was who she had become. She wanted a signet ring with the Grenville seal. She wanted a guest book on her hall table for signatures of the fashionable people who attended her parties. She wanted scrapbooks and photograph albums. It wasn't enough for her to write "Harry Kingswood" in her diary, for having been at her house for dinner, or beneath a photograph. The point hadn't been made, for either herself or others, unless she wrote "Viscount Kingswood" or "Lord Kingswood" at the very least.

She wanted her portrait painted. From the day she had first walked into Alice Grenville's house and seen the Sargent and the Boldini and the Lazlo, she wanted to have her picture done. She knew where in her drawing room she would hang it and could imagine herself lounging elegantly beneath it on her damask sofa surrounded by needlepoint pillows.

It was Bertie Lightfoot who suggested that Salvador Dali paint her, and the instant she heard his suggestion she knew how right it was, how unpredictable, how original, how like her. "That was my mother," she could imagine Diantha saying in years to come, regaling her friends with passed-down stories of the amusing and bizarre sittings that had taken place in the late afternoons in the painter's suite at the St. Regis Hotel.

Ann reveled in the exoticism of the court of the famed Spanish surrealist. The ends of his black waxed mustache turned roguishly upward to almost the corners of his eyes. She liked the scented candles, leopard-skin pillows, and bowls full of birds of paradise. An entourage, led by his red-haired wife, Gala, eyebrows plucked out and painted on in black arches of perpetual surprise, and handsome young men and pretty young women, convinced him daily of his genius.

"Let me peek. Let me peek," Ann would say playfully,

about the easel that faced away from her, but Dali would not, and her enticements, which bordered on the flirtatious, were of no avail. He was not interested in the opinions of his expensive sitters, only in his interpretations of them. If they were thrilled with the results, he was pleased. If they were not, he was indifferent.

On the day of the unveiling, Ann brought Billy with her, check in pocket. She passed in front of the picture and turned toward it. When her eyes met her image, she drew back, and her cheeks flushed for a moment. An outsider might have thought it was a flush of modesty. Someone who knew her, like Billy, knew it was a flush of displeasure. A look of hostility came into her eyes, as if she sensed that the artist recognized some hidden depths of herself that she preferred to keep hidden.

"I want everybody out of this room except Mr. Dali and my husband," she said to his wife and the assembled court, and the rage in her voice and the anger in her face made them retreat quickly and quietly to other rooms of the suite, where they listened in fascination through the doors to the screams of the disenchanted sitter. It was Billy's first encounter with the enormity of his wife's temper. He was startled by her crudeness. Her words were not used by women of his class. He blew out his lower lip, as he did when she did things that embarrassed him; it replaced the reprimand that he did not give.

Billy would have paid for the portrait and left it behind, treating it as a bad investment. Not Ann. She grabbed the check from her husband and tore it and threw the pieces at the bemused artist. "Never!" she cried. When she grabbed her mink coat off the chair where she had dropped it, she knocked over a vase of flowers but made no attempt to pick it up.

She thought, and Billy thought, the matter was at an end until she read in the papers a few days later that the artist was suing her and her husband for immediate payment. Billy was shocked to find themselves in a story in the tabloids.

"I'm going to pay it, Ann," he said. "I can't have this sort of publicity. It makes Dali more famous, and it makes us look ridiculous. You should have heard the razzing I got at the Brook Club this noon."

"You are not going to pay it," she said. It was a trait of hers that she would not back down, ever.

When the newspapers reached Billy at his office for a statement, he backed his wife's position.

"I looked at the picture," he said, "and walked away scared. It was like walking away from a monster. It was ugly and grim, and I feel Mr. Dali just sort of slapped it together. It is a heck of an unpleasant picture."

"Are you going to pay up, Mr. Grenville?" asked a reporter.

"No," answered Billy.

Dali, clever about publicity, kept the story alive in the papers. "The personal opinion of Mrs. Grenville is not for me so interesting. From an artistic point of view, it is not interesting at all."

The Grenvilles did not attend the court hearing and were shocked to be informed that they had lost the case and were ordered to pay the artist in full for the portrait. Billy, without consulting Ann, paid the money.

The picture was delivered to their house by the lawyer who represented them, never to hang over the damask sofa in the drawing room. One night, when Ann had been drinking, she slashed it, and it vanished to the rear of a closet in her bedroom.

"WHAT ARE all those pills?" Billy asked her one evening.

"Sidney," she answered, meaning Dr. Sidney Silkwood Skinner, as if the mysteries of medicine were beyond her, and the answer sufficed. Her daily intake of appetite suppressant spantules increased, and she began eating almost nothing. Obsessed with slimness, she allowed waiters and maids to remove her plates, the food fashionably untouched. You can't be too rich or too thin, Bertie told her the Duchess said, and she agreed.

At Voisin one afternoon for lunch, she looked across the crowded restaurant and saw, in a far corner, in deep conversation, Billy and a woman whose hat masked her face. She wondered why Billy never engaged her in intense conversation. Jealousy began to squirt its poison into her system. She gulped her second martini, and, combined with her pills, it prompted her to reckless action. Abruptly excusing herself from her luncheon companions, she charged across the restaurant, prepared for a public scene with the woman who was usurping her husband.

"Why, *hello*, what a surprise!" she said loudly as she approached his table, heavy irony in her voice. She was surprised that Billy did not blanch when he saw her. Then she saw that the expensively dressed woman was Cordelia, his own sister, with whom he was lunching. She realized, from the look on Cordelia's face, that they had been discussing her, and blushed. She would rather have come upon him with a mistress.

HER DATE BOOK was filled for weeks in advance. She liked to know that on two weeks from Thursday they would be dining with Eve Soby, black tie, and that a month from Friday they would be sailing on the *Queen Mary* for Europe. Tonight was Bertie Lightfoot's dinner to show off his brand-new apartment.

Ann took in the room at a glance. Like an art connoisseur having an instant and total reaction to a painting, she could reel off in her mind the entire guest list of a crowded room. The Chesters. The Dudleys. Billy Baldwin. Lady Starborough. George Saybrook. Thelma Foy. The Webbs. The

Chisholms. Cole Porter. Elsa Maxwell. Barbara Hutton. Nicky de Guinzberg. Lanfranco Rasponi. Dear, dear, dear, so much disinclination toward women, she thought. Basil some-one or other. Plant, maybe. She could never remember his name and didn't care much. He was petit, pale, unprepossessing, and poor, the type who could be counted upon to appear in a dinner jacket at the last moment when someone else dropped out. Ah ha, the handsome Viscount Kingswood, mercifully without Kay Kay Somerset. Things were looking up. She smiled her dazzling smile as she entered the room, aware, as she always was aware, that she understood how to enter a room better than anyone she knew.

"Bertie!" she cried out in greeting. Her voice was less a society woman's voice than the voice of an actress playing, and playing very well, the role of a society woman in a draw-ing-room comedy. Or drama. Early regional traces had long been obliterated, and a glossy patina of international partying had given her a sound so distinctive as to make people remark on what a lovely speaking voice she had. "It's heavenly! I'm mad about the color!" she said about the new apartment.

They were each other's favorite person, Ann and Bertie, and they kissed elaborately on both cheeks.

"Billy," said Bertie in greeting.

"Bertie," said Billy in greeting.

"Isn't this the apartment where Hillary Burden jumped out the window?" asked Ann.

"Mrs. Grenville chills the room again," said Billy.

"Come in. Come in. Who don't you know?"

When Harry Kingswood bowed to kiss her hand, in the Continental manner, Ann was astonished and thrilled to feel the wetness of his tongue on the back of her hand. As he raised his head, their eyes met, for an instant only, before she moved on to greet the other guests, but both sets were eyes of experience and recognition, and a sexual encounter was agreed upon without a word being exchanged. If he had been of less lengthy lineage, she would have resented his understanding of her availability, but it was, of course, the very thing that made her available.

"Hello, Elsa," she said to Elsa Maxwell.

Later, near the conclusion of the evening, she brought out a small Fabergé box and swallowed two pills she took from it.

"What are those?" asked Harry Kingswood.

"For sleep," Ann replied. "If I take them here, they will have started to work by the time we get home."

"Why not a brisk walk with the dogs to tire you out?"

"Not for me."

"Or warm milk with honey."

"You sound like the Grenvilles' doctor."

Billy appeared with her mink coat. Without knowing why, he resented Harry Kingswood. "Come along, mother of two," he nagged.

"Coming, father of one," she replied. "Goodnight," she said to Lord Kingswood.

"You must ring me when you come to London," he said. He knew she would. So did she.

"And how many heartbeats did you quicken this evening, my dear?" said Billy, in a sort of mock-caressing tone he sometimes adopted toward her, as they waited in front of the apartment building for their chauffeur to bring the car.

"You know I adore Bertie," said Ann irritably. "No one makes me laugh more, but I do think it's tiresome of him to palm off his arty friends on us at dinner. I mean, I was dying to talk with Harry Kingswood—he's supposed to have the best shoot in England—but I got stuck next to that Basil Plant with the tiny hands."

"The writer?"

"They say."

"What does he write?"

"Slender volumes no one reads."

"Overly shy, wasn't he?"

"I think shy people should stay home."

"Let's go to the country tomorrow."

"I told Elsa we'd go to the opening of Cole's show."

"Christ," Billy muttered.

"Didn't you have a good time?" she asked when they were settled into the back seat of their car.

"No, I had a terrible time," he answered.

"But it was a marvelous party! Why didn't you have a good time?"

"I feel uncomfortable with all those people. They all do things. They accomplish. After all, who are we? We're the couple with all the money whose name is in the papers too much for going out every night to too many parties."

"I wish there were eight nights in the week. I'd be out every one of them," said Ann.

"Look at Neddie Pavenstedt, my old Groton roommate. He's number-two man at the bank where my grandfather was president, and then my father, and where I was supposed to be after him. As for Basil Plant, with the tiny hands, his slender volumes get printed. I've never done anything. I feel like a failure, Ann."

"Oh, really," she said. It was a conversation she had heard before and was sick of before it began.

"Do you know what's happening to me, Ann? I only feel safe with people just like myself, out on the North Shore. I've become just who I swore I'd never be, one of those fourth-generation blank-faced men with sad eyes who laugh all the time. When I married you, I wanted you to save me from all that, and all that I did was get in deeper."

"How can you be a failure, Billy, when you have ten million dollars, and God knows how many more millions to come, après Mère? This is the most ridiculous conversation I've ever heard in my life."

"That's just the outsider in you talking. You don't understand."

"Oh, so I'm an outsider, am I?" she asked indignantly, readying herself for a fight.

"Let's not turn this conversation around to be about you,

Ann. It's so rarely I get a chance to talk about myself, and how I feel, and what I think."

"Oh, poor Billy, poor, poor Billy. Let's all feel sorry for Billy."

"God, I miss Bratsie. He's the only person who ever understood. Why did you have to die, Bratsie?"

"Because he fucked the foreman's wife, darling, and the foreman shot him dead, that's why."

"Ah, the meaning of life, as explained by the fashionable Mrs. Grenville."

"What's the new chauffeur's name?"

"Why?"

"What's his name, Billy?"

"Lee."

"Lee," she called out to the front seat. "We're not going home. We're going to El Morocco."

"No, we're not."

"Yes, we are. I'm not going home with you in this mood. And, Billy?"

"What?"

"Tomorrow tell what's-his-name to take his rosary beads off the rearview mirror. I can't stand that look."

WAY OVER EAST on Seventy-second Street, near the river but not on the river, in a block of fancified tenements occupied mostly by poor friends of the Astor family, who owned the block, as they owned a great many blocks in the city, my light burned late that night in the fifth-floor walk-up friends of friends of an Astor connection had arranged for me to call my home. My name, Basil Plant, appeared in the vestibule next to the buzzer system. The apartment, called a railroad flat, was tiny and somewhat squalid. A typewriter, reams of paper, a bulletin board with pink and blue and white file cards thumbtacked to it, and a wastebasket too full of discarded pages announced my writer's life.

In those days, as now, I never went to bed, no matter how late, or how drunken, or how drugged the evening had been without recording first my impressions of the people I had met in my multifaceted existence, seeing it all as bits and pieces of a giant mosaic that one day would fit together in a literary Byzantine pattern that would explain my life.

My bathroom cabinet was filled with the small bottles of Listerine, guest-sized tubes of toothpaste, and unused bars of Floris soap I took each weekend from the guest-room baths in the rich houses I was beginning to visit. I was always looking for economies. Ann Grenville was right when she said I wrote slender volumes no one read. The bitch. Even my aspirin bottles were purloined, and from one of them I took the four aspirins I invariably took before retiring after an evening of too much drink.

I was still smarting from Mrs. Grenville's snub, because I would have liked to become her friend. I like social climbers. They interest me. But she resisted me, right from the beginning. Neither my inquisitiveness nor my wit appealed to her. I looked at myself in my bathroom mirror. What I saw was a slender, fragile-looking, almost androgynous young man with a shy manner and a sweet smile. The loss was hers, I decided.

"Dinner at Bertie Lightfoot's," I wrote in soft pencil on a lined yellow tablet in my small, neat, and precise handwriting. "A last-minute replacement. Bertie gave me instructions to be interesting, and witty, and earn my bread and butter. It was his usual crowd of high-society people, the type who go out every night. On one side Natasha Paley, a Russian princess who works for Mainbocher. On the other the beautiful Mrs. Grenville of the social columns, who helped make Bertie Lightfoot the great success he is today. Brightly painted, she looked into her compact seven times during dinner, readjusting her face. She seemed to be engaged in secret smiles and looks with an Englishman called Harry Kingswood at the next table. My presence mattered very little to her. She picked up my place card, so as to read my name, and said, 'Bertie tells me you're a writer, and quite interesting,' and then sat back as if waiting for me to entertain her.

"I said to her, trying to hold up my end of the conversation, 'Weren't you in show business once?' I knew for a fact she danced in the line at the Copa. 'Briefly,' she answered, redoing her lips at the same time. 'But my family was furious, and then I married Billy Grenville,' conveying the impression she had been a rebellious deb. Then she snapped shut her compact, signaling the end of that conversation. I felt about her that her life began when she became Mrs. Grenville. She made no effort to conceal her boredom with me. So I got drunk. All that marvelous wine of Bertie's, Lafite-Rothschild.

"There is something about Mrs. Grenville, beneath her Mainbocher dress and perfect pearls, that made me think of a tigress in heat. I feel wantonness beneath her social perfection. I think she is bored, at least sexually, with her husband. Billy Grenville is very handsome. He doesn't have that overbred look so many of those North Shore people have, as if their mother and father were first cousins. Mrs. Grenville is a very silly girl."

BILLY FELT, in time, like a hostage, imprisoned in the relationship, and, like a hostage, he befriended his captor, but merely for the sake of survival. There were plans, furtive to be sure, for escape.

It was Ann who suggested to him that horses, the Grenville stables, Jacaranda Farm, twenty-five hundred acres in the Blue Grass country, the producer of three Kentucky Derby winners, would be his salvation.

"But I've never been seriously interested in horses," he protested. "That was always Grace's domain."

"Well, *become* seriously interested in horses. You own the farm, not Grace. Your father left it to you. I'll take care of Grace. It would be madness to just let the reins slip through your fingers, as you let the bank slip through your fingers."

It bothered Billy when she enumerated his failures to him. He looked off, away from her, out the window, thinking back to the days of his youth when his father made him, Saturday after Saturday, walk through the stables and paddocks, greeting people, talking horses, looking at horses, and the queasiness in his stomach returned to him that always returned to him when he thought of his greatly admired father.

"Look at Alfred Twombley," said Ann, citing the example of one of Billy's lifelong friends to prove her point. "He's made the most marvelous life for himself in racing. He works hard. He makes money. Everyone respects him. Why can't you do the same thing?"

Grace Grenville Grainger was in well-cared-for early middle age. Horses and dogs had always interested her more than people and society, and she lived a country life, happy that the business of the Grenville stables had fallen to her when her brother was indifferent to the management of his inheritance. "The thrill is in breeding rather than racing," she was fond of saying.

Grace made no preparations for visitors; they could take her as she was, or leave her, she didn't care. Not bothering to check her appearance in a mirror, or pick up fallen newspapers off the carpet, or puff up crushed cushions, she was on the floor cleaning up after her new puppy when Billy and Ann entered her living room.

"Grace, how could you?" cried Ann.

"How could I what?" replied Grace.

"Be down on your hands and knees like that, cleaning up."

"I'm cleaning up dog shit."

"Even so. Get someone to do it for you," said Ann.

The implication was quite clear. People like them, Grenvilles, did not do servants' work. It was not lost on either Grace or Billy that Ann had become more Grenville than the Grenvilles.

"I like this room, Grace," said Billy.

He was making conversation, Ann knew, dreading having to tell her that he was here to reclaim his inheritance. They were seated at opposite ends of a long sofa, slipcovered in well-worn chintz, facing a fire. All the bookshelves were untidily filled with horse books, dog books, and detective novels, some horizontally atop the vertical ones, and other books filled tabletops. The fireplace bench was heaped with magazines and newspapers, rendering it useless for sitting. A cracked Lowestoft plate, which they were using for an ashtray, on the cushion between them, was glued together rather messily. The glasses on the drink table, where Ann went to mix herself a Bloody Mary, were a mismatched lot, from a jelly glass to a chipped Baccarat goblet. The room annoyed her; only someone as rich as Grace could get away with a room like this. She knew that Billy was next going to say that it looked lived in.

"It looks lived in," he said.

Ann lit another cigarette and kept silent. She concentrated on how she would redecorate the room if it were her house. Her bracelet dropped off her wrist and fell on the floor by the fireplace. Grace picked up the fire tongs, retrieved the bracelet, and handed it to Ann on the end of her tongs. Grace sensed, before the conversation began, that there was a motive in the unexpected visit.

"There's a marvelous man on Second Avenue in the Eighties, Mr. Something, I have it written down, who could repair this plate for you so the crack wouldn't show," said Ann.

"What a lot of bother," said Grace, who didn't care about

the crack. Among themselves the sisters laughed at the grandeur of their sister-in-law.

Ann felt slighted, as she always did by her husband's sisters. Her makeup suddenly felt stale and caked on her face after the long drive. She was no longer in a good humor.

"Billy, why don't you go outside and look at the horses. I want to talk to Grace," said Ann.

Later Grace, who heard the language of the stables, and used it occasionally, to the hysterical dismay of her sisters, called their sister-in-law a cunt. What she actually said was that Ann gave new meaning to the word.

So it was that Billy Grenville began his new career in racing and breeding as the head of the Grenville stables.

ANN GRENVILLE stood outside the Colony Restaurant, under the green awning, and kissed the cheek of her mother-in-law and then the cheek of her sister-in-law Cordelia, with whom she had just lunched. As Alice Grenville's car drew up, Ann pulled back slightly the sleeve of her mink coat and quickly glanced at her watch.

"Wherever are you going, Ann?" asked Alice. "That's the third time in the last half hour I've seen you glance at your watch, and you made us gulp down our coffee."

"Doctor's appointment, Mère," Ann answered.

"You're awfully eager to get there," grumbled Alice, allowing Charles, her chauffeur, to assist her into the car. "Are you coming with me, Cordelia?"

"Yes, Mère. Goodbye, Ann."

As Alice Grenville's car headed for Madison Avenue, Ann took off in the direction of Park Avenue. Halfway to the corner, she looked back and saw that the car had turned uptown. She reversed her steps and headed back toward Madison Avenue, crossed, and walked swiftly toward Fifth Avenue. From her handbag she took out a pair of dark glasses and put them on, although there was no sun in the sky that day.

The Hotel Fourteen was her idea. She knew, from experience, that they asked no questions and catered to a clientele that was unlikely to have heard of her or any of the people in her group. It was next door to the Copacabana, and it had served, on more than one occasion, during her show-girl days, as a locale for a between-shows tryst with one of the garment manufacturers she sometimes saw when she was in financial distress.

She walked straight through the small lobby to the elevator as if she were registered as a guest. In an earlier period of her life, she had found the hotel elegant, but, with an eye grown familiar with elegance, she saw now that it was too gold, too red, too vulgar, but exactly right for the purpose at hand.

She stepped out of the elevator at the sixth floor and knocked at the door of Room 612 with a gloved knuckle. In an instant the door opened; its occupant had been waiting for her knock.

"Don't tell me I'm late," she said, walking in, dropping her mink coat off her, and dragging it along the carpeted floor. "Just ask me what I feel like."

"What do you feel like?"

"I feel like a call girl."

He laughed, bowed courteously, and kissed her hand. She felt the wetness of his tongue on the back of it. "Mrs. Grenville," he said.

"Lord Kingswood," she replied.

"A drink?"

"Let's not waste time on drinks."

"Good."

He wrapped his arms around her.

"Oh, I have been waiting for this," she said.

"And I."

"Oh, Harry, how did you know I like to be kissed on my throat, just like that," she said, her head back, her hands on his head, as he kissed up and down her lovely neck. "Oh, yes, handsome Harry, that is so nice. I do love the sound of kissing."

"Get undressed," he whispered.

"Unzip me," she answered, turning her back to him. With knowing fingers, he undid the hook and eye of her Mainbocher dress and slowly unzipped the back of her down past the hooks of her brassiere. "No, no, darling, I'll take off my own brassiere, thank you very much. You just sit down over there and watch. Oh, and Harry?"

"Yes?"

"You get undressed too. And I mean really undressed. None of that socks-on, shirt-on English stuff. Take off everything."

"Unbutton my fly for me," he answered.

"You English ought to learn about zippers," she replied, kissing him, as her expert fingers undid the seven buttons. "Oh, my God."

"What?"

"An uncoaxed erection."

Nothing excited Ann Grenville more than to watch a man see her breasts for the first time. They were, she knew, perfect, and the look of lust that came over Harry Kingswood's face at the sight of them and the expectation of touching them filled her with passion that matched his own.

"Harry?"

Harry Kingswood's face was buried between her breasts, too occupied to reply, but his bare shoulders made an answering gesture.

"You're not in any great hurry, are you?"

He shook his head, his tongue traveling from the bottom of one breast to her large excited beige nipple.

"Oh, good. I hate wham, bam, thank you, ma'am."

She lay back in the center of the double bed in Room 612 of the Hotel Fourteen and watched as this direct descendant of the fifth wife of Henry VIII entered her with the precision of an expert and for an hour held back his own arrival until she had been thrice satisfied.

"My God," she whispered when they had concluded. "And the missionary position! It's nice getting back to the basics."

Harry Kingswood laughed, at the same time fondling her breast.

"Let's hear it for love in the afternoon!" said Ann. "Do I look beautiful?"

"You do."

"I feel beautiful. What are you doing tomorrow afternoon, and the next, and the next?"

"I hope I'm going to be meeting you in Room 612 of the Hotel Fourteen."

She lifted his hand from her breast to kiss it and noticed the time on his wristwatch. "I have to dress, Harry. I still have to have my hair done. Billy and I are going to Eve Soby's party tonight, and Billy gets furious if I'm late."

"I'm going to Eve Soby's, too," said Harry.

"If you feel a hand between your legs under Eve's table-cloth, it'll be me," said Ann, dressing.

Harry Kingswood looked at Ann in delight. Each understood they were embarking on a love affair, without commitment or any thought of upsetting either of their marriages.

"The shooting season starts next month. Have you told Billy about coming to England yet?"

"I will tonight."

"I WISH YOU wouldn't sit on the bed. It's been fixed for the party, and you're wrinkling the coverlet," said Ann irritably.

"Too bad you're not fixed for your party," answered Billy, turning on the satin-and-lace coverlet, wrinkling it more.

"I'm not well," she replied, in self-defense.

"You stayed out all night dancing and drinking, and then you took a handful of sleeping pills at dawn."

"I did not."

"Do you ever think about this ridiculous marriage we have?"

"Billy," she said. Her voice was now placating. "There are people arriving any minute for cocktails. There's the bell now. Please go down and greet them. It'll take me twenty minutes at least. My eyes are all puffed."

"You're full of sleeping pills."

"Please, Billy. Our friends are arriving."

"Your friends. I think I'm going to walk out the front door as they're walking in and go to the Brook Club."

But he didn't. "How very pleasant this is," he said, entering his living room, to greet the already arrived Harry Kingswood. They were to have drinks there and dine at Maud Chez Elle, a restaurant then much in fashion, and go on to dance at El Morocco. Billy and Harry had the outward camaraderie of two members of the same class who recognized each other's equality, but there remained, nonetheless, an unease between them.

When finally Ann entered the room, fastening a bracelet —late, sure, unhurried, beautiful—for the evening of revelry ahead, Billy was astonished, as he always was astonished, at how she was able to pull herself together. Later, after midnight, he disengaged himself from the celebrants at El Morocco, waving goodbye to Ann and Harry Kingswood on the dance floor, and went home. He was, those days, up early and out at the track at Belmont for the morning workouts.

Billy often said that some of his best ideas came to him at breakfast. It was for that reason that he liked to breakfast alone, very often staring off into space while sipping his coffee or munching his toast. It was at such a moment that his troubled feelings connected the fact of Harry Kingswood's visit and his wife's duplicity. With the taste of strawberry preserve still in his mouth, he bolted from the room.

Upstairs, in their darkened bedroom, all signs of daylight were shut out, and would be for hours to come. He watched his wife in restless sleep, her arms embracing a pillow, one strap of her satin-and-lace nightgown fallen from her shoulder. On her bedside table were no clues of duplicity, if that was what he expected to find, only an apothecary of prescriptions, and lists and notes of things to be done, for her relentless pursuit of social life, when her day would finally begin.

"Why are you staring at me?" she asked, without opening her eyes, or changing her position, which was faced away from him.

"I'm not staring at you," he answered, backing away from their wide bed as if he had been caught stealing.

"Yes, you are," she said, from her sleep.

"I forgot something," he mumbled with a note of apology in his voice and withdrew from the room, not having spoken what he intended to speak. A new maid, observing the morning rules of silence, nodded to him as he left the room but did not speak either.

Outside the house the chauffeur, Lee, waited with the car and all the morning papers for Billy to read on his way out to the track.

"I'm going to walk for a bit before we start out," Billy said to his driver and proceeded toward Park Avenue. At the corner he stood through two light changes before crossing and failed to notice an acquaintance who greeted him. He was unused to examining his feelings and could not tell if the deep distress he was experiencing was because he loved his wife so much, or because his wife had not valued sufficiently the name and position that he had bestowed upon her. He wondered how many of their group knew of the liaison. He wondered if he had been made to look a fool.

That night, back at El Morocco, after another cocktail party, and another dinner party, Billy, drunk, finally said what it had been on his mind all day to say, but, out of sheer weakness, he ascribed his accusation to others. "Someone came to me with a s-s-story about you," he said.

"Who?" she instantly demanded.

"D-d-don't you want to know w-w-what was said before

w-w-who said it?" he asked. His speech was interrupted by an occasional stammer, a slight impediment of childhood, long since overcome, that reappeared only during intoxication.

"What, then?" she asked, knowing in advance what he was going to say. She had meant to tell him of her plan to visit Harry Kingswood, to shoot, but the moment had not presented itself.

"A-d-d-dultery," he replied.

"Really, Billy," she laughed. "How drunk are you?"

"Who said I was d-d-drunk?"

"You begin to stutter."

"I d-d-do not."

"Yes, you d-d-do."

During scenes she focused on things. She looked at the candlelit flowers, leaned forward and moved a rose, surveyed it with satisfaction, as if it made a difference. But there was no scene. They sat on interminably, nearly never speaking, watching, like a movie, the drama of nightclub life. Once they had thought there would never be enough time for them to say all the things to each other they had to say. She placed her hand over his finally and squeezed it. She wanted his feelings for her to remain constant, even while hers expanded to include others.

"I love you," she said.

"You don't love me, Ann," he replied, no longer drunk. "You just love the life that happens around me."

What he said frightened her. She lipsticked her mouth crimson, using the blade of her table knife as a mirror. Billy found her gesture vulgar and exciting. It was when he liked her best. At home later, enticing him to sexual frenzy, she erased his suspicions of infidelity. With the outpouring of her lover still within her, she received the fresher outpouring of her husband. And peace prevailed again.

A few nights later they went to a ball on the North Shore. A Hutton heiress was being presented to society in an indoor tennis court attached to a guesthouse on one of the great estates still in full swing. Young couples wandered about in the formal gardens. Ann took in the scene at a glance. The Eburys. The Phippses. The Hitchcocks. The Schiffs. The lot of them. The cream of the North Shore. She felt she had never seen anything so beautiful, and she valued her life and her marriage. Hello, Sass, she said. Hello, Titi. Hello, Molly. Marvelous dress, Brenda. Kiss-kiss, Lita.

She wandered about with Billy in tow. In the guest house —nicknamed the Playhouse—were a living room, a dining room, many bedrooms, and a vast music room with acoustics so perfect that combinations from the New York Philharmonic often came to play for the musically inclined hostess. Billy told her that the family used the Playhouse mostly as a guesthouse and a place to relax after tennis. Its courtyard, he said, had been brought from Fotheringay Castle in Scotland, and its cobblestones were the very ones Mary Queen of Scots had walked over on her way to the guillotine.

"Enjoy it," Billy said about the ball and the estate. "It's the end of an era. No one will be able to afford to give parties like this or live on places like this for long."

The orchestra played "Full Moon and Empty Arms." She sang into his ear as they danced, "Full moon and empty legs." He laughed with delight and remembered their first meeting in El Morocco.

"This is where I want to live, darling," whispered Ann into Billy's ear.

He laughed again.

"I don't mean this whole vast place," she said. "I mean the Playhouse, and the grounds around it."

"What about old lady McGamble? Don't you think she'd have a thing or two to say about that?" asked Billy, who never quite understood her sudden passions for having to have things instantly, not always with the best results. He still smarted over her squabble with Salvador Dali.

"I had a feeling about this house the minute we drove up the drive," she said. "It was meant for us. I can feel us living here. It would be perfect for the children. We can't go on staying at your mother's house every weekend. I think we've worn out our welcome there. I know her servants all complain about me, not that I care one damn bit about that, but it's time for us, Billy, to have a weekend place of our own."

THE WALKING ring outside the Saratoga sales pavilion was dark except for the orange glow of a hanging lantern on a stable door. The bidding was over on the yearling Thoroughbreds that had been walked around the ring on the last night of the sale. About a hundred yards away in the garden of the Spuyten Duyvil bar, horse breeders and buyers from around the world were drinking whiskey and talking horses. The main topic of conversation was the record price paid by the neophyte breeder Billy Grenville for a yearling colt he had already named Tailspin.

"You've got an eye like your father's," said Sunny Jim O'-Brien, the old horse trainer from the Grenville stables who had known Billy since he was a child and had been brought reluctantly to Saratoga by his dashing father.

"Do you think so, Jim?" asked Billy. "Really?"

"A chip off the old block," replied Sunny Jim, knocking back the only whiskey he allowed himself. "This Tailspin of yours is a winner, and you spotted it the instant you saw him. Your father had that instinct with Ishmael."

"This Tailspin of *ours*, you mean. We're going to do the same things, you and I, that you and my father did. Come on now, Jim, break your rule and have another drink. This is a night to celebrate."

Alfred Twombley and Piggy French, the two biggest names in racing, joined in the celebration. It thrilled Billy that old Sunny Jim thought he approximated his father. All his life he only remembered disappointment in his father's eye. He wished his father had lived longer.

ANN COULD NOT believe that she was in the company, for the weekend, of one of the English princesses. Sometimes she marveled at her life, to herself only, for she would not have admitted, even to her husband, that she did not take in stride whatever happened to her. It was times like this that she missed her mother. Her mother would have understood, her mother would have been overjoyed. She felt, alternately, thrilled and disappointed: thrilled with the event, disappointed with the person. She wanted the princess to be slimmer. She wanted her country tweeds to be less country, and her diamond pin to be more country. The perfection of royalty interested her. She was determined to buy herself an amber cigarette holder when she got to London, at Asprey's, like the one the princess had, and she stared and stared at her until she was able to memorize exactly the way the princess held the holder, in an elegant way she had not seen before, and the way she inhaled and the way she exhaled.

She took up her camera and, almost surreptitiously, snapped a photograph of the princess, who was in conversation with Harry Kingswood, listening to him explain the history of Kingswood Castle. Ann liked the way it looked, the informality of it, the princess in a tweed skirt and a silk blouse and walking shoes for the tour of the gardens and the grounds that was about to come. It was not a way many people saw her, and Ann could see the picture of the two of them, Harry and the princess, sitting on the chintz-covered sofa, in conversation, on one of the pages of her scrapbook. She took another picture, feeling braver, and then another. She wished the camera did not click so loudly. What a marvelous gift this will be for Harry, she thought to herself, as if she were a historian preserving an important moment of history, unconscious, in her zeal, of the looks the other guests were giving her to desist from her mission. There was silence in the room, but the clicking of the camera persisted. Looks of royal displeasure were to be evermore preserved in the scrapbooks of Ann Grenville. She was by this time aware of her faux pas, but she could not stop herself until the roll ran out, and the roll, alas, was of thirty-six exposures.

"I feel, Harry," came the royal voice of the royal princess, in ice-water tones, "that I am on duty at a charity bazaar being click-click-clicked away at instead of being a guest in your house. *When* is she going to stop taking my picture?"

Ann blushed in embarrassment, knowing that all eyes were upon her. From the sofa where the princess remained seated, she heard muffled excuses from Harry for her. "American, you know. She didn't know, ma'am."

Her love affair with Harry, so successful in New York, had, like some wines, not traveled well. "I say, Ann," said Harry, bearing down on her, in a hissing whisper, "this sort of thing is just not done. For God's sake, put that camera away!"

That evening Ann pleaded a headache and did not come down to join the house party for dinner. The telephone was located, for facts only, not confidences, in an upstairs hall of the castle, with not even a chair by it, lest one linger. By now Ann was familiar with Harry Kingswood's frugality. The next morning, before the other guests arose, she left by car for London, reliving the scene all the way, wondering if they were laughing at her, hoping the story would not get back to New York, knowing she would never see Harry Kingswood again. She understood instinctively that when one was married, love affairs had a natural termination. She flew to Rome and looked forward to a reunion with Billy.

Thereafter her passion for the English abated. Later, in another city, introduced to the same princess again, she gave no recognition of ever having met her before as she bowed her head and bobbed her curtsy.

*   *   *

"His ROBES, my dear, are made for him in Paris by a couturier. They shimmer and sparkle and are said to outdo in
grandeur the robes of the Pontiff. Don't you love it? Fulco
told me." Lipsticked already, Ann took a comb from her bag
and ran it through her hair, automatically.

"He's a priest?" asked Billy.

"No, no, a monsignor, and a great wit and diner-outer. I
mean, everyone knows him."

"He's American, you say?" Billy did not share his wife's
passion for European society, and the endless stream of gossip
that she brought back with her each day from her forays into
the palazzos of Rome went, for the most part, in one ear and
out the other.

"Yes. He married Tyrone Power and Linda Christian. I told
you that. But, now, listen to this!"

"I'm listening."

"He has arranged an audience for us with the Pope, and I
have bought a black lace mantilla that is so divine, and I
thought I'd wear that black dress that I wore to your sister's
party in London."

"But we're not Catholic."

"You don't have to be a Catholic to have an audience with
the Pope, for God's sake."

"When?"

"May fifth."

"May fifth?" Five, five, five, five. The fifth day, the fifth
month, 1955.

"That's what I said. May fifth. Ten A.M."

"I can't go."

"Why can't you go?"

He turned away from her, embarrassed to tell her what day
it was. "That's the day that . . ."

"What day? Oh, for God's sake, Billy, do you mean the day you're supposed to die?"

"I know it sounds insane, but I've never forgotten what that fortune-teller in Tacoma said. Five, five, five five. It seemed so far off then, and now here it is upon us."

"You don't believe that?"

"No, of course I don't, but I do, too."

"Well, if you're going to die, what better way to do it than to see the Pope first? It'll pave the way *right* to heaven for you."

"What will we talk to the Pope about? The latest parties?"

"It won't be just *us*, for God's sake, there'll be others, and afterward the monsignor is giving a lunch for us at the Palazzo Doria."

IT RAINED steadily on the morning of the papal audience. Eruptions of thunder preceded daylight, and rain beat angrily on the windows of the Grenvilles' suite at the Grand Hotel in Rome. Awakening late, after a night of too much drink, each was reminded of the morning of their wedding day in Tacoma twelve years earlier. Both bad-tempered, they dressed and drank coffee in silence. Why, Billy wondered, had they sat up until four drinking brandy at Bricktop's with a strange trio from Pasadena whom they had never seen before and would, probably, never see again? Why was it they always were out, out, out?

Below, in the downpour, there were at least thirty people ahead of them waiting for taxis in the drive-through of the hotel, and the hour of the audience was fast approaching.

"Whatever will I tell the monsignor?" wailed Ann.

"That we sat up until four drinking brandy at Bricktop's with a *ménage à trois* from Pasadena that you picked up. The

Pope will understand. So will the monsignor in his couturier robes," said Billy.

"Sometimes I hate you," she said to him. Their eyes met in mutual discord.

"It looks hopeless," said Billy, about the taxi situation.

"I can't understand why you didn't hire a car and driver when you knew perfectly that we had to be at the Vatican by ten." She, feeling mocked, was ready for a fight.

At that moment a car and driver went by and then stopped abruptly. A woman called out the window, "Is that really you, Billy Grenville?"

"Esme!" cried Billy. "I simply don't believe it! Could you drop us at the Vatican? We're late for an audience, and there's not a taxi in sight, and we're soaked."

Esme Bland, who had always loved Billy Grenville from afar, had never voiced her opinion on the subject, even to her great friend Cordelia, but she thought Billy had wasted himself on Ann.

"You have met Ann, haven't you, Esme?" asked Billy when they were settled in the back seat.

"Yes," replied Esme.

"At Cordelia's," said Ann.

There was a silence.

"It's raining cats and dogs," said Billy finally.

"My mantilla will be ruined," said Ann.

"Here, take my umbrella, Ann," said Esme.

WHEN THEY LEFT the Vatican, the sun was shining brightly on St. Peter's Square.

"He was adorable, just as cute as he could be," said Ann about the Pope.

"His flock will be touched by your description," replied Billy.

"Now I'm stuck with this damned umbrella of Esme's," said Ann.

"Why don't we wander around the cathedral a bit," said Billy.

"We haven't time," said Ann, looking at her wrist.

"I can't imagine having to report to Mère that we've been here and haven't looked at the *Pietà.*"

"Billy, we're due for lunch at Monsignor Herrick's at the Palazzo Doria," said Ann.

"I'm not going to lunch at Monsignor Herrick's at the Palazzo Doria," replied Billy, repeating her words exactly, diminishing them in importance.

"Of course you are."

"I'm not," he said. He was quiet, and his face did not have the stubborn look it assumed when he took a stand on something. She looked at him in the May sunlight, crowds of tourists jostling them, and realized she did not understand his withdrawn mood.

"What are you going to do?" she asked.

"I'm going to look at the *Pietà,* and then I'm going back to the Grand Hotel and order a chicken sandwich in the room, and then I'm going to lie on my bed and look off into space."

"Simonetta d'Este's going to be there for lunch, and the Crespis, and Princess Ruspoli," went on Ann enticingly, as if he, like her, would have his mind changed by titles.

"You should be in hog heaven."

"Does this have anything to do with that damn fortune-teller?" she asked in a mocking voice.

"I'll put you in a taxi, Ann."

LATER, AFTER the lunch, Ann returned to the hotel, bubbling with gossip about what he had missed and thrilled that she had gotten them invited that evening to a ball at the

Pecci-Blunts. Billy said he didn't want to go. His refusal exasperated and infuriated her.

"Let's not get into a fight over this, Ann."

"I did not come all the way to Rome to sit here in this room because in 1943 some fortune-teller in Tacoma, Washington, told you you were going to die today. It's the most ridiculous thing I've ever heard of. If fortune-tellers know so damn much, why do they always live in some filthy hovel?"

"You don't have to sit here. Go to the ball. Enjoy yourself. I'm quite content here."

"I may be quite late."

"That's all right."

"It gives me the creeps, all this silence and gloom."

HE WORE A MAROON polka-dotted dressing gown over his undershorts and shirt. The only light on in the room was the lamp between the double beds. Lying on one of the beds, he read the international edition of the *Herald Tribune* and the *Rome American*. He listened to the radio. He napped. He thought about his children. He thought about his father. He wondered why, with so much, he felt so dissatisfied with his life. He wondered, as he always wondered, in his rare moments of introspection, if he would have amounted to anything if he had not inherited so much money. He felt that the deference he received from people, for the name and fortune he possessed, was unearned and undeserved, and he wondered if others thought this about him.

He started to say the Lord's Prayer, but he felt embarrassed, as he always felt embarrassed, when he prayed outside of St. James' Episcopal Church, which he attended only for weddings and funerals. He felt the urge to get off the bed and get down on his knees to say the prayer, but he thought how extremely foolish he would feel if Ann should happen to walk in the door at that moment, even though he knew it was highly unlikely that Ann would ever leave her ball for any reason. He wondered if he minded dying, and it surprised him that, yes, he did mind, although only yesterday it had not seemed such a terrible loss to him.

Then he heard the bells from the Campanile begin to sound across the city, ringing the hour of midnight. The day was over. He had lived. The gypsy fortune-teller from Tacoma was wrong. He leaped up from the bed, joyous again with his life, and picked up the telephone and asked the operator to connect him with another hotel in the city. He asked the operator in that hotel to connect him with the room of one of its guests. He could hear the telephone ring several times, and then it was answered by a sleepy voice.

"Esme?" he boomed. "It's Billy. Get up. Get dressed. Let me come and pick you up and let's go out somewhere for a drink!"

"SHE'S NOT AFRAID to lose control, you know. I am," said Billy to Esme about Ann. They sat in the spring night in the bar on the roof of Esme's hotel.

"Why do you stay with her?" asked Esme.

"There was a time when I loved her, and during that time I was the happiest that I ever have been," he replied.

"That was then. This is now."

"You will not admire me if I tell you why."

"Don't worry about that."

"I'm afraid of her. There is something reckless about her."

"Reckless?"

"Once, when I was courting her, I went to the apartment she was living in, in the thirties somewhere, Murray Hill. She was a dancer in those days. For some reason the street door was open, and I went right through without ringing her buzzer, and ran up the flights of stairs to her apartment, and rang her bell. I was carrying flowers. She opened the door and she was holding a gun pointed at me, and there was on her face a truly horrible look, like a woman who had lost control completely, slack and loose and ready to kill. And then she recognized that it was me, and in an instant she pulled herself together and tried to turn the whole thing into an enormous joke, saying that the gun was not really a gun at all, but a starter's pistol for races. I never knew who it was she was expecting, probably some boyfriend she was trying to break off with now that I had come into her life, but I have never forgotten the look on her face."

"Did you ever talk about it with her?"

"She always made light of it. I think it embarrassed her that she had shown me her dark side so blatantly, but I was madly in love with her then, and she almost made me believe that I had imagined the moment."

"Could she kill, do you think?"

"Dear God, Esme, we're talking about my wife."

"Could she?"

"On safari, none of the natives wanted to be with her. She shot first and looked later, they said. Nothing ever happened, of course, but she appeared dangerous to them, and I understood their feelings."

"Is she a good shot?"

"She has an itchy trigger finger."

"That's not the same thing."

"She doesn't wait. There is a recklessness about her."

"You must leave her, Billy."

"She never forgets an injury, Esme. She would eventually find her revenge."

"But what kind of a marriage is it you have?"

"She enjoys being Mrs. William Grenville, Junior, and will never give up being that unless an Italian prince or an English lord or the Ali Khan asks her to marry him."

Esme looked away from Billy and sighed deeply.

"Is that a sigh?" asked Billy.

"I suppose it is," she answered.

"Will you translate it?"

"I would have enjoyed being Mrs. William Grenville, Junior, too, you know, but I would have been a very different one."

"Oh, Esme."

"IT'S TIME FOR US to go back home, Ann," said Billy. They were on the Riviera staying at Chateau de l'Horizon as the guests of Ali Khan.

"No, no, not yet, Billy," pleaded Ann.

"Well, I'm going back to New York."

"Please, Billy, just stay for the Marquis de Cuevas's ball in Biarritz, and then, after that, I promise you I'll go back."

"Every time I want to go home, you tell me of another party that's bigger and better than the last party. There's always going to be another party."

"Just this one, Billy, and then we'll go. It's costume, and they want us to be in the Dante's *Inferno* tableau. It's going to be such fun. I'm going to be a devil all in red and carry a pitchfork. Ali's part of the tableau. And they want you to be dressed as—"

"Listen to me, Ann."

"Don't you remember how much you used to like me in my little cat costume?" She sensed a difference in his ardor toward her and applied herself to attracting him.

"YOU DON'T LIKE costume parties, Mr. Grenville?" asked Simonetta d'Este. Billy had withdrawn from the spectacle, watching the ballroom below from the splendid isolation of a rococo balcony. She was an elegant Madame Du Barry in court finery, powdered wig, and magnificent pearls.

"Why do you say that?" asked Billy.

"Your white tie, your tails, your red sash across your chest. It's what all men wear who hate costume parties but go to please their wives."

Billy laughed. "I suppose you're right."

"I'm Simonetta d'Este."

"I know."

"Do you hate to dance too, Mr. Grenville?"

"My name is Billy."

"I know. Do you hate to dance too, Billy?"

"I dance rather well, I think. Would you like to?"

"I've sought you out. Of course I would."

TO BE PART OF the Dante's *Inferno* tableau at the de Cuevas's ball in Biarritz was of great importance to Ann Grenville. Among the dozen red-clad participants of Hades were some of the oldest titles in Europe as well as the kind of names that dazzled the readers of Fydor Cassati's column back in New York. For her it represented a triumph of social acceptance that she felt she had never achieved in the New York and Long Island circles of her husband's family. In the group of international partygoers and pleasure seekers that was then beginning to be called the Jet Set, people who got on airplanes and went to parties the world over, wherever the season was, she was accepted as the beautiful and witty Mrs. Grenville of the famous New York family, and who she was before she became who she had become was of no consequence, as it was on the North Shore. She was on this night at the peak of her beauty and fame.

For days preceding the ball, the merrymakers rehearsed

their entrance with the dedication of courtiers, as if winning a prize for best tableau were a thing that mattered.

And win they did, the dozen devils of Dante's *Inferno*, amid hugs and kisses and toasts and congratulations. Ann, delirious with her success, looked among the celebrants for her husband, wanting his approval, needing his approval, knowing he would brag about her back in New York, to his mother, to his sisters, to his friends. She took a drink from a passing tray.

"Have you seen Billy?" she asked someone.

"He's dancing, I think," was the reply. She drank her drink and drank another.

"Have you seen Billy?" she asked someone else.

"He's dancing, I think," came the reply.

"Which room?"

"The nightclub." She drank another drink. He had, she realized, not seen the tableau, nor witnessed her moment. Her eyes flashed dangerously at the marital slight. The pills she had become used to taking—to wake, to sleep, to diet, to remain calm—and the liquor she drank combined to free the latent savagery within her.

IN ANOTHER room of the de Cuevas villa, fitted out for the evening as a nightclub, Billy Grenville danced with Simonetta d'Este, oblivious to the pageantlike festivities of the ballroom. It was a romance, but the romance of a party, without sex, without kisses even. Champagne, banter, laughter, dancing.

". . . and *I* thought that when the audience with the Pope was scheduled on the very day that the fortune-teller told me was going to be my last, it was a sure sign that she was right."

"What a marvelous story this is," said Simonetta. "No wonder you didn't come to that silly lunch at that silly monsignor's. I would have done the same thing. You were preparing yourself, in case."

"Exactly. And at midnight the Campanile rang. You can't imagine the relief. I never believed it, but at the same time I did, and it'd been hanging over me."

"And now you have a new life ahead of you."

"That's what I've been thinking. You're a wonderful dancer."

"So are you."

Eyes closed, abandoning herself to the music, Simonetta d'Este was unprepared for the force with which Ann Grenville grabbed her from behind by the shoulder and yanked her away from her husband.

"Bitch!" screamed Ann.

"Ann!" cried Billy.

Not satisfied, Ann grabbed Simonetta again, tearing the front of her Madame Du Barry costume and breaking the strands of precious pearls that were around her neck. Pearls fell all over the floor of the darkened room.

"Ann, for God's sake," said Billy.

"You stay away from my husband!" screamed Ann.

The orchestra stopped playing. The room was in silence as people crowded around to witness the melee, stepping on the scattering pearls. Billy grabbed Ann, but she pulled herself away from him, then turned on him, scratched his face, and tore his tie away.

"Please, Mrs. Grenville," pleaded Simonetta d'Este.

"I know your tricks," screamed Ann, attacking the woman again. She was out of control, and people stepped away from her.

"Someone, call the police!" It was the outraged voice of the Marquis de Cuevas, who, dressed as Cardinal Richelieu, pushed his way into the crowd surrounding the fight. "Get these people out of my house!"

Drunk and shamed for the scandal she had created, but convinced of her rightness in the matter, Ann retreated to the Hotel de Palais, where they were staying. Her purse lost, still in her red devil costume, she made her way across the white-and-gold lobby, aware, by the looks she was receiving, that word of her social debacle had preceded her return in the early-morning hours. Her face assumed the look of hauteur as she demanded the key to the Grenville suite.

"If my husband should return," she said to the hall porter, in the measured words of drunkenness, "please inform him he is to seek accommodations elsewhere."

Once inside, she locked the several doors of her suite, after hanging Do Not Disturb signs on the exterior handles. In a standing gold-framed three-way mirror, she caught sight of herself. What she saw was not the elegant lady of international society that she had become, but who she once was— a chorus girl in a chorus-girl costume looking like a chorus girl. In addition, her stockings were ripped, her makeup was smeared, her hair was in disarray. To her own snobbish eye she looked common and aging, and it reawakened her terrible rage toward her husband. She pulled his suitcases from closets and piled his clothes inside. She opened the door of the suite and pushed his luggage into the hall, bags half closed, sleeves hanging out, his brushes and shoes thrown after them.

Mollified somewhat, she sat on the edge of the tall, deep, old-fashioned bathtub and took several pills. Sleep, she knew, would obliterate the night for her, and she would deal with tomorrow when it came.

Billy, unable to get another room in the crowded hotel, too embarrassed at that hour to telephone friends with villas to get a bed for the night, used his key and entered the suite, bringing in his luggage, shoes, and brushes from the hall outside. He made up a bed for himself on a sofa in the sitting room. When he went into the bathroom, he found his wife passed out in the tub, still dressed in her costume of the evening.

The tub was too deep for him to lift her out and carry her to her bed without awakening her. He took her shoes off and went into the bedroom to get a pillow to place under her head in the tub and a sheet to cover her.

Ann awakened to see Billy coming down on her with a pillow in his hands. Drunk and drugged, she thought he meant to kill her, and a piercing scream was heard up and down the corridors of the staid Hotel du Palais.

Police were called for the second time. "My husband tried to kill me," said the hysterical Ann to the prefect. "You must believe me, he tried to kill me. He was going to smother me, but I awoke, just in time, to see him coming down on me with a pillow in both hands. He was going to put it over my mouth."

"I found my wife passed out in the bathtub," said Billy to the prefect. "If you ask any of the people who were at the ball this evening, they will tell you that she had too much to drink. What I was doing was trying to make her comfortable in the tub, as it was apparent she was going to spend the night there."

By morning the Grenvilles had departed Biarritz by separate cars.

PART
THREE

dultery was not the straw that broke the camel's back. The marriage survived their mutual infidelities, as did the marriages of most of the couples in the circles in which they traveled, in both New York and Europe. However, Ann's public displays of jealousy and erratic behavior caused much speculation that she was either mad or taking too many diet pills, and his friends wondered for just how long poor Billy Grenville was going to put up with his beautiful wife's unfortunate scenes. Even the most casual observer of their lives knew that the marriage was in poor straits. The fact that Fydor Cassati, the society columnist, had not reported on it was attributable to his deep affection for Billy, who had always treated him as a fellow gentleman and not as a newspaper writer, playing golf and tennis with him and inviting him to lunch at the Beach Club in the summer. There was hardly a person in café society who had not heard that Ann had thrown a drink in Rita Sinclair's face at El Morocco over an imagined flirtation with Billy, and that Billy, shamefaced for his wife, had taken her home. The debacle in Biarritz had stunned the international assemblage, and the resulting gossip and publicity on both sides of the Atlantic were agonizing for Billy, who worried always about what his mother would think.

Walter Winchell, who had written items about Ann Grenville when she was a show girl, reported in his column that "the veddy social Grenvilles of sassiety and racing circles have Reno on the beano." Finally they separated. Billy's friends

175

breathed a sigh of relief. He moved out of the house into the Brook Club, where according to Doddsie, the night porter, he spent long and sullen evenings alone in the bar. He returned to the house only to see the children, at a specified time in the late afternoons, and it was a condition of his visits that Ann not be in the house at the time, because she created embarrassing scenes in front of the servants. Whatever his family said among themselves was not known, but they remained noncommittal to people who questioned them about the separation. When Billy asked Ann for a divorce, she became hysterical and told him she would never grant him one.

To the surprise of all, themselves included, apartness diminished rather than enhanced them. They did not stand up singly as they had as a couple. With all his social perfection, and good looks, and excellent manners, there was a blandness of personality about Billy that made him less interesting alone than as a partner to the firebrand he had married. He missed, he discovered, the relentless social life that Ann was expert at arranging for him. He missed also, he discovered, the comforts of the beautiful house that Ann had put together for him. He liked comfort, but he liked comfort arranged for him; he did not know, nor want to cope with, the intricacies of arranging it himself. The Brook Club was fine for the moment, but its bylaws forbade him to stay on there indefinitely.

Ann appeared on the scene with great fanfare as the latest companion of the notorious womanizer, Ali Khan. They were photographed in nightclubs and at the yearling sales in Saratoga, on her husband's home turf, but her stature as his companion was lessened by his continued attachment to the film star Rita Hayworth. There followed an Italian prince, with whom she had dallied in Rome, but he found her less exciting, and more demanding, now that she was available, and he returned to Italy.

All their friends expected a divorce, but to everyone's surprise they appeared together smiling and lovey-dovey at a large party at Alice Grenville's house a few weeks later attended by all the members of Billy's family. They did not so much reconcile as go back together. The marriage was over but endured with decreasing ties. Each recognized the other's signals of conclusion. She began to smoke in bed again, a habit that enraged him. He no longer lifted the toilet seat to pee, a habit that enraged her. First she wanted separate newspapers. Then she wanted separate bathrooms. Eventually she wanted separate bedrooms. After they stopped loving each other, or even liking each other, they continued, on occasion, to be attracted to each other, although rarely at the same time, so that lovemaking, on those occasions, was often unsatisfying and unpleasant.

BILLY SAID HE was having lunch at the Brook Club with Teddy Vermont, but when Ann called the club she found that he was not there and had not been there, and Teddy Vermont was in Lyford Key with Alfred and Jeanne Twombley. A look of displeasure passed over her face. Distracted, she knotted and unknotted the sleeves of the sweater that hung fashionably over her shoulders. She thought back on the conversation of the morning.

"The Haverstrikes are here from California, and I said we'd meet them for lunch at '21,' " she had said.

"Can't," he had replied, brushing his hair with two brushes.

"About the safari."

"Still can't."

"Why?"

"I'm having lunch at the Brook Club with Teddy Vermont."

"Teddy Vermont?" She did not know Teddy Vermont.

"Groton," he had replied, explaining him, removing him from her sphere.

"What does Teddy Vermont own? The state?"

"You should be on television with your wit—*Leave It to the Girls*," he answered, walking out the door.

She suspected him of infidelity. Jealousy flooded her insides with its vile juices. It was Simonetta d'Este, she suspected, a princess, tall and dominant, as she was, strong, as she was, pedigreed, as she was not. She felt the insecurity of her position, unloved by both his family and his friends.

"IT'S NOT A good idea for us to go out anywhere alone, Billy. It would be misinterpreted, and I'm not keen about having a public encounter with the terrible-tempered Mrs. Grenville."

"Please, Esme."

"No, Billy."

"How about Hamburger Heaven, then? Isn't that innocent enough? We could have met there by chance."

"All right."

"IT'S HARD, YOU know, when you've done something as unpopular as what I did, marry someone no one approved of, not a single person, not even Bratsie, to say, 'Yes, everybody, you were right, all of you, and I was wrong.' It takes a bigger person than I am for that."

"What is your alternative, Billy?"

"The horses, I suppose. I have that. The farm is making money. And Tailspin, you've heard about Tailspin. He'll be a champion."

"Mr. Grenville?" They were being interrupted.

"Yes?"

"I'm Ashton Grimes."

"Hello." Billy could not remember who Ashton Grimes was.

"From Buckley School. I'm Third's teacher."

"Of course. How are you?"

"I don't mean to interrupt."

"Quite all right."

"I had hoped to see you at Parents' Day, and I thought we could talk then."

"Yes, I was in Europe." He was, he remembered, in Biarritz on the day. "This is, uh, Miss Bland. Ashton Grimes."

"Hello."

"He's not doing well, Third, is he?" asked Billy.

"He's not."

"What shall we do about it?"

"I think we must meet, Mr. Grenville. Something must be done. He is, uh, disturbed."

"May I call you tomorrow?"

"Yes, of course. Goodbye, Miss Bland. Goodbye, sir."

"He is disturbed, I suppose, about his mother and father," said Billy. "I've often wondered if they hear us, the fights, the screaming. I guess they do, and the servants, too."

"What are you going to do?"

"I never did well in school either, in my time. And then my father would give a gymnasium or a dormitory, and everything would work out all right."

"It's not the same."

"No, it's not the same."

"That teacher is telling you your son needs help, Billy," said Esme Bland, who, if asked, would know what to do.

"I have to go," said Billy. "The adulteress is expecting me for dinner."

‡   ‡   ‡

"GET YOURSELF a smart lawyer, just in case," advised Babette Van Degan, who had received the largest divorce settlement in the history of New York, and Sam Rosenthal was the smart lawyer Babette Van Degan advised her to get. There was something about Babette, despite her appearance that never outgrew her brassy show-girl look, that made you take her advice in matters of finance and legalities.

"Tell me about him," said Ann.

"He is a snake, a liar, completely dishonest. He will be perfect for you."

"Where is he from?"

"Oh, Minsk. Or Pinsk. One of those places."

"I meant what firm."

"His own."

Ann didn't really have to be told who Sam Rosenthal was. Every wife in New York in a precarious marriage to a rich man knew who Sam Rosenthal was. She went to his office in Rockefeller Center. His intense black eyes showed white between the bottom of the iris and the lower lid, giving a hypnotic effect. His black eyebrows met in the center.

Sam Rosenthal knew who the Grenvilles were and how much they were worth. "A lotta simoleons," he said. He told her the name of a private detective who would be able to find out for her whether Billy was having an affair with Simonetta d'Este. She told him she wanted to keep their marriage together, not divorce. He advised her, when that moment came, to ask so much money that Billy would prefer to keep the marriage going. "Those old New York families like the Grenvilles would do anything rather than break up the fortunes," he told her. She liked Sam Rosenthal and felt she had made a friend.

"This is my private telephone number," he said to her, handing her a card. "They will always know where to reach me, day or night. Put it in your book in case you ever need me."

♣   ♣   ♣

"Mrs. Grenville will be down directly, sir," said the maid.

"Thank you," replied the man, whose name was Mc-Carthy. He liked to guess people's names from their looks, and very often he was right. He guessed the maid's name was either Mary or Margaret. He knew she was Irish, like himself. He knew she had been to Mass that morning; the ashes of Ash Wednesday thumbed into her forehead by some Catholic priest paid tribute to that. He guessed that she was new in this grand household where he found himself, by invitation, and he guessed correctly. He guessed also, correctly again, that the word "directly" in Mrs. Grenville-will-be-down-directly had been taught her to say, like a line in a play concerned with gracious living. He would have lingered with her in conversation until Mrs. Grenville appeared, but she did not and so he did not. Pretty little thing, he thought when she left the room. She closed the door to the hallway, leaving him free to prowl the room. He wondered if these people called it a living room or a drawing room. His eye, unschooled in art, nevertheless recognized value, and he judged the pictures on the wall to be "museum-quality," as he would later describe them to his partner, although this estimation, which was correct, was arrived at more from the elaborate gilt frames than from the pictures themselves.

In a corner was a discreetly placed drink tray bulging with the right liquors, wines, and brandies. In an instant he lifted a decanter, cut-glass with a silver necklace identifying it as Scotch, gulped from it, and replaced it in a movement so swift that an observer, had there been one, which there was not, might have missed it. He heard voices on the stairs outside and seated himself on a *bergère* chair covered in gray silk, obscuring its delicate lines with the extra weight that he carried and always meant to rid himself of. He placed his left ankle over his right knee, and then shifted to his right ankle over his left knee, and then placed both feet on the floor, tapping the sole of his Thom McAn shoe on the Portuguese carpet. Finally he reached over and picked up a magazine that had been left open to a particular page. If it appeared incongruous that this red-faced, white-haired, stout man in an inexpensive three-piece suit should be reading *Harper's Bazaar,* the incongruity was soon dispelled by his very real interest in the page he happened upon. There, elegantly seated in the very *bergère* chair in which he was now seated, was Mrs. William Grenville, Junior, photographed by Louise Dahl-Wolf in a setting of such high fashion and high style as to remove it almost from reality. He wondered if it had been placed there for him to see.

From outside the room he heard:

"We'll be four for lunch, Mary."

"Yes, ma'am."

"You'll have to help cook serve."

"Yes, ma'am."

"What's-her-name left."

"Yes, ma'am "

"Just walked off the job."

"Yes, ma'am."

"What's that smudge on your forehead?"

"Ashes."

"What?"

"You know, Ash Wednesday."

"Wipe it off before the duchess comes."

"Yes, ma'am."

Mr. McCarthy guessed, correctly, that the next time he was in this house, Mary would have left, like what's-her-name. The door to the room—living room? drawing room? —opened, and Mrs. William Grenville, Junior, entered, her expensive perfume preceding her. Tall, striking, blonde, lipsticked, exquisitely bosomed, she observed him observing her.

"I'm sorry to have kept you waiting, Mr. McCormick," she said, advancing toward him, offering her hand, "but we have had a crisis in the kitchen."

"McCarthy," he corrected her.

"I beg your pardon. Mr. McCarthy. I have guests for lunch, and the little waitress has simply walked out." Her gaze became distracted by a misplaced iris in a flower arrangement, and she repositioned it to her satisfaction.

"Do please sit down," she said. "I see you've seen my picture. Do you think it's good? I'm terribly pleased with it, although my mother-in-law thinks I am too much in the papers and magazines. She is of that school that thinks a lady's name appears in the papers only three times in her life."

Mr. McCarthy sensed that she was having difficulty getting around to the purpose of the meeting between them.

"Are you interested in protection for your home, ma'am?" he asked, helping her out.

"Do you mean like guards? Heavens, no! Is that what you thought?"

"We do that sort of work."

"I heard of you through Mr. Sam Rosenthal."

"Ah, yes, Mr. Rosenthal. We do a great deal of work for Mr. Rosenthal. It's that sort of thing?"

She walked away from him toward the window. Seeing her from behind was as nearly pleasurable an experience as looking at her face-on for Mr. McCarthy. Every proportion was perfect. Her legs. Her back. Her well-exercised buttocks beneath her smart wool dress. She looked around at him from the window. The part of herself that she totally understood was her physical presence, and she was never displeased, during any circumstance, to know that it was being admired. She was not seductive to him, had no wish to be, but she warmed toward him when she realized he had responded to her.

"I have reason to believe that my husband is being unfaithful to me," she said. If it had been a play, and she had been its author, she would have assigned to the private detective the line "He must be mad," referring to the deceiving husband, but it was not a play, and he did not say that line, but he thought it, or at least his own version of it.

"I would like to have him followed—discreetly, of course. You see, I love my husband. There is no thought of divorce, but I am most anxious to protect my marriage. I trust this is all confidential, what we are discussing?"

"Completely."

"I do not want him to be aware that I suspect him."

"No problem there."

"His office is on Wall Street, but he lunches most days uptown at the Brook Club, or the Racquet Club, or the Knickerbocker Club. The thing is, of late he has not been returning to his office in the afternoons, and I would like to find out where he is spending his time."

"Do you have a suspicion of a particular person?"

"I do."

"Good."

"What do you mean, good?"

"I don't mean good in that sense. I mean if it's a case of general philandering, it's a more difficult thing to pinpoint."

"I would prefer philandering. There is no threat in philandering," she added softly. She looked down at her vast ring, which he would later describe to his partner as a skating rink, as if it were a symbol of her marriage. When she looked up at him, she smiled sadly and blinked a tear away from her eye. Mr. McCarthy was absurdly touched, even though he realized he was witnessing a performance rather than a true emotion. He sensed, and quite rightly, that it was fear of loss of status and position that concerned her.

"Her name?" he asked.

She turned her back to him again and looked past the elaborate gray silk curtains to the street outside. Her slightly flushed face and stiffened back belied her serenity.

"She is called Simonetta d'Este."

He reached for his pad and pen.

"*Princess* Simonetta d'Este," she continued.

The correct spelling would come later. He did not interrupt her for that. He sensed that she felt rage toward this woman who threatened her marriage but at the same time was impressing him with the caliber of woman who was capable of unseating her. He realized she liked to have credentials established.

"What aroused your suspicions?"

"As to adultery or to the particular person?"

"As to adultery, ma'am."

"That's very embarrassing."

"Lipstick on a handkerchief, that sort of thing?"

"I smelled another woman on his fingers."

The detective turned scarlet.

They exchanged particulars: the address and marital status of the princess; the rates of his private detective agency, which she already knew from Sam Rosenthal, she said, anxious not to be overcharged. From below a doorbell rang.

"My God, she's early," said Ann Grenville, glancing at a clock on the mantelpiece. Her assurance seemed to leave her, as if figuring out how to get rid of one element of her life before another entered. "You see," she said to the private detective, who suddenly looked to her exactly like a private detective, as if he were wearing a badge proclaiming himself to be just that, so that explanations would have to be made, "it's the Duchess of Windsor coming to lunch, and, uh . . ."

"And you would like me to make a hasty exit down the back stairs, so as not to be seen, is that it?"

As she shook his hand in hasty farewell, she said, "I would like photographs."

IT WAS A RARE family outing: Alice Grenville, Billy and Ann, Diantha and Third. They were sitting in the Grenville box at the Belmont track watching Tailspin. Alice detected, but did not address, the strain she felt between her son and his wife. After the race, and photographs, and congratulations to the jockey and trainer, Ann wandered off to greet friends in the bar, and the children were taken by their nanny to buy hot dogs.

"What's the matter with Ann?" asked Alice.

"Nothing," replied her son, waving to the reporters and photographers in a gesture concurrently friendly and dismissive.

"Don't say 'nothing' to me, Billy. I'm your mother."

"She's jealous."

"Of whom?"

"Simonetta."

"With reason?"

"No."

The closeness that had once existed between them had never been the same since the night she had refused to sanction his marriage. She sensed his unhappiness now and wanted to reach out to him, but dared not. For an instant their eyes met.

"Marvelous about the race," she said rather than what she wanted to say, raising her field glasses and watching the track.

"Wasn't it?" he replied, hollow-voiced.

"I think Tailspin's going to win the Triple Crown next year."

"Wouldn't it be marvelous."

"I'm proud of you, darling."

"Thanks, Mère."

"Your father would have been, too."

"Do you think?"

"Oh, yes."

He sounded better. She felt better.

INSIDE, AT THE members' bar, Ann ran into Babette Van Degan. They sat down at a table together and ordered daiquiris. Babette munched peanuts as she watched her old friend.

"Why the morose silence?" she asked.

"Oh, I don't know. *La vie*," answered Ann.

"What did you think of Sam Rosenthal?"

"His eyebrows meet in the middle."

"You're not seriously thinking of divorce, are you?"

"Murder, yes. Divorce, no," Ann answered.

They roared with laughter.

"I won a bundle on your horse," said Babette.

"Good," said Ann. "I know you need the money."

They laughed again. Ann felt better.

"How's your son?" she asked, lighting a cigarette.

"Just got kicked out of another school," replied Babette. "How are your kids?"

"Oh, fine, I guess," said Ann.

THE COFFEE SHOP of the Astor Hotel on Times Square was jammed with a jostling crowd of conventioneers. Perfect, Ann thought to herself as she inched her way through to the booth where private detective Danny McCarthy waved to her. Better to meet here, she reasoned, near his office, than to risk meeting again in her home, especially as there were photographs to be viewed.

She wore a raincoat, a last-minute decision, leaving behind her mink coat, and she was glad not to stand out. She turned her ring around on her finger, stone inward.

"Coffee?" asked the waitress, pouring and spilling it over into the saucer.

"Bring me a clean saucer," Ann said to the waitress. It was a thing that always annoyed her exceedingly. She never allowed herself to remember that she had once, briefly, been a waitress in a coffee shop herself, at Crowell's Pharmacy in Pittsburg, Kansas. Greetings with Mr. McCarthy completed, her favorite kind of sandwich ordered, she settled back for the business at hand. The photographs were handed to her in an eight-by-ten manila envelope.

"Urse Mertens! Is that you? Urse?"

Before she raised her eyes from the six black-and-white photographs of Billy and Simonetta d'Este sitting on a bench in Central Park, at opposite ends of the bench, turning to face each other, talking only, not provocative in the least, near the children's playground, where her children were probably playing, Ann knew that the voice that addressed her belonged to Fredda Cunningham of West Quincy Street in Pittsburg, Kansas. At first she pretended not to hear as she perused the enlargements handed to her by Mr. McCarthy. She regretted her decision to dress down for the occasion. Her mink coat would have made her less approachable. Beneath the table she turned around to the outside the flawless emerald-cut pink diamond that she had turned inside for the meeting with Mr. McCarthy. It was too confusing a situation to cope with, explaining to Mr. McCarthy who Fredda Cunningham was, explaining to Fredda Cunningham that Mr. McCarthy was not her husband.

"Urse?"

"Are you speaking to me?" she asked, looking up at the childhood acquaintance she had once longed to be accepted by. There was grandeur in her voice. She brought her left hand up to her face, and the huge diamond, the skating rink, as Mr. McCarthy had described it to his partner, dazzled brilliantly in the fluorescent light of the coffee shop. Fredda, embarrassed, crimsoned.

"I beg your pardon," said the flustered Fredda. "You reminded me of someone I once knew."

Ann smiled pleasantly, acknowledging the woman's error. Standing behind Fredda was a man. Every instinct within her told her not to look at him, but she did. It was Billy Bob Veblen, the best-looking boy in Pittsburg High, with whom she had once "gone steady," with whom she had made plans and promises, to whom she had . . .

Again she smiled pleasantly at the two staring people as if they were strangers. The cheese-and-bacon sandwich she had ordered arrived, unexpectedly open-faced, like the cheese delight from Crowell's Pharmacy in Pittsburg, Kansas. Ann, beneath her makeup, flushed and dared not raise her eyes, lest the same thought occur to them.

"Sorry to have bothered you," said Fredda Cunningham.

"Not at all," answered Ann. They moved on past her and went to the cashier, where they paid their check.

"That was her," said Billy Bob Veblen to Fredda Cunningham, and his voice carried back to the table where Ann sat with the private detective she had hired to follow her husband.

Although he was impassive throughout the encounter, the moment was not lost on Mr. McCarthy, whose dress and girth belied his sensibilities. How does it feel, he wondered, to snub old friends? He made a mental note of the name Urse Mertens, and of the name tag of the conventioneer, William R. (Billy Bob) Veblen, Mathieson Aircraft, Pittsburg, Kansas.

"Is this it?" asked Ann about the photographs. She didn't know if she was pleased or disappointed that they were so nonincriminating.

"He's clean as a whistle," replied Mr. McCarthy about the husband Ann Grenville thought was deceiving her.

IF IT HAD BEEN Fredda Cunningham alone, Ann would have run after her, through the lobby of the Astor Hotel, to set things straight. She possessed a vivid imagination and could have thought of something that would have explained, in a reasonable way, her rude behavior to her childhood friend. She would, she thought at that moment, even enjoy bringing Fredda up to her house and watching the richest girl in Pittsburg, Kansas, react to the magnificence of her life.

But Billy Bob Veblen. That was something else again. What could she say to him that would not upset, irretrievably, both their lives, and other people's as well? That he should reappear like that, in a coffee shop she had never entered before and would never enter again! She wondered if her life was closing in on her. She had simply ceased to remember that Billy Bob Veblen had played a part in her life.

"WHAT'S A SAFARI, Daddy?"

"It's a hunting expedition."

"Hunting what?"

"In this case, Bengal tigers."

"Here on Long Island?"

"No, no, no, India. Now run along, Third. Nanny's calling you."

"Night, Mummy."

"Goodnight, Third."

"Hug him," said Billy to Ann.

"I can't wait for my son to grow up so he can take me out dancing," said Ann, embracing her child. It was a thing she often said when moments of affection were required. It implied that then, in his young adulthood, would her motherhood come into flower.

At the last minute Billy backed out of going on the safari. Tailspin was running at Santa Anita, and old Sunny Jim O'Brien, the trainer, thought he should be there, he said. Ann didn't believe him. She wanted to back out too, but she knew she would never be asked again if she backed out at the last minute after all the elaborate arrangements had been made. The Haverstrikes had already left, and the Maharajas of Patiala and Alwar were expecting them in India on the eleventh. Besides, she loathed California; too many people in the film business remembered her from her chorus-girl days. By this time she had settled into her success. It was part of her. She didn't like people who remembered her from earlier periods.

In London, en route to New Delhi, she picked up a twelve-gauge double-barreled shotgun at Churchill's. Billy had ordered it for her after last year's safari, made up to her specific measurements, to decrease the kickback on her shoulder. Engraved on it was "To Ann from Billy, with love." She felt very touched by his thoughtfulness and wired him thanks in Pasadena.

Dressed in exceedingly smart huntress attire, she managed to be the dominant figure of the safari, admired greatly by the men but disliked by the women, including the maharanee, whose servants she thought nothing of ordering about.

"Open the safe and get me my jewels," she said.

"I cannot open the safe unless the maharanee is present, madam," said the steward.

"I said, open the safe."

"I cannot, madam."

"I order you to open the safe."

Mrs. Haverstrike suspected her husband of having an affair with Mrs. Grenville. Heretofore Mrs. Oswald Haverstrike, of Hillsborough, California, had not begrudged Ozzie the occasional dalliance. He knew the rules and played by them; that part of his life was kept far afield from their life together. However, Ozzie's dalliance with Ann Grenville was more than she was willing to put up with, happening under her nose as it did. It terminated with an emerald-and-ruby necklace that Ozzie purchased for Ann in New Delhi.

Ozzie Haverstrike said she became excited and rattled when a tiger was in the neighborhood, but she shot the biggest tiger of the safari, a ten-foot Bengal, the first woman ever to shoot a tiger of that size in the territory. Her reputation as an excellent shot, accompanied by the photograph of her and her prey that became so famous after the tragedy, preceded her back to America.

IT WAS NOT that she was lunching with Ali Khan that was incriminating. They had picked a public place frequented by people they knew, and, it could be reasoned, if they had anything to hide, they would have sought an out-of-the-way bistro. It was an attitude of passion toward the Moslem prince that she knew Felicity had seen. She felt herself crimsoning. Always a clever strategist, she knew she could outargue Felicity in a showdown with Billy, but she knew that Felicity had not misread what she had witnessed.

"When she saw me, she blushed," said Felicity. "You can't even say she blushed. She turned beet-red. She looked frightfully common, actually."

"You've never liked her," said Billy.

"You're quite right, I never have, not from the first day," replied Felicity. "But I do like you, little brother."

TAILSPIN WAS the coming three-year-old that season, his earnings just under a million dollars, a record for that time. He was setting record after record and was spoken of as a Triple Crown contender. The public took to the horse with the same affection they had taken to Man o' War, and Billy Grenville, after years of nonaccomplishment, was considered, along with Alfred Twombley and Piggy French, one of the most successful breeders in American racing.

Alice Grenville felt that he was living up to the high expectations of his father, and Billy basked in her approval, as well as the approval of his sisters.

Ann felt it was she who had reawakened Billy's interest in the family sport and was proud of his success at the same time that she was frightened of his newfound independence. More and more she was at the track for the big races, and the photographs of Billy and Ann that appeared on the sports pages and newsreels after the big wins, hugging and laughing, made them look like one of the most glamorous and in-love couples in the country.

DIANTHA AND Third preceded Billy and Ann to the country that Halloween weekend. The chauffeur, Lee, picked them up at their schools in New York and drove them and the new cook, Anna Gorman, out to the house in Oyster Bay. Billy and Ann came down later, after a cocktail party she had wanted to attend and he didn't. For him the party had not been amusing. He was sick to death of the International Set, the titled Europeans that Ann found so irresistible; more and more he preferred the company of the people he had grown up with on Long Island. He was angry when he heard her invite Dougie DeLesseps to lunch on Sunday when she knew that he did not enjoy having guests on the weekends.

"I'm not going to be there," he said.

"Fine," she answered.

They drove in Billy's specially designed car, a Studelac, which combined the sleek design of a Studebaker body with the powerful force of a Cadillac engine. Driving it was one of the things he most enjoyed doing, and part of each weekend in the country was spent in solitary journeys to the farther reaches of Long Island, enjoying the stares of passersby. A few days before, he had returned from Kansas, where he had treated himself handsomely, from Tailspin's million-dollar earnings, to a gleaming silver four-seater airplane, for further solitary pursuits. If it occurred to Ann that Billy was spending more and more time away from her with his cars and plane and, of course, the horses, which had become a sort of obsession with him, she did not mention it.

They were arguing, as they often did when they drove. It was either that or silence. Billy was distressed to have heard at the cocktail party that a photograph of Ann, and Ali Khan, and Mrs. Whitney, taken at the yearling sales in Saratoga, had come out that day in a new issue of *Town and Country*. It was certain, he said, to pour fuel on the much-circulated story in racing circles that Ann was having an affair with the Moslem playboy. A few weeks earlier Billy had enraged Ann by ordering the caretaker at the country house to drain and clean the swimming pool after Ali Khan had swum in it.

Ahead of them, in the center lane of the Long Island Expressway, an old couple in an old car, unsure of their exit, had simply stopped in the road to consult a map. Billy, traveling too fast and directing his attention toward Ann rather than the expressway, did not see them.

"Billy!" screamed Ann.

At the last second before crashing into the rear of the old people's car, he swerved out of the way, narrowly missing a truck. The Studelac screamed to a stop at the side of the expressway, and they looked at each other, ashen-faced and breathing heavily, knowing they had come very close to death. He thought of the fortune-teller in Tacoma and wondered if she had been off in her dates by a few months. Do people who are about to encounter catastrophe meet warning signals along the way?

Resting his head on the steering wheel, Billy said, "Let's go to Rothman's and have a few drinks and dinner."

"But I told the new cook we'd have dinner in," said Ann.

"The hell with the new cook. We just almost died."

The owner of Rothman's knew the Grenvilles and instantly

found them a choice table in the bar, even though it was Friday night and people were lined up waiting for their reservations. He liked it when the social crowd from the North Shore stopped in on their way to and from their country houses, and he made room for them ahead of his regular customers. Neither the cold and perfect martinis that were speedily produced nor their brush with disaster made conversation easy for them. It distressed Ann to be observed dining in silence, even by servants or waiters. She had heard that the Duchess of Windsor recited the alphabet to the duke, in various conversational attitudes, when they had nothing to say to each other in public, but she dared not try that on Billy, especially in the mood he was in. Instead she kept a running commentary on the other diners.

"Dear God, look at that woman with high-heeled shoes and socks," she said.

"Hmmm," replied Billy.

The piano player played "Full Moon and Empty Arms." Once it had been a favorite of theirs. "Full moon and empty legs," she sang to him, but he did not laugh, as he used to when she sang that lyric.

The waiter served.

"What is this?" she asked. "Whitebait?"

"Whitebait."

They ate in silence.

"Oh, look," she said, thinking finally to engage him. "There's Eve Soby. Drunk. Again. Hello, Eve."

"If all else fails for you, Ann, you could always write a column," he said unkindly. *"Urse Mertens's New York."*

A flash of anger passed over her face at his mockery. She hated that name and regretted having once told Billy that she had been born with it. Her appetite ruined, the food followed. An eggplant soufflé dwindled cold on her plate. The Camembert hardened. The lemon ice melted. Only the wine was touched, but its excellence went unheeded. An error in the bill was ignored, and they left the restaurant in silence.

☙   ☙   ☙

WHEN THE house the Grenvilles lived in on Long Island had been part of the vast Helena Worth McGamble estate, it was always called the Playhouse, and the name remained even after Billy Grenville bought it as a weekend house for himself, Ann, and their children.

A curious condition of the sale was that Billy Grenville honor an agreement Helena McGamble had made with the New York Philharmonic allowing them to use the indoor tennis court as a recording studio for seven years. Billy, always honorable, adhered to the agreement, but Ann Grenville, who had pressured Billy into buying the house in order to break away from the restrictive weekends at Alice Grenville's house in Brookville, found the sounds and presence of the members of the orchestra, on the rare occasions they were there, annoying and tiresome. She quarreled constantly with Ralph Wiggins, the guard hired by the Philharmonic, who lived in the caretaker's room on the far side of the tennis court, for refusing to undertake chores she asked him to do on behalf of the Grenville family and was always urging Billy to abrogate the agreement.

THE COBBLESTONES in the courtyard of the Playhouse had been packed and brought over from Fotheringay Castle by Helena Worth McGamble's father, Frank Worth, when he had dreams of creating a dynasty through his favorite daughter. What she noticed as the headlights of Billy's Studelac flashed over the cobblestones when the car pulled up to the front door was that the gardeners had not been doing their job sufficiently; the late-fall leaves were blowing messily around the courtyard, and if there was one thing Ann Grenville could not stand, it was for things not to be looking their best.

She was startled also to see Ralph Wiggins enter the courtyard as if he had been waiting for the sound of the car. He went straight to Billy's side of the car, opened the door for him, and greeted him. Ralph Wiggins never came around to this side of the house, and both Billy and Ann looked at him as if something might be the matter.

"I'm sure there's nothing to worry about, Mr. Grenville," he said, "but there's been a break-in at the cabana by the pool, and I wanted to tell you without the children or the new cook hearing about it."

"That's very kind of you, Ralph," said Billy, getting out of the car. Neither of them ever brought luggage for the weekend, as they kept their country clothes here. This weekend, however, because of Edith Bleeker's dinner for the duchess the next night, Ann had brought an elaborate evening dress as well as her jewel case, and Billy went around to the trunk to get her things out.

"But there's nothing to take in the cabana," said Ann.

"I don't think anything was taken, except perhaps some food from the refrigerator, and the window was broken," Ralph answered.

"I'm cold," said Ann.

"Go on in," said Billy. "How did you happen to notice it, Ralph?"

"The Oyster Bay police came by this afternoon before the children arrived, and I was the only one about. The Eburys across Berry Hill Road have had an intruder, and so have the Twombleys, so we took a look around, but that was all we could find."

"Perhaps I should drop in on the police tomorrow," said Billy, not allowing his deep fear of intruders to show. Since he had been briefly kidnapped at ten, the fear was always with him.

"I don't think it's anything to worry about, Mr. Grenville, but I wanted you to know."

"Thank you, Ralph."

"If you'd like, I'll put your car in the garage for you, and I'll leave the keys in the kitchen with the new cook."

"Thank you."

THE NEXT morning, Ann Grenville, who usually slept until noon, in troubled Seconal slumber, arose early and appeared in the dining room, to the amazement of her husband and two children. Her beauty, which was considerable, was not yet in evidence, her eyes still puffed from the early rising and her expert ministrations at her makeup table not yet attended to.

"Do, please, remove the milk bottle from the table," she called into the kitchen to her new cook. A milk bottle on a dining table, or catsup bottle, or mustard, reactivated an erased memory of an earlier life and filled her with irritation.

Billy returned to his newspapers while coffee was poured for her. With no columns, Saturday papers bored her.

"Daddy's going to take me flying in the new plane tomorrow," said Third.

"Nice," replied Ann, drinking her coffee. "Do not feed the dog toast, Diantha."

"Why are you up so early, Mommy?" asked Diantha.

"Hairdresser in the village for the party tonight."

"Are we having a party?"

"Mrs. Bleeker's having a party." She loathed morning conversation.

"Is it a costume party?"

"Why would Mrs. Bleeker be having a costume party?"

"It's Halloween."

"Oh." She had forgotten it was Halloween. Pumpkins and

candy and trick or treat had all slipped her mind. Damn that nanny for leaving.

Billy's words, when he spoke, were inappropriate to the situation, but his words, and hers, when they spoke to each other, had been inappropriate to the situation for a long time.

"I don't suppose there's anything in that pharmacy by the side of your bed so simple as an aspirin?"

"I told you not to drink those two brandies."

"Is there?"

"Is there what?"

"An aspirin."

"Of course there's an aspirin."

"Where?"

"Look for it. You don't think I'm going to look for it for you, do you?"

"No, that's one thing that never crossed my mind."

When the telephone rang, Billy thought it would be the mechanic from the hangar to tell him if the new plane was ready to fly. The children thought it would be the riding teacher about the trials for the horse show. Ann thought it would be the hairdresser in the village calling to confirm her appointment.

"Hello?" she answered as if she knew who it was going to be. "Oh," she said, surprised. "Mère." When she married into the family, Ann had picked up the habit of calling her mother-in-law what Billy and his sisters called her, although there was never a bit of affection shared between the two Mrs. Grenvilles, only carefully observed amenities. Ann relinquished the telephone to her husband and went about the day's business.

"What did your mother want?" she asked Billy later.

"She's canceled out of Edith's party tonight. She's not coming to the country this weekend. She's decided to stay in New York."

Ann was delighted, although she didn't say so. She always felt inhibited at parties when her mother-in-law was there.

Later, looking for signposts along the way, people wondered whether if Alice Grenville had *not* canceled out of Edith Bleeker's party, the tragic event that followed it might not have happened. Certainly, Ann would not have made the scene she made with her mother-in-law present. She was known to be frightened of her. And the scene she made, everyone who was there agreed, no matter what they said to the police afterward, must have led up to what happened.

HER GARDEN was closing down for winter. There were early chrysanthemums, late dahlias, and a few surviving roses. Ann leaned over and plucked off two dead dahlias and lay them on the edge of the bed for the gardener to find. "I can't bear them when they turn brown like that," she said. Ann was proud of her garden, and liked nothing more on a weekend than to walk guests through it and point out this flower and that bed, and talk about annuals and perennials in the way she had observed English ladies doing it.

"I am talking to you," said Billy, measuring his words in quiet fury.

"I'm listening. I'm listening," she replied. "Go on."

The situation did not warrant his stalking off in a state of agitation, but she knew it was what he was considering.

"About the car," she helped him. "The Studelac, wasn't it? The prowler broke into the Studelac, you were saying. He'd probably never seen one before. That's all. What was taken?"

"Nothing, actually," he said finally. "After all, what is there to take in a car? Maps. Gloves. Dark glasses. I mean, that's not the point, what was taken. The point is, there was someone here, several times, in our garage, and in the cabana by the pool."

"Kids, probably. The caddies from that Jewish golf club through the trees."

"I wish you'd take me seriously."

"Look at that marvelous rose still blooming this late in October. I'm going to cut some flowers for the table."

"I'm going out to look at the new plane."

"No, not now, Billy. I told the new cook we'd have lunch at one with the children, and it's lamb chops, so don't go off now."

She looked after him as he walked toward the house. The prowler, real or imaginary, did not seem to her the problem with Billy. What, after all, was a prowler to them? A call to the Oyster Bay police station to report it, or, at most, the hiring of a guard to patrol the grounds, as the Twombleys had done, and the matter of the prowler would be at rest. People who lived behind gates and high walls must expect to be preyed upon. It was in the natural order of things. Did not Alice Grenville keep an unheard-of amount of money in the wall safe behind the Constable painting in her bedroom ever since the attempted kidnapping of Billy over twenty years earlier, simply to be prepared in the case of an emergency? The trouble with Billy had more to do than with prowlers, she knew. It had to do with their marriage. Uncourageous, except for his single incident of bravery in wartime, he could not bring himself to keep after her about the divorce he wanted, and, in frustration, seized upon the prowler as something to brood about.

With her blunt garden scissors she clipped the October rose, and another, open to full lushness, and searched for more. She could, she knew, cajole Billy through this period of marital unrest. Settled now, even complacent, in her own success, she was, to her very marrow, Mrs. William Grenville, Junior, and nothing was going to disrupt that fact of her life, even if it meant giving up her lover. She would miss Ali Khan, but she could do without him.

"Mommy."

"Mommy."

From the house Diantha and Third called her for lunch, excited to be sharing a meal with their parents.

♣   ♣   ♣

"WHAT'S THE new cook's name?" Billy was leaning against the door to Ann's room, still in his maroon polka-dot dressing gown.

"Anna, I think. Or Annie." She was seated at her dressing table, putting on her makeup.

"Which?"

"What difference does it make?"

"It makes a good deal of difference. It's one of the reasons we have a new cook every two weeks." There was a tone of annoyance in his voice. "In my mother's house—"

"Oh, for God's sake, spare me that old chestnut about your mother having her cook for thirty-two years, and her butler for twenty-eight, and her maid for seventeen."

"My mother knows how to treat them properly, and that's why they stay with her."

"Do you want to move back home?"

"You are a pain in the ass, Ann."

"You're always disagreeable after you come. Does your wop princess ever tell you that?"

She leaned toward the mirror and rubbed her finger back and forth across her lip, evening her lipstick. Her eyes met his in the mirror. She watched him turn sulkily and walk across the hall to his own room and regretted she had mentioned Simonetta d'Este.

"Billy," she called after him.

He didn't answer.

"It's Anna," she called again.

"What's Anna?" He appeared again in her sightline in the mirror.

"The cook's name. It's Anna. Anna Gorman. Fifty-six years old. From the Creedon Domestic Agency. Good references. Last worked for a Mrs. Slater of 563 Park Avenue, *not* the Mrs. Slater we know. Why this great interest in the cook's name?"

"I want to show her how to lock the doors after we leave."

"You'd better get dressed. We can't drift in late tonight. Edith wants everyone there at eight sharp, before the duchess comes down."

"I still want to talk to the cook about locking the front door. It's tricky."

"How do I look?" She stood up and turned around toward him.

" 'Mrs. William Grenville, Junior, was in powder-blue satin by Mainbocher,' your friend Elsa Maxwell will write."

"Balenciaga. I'm branching out. And Elsa Maxwell was not invited."

"No rocks tonight?"

"If there is this prowler around, as you insist, I'm not going to put on my jewels until I'm in the car."

"Anna!" she called out. "Anna!"

"What's the matter?" asked Billy, crossing over from his room, adjusting his black tie.

"Where the hell is she?"

"She's in the kitchen eating her dinner. What's the trouble?"

"There're some things I want her to do after we go out."

"That's no reason to yell for her like that. I thought something was wrong."

"Oh, go tie your tie," said Ann.

"Did you want me, Mrs. Grenville?" asked Anna Gorman, opening the door into the small hallway that separated their two bedrooms.

"Mr. Grenville said I was interrupting your dinner. I am sorry," said Ann in exaggerated friendliness.

"That's all right, missus," said Anna. Anna Gorman had heard a thing or two about Mrs. William Grenville, Junior, at the employment agency.

"We'll be leaving in a few minutes, Anna, and there are a few things I wanted to go over with you. You see, we can't be late, because we're going to a dinner for the Duchess of Windsor, and all the guests must arrive before the duchess comes down."

Behind the cook's back, Billy Grenville shook his head slowly in disapproval of his wife's name-dropping in front of a servant, a thing he would never have done himself, and returned to his own room to finish dressing. His head-shaking was not lost on Ann, and it added to her annoyance that the cook did not seem impressed with her social disclosure.

"The chauffeur's bringing the children home from the riding instructor's Halloween party at about eight-thirty."

"Mr. Grenville told me."

"Tell the children to go right to bed, no television. Mr. Grenville's going to take Third flying in the new plane in the morning, and he won't if he stays up late. Also, would you telephone this number in the city and say that Third is in the country with his parents for the weekend and cannot come to Bobby Strauss's birthday party tomorrow. If the nurse hadn't left, she'd be doing this."

"Yes, Mrs. Grenville."

"I bought a lot of cosmetics in the village this afternoon. I wonder if you'd unwrap all those packages for me and throw away all the papers and strings."

"Yes, Mrs. Grenville."

"When you pick up my clothes and straighten up the bathroom, I wonder if you'd do me the most enormous favor, Anna?"

"What's that, Mrs. Grenville?"

"The laundress—what's her name?"

"Lil."

"Lil, yes. She creased my sheets when she ironed them,

and I simply cannot bear to have my sheets creased. She's supposed to fold them over her arm and carry them to the bed to change. Do you think you could run the iron over them, just this once, and I'll explain it again to Lil when I see her on Monday."

"I'm just the cook, Mrs. Grenville."

"Yes, of course, but I just thought if you had a few minutes to spare after we leave and before the children get home, you might, uh, you know, run the iron over the creases, and also, about the lights, leave all the lights on in the house, don't be worried about the electric bill, the people who rent the indoor tennis court pay all the electricity bills, and if there's a prowler in the area, as Mr. Grenville seems to think, he won't come near a house that's all lit up."

"I'll light it up like the Catholic church," said Anna.

"What?"

"Just an expression, missus."

"Now, the telephone number where we'll be having dinner at Mrs. Baker's is——"

"Mr. Grenville gave me the number, missus, in case he received a call."

Ann let this fact register but said nothing. Instead she picked up her brush and brushed hard her already brushed hair. She wondered from whom he was expecting a call.

"Is there a guard on the place, Mrs. Grenville?"

"No, there's not, but the Oyster Bay police patrol the grounds every hour or so, and there is a guard that the people who rent the indoor tennis court have, called Ralph, or something. We're going to be late. Billy, are you ready? Hand me that bag with my jewels, would you, Anna?"

"Here, missus," said Anna, handing Ann the bag.

"And you won't forget about the sheets, will you?" she said, finishing the conversation and sweeping out of the room.

Anna Gorman looked after her, shaking her head slowly in the same way Billy Grenville had. She turned toward the unmade bed with its upholstered headboard and creased linen sheets, and resignedly stripped them from the bed. On Monday, she decided, she would call the Creedon Employment Agency in Manhattan.

THE CAR was parked in the cobblestone courtyard, and Billy Grenville was seated behind the wheel smoking a cigarette. Beside him on the seat was a revolver.

"What in the name of God are you carrying a gun for?" asked Ann as she opened the door of the car and got in.

"The garage has been broken into. The cabana has been broken into. I'm not taking any chances," said Billy.

"But nothing was taken, except some food in the cabana," said Ann. "It's probably kids."

"I think it's someone who's living in the woods there," said Billy, pointing in the direction beyond the garden and the swimming pool. "I'm going to set a trap for him."

"Oh, Billy, for God's sake, if you're so concerned, you should have hired a guard," said Ann. She did not press her point and suggest that if he was so concerned about the prowler, they should remain with the children and stay home from the party instead of leaving them alone in the house with a brand-new cook. She particularly wanted to go to this party to show all the North Shore families that the Grenville marriage, despite all the rumors to the contrary, remained on a firm footing. "What are you stopping for?"

"I'm going to turn on all the driveway lights down to the road."

The lights shone on the rhododendron bushes that lined the long driveway. Ann shivered, wondering if anyone was standing behind one watching them drive away. From her gold minaudier she took a cigarette and matches. Ignoring Billy's outstretched lighter, she lit her own cigarette with a match. The matchbook, she saw in the flash of flame, was from an obscure French restaurant where she had lunched the day before with Ali Khan. Billy, meanwhile, withdrew his gold Zippo.

"Those lights are so bright."

"That's the point."

"Anna will say it's lit up like a Catholic church."

"What?"

"Just an expression, missus."

"I don't know what the hell you're talking about."

"It's quicker to go 25A than Berry Hill Road," said Ann as the car turned out from the driveway.

"You don't have to tell me how to get to Edith Bleeker's house. I've been going there since I was ten years old."

"Right," said Ann, twisting the rearview mirror around to watch herself put on her earrings. "Just don't tell me that story again of Bratsie's tenth birthday party."

"I wish you wouldn't twist the rearview mirror around like that when I'm driving," said Billy. "It's very dangerous."

"If you'd put a mirror on the back of the visor as I've asked you to, I wouldn't need to use your damn rearview mirror."

"Poor Bratsie," said Billy quietly, as he always did when Jellico Bleeker's name came into the conversation.

"Necklace, earrings, ring, bracelet, brooch," Ann said, checking off her jewelry in the rearview mirror. "I hate this damn clasp Jules Glaenzer talked me into. It pinches my earlobe."

"Did I tell you I drove by your old house in Pittsburg, Kansas, last week when I was picking up the new plane?" asked Billy. "West Quincy Street, I think it was."

Ann's face reddened in the dark car. She had, even before meeting the family she married into, disengaged herself from her past. She disliked being from a place for which apologies had to be made. "And just what is that supposed to mean?"

"Nothing, really," said Billy. "It just seemed like a natural segue from your sapphires pinching your earlobes."

"You're a shit, Billy," she said, lighting another Camel.

"I want a divorce, Ann." The words held no threat for her, as they once had. Too often spoken and never acted upon, they had become part of their conversational discord.

They arrived at the gates of Edith Bleeker's estate on Viking's Cove. "Look," said Ann quietly. "I don't want to be the first one there. Let's drive around for a few minutes before we turn in at Edith's."

Billy dutifully backed the Studelac out of the drive and took off in the direction of Locust Valley.

"Did you hear what I said?" he persisted.

"Do I feel the presence of Princess Simonetta d'Este in this domestic crisis?" asked Ann.

"You keep Simonetta out of this," he said.

She did not want to let him know that she had been having him followed by private detectives and wished she had not introduced Simonetta d'Este's name into the conversation.

"I want a divorce, Ann," he repeated. The calmness of his request began to unnerve her.

"His own kind. That's what they'll say about Simonetta d'Este. So much more suitable than the show girl. What his mother always wanted for him."

"I am waiting for an answer," said Billy.

"You know my price and my conditions," said Ann nervously, taking a gold-and-diamond compact from her gold-and-diamond minaudier. She opened it, looked at herself in the mirror, and began powdering her face.

"I haven't seen that before," said Billy.

"Seen what?"

"That compact."

"Of course you have."

"Who bought you that, Ann? My old roommate Neddie Pavenstedt? Or that greaseball Ali Khan?"

He wound down the window of the car.

"What are you doing that for?" she asked. "I'm cold, and it will blow my hair."

"To do this," he answered. He reached over, pulled the compact out of her hands, and threw it out of the window as he sped on. Again her face reddened in the dark car, this time with rage.

"The duchess will say what lovely color you have tonight, Ann," taunted Billy.

"I'm going to get even with you for this," said Ann, stabbing her cigarette butt into the ashtray where, unextinguished, it continued to emit smoke. She lit another.

"And do me a favor, will you? Don't curtsy to the duchess. It's so tacky."

THEY TURNED through Edith Bleeker's massive wrought-iron gates, each supported by a red brick column surmounted by a stone griffin on a ball of stone, and drove silently up the long white-pebble driveway to the porte cochere extending from the entrance of the enormous red brick house over the adjacent driveway. The air of the Studelac was clouded with the smoke of Ann's Camel. The outdoor staff, dressed for the occasion in black mess jackets and ties, lined up to park the arriving cars. Ann drew deeply on her cigarette one last time, as if she wanted more out of it than it could give her.

Billy, lugubrious no longer, sprang from the car when his door was opened. Edith Bleeker's was a house he always enjoyed coming to, and he never was not filled with childhood memories when he reached up to push the bell that hung from a cord in the ceiling of the porte cochere. "Bratsie and I used to stick pins in this bell on Halloween when we were kids, and the bell rang inside interminably, and Edith would have a fit, but Brats and I would run like hell, and . . ."

But Ann was never interested in Billy's endless reminiscences of dead Bratsie Bleeker and was not listening. Instead she was mourning for her gold-and-diamond compact given to her only the day before by Ali Khan.

"Good evening, Mrs. Grenville," said the old and distinguished butler, Dudley, who bowed formally at the entrance.

It was a mark of distinction on the North Shore to be person-
ally greeted by Edith Bleeker's celebrated butler. He was an
indispensable contributor to the success of Mrs. Bleeker's frequent entertainments, so highly thought of that the late
George Bleeker's will provided generous bonuses for every five
years that Dudley remained in his widow's service. He knew
all the connections and cross-connections of the North
Shore, but of no one was he more fond than Billy Grenville.

"Good evening," answered Ann, not looking at him as she
passed him and entered the hall. She walked straight to a gilt
Chippendale mirror over a console table and eyed her wind-
blown hair critically in it.

"Good evening, Junior," said the butler.

"You know, Dudley, you're the only person who can get
away with calling me Junior still," said Billy affectionately.

"I've known your husband since he was ten years old, Mrs.
Grenville, when he used to come here for poor Jelly's birthday
parties," said Dudley.

"Don't tell me we're the first ones here?" asked Ann in
reply.

"Mr. Freeman's already in the drawing room," replied Dudley.

"The piano player, you mean?" asked Ann.

"Yes," said Dudley. "Mrs. Bleeker has had him learn all
the new tunes from *The Boy Friend.*"

"We're the first ones here," said Ann, looking at Billy.

"You wanted to be on time," replied Billy.

"I stupidly have come off without my compact, Dudley,"
said Ann. "Do you suppose I could go upstairs?"

"Of course," said Dudley.

"You go on, Billy. I'll join you," said Ann, walking up the
sweeping staircase.

"Say, Dudley?" said Billy in a confidential voice when Ann
had disappeared from sight.

"Yes, Junior," answered the butler, moving closer.

"I may be receiving a call later."

The doorbell rang. Other guests were arriving.

"I'll find you, sir," said Dudley.
"Long distance," said Billy.

OUTSIDE THE drawing-room windows the grounds and gardens were flood-lit, and beyond, ships bearing freight sailed silently by on Long Island Sound. Only the piano player, hired for the evening, found the breathtaking sight more compelling than the guests.

"Everyone's been to the vault, I see," observed Ann, surveying the jewels in the room, knowing her own stacked up. She was, she knew, madly chic, just as Fydor Cassati often described her in his column. She heard the sound of her satin and smelled the scent of her perfume and caught the gleam of her diamonds. She looked down the front of her strapless dress at her lovely breasts, and pleasure filled her. She breathed in deeply. She was ready to make her entrance.

"Who is that marvelous-looking creature?" asked Lord Cowdray, pointing his whiskey glass toward the entrance doors of the room where Edith Bleeker stood to receive her arriving guests.

"Which?" asked Tucky Bainbridge, following his gaze toward the gathering assemblage of the proudest peacocks of the North Shore of Long Island—the Phippses, the Hitchcocks, the Schiffs, the Guests—spilling in one upon another, the nobility of North America, or so they thought, honoring their hostess's request for promptness in arriving before the Duchess of Windsor.

"Brightly painted. Blazing jewels. Sweeping in," said Lord Cowdray. "Ravishing."

"Oh, her," said Tucky, putting withering scorn into the two words. "That's Ann Grenville."

"Now that's the way a woman should enter a room," he went on, not taking his eyes from her.

"Her Copa training, no doubt," said Tucky sourly, losing

interest in her assigned task of pointing people out to the visiting Englishman.

"Her what?"

"She used to dance at the Copacabana. We call them the prince and the show girl out here. Hello, Brenda," she called to Brenda Frazier.

"I do hope Edith has seated me next to her."

"To Brenda?"

"I meant Mrs. Grenville."

"If not, don't fret, Lord Cowdray. When she hears your title, she'll seek you out."

"Not one of your favorites, I take it?"

"The life and death of every party. How Billy Grenville could have thrown himself away on her is something I'll never understand," said Tucky.

"Billy Grenville who owns Tailspin?"

"The very one."

"The best horse in America. Is that Billy Grenville next to her?"

"Yes. He's got the class, and she's got the brass."

"They appear ideally suited."

"Just an act. Lord Cowdray. Just an act."

I WAS ALWAYS reading in the social columns of the brilliant conversations that took place at Edith Bleeker's dinner parties, but what I heard was nothing more than desultory chatter, where they had been, where they were going, that sort of thing. "Were you at Cornelia's?" "Ghastly." "Who was there?" "Taytsie and Winkie and the Delissers, and old Mrs. Altemus with all the white powder and bright red cheeks."

But I can tell you this much about that night: Ann Grenville was surprised to see me in that grand house at that august gathering. From across the room I could see the wheels work-

ing in her social climber's mind. What in the world is Basil
Plant doing *here* at Edith Bleeker's? she was thinking. Edith
Bleeker's parties, like Alice Grenville's, were closed to newcomers and outsiders. Even the recent successes of my slender
volumes, particularly *Candles at Lunch,* thirteen weeks on the
New York Times best-seller list and soon to be a major motion
picture, did not qualify me for social entrance to Viking's
Cove. However, my success had made me a favorite of certain
of the North Shore ladies with literary leanings, particularly
Jeanne Twombley and Petal Wilson, and I was spending that
weekend with the Twombleys when Alfred was felled by the
flu at the last minute and Jeanne pressed me into service as
her escort. That's how I got there and bore witness to Ann
Grenville's performance.

Once, urged on by Bertie Lightfoot, who was intent on
launching me, Ann had traipsed up flight after flight of dark
stairs that she complained smelled of cat urine to the tene-
ment flat way over east on Seventy-second Street where I
then lived and worked. Once there, the style of it surprised
her; she had hardly expected to see a gesso console table in a
fifth-floor walk-up. It was, I told her, a gift from Kay Kay
Somerset, who was redecorating and getting rid of things. We
drank red wine and gossiped about Salvador Dali and her
portrait, and Bertie, and people in society, and laughed a
great deal. She could see the possibility of me as a witty
addition to her dinner parties, but something about me made
her cautious. I think she felt that I saw through her the way
Dali had, past the soda fountain waitress, into her self. She
never did invite me.

"Ah, the beautiful Mrs. Grenville," I said when our eyes
met, and I crossed the room to greet her, whiskey spilling
over a bit from my glass onto Edith Bleeker's Aubusson carpet.

"Hellohowyou," she answered, all in one word, in that chi-
chi voice of hers, the way she had heard Billy's sisters do
when people spoke to them they didn't want to talk to. She

moved on away from me to greet Neddie Pavenstedt, leaving me with egg on my face. I looked after her, my eyes boring into her splendid back, and made a mental note for my journal.

IT WAS THE duchess only; the duke was not there. She said business in Paris had delayed him from making the trip in time. His absence in no way diminished the splendor of the occasion; she had eclipsed her royal husband as a social curiosity. It was not yet fashionable to decry the Duchess of Windsor. That would come later, after the duke died, and the sum total of his wasted life was laid bare. At the time of which we speak, the duke and duchess were considered to be exquisite still, and those who basked in their light acquired a patina of exquisiteness themselves in the upper echelons of New York society.

"Wallis," said Edith Bleeker, taking her guest of honor around her drawing room, "you know this attractive couple, I know. Ann and Billy Grenville. Billy Grenville was my son Jellico's best friend." In death Bratsie Bleeker had taken on a nobility he had not possessed in life, and the shabby circumstances of his unsolved murder had passed from memory.

"Hello, Billy," said the duchess, extending her hand. "How's your divine mother?"

"She's well, Your Grace," said Billy, inclining his head.

"Do give her my love." She moved and spoke as if she were a royal presence, which is what she believed her marriage had made her. Ann watched her, glowing in her reflected glory. She was in green. Ann knew that her dress was from Dior, and that the emeralds at her neck, on her ears, and at her shoulder were Queen Alexandra's emeralds, left to the duke for his future queen when he was the Prince of Wales. She also knew they had been reset in Paris at Cartier's, secretly, so that they could not be reclaimed by the English royal family as part of the Crown Jewels. The man from Cartier's who had made the ear clip that pinched her lobe had told her that. It was the sort of information that Ann always knew.

"Good evening, Ann," said the duchess. "What marvelous color you have this evening."

Ann Grenville had never looked so lovely as now. It thrilled her that the Duchess of Windsor should call her by her first name, and the mixture of excitement and success of the moment enhanced her already striking appearance. She bobbed a curtsy, somewhat less deep than she would have liked to give, and the duchess beamed at her for this recognition. "It's lovely to see you again, ma'am," said Ann. She wondered what her mother would have thought if she had witnessed this familiarity with the famed romantic figure she had admired so extravagantly.

She longed to prolong the conversation. She knew that the duchess found her more entertaining than the Long Island ladies, and she enjoyed the feeling that it gave her. Although it was not a thing she discussed, even with Billy, she was aware that the ladies of the North Shore, like Tucky Bainbridge for instance, did not care for her and tolerated her only because she was married to William Grenville, Junior, whose position in the society of New York and Long Island was as inviolate as any of theirs. With the men, it was another thing. It was only to Babette Van Degan, who was never asked anywhere anymore, that she confessed she saw a parallel between her marriage to Billy and Wallis Simpson's marriage to the Prince of Wales.

"I'm so sorry you missed the race at Belmont, ma'am," said Ann, placing her hand on Billy's arm with wifely pride. "It was thrilling."

"We read all about Tailspin in Paris," said the duchess. "It's so exciting for you, Billy."

Billy Grenville was constantly astonished by the performance of marital bliss his wife was able to enact in the presence of others, always managing to confuse the skeptics who were certain that the stormy union had run its course. As always he fell into step with her performance, and the conversation between the duchess and the attractive Grenvilles became animated and filled with laughter, prompting the duchess to say about them, to Edith Bleeker, that they were an ideally suited couple.

"It's NOT FUNNY, darling. Poor Ann is terribly worried about the prowler. He broke into Billy's car last night."

"She's not so worried she'd miss a party. After all, who's home with the kids if she's so damn worried? Some new cook who just arrived."

"She was never going to get mother-of-the-year award."

"I don't believe that prowler story anyway. I bet it's Ann. Ann always has to create a drama with herself at the center of it."

"But of course there're prowlers, darling. It's the North Shore. People like us are fair game."

"It's only food he's after. He's probably just a vagrant."

"I have the most marvelous idea," said Kay Kay Somerset.

"What's that?"

"Why not set a trap for him?"

"What kind of trap?"

"If all he's after is food, make him a sandwich and leave it in the fridge of your pool house, and sprinkle some sleeping pills on it, in the mayonnaise or something, and he'll fall asleep, darling, right there on the chaise by your pool, and the police can catch him, snoring away, and take him off to the slammer *toute suite.* Now how's that for the idea of the evening?"

"Did you hear Kay Kay's idea for the Grenvilles' prowler?" asked Tucky Bainbridge, screaming with laughter. "Kay Kay said to put sleeping pills in a sandwich. Don't you think it's divine?"

"God knows, and so does everyone else, that Ann has enough sleeping pills around to fell an army of prowlers."

AFTER ELEVEN the telephone rang in the house in Oyster Bay. Upstairs Anna Gorman put aside reading *The Messenger of the Sacred Heart* and wondered about people who called that late. There was no telephone in the room where she was sleeping, and she felt quite sure that by the time she rose and put on her robe and went downstairs to the telephone in the hall, whoever was calling would have hung up. The night outside was dark and wet, and the house was strange to her, and she decided not to answer it. Instead she switched off her bed light.

LATER IN THE evening, after dinner, Dudley, the butler, whispered in Billy's ear that there was a telephone call for him.

"Is it the cook from the house?" Billy asked Dudley, knowing it wasn't, for the benefit of his companion.

Dudley, who was used to the complicated affairs of the people he served, met Billy's eyes and mouthed the words "long distance."

"Excuse me, Brenda," Billy said to Brenda Frazier. "There's been this damn prowler."

Across the room Ann talked to Lord Cowdray about Princess Margaret and Peter Townsend, her equerry, if she would marry him or if she wouldn't. It was a conversation that Ann could carry on in great detail without giving her full attention to it. She watched the butler whisper in her husband's ear, and she kept on talking. She saw her husband nod his head, and she kept on talking. She met her husband's eye as he glanced furtively at her and looked away again, and she kept on talking. She followed with her eyes as her husband left Edith Bleeker's drawing room, and she kept on talking. She listened to an illicit proposition being made to her, and she let the Englishman know it might be a future possibility.

"You will ring me when you are in London next?" he asked her.

She smiled at him. "Excuse me, will you?" she said and rose and walked out of Edith Bleeker's drawing room.

WHATEVER the conversation had been, it was brief. By the time Ann quietly opened the doors of the library, she saw her husband across the room standing by the desk with his back to the door. He was speaking into the telephone in an extremely low voice, but she was able to hear him say, "Goodnight, my darling, sleep well," make a kissing sound, and end the conversation with "I love you, too."

Ann threw the Baccarat glass containing Scotch and soda that she had carried with her from the drawing room. It narrowly missed Billy and crashed into a Lowestoft platter on a teakwood stand that separated the leather-bound copies of Melville from the leather-bound copies of Dickens on the shelves of Edith Bleeker's library, smashing the armorial platter into worthless fragments.

Within an instant she was across the room and pulled the telephone receiver out of his hand. "Listen to me, you wop whore!" she screamed into the instrument. "You leave my husband alone!" If it was Simonetta d'Este, she heard no more, as Billy broke the connection.

"Are you out of your mind?" he said to her.

"How dare you embarrass me like this?" she screamed at him, at the same time slapping his face.

"You understand, don't you," he said to her, grabbing her hand from his face and holding it hard, "that if you make one of your scenes in Edith Bleeker's house, it will be the end of you on the North Shore. Not of me, mind you. Just you."

She knew what he said was true.

"All that Jet Set trash at de Cuevas's ball may have forgiven you for the scene you made there, but you won't get away with it here."

Behind them the doors to the library opened, and Edith Bleeker, the grande dame of Long Island, walked into her room. In the hallway outside stood Basil Plant and Kay Kay Somerset and Jeanne Twombley staring into the room as more guests arrived to look in.

"Edith, my darling, I am sorry. This is totally my fault," said Billy Grenville. "My elbow must have hit this beautiful platter, and I knocked it off the stand. We seem to have caused quite a spectacle at your lovely party, and I would very much appreciate it if you would excuse us and allow us to leave through the kitchen, and I will be in touch with you tomorrow to make amends and restitution for the damage I have caused."

Edith knew, as did everyone else, that Billy Grenville was covering for his wife. Tucky Bainbridge was sent upstairs to fetch Ann Grenville's fur jacket, and Dudley retrieved Billy's coat from a hall closet. Stan Freeman, accompanied now by a bass and drums, struck up some of the tunes from *The Boy Friend,* and Mrs. Sanford grabbed Lord Cowdray to dance with her, and other guests followed suit, anxious to keep Edith Bleeker's party from being destroyed by the disgraceful fight of the Grenvilles. Long after their flight into the cold October night, the Grenvilles were discussed in various corners of Edith Bleeker's drawing room. Many of the conversations ended with the words "Poor Alice," meaning Billy's beloved mother, Alice Grenville, who had never from the beginning approved of her son's misalliance with the Broadway show girl who wanted so terribly to be part of the Grenvilles' world.

THEY DROVE over the Long Island roads from Viking's Cove in Locust Valley to Oyster Bay in murderous silence. Ann stared out as the windshield wipers made a swish sound, back and forth, back and forth. She dared not tell him he was driving too fast. She feared he might stop the car and strike her if she cautioned him about his speed. She pulled her sable fur around her and sat as far away from him as she could.

She knew she had gone too far. Inwardly she always suffered from remorse when she lost control and created scenes in public. For someone who cared so much about belonging, she could not understand about herself why she continually sabotaged herself socially. She wondered if there was a connection between it and her menstrual period, which she could feel was beginning.

The speedometer on the dashboard hovered at seventy-five. The dark roads were wet, and she closed her eyes and tried to remember exactly how much she had had to drink. Usually she nursed a single drink for the entire evening when she was out with the North Shore group, but the talk about divorce in the car on the way to the party had unsettled her. There were two Scotches before dinner, she counted, and white wine with the fish, and red wine with the beef, and champagne with the sweet, while most of the food was left fashionably uneaten. No brandy, she had turned down the brandy, but there had been another Scotch, or maybe two, not counting the one she had hurled across the library that had broken Edith Bleeker's Lowestoft platter. She shuddered at the thought and forced it out of her mind. She wondered if the pills she took that Dr. Sidney Skinner prescribed for her—for diet, and nerves, and sleep—could have had an adverse effect on her system combined with all the liquor she had had.

He turned off 25A onto Berry Hill Road without looking left or right, but the wet roads were empty. As they pulled into the driveway, she could see that they had made the trip in only sixteen minutes. The lights were brightly lit along the long driveway, reminding them both of the prowler. In her corner of the front seat, Ann removed her earrings, her rings, her bracelet, her brooch, and her necklace, placed her jewels in the leather bag she had put into the glove compartment, and put the bag in the pocket of her fur coat. The car pulled into the courtyard and around to the side door of the Play-house.

For a few seconds they both sat in the car and surveyed their house. The bare branches of the large oak tree to the left of the side door scratched the roof of the house over Ann's room, and dead brown leaves, soaked by the rain, covered the cobblestones of the courtyard.

"Who were you talking to on the telephone, Billy?" she asked.

"None of your business," he answered.

"Are you going to put the car in the garage?"

"No."

"Are you going to turn off the driveway lights?"

"No."

They opened the doors of the car and got out. Billy walked up to the side door, put his hand on the knob, and found it locked. She saw for the first time that he was holding his revolver.

"Shit," he said.

"What?"

"It's locked."

"Of course it's locked. You gave what's-her-name locking instructions for fifteen minutes before we left."

"I forgot to bring a key."

"Great."

"You didn't bring one?"

"Of course I didn't bring one."

"How the hell are we going to get in?"

"Wake up cookie."

He ignored her and walked over to the window of his bedroom and peered in. The curtains had been drawn, but the window was unlocked, and he pushed it up and crawled in. Ann stood outside in the wet courtyard, uncertain if she was supposed to enter the house in the same fashion or if Billy would return and open the door for her. A chill went through her, and she felt frightened, as if someone were watching her. Then the front door opened.

"Lock all the doors and leave the windows open!" said Ann sarcastically, to hide her fright. "Guaranteed to fool all the burglars in the neighborhood."

"Why don't you shut your big fucking mouth," said Billy at the door. "Don't you think you've had enough to say for one night?"

She walked into the narrow hall past Billy. Her bedroom was to the right and Billy's was to the left. She went into her room and took off her fur jacket, removing the bag of jewels from the pocket. She placed it on her dressing table. She switched on a lamp in the room and saw that Anna had unpacked her cosmetics, as she had asked her to, and had repressed her sheets so that the offending creases had been removed.

"I don't suppose your motherly instincts would include going upstairs to check on the children?" asked Billy.

"You go upstairs and check on the children," she replied. "You're the one with the gun."

"I wonder if I always thought this was a creepy house," he said, "or if it just seems creepy to me tonight."

"Billy."

"What?"

"Bring me back a beer, will you?"

"Funny."

"What?"

"I thought you were going to say bring you back a gun."

They looked at each other for a minute. He turned away from her and opened the door of the bedroom hallway that led into the front hall of the house. To the right was the dining room and kitchen. He switched on the lights. Across the hall was the paneled living room that looked down on the indoor tennis court. He entered the living room and switched on the lights. He crossed the length of the living room. Beyond it was another hallway. He switched on the lights in the hallway. To the right were the double doors that led to the vast music room. To the left was a stairway that led upstairs to where the children and the cook were sleeping. He switched on the stair light and walked upstairs. At the top of the stairs he turned on the upstairs hall light and entered Diantha's room. He pulled her blanket up over her and kissed her on the cheek. She sighed in her sleep and hugged the dog that slept next to her. Then he walked into Third's room and looked down at his son. He turned back to the hall and then walked over to Third's bed and leaned down and kissed him.

"Goodnight, little boy," he whispered.

"Night, Daddy," whispered Third.

"Why aren't you asleep?" he asked.

"Are you going to take me flying tomorrow?"

"Yes, yes. Now go to sleep."

He retraced his steps through the house, turning out all the lights he had turned on. Passing through the living room, he walked to one of the windows and peered out at the grounds as if he expected to see someone out there.

"WHAT WAS THAT called?" she asked.

"The final fuck," he answered.

He was different to her. She did not understand why he

seemed to be in control, but she did not change her performance.

"Good, I won't have to fake it anymore," she said, preparing herself for bed, putting on the black brassiere that she always wore beneath her nightgown, for the support of her beautiful breasts.

"I'll say this much for you, Ann—you've still got great tits."

"Such gallantry," she replied.

"Let's talk divorce."

"You want a divorce, Billy? Fine. Shall I go over the figures? I want five million dollars. Plus this house. Plus the house in New York. Plus full custody of the children. When you're ready to talk my language about divorce, then we'll talk divorce. Now go to bed. We have people coming for lunch."

"Those aren't the kind of figures I have in mind, Ann."

"What do you think this has been like for me, this marriage? How do you think it feels to know that your mother and sisters loathe me, have always loathed me, will always loathe me, even if we should happen to stay married fifty years?"

"All the more reason to divorce."

"I don't want a divorce."

He picked up his revolver, which he had placed on her bedside table, and started for the door.

"Did I tell you I saw your old house on West Quincy Street in Pittsburg last week?" he asked.

"Yes, you did," she replied. She was sitting at her dressing table. She swallowed a few sleeping pills with some beer, which she drank from the bottle.

"I went to the cemetery, too," he said, "and looked up the Mertens plot. I didn't know that, uh . . . ."

She watched him in the mirror as she applied cold cream to her face. There was something about his voice and manner that gave her a feeling of warning and apprehension.

"You don't look as well nude as you used to," she interrupted him, hoping to deflect the conversation away from her past, that part of her life that she no longer considered part of herself.

". . . that you had a little brother. Odd you never mentioned him," continued Billy, not feeling uncomfortable in his nudity.

"He was only three when he died," said Ann, relieved. "I never think of him."

"Claud his name was, in case you forgot."

"I didn't forget. Why this great interest in my family all of a sudden? You haven't evinced much curiosity about my background all the years we've been married."

"Curious," he said, reflecting on the word as he spoke it.

"What's curious?"

"Life."

"What are you babbling about, Billy? You'd better go to bed. It's very late. Aren't you taking Third flying in the morning?" She lifted the bottle of beer to her lips and took several deep swallows, all the time not taking her eyes off him in the mirror. She knew there was more he had to say; her curiosity was intense but her desire not to hear any more of it was equally intense.

"Don't you think it's odd, in the overall scheme of things, I mean, that the particular airplane that I wanted to own should be manufactured in the very tiny little town in the southwestern corner of the state of Kansas where my wife was born?"

"Are we getting mystical at one o'clock in the morning? Fate? Is that going to be next?" She got up from her dressing table and went into the bathroom, wanting to get away from him, and began brushing her hair in the bathroom mirror away from his gaze.

"I said to them, at the aircraft plant, that my wife was from that town, I believed." He walked across her room and leaned against the bathroom door, again watching her in the mirror.

"I wish you'd go to bed, Billy," she said. "I want to put in my Tampax."

"I said her name was Urse Mertens, but no one seemed to remember you."

"I left there years ago, Billy."

"Except one fella. He remembered. He didn't speak up at the time, though. He was an accountant with the firm, not one of the big honchos, as he referred to them later when he called me at the Vel-Fre Motel. We had dinner in a Chinese restaurant on South Broadway, new since your time, right next to Crowell's Pharmacy. He said you used to be a waitress at Crowell's when you were in high school."

"I'm going to close this door."

"Four pens in his breast pocket, that kind of person. He's the one who took me out to the cemetery. Nicely attended, your mother's grave, and little Claud's. He called you Urse. Urse Mertens, he said. Funny. You don't look like an Urse Mertens."

"If you're just deciding that you married beneath you, Mr. Grenville, that's something your mother and sisters tried to tell you years ago," she answered.

"Aren't you curious to know what his name was? Billy Bob Veblen! He said he went to high school with you."

Ann stared at her husband. She could begin to feel panic rising within her.

"He said he was in *Lady Windermere's Fan* with you."

She continued to stare.

"HE SAID HE WAS MARRIED TO YOU!"

Hatred and wrath, which had been accumulating within her for the whole evening, suddenly boiled over. "THAT IS NOT TRUE!" she screamed.

He grabbed her by her arm, pulled her across the room to her bed, pushed her down on it by her shoulders and leaned over her, breathing heavily, poised to enter her or kill her. He was what he thought he would never be, out of control. Saliva dripped from his loose mouth onto her. The thought of striking her, and worse, went through his mind.

"He said he joined the Marines and when he came back, you had vanished from the earth, as far as he knew. He didn't know you had changed your name to Ann Arden. He said he never got a divorce from you."

"No," she screamed.

"You know what this means, don't you? This is not a moment that either of us should be deceived by. We're not even married! You're still Mrs. Billy Bob Veblen, the bigamist, from Pittsburg, Kansas!"

Pushing down on her, he heaved himself upward, off her and off the bed, terrified by the thoughts of violence that had entered his head, that he knew she had read. She snaked her body away from him while they continued to stare at each other.

"What has happened to us?" he asked, aghast.

"You're drunk," she said.

"No, I'm not," he replied.

She was not listening. Why had she not paid more attention to him when he told her he was going to Kansas to buy his airplane? She dreaded to think of Alice Grenville's reaction to her earlier marriage. She wondered if even Sam Rosenthal, the divorce lawyer who had been so sympathetic to her marital plight, would have the same regard for her when he heard there had been an earlier marriage that she had never dissolved.

Billy walked to the window and peered out at the cobblestone courtyard. He thought he heard footsteps outside.

"You know my motto, don't you?"

"What?"

"Shoot first and ask questions later."

"What are you talking about?"

"The prowler."

⚘   ⚘   ⚘

UPSTAIRS, at the other end of the house, Anna Gorman, the new cook, whose duties this night included keeping an eye on the sleeping children, heard voices below. They were not the voices of conversation; they were the voices of combat. She picked up her ticking clock from the bedside table and saw that it was half past two in the morning, then remembered that she had forgotten to reset her clock from Daylight Savings Time to Eastern Standard Time. Spring forward, fall back, she remembered, as she turned the hands back an hour, all the time listening to the sounds below.

The door to her room was ajar, as were the doors across the hall to the rooms of Diantha and Third. Anna Gorman rose, shivered in the cold, pulled her heavy wool comforter around her, and knotted its braided cord. She slipped her feet into fleece-lined slippers and padded to the door.

A flight of stairs and the length of a long living room and hall below separated her from the bedrooms, across the hall from one another, of Mr. and Mrs. Grenville, but through some quirk of construction in this house that was conceived to be a playhouse and not a domicile, with its indoor tennis court and music room, the sounds of anger and reproach traveled eerily across rooms and up the stairs. Anna Gorman, who believed in God and family, felt that it was her duty to close the doors of the children's rooms, not only to assure their sleep but to shield them from the ugliness below should either of them awake.

Diantha, she saw when she peered into the dark room, was already awake. With her in the bed, listening to the fight below, was Third. Between them was Diantha's dog, Sloppy.

As SHE OFTEN did in moments of panic and despair, Ann missed her mother, the only person who had ever understood her completely, the only person with whom she had never had to pretend to be anything other than what she was. That Billy Bob Veblen, long since forgotten, should reenter her life twelve years into her marriage and bring her enviable existence crashing down was inconceivable to her. Her mother had discovered her all those years back engaged in sexual intercourse with Billy Bob Veblen, the captain of the Pittsburg High football team, the handsomest boy in the school, on the davenport of the front room of the house on West Quincy Street. To her surprise there was no reprimand. Or punishment. What her mother said she had never forgotten. "Don't waste it here," said Ethel Mertens, meaning Pittsburg, Kansas. "That's the mistake I made." Her elopement several years later from Kansas City across the state line to Oklahoma, before Billy Bob Veblen enlisted in the Marines, was the event that precipitated her mother to move her to New York.

"As they say in the movies, 'My lawyers will be in touch with you,' " said Billy to his ominously silent wife. He began to whistle as he turned to walk back to his room.

Her lips curled back from her teeth. Her eyes flashed dangerously and Billy saw the fiery gleam that he had come to dread in them, like a flash of lightning in the sky preceding terrifying thunder. She made an inarticulate, almost animal sound in her throat. "I'm glad you're leaving," she snarled at him. Her voice was low and guttural. All traces of tonal culture evaporated. "I'm glad you're leaving." She repeated the words, her crescendo building. Nothing could stop the savage force of her rage. *"I'm glad you're leaving!"*

Billy watched her distorted face as she screamed up at him from her bed, like a caged animal.

"I hope you don't think you're being impressive," he said quietly as he turned and walked back to his room, unaware that his earlier words to her about the prowler had set in motion a lethal train of thought. His bed had been turned down. His pajamas and dressing gown had been laid at the foot of the bed. His slippers, velvet with embroidered initials, from Lobb in London, were on the floor by the side of the bed. He walked to the window and opened it to the cold night, looking across the cobblestone courtyard as he did so. For an instant he thought he saw a shadow moving toward the house, but decided that it was the branches of the large trees that surrounded the courtyard, still lit by the bright exterior lights that he had not turned off.

His armpits felt moist, even in the cold; the result, no doubt, of the triumph of his disclosure to Ann, the secret that he had nurtured within himself for over a week now, sharing it with no one, not even his lawyer, saving it for just the right moment. He felt exultation within himself for the freedom that was at hand for his life. He walked into his bathroom, turned on both taps full blast, and stepped into the shower.

She walked to the door of her bedroom when she heard the sounds of his shower. The room was chilly, and her shoulders were cold in the diaphanous silk-and-lace nightgown she wore. At the foot of her bed Anna Gorman had laid out a matching bedjacket and slippers. She put on the bedjacket and noticed in the mirror, even in the calm of her resolution to act, that the jacket concealed the black brassiere that she always wore to sleep. She slipped her feet into the satin slippers and walked out into the narrow hallway that separated their two bedrooms. The door to Billy's room was closed. Beyond it the sounds of the shower continued. She opened the door of the bedroom hallway that led into the front hall of the house.

Immediately to the left of where she was standing in the hall was a narrow curved stairway that went down to the basement area and the tennis court. At the top of the stairway she turned on a light and went down the stairs to another hall off which there were several closed doors. One led to a wine cellar. Another led to a fur vault. The third led to the gun room, where guns and ammunition were stored in glass-fronted gun cabinets. There were guns for skeet, and guns for duck and pheasant shooting, and guns for big-game hunting.

From a hidden drawer in one of the cabinets she took a ring of keys, then opened the gun cabinet. The third gun in on the rack was the expensive double-barreled weapon that Billy had purchased from Churchill's in London as a gift for her.

She took it out of the case. From a drawer beneath she took out a box of ammunition and loaded both chambers. Shoot first and ask questions later. Those were Billy's very own instructions about the prowler. She took several extra rounds of ammunition and stuffed them into her black brassiere. She turned off the lights and shut the door behind her and walked up the narrow stairs. At the top she turned off the light, reentered the hallway that separated her bedroom from Billy's, listened at his door to the continuing shower sounds. She walked into her bedroom and placed the heavy gun on a slipper chair next to her bed. Her finger, ringed and manicured, brushed past the cold metal of the engraved inscription, "To Ann from Billy, with love," as on a wedding band.

Billy walked into his bedroom from the shower, naked still. He intended to put on his pajamas and drop into bed and go to sleep. He was planning to take Third up in the new plane for the first time in the morning, and it was getting late.

From across the hall he heard Ann scream. "Help!" she shouted. "Don't! Please! Please don't!"

He remembered the feelings of being grabbed by a kidnapper when he was ten years old. He moved with speed but felt as if he were moving in slow motion and opened the door to his bedroom. In hazy darkness his eyes locked with the eyes of his wife holding her double-barreled shotgun aimed at him. Their throats tightened. The roofs of their mouths went dry. In their brains was a screaming silence. Never were they more as one. Only then did it occur to him that the message in his fortune cookie at the Chinese restaurant in Pittsburg, Kansas, had been blank. He turned away from her.

A massive reverberating roar filled the room, followed almost instantly by a second massive reverberating roar. Rockets' red glare. Bombs bursting in air. The nude body was knocked backward and fell with a resounding thud onto the carpeted floor. Blood soaked the carpet.

Yet death was not instantaneous for William Grenville, Junior, merely painless, and, for the fifteen minutes left to him before expiration, thoughts of the dying variety passed through whatever thought process was left to him. He saw himself as a son, a brother, a lover, a husband, a father, and a man. With total clarity he recognized himself as a passive figure of fate whose death would catapult him into a notoriety he had, mercifully, never achieved in life.

On the other side of the indoor tennis court, Ralph Wiggins, the guard hired by the New York Philharmonic, was awakened by the double blast. He sat straight up in the narrow single bed in the bedroom of what had once been a caretaker's apartment. He knew for a fact that he felt fear and did not want to get up and investigate. His thoughts were on the prowler. The Oyster Bay police had said to call at any time of day or night if there was any sign of him. He waited. He listened. There was only silence. He was nearing retirement age, and there was a pension to be considered. He decided to wait and do nothing until he was sure.

Upstairs, at the far end of the house, Anna Gorman, the new cook, heard the shots. First one, then another. There was no scream. There were no sounds after the shots. She did not know these people. She did not want to be involved with them. She knew only that on Monday morning she would be back at the Creedon Employment Agency on East Thirty-sixth Street. She wondered only about the little children across the hall. If she heard them get up from their beds, she would get up. Otherwise she would stay where she was. Whatever happened, it was not her responsibility.

"I'M SCARED," said Third.
"Don't talk," whispered Diantha.
They listened. They heard nothing.
"I have to go to the bathroom," said Third.
"You can't."
"Do you think the new cook heard it?"
"If she did, she would have been in here."
"Do you think it's the prowler?"
"Stop talking, Third. Just listen."
"Where's the dog, Diantha?"

HE WONDERED if his children would be scarred by growing up in the shadow of a disgrace and scandal in which he had been an active participant. He thought of his mother. He thought of the fortune-teller in Tacoma, who had known what she was talking about even if her dates were off by a few months. He thought of poor Esme Bland whose telephone call at Edith Bleeker's party had set this evening in motion.

"Dear God," he heard his wife say. "Dear God." And then he heard her repeat it again. "Dear God." He heard her shotgun fall to the floor. He heard her go to the telephone and ask, not for the police, not for an ambulance, not for a doctor, but for a lawyer called Sam Rosenthal.

♣   ♣   ♣

SHE HAD PUT the telephone number in her address book under L for lawyer instead of under R for Rosenthal in case Billy should ever go through her book to look for a number and come upon it. She found his initials, S.R., between the Lafayette Cleaners and Lord and Taylor. She picked up the telephone by the side of her bed and gave the number in New York City to the operator in a voice of complete calm. He had told her it was his private number, and whoever answered would always know where to reach him day or night. She heard the number ring once, twice, three times.

"Mr. Rosenthal's residence," came a voice that she knew was an answering service.

"I must speak to Mr. Rosenthal."

"I'm sorry. Mr. Rosenthal is away from the city for the weekend."

"Can you tell me where he is."

"Mr. Rosenthal is in Westhampton."

"Will you give me the number please."

"May I ask who is speaking?"

"This is—." She didn't know what to call herself. If she did not give her right name, he would not know it was she. On the other hand, she did not want to call herself Mrs. William Grenville, Junior. She heard Diantha's dog, Sloppy, scratching at the hall door. She looked through her open door across the narrow hallway into Billy's room and saw his naked body lying face down on the floor. She knew that she had to act quickly. "This is Ann Grenville."

"Will Mr. Rosenthal know who you are?"

"Yes."

"I am not at liberty to give out Mr. Rosenthal's number, but I will call him in the morning and give him your number if you will give it to me."

"I must talk to Mr. Rosenthal *now!*"

"It is almost two o'clock in the morning."

"I don't care."

The answering service operator paused. "Give me your number, Ann, and I will call him."

As HIS EYEBALLS receded upward into his head, he thought of his friend Bratsie Bleeker, also shot dead, also in ignominious circumstances, and he knew that once more vengeance would not be sought. And then he died.

SHE STEPPED into the front hallway and listened. There was silence in the house except for the dog. She picked it up, took it in the kitchen, and closed the door. She moved to the left and went down the narrow curved stairway that led to the basement area and the tennis court. She walked past the wine cellar, past the fur vault, and entered the small room where the guns and ammunition were stored. She reached into her black brassiere and took out the extra rounds of ammunition that she had stuffed there. Some of the rounds fell on the cement floor, others on the shelf of the gun rack. Upstairs she heard a telephone ring. She raced back to the stairs, ran up them, crossed the front hall, opened the door that led into the narrow hall that separated the two bedrooms. To the right of her was Billy's body. She went into her bedroom and picked up the receiver before it rang a third time.

"Yes?"

"Ann?"

"Sam?"

"Yes. What's the matter?"

"Oh, Sam." The tears, the panic, the hysteria that she had held in abeyance since she blew off her husband's head came to the fore.

"I can't understand you, Ann."

"It was an accident, Sam. I swear it was an accident."

"You must pull yourself together, Ann, or I cannot be of any help to you."

"I'm trying."

"First . . ."

"Yes?"

"Does anyone else know?"

"No."

"All right, now tell me exactly what has happened."

"Billy's dead. I shot him."

"Start from the beginning, Ann."

RALPH WIGGINS had not heard a sound for over fifteen minutes, and he was beginning to believe that it had been the backfire of a car or truck that he had heard and not gunshots. He had pulled on his trousers and flannel shirt and boots and placed the loaded .38 revolver on the bureau of his bedroom. He had never fired a gun, although he had kept that information to himself when he applied for the job of watchman in the sylvan surroundings of the McGamble estate. He sat down on a wooden chair and began to untie the laces of his boots, ready to return to his bed for the rest of the night. From the other side of the indoor tennis court came the sounds of screams, hysterical screams. Again he froze. This time he knew there was no doubt. He rose from the wooden chair, picked up the revolver, and held it in his hand as he walked to the telephone. He picked up the receiver and dialed 0.

"Operator," replied a harassed voice.

"This is the night watchman at the Grenville house on Berry Hill Road," he said in a low voice. "I need the police."

"There is a hysterical woman on the other line, and I cannot understand a word she is saying, except the Grenville name," said the operator.

"Get the police. There is trouble here."

SHE REMEMBERED the instructions Sam Rosenthal repeated and repeated in her ear over the telephone, with complete calmness, as if death by gunshot were a thing he was used to dealing with.

"If there are any lamps or hall lights on, turn them off. You must be in darkness when the police arrive. . . .

"Listen, carefully. Tell them you heard the dog bark. It woke you. Then you heard a sound. Outside. Maybe in the tree. Maybe on the roof. It doesn't matter. You heard a sound. And Billy must have heard the same sound in his room. You both must have gotten up to investigate the sound at the same time. . . .

"Remember this, Ann. About the gun. Your husband insisted you go to ged with a gun by your side because of the prowler. Having a gun was his idea. . . .

"Now, you must both have opened your bedroom doors at the same time. You saw the shadow of a man standing there. You fired. Once. Twice. And then you realized it was your husband that you shot. . . .

"Be by your husband's body when they find you. And don't forget about the lights."

"No," she answered. "Turn out the lights."

"Now, Ann, listen."

"Yes?"

"Are you going to call the old lady, or am I?" he asked.

"I can't. I can't," she said, hysteria beginning to break through her forced calm.

"I'll do it. We're going to need some blank checks. Some signed blank checks."

"Oh, my God," said Ann.

"Who else from the family should I call, Ann? There should be someone to arrive at the house shortly after the police. The sister, Felicity. Doesn't she have some sons? Doesn't she have a house out there near you? I'll call Felicity. Now hang up, Ann. And pick up the telephone and get the operator. Tell the operator there has been a terrible accident and you need the police. Answer no questions when the police arrive. Just keep repeating over and over again that you thought Billy was the prowler. I'll take care of everything else."

THE PRISMS on the great chandelier in the main hall of Alice Grenville's house sounded—coldly, not musically—as if a wind passed through them. Alice Grenville, waking, opened her eyes an instant before the telephone rang in her darkened bedroom. She remembered for the first time in years when the chandelier had fallen on a workman and killed him. Instantly alert, she did not take the time to turn on her bedside lamp before picking up the receiver.

"Hello?"

"Mère." It was Cordelia. It was trouble.

"What time is it?"

"Late. Early. Mère—"

"What's happened? Are you crying?"

"You must wake up completely."

"I am awake."

"Turn on your light."

"Tell me what's happened, Cordelia."

"Something terrible. I can't even say it. Something so terrible. I'm driving into town to be with you, but I was afraid someone might call to tell you before I got there."

"It's Billy, isn't it?"

"She shot him, Mère. She killed him!"

The blood drained from Alice Grenville's face. She felt as if she were going to faint. "Oh, my darling Billy. Oh, no. No. No. It is not possible."

"SHE WAS SAYING, 'Please help me, please help me, something terrible has happened,' " said Ralph Wiggins to the detective in the courtyard of the house. "You can see her through the window on the floor, but I can't open the door."

"See if you can climb in that window that's open to the left of the front door," said Detective Kramer to one of the policemen. "Then come around and open the door. You and you," he called to two other policemen who had just driven up, "search the grounds."

When the police entered the house, they found Ann Grenville lying over the naked body of her dead husband. She was screaming his name over and over. So covered with his blood was she that at first Detective Kramer thought she had been shot as well. They tried to pull the hysterical woman away from her husband's body, but she would not let go. It was as if she were trying to breathe life back into him.

"Who shot your husband?" asked Detective Kramer.

Ann Grenville screamed.

"Wipe the blood off her face," said Kramer to a policeman. "Mrs. Grenville, please, tell us who shot your husband."

Hysterical and screaming, she was incoherent.

"Search the house," said Kramer. "See if there's anyone here."

He began to rise, then saw the woman reach out to him from the floor where she was lying.

"I shot him," she whispered. "I thought he was the prowler."

Detective Kramer stared at Ann Grenville as if he had not heard her correctly. "You shot your husband, Mrs. Grenville?"

She nodded through her sobbing.

"This is your gun?" he asked.

"I thought he was the prowler," she repeated.

"Why did you think he was the prowler?"

"I heard a sound, and it woke me."

"What kind of sound?"

"The dog barked."

"The dog? What dog?"

"There's a dog tied to a kitchen chair," said one of the policemen.

"I mean, I heard a sound outside or on the roof," she said.

"You were in bed asleep when you heard the sound?" asked Detective Kramer.

"Yes."

"And when you got up, you grabbed your gun?"

"Yes."

"Are you in the habit of going to bed with a gun, Mrs. Grenville?"

She feared that the man who was questioning her did not believe her. "My husband insisted. There was a prowler in the area. Our cabana had been broken into, and my husband insisted when we got home from Mrs. Bleeker's party that we both arm ourselves. He got the guns out of the gun room in the basement when we came home from the party."

Detective Kramer nodded to one of the policemen to check the gun room in the basement. "When did you put on your negligee, Mrs. Grenville—before or after you grabbed your gun?"

"What?"

"You are dressed in a negligee. I was curious at what point in your fear of the prowler you remembered to put it on."

"I sleep in my negligee."

"Oh?"

"Yes, my shoulders get cold on these October nights, and I sleep in a negligee."

"I see," said Detective Kramer, staring at her, disbelieving her story.

Ann Grenville was breathing heavily. She looked at the detective as if he were an enemy.

"One other thing, Mrs. Grenville."

"Yes?"

"I notice that under your nightgown you are wearing a black brassiere. Do you sleep in your brassiere too?"

"Yes, always. I have always slept in a brassiere."

A policeman interrupted the detective.

"Detective Kramer?"

"What is it?"

"There's children upstairs, and the cook."

"Put Mrs. Grenville in her bedroom," said Kramer. "Get Inspector Pennell on the telephone. I'll talk to the children and be right back."

FELICITY'S SON, Tommy Ashcomb, age nineteen, drove up the driveway of his Uncle Billy's house in Oyster Bay. He had never seen the long driveway so lit up. He knew that his young cousins, Diantha and Third, were asleep in the house and that he must get them out and back to his mother's house in Glen Cove before they were told what had happened. He was to wait until the local doctor, Dr. Curry, came to sign the death certificate and make sure the doctor gave his Aunt Ann, the sexpot, who had once tried to seduce him, or so he claimed, a shot to calm her hysteria.

Ahead of him he saw that the entire courtyard was filled with police cars, at least twenty of them. His heart began to beat rapidly. He pulled his car over to the side of the driveway. As he turned off the ignition, a policeman approached his car and shone a bright flashlight in his face.

"Who are you?" asked the policeman.

"My name is Tom Ashcomb. I am the nephew of Mr. Grenville."

"What are you doing here?"

"I have been asked to identify my uncle's body and to remove the children from the house."

ALICE GRENVILLE sat on the side of her bed and picked up the telephone again.

"I would like to talk to Sands Point, Long Island," she said to the operator. "The number is 555-8121."

She waited for what seemed an eternity.

"Please, God, let him be there," she whispered to herself. "Please, God, don't let a servant answer the telephone."

"Governor Milbank's residence," said the sleepy voice of the butler. At the same time, on another extension, a woman's voice said, "Hello? What is it?"

"Marie! Oh, thank God, you're there. It's Alice Grenville. I am sorry to call you at this disgraceful hour, but it is a matter of the utmost urgency that I speak with Payson."

"THE WOMAN IS utterly hysterical," said the police officer over the telephone to Inspector Stanley Pennell. "When we entered the house, we thought she had been shot as well as

Mr. Grenville. We had to pry her away from his body. She was clinging to him, saying she loved him, and she was covered with his blood. She is a possible suicide, and we think that there should be a nurse sent out from the village to sit with her while the investigation is going on."

ALICE GRENVILLE dialed the telephone again, looking up the number in an address book that she kept by her bed. When she spoke, she spoke very rapidly.

"Charles? Charles, you must wake up. It's Mrs. Grenville. I need your full attention, Charles. Do you need to put water on your face? . . . It's two-thirty in the morning, Charles. That's what time it is. I want you to go to the garage and bring one of the cars here to the house. It is not necessary that you get into your uniform. It is preferable if you do not, in fact. Don't bring the limousine. Or the convertible. The Ford, or Chevrolet, whichever it is that you market in, bring it. Come to the front door of the house, but don't ring the bell. I will be there waiting for you. There will be an envelope that I want you to take out to Mr. Billy's house in Oyster Bay, and I want you to give that envelope to Felicity's boy, Tommy Ashcomb, and no one else. There has been a terrible tragedy, Charles, and I am counting on you."

She hung up the telephone. She locked the door of her bedroom. She moved behing the marquetry table covered with photographs in silver frames and pulled away from the wall a Constable painting of Salisbury Cathedral that hung on hinges and concealed a safe. Quickly she worked the combination, and the door sprang open. She lifted out her jewel box and placed it on the table. Then she reached inside again and began taking out packets of money that had been sitting in the safe for more than twenty years, since the kidnapping scare. She placed the money in a large manila envelope, ten packets of five thousand dollars each. She went into the bathroom and moistened a washcloth, which she then wiped over the glue portion of the envelope and stuck it. She dressed herself in a warm robe and walked down the stairway three flights below to wait for her chauffeur to take the money out to the house on Long Island.

"ON WHOSE ORDERS did you give her a shot?"

"She was hysterical."

"I repeat, on whose orders did you give her a shot?"

"No one's orders. She was hysterical."

"You are aware, are you not, that a death by shooting has taken place in this house?"

"What is it that you are saying, officer?"

"I am saying that in a homicide, when a person is hysterical, that is when we get the information that we most need."

"I don't know anything about that."

"How long will she be out, doctor?"

"Several hours."

"Swell, doctor."

"THERE'S ENOUGH bottles of pills in this room to fill a couple of bags," said Mary Lou Danniher, the nurse from Oyster Bay.

"Then fill a couple of bags, nurse. Just don't let Mrs. Grenville near a pill when she comes to."

"Oh, my God," said Mary Lou Danniher, looking for the first time at the body on the floor. "Is that Mr. Grenville?"

"That was Mr. Grenville." The only thing alive about him was the ticking watch on his left wrist.

"Don't you think you could cover him up? At least his private parts."

"They're still taking pictures."

"They don't have to take a picture of his private parts. You can't expect me to walk back and forth by a naked man for the rest of the night. I mean, it's not proper."

"Say a rosary, Nurse Danniher."

"WHAT IS THE name of that doctor of hers with the slim mustache? The one she went to when Archie Suydem wouldn't give her the sleeping pills she was always asking for?" asked Alice.

"Oh, yes, the Park Avenue one. They all go to him. Babette Van Degan. All of them. Oh, what is his name? Skinner! That's it. Dr. Sidney Skinner. Why?"

"Get him for me on the telephone."

"Mère, it's three o'clock in the morning."

"Tell him it's Mrs. William Grenville, the mother-in-law of Mrs. William Grenville, Junior. Tell him it's an emergency. I guarantee you he will be here in twenty minutes."

"When do you want to see him?"

"In twenty minutes."

"Why?"

"I am going to send him out to the house in Oyster Bay and put him in charge of her. She cannot, must not, be put into the hospital in Mineola, where she would be under the jurisdiction of the Nassau County police. Mr. Rosenthal and Payson Milbank both feel it will be better all the way around if she is put into Doctors Hospital here in the city."

"Why are you doing all this for her, Mère?"

"Make the call, Cordelia."

"Yes, Mère. Did you know they fought terribly at Edith Bleeker's party? Did you know she threw a drink at him and smashed one of Edith's Lowestoft platters? We're in a scandal, Mère. A terrible, terrible scandal."

"Make the call, Cordelia. I'll deal with Edith Bleeker in a few hours when she wakes up, and I'll guarantee you there won't be one word about that fight."

IT SEEMED TO Ann that Edith Bleeker's party had been long, long ago, not yesterday, and that her present agony had lasted longer than her childhood, her career, and her marriage, and would go on forever. Stripped for once of artifice and social veneer, she had, in her fragility and stillness, a pathetic quality, like an abandoned foundling. She looked as if she belonged nowhere, frightened and homeless, grandiosity behind her, uncertainty ahead.

"Please," she whispered.

"What is it?" asked the nurse.

"Why is there a siren?"

"It's the ambulance, Mrs. Grenville."

"For my husband?"

"No, Mrs. Grenville. They already took Mr. Grenville's bod—They already took Mr. Grenville."

"Is it for me?"

"Yes, ma'am. They're going to take you to the hospital."

"Where's Dr. Skinner?"

"He's in the living room talking with the police, ma'am."

"What's all that noise outside?"

"What noise?"

"All those people talking in the courtyard."

"The media," said the nurse, pleased with herself for knowing the new word that was coming into the language.

"The what?"

"The press. The photographers. The television cameras."

"Will I have to go past them when they put me in the ambulance?"

"It'll just be for a few seconds."

"There is something I want."

"What's that, Mrs. Grenville?"

"Cover my face with a towel."

"But—"

"Please." There was a begging tone in her voice. "I don't want them to take my picture."

"She wants her face covered with a towel," said Anna Gorman to the nurse in an ordering tone, from the corner of the room where she had been standing.

"Then you cover it for her."

"Anna? Is that you?" asked Ann.

"I'll cover it for you, missus."

"Where are my jewels?"

"Your what?"

"My jewels that I wore to Mrs. Bleeker's party last night."

"I don't know, missus."

"They should be in a bag on my dressing table."

"Here they are."

"Give them to me, Anna. I want to take them with me."

What Anna Gorman thought, but did not say, then or ever, was that Mrs. Grenville had asked for her jewels but had not asked for her children.

Those wounded creatures watched from above. Covered and carried, their mother did not have to meet their eyes peering from an upstairs window. Lying still as death beneath her linen towel, she listened to the thousand clicks of camera shutters and heard the sounds of the press jostling each other inches from her stretcher to view her inert form.

The task of telling her children that their father was dead had not been hers. Nor had it been their cousin Tommy Ashcomb's, though he had come to the house to take them away. Nor their Aunt Felicity's, to whose house they were eventually taken. Detective Kramer of the Oyster Bay police assumed that difficult duty.

From the moment he entered the house of death, Kramer began to have the feeling that other forces were taking over an investigation that was his. Lawyers, doctors, and snobbish relations of the deceased addressed themselves to decisions and plans that were not of his making. Smarting still with anger that Dr. Curry, acting on unknown orders, had administered a shot to Mrs. Grenville that rendered her insensate for six hours, incapable of being questioned during her period of hysteria, when inconsistencies in her story might have led somewhere, Detective Kramer was not to be thwarted in his questioning of Mrs. Grenville's children. He did not believe her story that she had mistaken her husband for a prowler.

WHEN KATHLEEN MCBRIDE was preparing to go to the seven-o'clock Mass at St. Patrick's Church in Glen Cove, she listened to the early news on the small radio that her employer, Edith Bleeker, had given her for Christmas. "A gunshot early this morning," said the newscaster, "took the life of William Grenville, Junior, thirty-five-year-old financier, sportsman, and owner of the great racehorse Tailspin." Kathleen McBride gasped. "District Attorney Sal Scoppettone of Nassau County said the gun was fired by the victim's wife, Ann Arden Grenville, thirty-two, who told investigators she thought she had aimed it at a prowler."

Kathleen saw out the window that the chauffeur had parked the station wagon to take all the maids into the village for Mass, and she was torn between her desire to receive communion and her strong feelings of obligation toward Mrs. Bleeker, for whom she had worked for twenty-three years. Kathleen knew all about the young Grenvilles; there wasn't a servant in the house who hadn't heard about the fight Mr. and Mrs. Grenville had had in the library last night, humiliating poor Mrs. Bleeker in front of the Duchess of Windsor, for whom she wanted everything to be so perfect, not to mention breaking Mrs. Bleeker's beautiful platter.

"Healy's waitin' with the car, Kathleen," came Mary Whelan's voice through the door.

"You go ahead without me, Mary," replied Kathleen, removing the pin from her hat.

"You gonna miss Mass?" asked Mary's shocked voice through the door, implying that mortal sin was about to be committed.

"You go ahead, Mary. I'll go to the eleven."

Kathleen knew she was within her rights to go into the darkened bedroom of Mrs. Bleeker and awaken her with the news of Mr. Grenville's death, even though Mrs. Bleeker had not planned to arise until eleven, in time to attend Mrs. Slater's luncheon for the duchess. Kathleen remembered another time five years earlier at the plantation in South Carolina when she had had to awaken Mrs. Bleeker to tell her that Bratsie was dead. Funny, she thought, as she made her way through the halls to Mrs. Bleeker's room, the duchess was there that weekend, too.

Standing outside the bedroom when she arrived there was Dudley, the butler.

"Did you hear?" asked Dudley.

"Terrible thing," answered Kathleen.

"The police have requested a copy of the guest list from last night's party," said Dudley.

"Whatever for?"

"They intend to question each guest."

"What about?"

"The fight."

"Dear God."

"What is it? What's the matter?" came the sound of Edith Bleeker's sleep-filled voice.

"There's been a tragedy, ma'am," said Kathleen as she entered the room.

"THAT LITTLE incident that happened in my library last
night between them, with the glass and the platter and so
forth, we must forget that ever happened," said Edith Bleeker
to Jeanne Twombley over the telephone from her bed. "Kathleen, this coffee is cold. Excuse me, Jeanne. I talked to Alice,
the poor darling. She called me an hour ago, and she had
talked to the governor and a Mr. Sam Rosenthal, and they
both advised her, separately, to ask us *not* to mention the
fight when the police question us. You know what it will be
like if something like that gets in the papers. Will you tell
Petal? And Tucky? I've already called Neddie Pavenstedt, and
he's going to play golf with Lord Cowdray at Piping Rock and
will tell him. Just say they were an ideally suited couple. Fine.
You're going to be at Elsie Slater's for lunch, aren't you? I'll
see you there. Oh, and Jeanne?"

"Yes, Edith?"

"That Basil Plant you brought to my house, the writer. He
won't talk, will he?"

"Basil? Never, darling. He's one of my best friends. I trust
him implicitly."

Jeanne Twombley was right about me. I wouldn't talk to
the police about the fight I had witnessed between Ann and
Billy Grenville. I wouldn't waste what I had seen and heard
on the police. I had a book to write.

DURING THE DAYS that followed, all of New York, and
much of the country, waited with fascinated impatience for

each day's newspaper, radio, and television revelations in what quickly became known as the Grenville case. As far afield as London, Paris, and Rome, men and women who had known the couple discussed the tragedy in shocked tones, avid for more details. They read the coroner's reports on the body of William Grenville, Junior, describing minutely the terrible wound that he had suffered, and gasped that he had still lived for fifteen minutes. They pored over diagrams of the Playhouse, saw the narrowness of the hall that separated the bedrooms of the ill-fated couple, and wondered among themselves how it was possible that the celebrated markswoman, who had so recently bagged a ten-foot Bengal tiger, could have mistaken her nude husband for a prowler at such close range. Might it not, they asked each other, have been one of her children she fired at without calling out, "Who goes there?"

Fydor Cassati, the society columnist, who had been Billy's friend, recounted, on the front page of the Hearst paper, the insane jealousy of Ann Grenville. Her fits of temper, he wrote, were enough to put the fear of God in a platoon of British grenadiers. Stories that hitherto had not been published, because of his great affection for Billy, were now there for all the world to read.

"People believe she is guilty, and they want to see her tried like any other criminal," said Kay Kay Somerset to Petal Wilson.

AT SIX O'CLOCK Monday morning Dr. Sidney Silkwood Skinner walked into Room 1010 of Doctors Hospital in New York City, tapping on the door slightly as he entered to announce himself. He saw that during the night bars had been placed on the windows of the room but made no comment.

Ann Grenville, who usually slept until noon, was up from

her bed, sitting on a visitor's chair, dressed for the street. She was wearing a wide-brimmed black hat under which her hair had been totally concealed. On her lap was a black broadtail coat, a black alligator bag, and black gloves. In her hands was a pair of black-lensed dark glasses of the style favored by film stars incognito. An empty coffee cup was on a table by her side.

"Do they think I'm going to jump?" asked Ann.

"What?" said Sidney Skinner, although he knew what she meant.

"The bars on the window."

"Orders from the police," he said. "It was hard getting you out of Nassau County, you know."

"Have you seen any newspapers?"

"No," he lied. "Are you ready?"

"Yes," replied Ann.

"Did you sleep?"

"No."

As if she sensed that he thought she looked bad, she reached into her bag and pulled out her compact. She opened it and stared at herself in the mirror. Her skin was sallow and liverish. Even when she made her mirror face, which she felt presented her at her best, she could see that even in so brief a time she had aged considerably. A shudder went through her. The sight of herself in the mirror, looking as old as her mother had looked at the end of her life, was at that moment more terrifying to Ann than the widowhood that stretched before her.

"Don't put on any makeup, Ann," said Dr. Skinner sharply.

"I'm not going to put on any makeup, Sidney," replied Ann just as sharply.

"What I've told them at the desk is that I am taking you to an interview with Inspector Pennell of Nassau County at your mother-in-law's house."

"Will there be press outside?"

"I am taking you in a wheelchair down the freight elevator to the basement and then out a side door to Eighty-eighth Street. My car and driver are there. Ready?"

The streets were wet and dark. Ann and Sidney drove in silence for the most part. She looked out the window of the Lincoln as the streetlights turned off and the first rustlings of morning began. A girl in an evening dress got out of a taxi and raced past her doorman before daylight came. White-aproned men unloaded crates of oranges in front of Gristede's market. A young couple unloaded weekend luggage from the rear of a station wagon. She wondered if she had valued life enough when it was there at her disposal.

"The front door of the shop will be open," said Sidney, "so you can walk straight in without having to wait on the street for someone to answer."

"You think of everything, Sidney," said Ann.

"Caruso will be ready for you. I've asked him not to talk with you, just to do what has to be done as quickly as possible. He said it will take an hour. There is a possibility that a few other customers will come in at seven-thirty, some women executives from the department stores who have regular appointments at that time that he was not able to change, but he will take you in a private room. The only time that you might encounter anyone is when you leave. Wear your hat and dark glasses then. The car will be parked right at the front door of the shop."

"You understand why I'm doing this, don't you, Sidney? I mean, you know, don't you, that it has nothing to do with vanity?"

"It's an awful risk, Ann, when the police haven't even questioned you yet."

"I don't want it known that my hair turned white overnight, Sidney. I don't want Alice, or Cordelia, or any of those sisters, or, God knows, the police, to know that my hair turned white overnight."

"It could be interpreted as grief," he said.

"They would interpret it as guilt," she corrected him.

Dr. Skinner looked at her sideways and wondered if that was her interpretation.

"And call Bergdorf's, Cordelia," said Alice Grenville. "Get Jo Hughes. We'll need black hats, veils, dresses. She'll know exactly what to get. Ask her to bring them up to the house this afternoon."

"Yes, Mère."

"And Grace."

"Yes, mère."

"The maids want to go to the funeral. They should be seated behind all the family but in the side aisle."

"Yes, Mère."

"Make sure they all have black hats. If they don't, call Altman's and order what they need."

"Yes, Mère."

"Felicity!"

"Yes, Mère."

"Please don't look out the window like that. One of those reporters will photograph you with a telephoto lens."

"I'm sorry, Mère," said Felicity, closing the curtain. "I heard commotion outside."

"More flowers, probably. Or those awful press," said Alice.

"It's Governor Milbank arriving, Mère," said Felicity.

"Oh, Payson, thank God," said Alice.

"Did you know Governor Milbank was coming?" asked Felicity.

Alice did not answer her daughter.

The governor entered the reception room off the front hall, where Billy's casket had been placed against the wall opposite the fireplace in the same spot where his father's casket had been placed. Floral arrangements were behind and on either side of it. The main hallway beyond under the chandelier was also filled with great profusions of flowers. The governor went directly to the kneeler in front of the closed casket, knelt, and bowed his head in prayer. Rising, he turned toward the fireplace, where Alice Grenville stood with her daughters and her triplet sisters.

"My dear Alice," he said. "I am so terribly sorry. I remember so well when he was born, and Woodrow Wilson wrote him a letter welcoming him to this world. Do you remember?"

"We must find that letter and give it to Third," said Alice to her daughters.

The governor greeted Alice's sisters and daughters. He looked above the fireplace to the large portrait of the triplets that had been painted more than half a century before. Alice followed his gaze.

"I'm the one with the green ribbon," she said.

"Sargent, isn't it?" asked the governor. "Marvelous."

His mission was not to admire the paintings, however, and his gubernatorial time was precious. He looked at Alice, and she understood his look, and took him by the arm and led him out of the reception room into the main hall, knowing that he wanted to talk to her privately.

"There are people everywhere," she said. "Every room is full. Relations are arriving by the hour from everywhere. Perhaps up to my room. There won't be anyone there."

"Fine," said the governor.

"Cahill," Alice called to her butler.

"Yes, ma'am."

"See to it that the secretaries write on each card exactly what the flower arrangement is, and then enter it into that book I've left on the hall table."

"Yes, ma'am."

"This house has the first private elevator in New York, Payson," said Alice Grenville.

"Let's walk up the three flights, Alice."

"We're getting old, Payson."

"We've got thirty years more in us, you and I, Alice. Maybe more," answered the governor.

They sat in her room, away from the green-canopied bed, on two chintz-covered chairs beneath the Constable painting of Salisbury Cathedral.

"You never know what to do when your children bring home these second-rate people and say they're in love with them. You want to scream out, at the top of your lungs, no, no, no, no, no, no, it must not be! There was nowhere for this to end but in disaster."

"You must understand, Alice," said the governor, "a case like this is a criminal lawyer's dream. A national reputation will be made. What is more fascinating to the American public than the rich and powerful in a criminal circumstance? Look at the newspapers. Listen to the radio. Watch the television. The country is consumed with curiosity."

"She took my only son's life, Payson."

"And in order to save hers, they will take his again," replied the governor, taking her hand in his to give her comfort.

"How so?"

"They will put your son on trial. All the dirty laundry of their marriage will be brought out. They will dig up every perverse aspect of his character, every marital infidelity, his drinking habits, his bedroom habits, his bathroom habits, for all I know."

"Oh, my God."

"Yes."

"What are you suggesting?"

"Stand behind her."

"You must be mad!"

"Believe her story about the prowler."

"She killed my Billy."

"Embrace her for the world to see."

"But she is guilty."

"There will be a shift in sympathy. You will see. In a few

months, when the shock of this terrible tragedy wears off, they will begin to forget Billy, and it will be Ann's tragedy that will take its place."

"The chorus girl from Kansas and the millionaire's son."

"That's it exactly. In time they will root for her, not for you."

"It's so unfair."

"The healing process can't begin with the trial looming ahead like a dark and evil cloud, and either way, whatever happens, there is no winning. If Ann goes to prison, it will only scar the children more than they have been scarred already."

"You know what this will do, Payson? It will bind us to that woman more closely than if she had been born one of us."

SIDNEY SKINNER burst into Room 1010, radiating good news. From her bed, the aged Ann Grenville turned slowly to look at him. In her hands was a newspaper she had bribed a nurse to bring her, with graphic details of the killing. All her life she had wanted to be famous, and now she was, but the fame that had found her at last was not the variety she had craved.

"There is good news, Ann," exclaimed the doctor, at the same time seeing the forbidden newspaper on the bed. "I have just had a call from Sam Rosenthal."

"What has happened?" she asked.

"They have found the prowler!"

Ann stared at him unable to believe what she was hearing.

"It is as you said. There *was* a prowler, and they have found him," said Sidney.

She wanted to know and was afraid to know what the prowler had said. She wanted him to go on. He, in turn, wondered if she was too sedated to absorb the glad tidings he was bringing her.

"I cannot believe the terrible stories that Fydor Cassati has written about me in his column," she said.

"It doesn't matter about Fydor Cassati," said Sidney Skinner. "What matters is that the prowler has been caught."

WHEN ALICE GRENVILLE hung up the telephone from Iphigene Sulzberger, whose family owned the *New York Times*, and Betsy Whitney, whose husband owned the *New York Herald Tribune*, she next called Millicent Hearst, the long-estranged wife of William Randolph Hearst, the newspaper baron, for whom Fydor Cassati was such a star, selling more papers than any other with his daily coverage of the Grenville case.

"Millicent," she said.

"Oh, Alice, my dear, I am so terribly sorry about your tragedy," replied Millicent Hearst. A onetime show girl and beauty, she was captivated with society in New York. While her husband romped and built castles in the West for the actress Marion Davies, she, the mother of his five Hearst sons, enjoyed the homage paid to her by the society columns of her husband's papers. "I saw dear Billy only weeks ago at the Belmont Ball, and he was in such marvelous form with all the great success he was having in racing. I can't bear it that you are suffering so much."

"Yes," replied the mother of the slain Billy Grenville. "Thank you, Millicent." Wanting to rush through the condolence, she allowed it its full course for the favor she was about to ask. She had never had Millicent Hearst to any of her parties, nor had she ever contributed to the Milk Fund, which was the charity dear to Millicent's heart, but she resolved then and there to do both if she got what she wanted.

"What I'm calling you about, Millicent, is Fydor Cassati,"

said Alice, getting straight to the heart of the matter. "My son was so fond of him, and he is indeed such a charming fellow, but we feel that his columns these past few afternoons, since Billy's death, have been excessive and unfair."

"But Fydor adored Billy," protested Millicent.

"Apparently he did not adore Ann," replied Alice.

"But I have no say over what he writes in his column," said Millicent.

"Nonsense," said Alice firmly. "Your husband owns the paper. Please, Millicent, make him stop. What happened in Osyter Bay on Saturday night was an accident, and his columns are suggesting that my daughter-in-law shot my son on purpose."

"Willie owns the papers, Alice. I have no say," she said again.

"That's not so," persevered Alice Grenville. "You got Fydor the job, after all that nasty business in Washington, with the tar and feathering, just as you got Elsa Maxwell her job. And Cobina Wright. They will do anything for you, those people. Make him stop! Oh, and Millicent, when the mourning period is over, my daughters and I will attend your next benefit for the Milk Fund and contribute handsomely to it."

"She didn't know it was loaded," said Kay Kay Somerset, screaming with laughter.

"Kay Kay!" said Petal Wilson, adjusting her makeup in the mirror of the ladies' room at El Morocco.

"It could have been worse, I suppose," Kay Kay went on, reapplying lipstick in the same mirror.

"What do you mean?" asked Petal.

"She could have killed Tailspin," answered Kay Kay, screaming with laughter again.

"Kay Kay!"

"Billy told Brenda he had changed his will."

"No!"

"*And—*"

"Go on. I'm riveted."

"Not a word of this to anyone. Promise?"

"On my life, darling."

"He said the children would get it all, leaving Ann out completely."

"How could he do that? With widow's share, and all that."

"He had the goods on her, finally. He was going to divorce her."

"How much should I tip her?" whispered Petal, indicating the ladies'-room attendant.

"A quarter's plenty," said Kay Kay.

"Are you going to the funeral?"

"Of course, darling. It's the funeral of the decade."

STILL DAZED in sedated slumber, Ann Grenville planned her husband's funeral. She wanted to wear black veils and her Mainbocher black dress from last season with only a single strand of pearls and the diamond circle pin that Billy had given her before they were married. She wanted to have her nails done, plain, no color; Blanchette could come here to the hospital to do them. She would wear only her wedding ring, she decided; her engagement ring was too big. She would sit in the reception room off the main hall of her mother-in-law's house off Fifth Avenue for the prayers before the pallbearers put the casket into the hearse to take it to St. James' Church for the service. Names went through her head of the men she wanted to be her husband's pallbearers.

"The hymn!" she cried out suddenly.

"What?" asked Miss Toomey, the nurse, who had been snoozing in her chair in a corner of the darkened room.

"What was the name of that hymn?"

"What hymn, Mrs. Grenville?"

"From Groton, that hymn. The one Billy liked so much."

"I don't know, Mrs. Grenville."

"About God and honor, that kind of thing."

"Oh."

"I want that sung at the service."

"Yes, ma'am."

"THE DUCHESS will be in directly," said Cecil, her butler, to Inspector Stanley Pennell and Detective Kramer in the living room of the Duchess of Windsor's ornate suite on the twenty-eighth floor of the Waldorf Towers. There were flowers everywhere of different varieties and heights but uniform color, as if Constance Spry, her florist, had advised her gift-givers that this season the duchess favored yellow and white. Invitation cards leaned against a mirror over the fireplace.

"What do we call her?" whispered Detective Kramer to Inspector Pennell, eyeing the elaborate gold furniture.

"I should have asked that Cecil," whispered back Inspector Pennell.

Three English pug dogs yapped and snapped at the intruders.

"I hate these fucking little dogs," whispered Detective Kramer.

"Shhhh," said Inspector Pennell.

Two of the dogs, exhausted, retired to their bamboo baskets and curled up on needlepoint cushions that bore their names. The third continued to be unpleasant to the inspector and his assistant, letting him know that their call on his mistress, official though it might be, was inappropriate.

"Disraeli, you naughty boy!" cried the Duchess of Windsor to her dog as she entered the room. "You must forgive this naughty beast, Inspector Pennell. He is just protecting his mummy. Aren't you, you naughty thing? Yes, you are. Kiss, kiss, kiss. Yes. Now you go over there to your basket and lie down. Oh, please, do sit down, Detective Kramer. Would you like to smoke?" she asked, opening a gold box with a royal seal and offering it to them. "Or a drink?"

The sheer social power of her overwhelmed the room. Wafts of expensive perfume surrounded her. Earrings, brace-let, pin, and rings matched. She sat perfectly and with a gesture turned the meeting over to them, as if she were in their power, but they knew, as she did, that they were in hers.

"We are here, uh, Duchess, because of the, uh, sad—"

"Yes, yes, I know," she said. "What a sad occasion this is. Poor Alice Grenville, his mother. Such an old friend. I talked to her today. She is bereft with the tragedy."

"You talked with Mr. and Mrs. Grenville on the night of the party, I understand?" asked Inspector Pennell.

"Yes, I did, and he was in such good spirits. You know about his horse, Tailspin, don't you? Well, he was so ex-cited."

"There is a telephone call, your grace," said the butler.

"No, no, I can't, Cecil. You see, I have the inspector."

"It is Mrs. Bleeker, Your Grace."

"Would you excuse me, Inspector? I must take this call. Would you ask these gentlemen again, Cecil, if they would like something to drink. Hello, Edith. Yes, darling. Of course. They're here now. Yes. Uh-huh. Fine. Now about tonight. That nice Jimmy Donahue is picking me up. We're going to Thelma Foy's for cocktails, for an instant only. She has the Stamirskys, whom I long to see. I don't think long dress, do you? Under the circumstances? Right. Then we'll drop by poor Alice's. And then meet up with Serge Obolen-sky for dinner. Maud Chez Elle, Serge thought. Somewhere quiet. I told Kay Kay Somerset no El Morocco until after the funeral. Strict orders from David. Now about the funeral. Do you want to go together? Fine. I'll be ready. And after, there's lunch at Kitty Miller's. Yes, yes, I won't forget. Say it once more. Fine. Fine. Goodbye, Edith. . . . I am sorry, Inspector. Forgive me. Oh, look at the time it's getting to be. Has the hairdresser arrived, Cecil? It's such a tragedy, the whole thing. They were an ideally suited couple, Inspector."

Detective Kramer wrote in his notebook the words "an ideally suited couple" and nodded his head quietly.

"What is your impression of Mrs. Grenville, Duchess?" asked the inspector.

"Alice Grenville?" asked the Duchess.

"No, I meant Ann Grenville," replied Inspector Pennell.

"Oh, Ann." She had an urge to say that Billy Grenville had told Brenda Frazier on the night of the shooting that he had changed his will, cutting out Ann, but she did not. "For bringing together all kinds of people in a gay, airy, but flawless setting, I have never known anyone to equal Ann Grenville," she said instead to the bewildered detectives. "She mixes people like a cocktail, and the result is sheer genius."

"Yes, ma'am. Thank you, ma'am," said Inspector Pennell.

The afternoon editions quoted Inspector Pennell quoting the Duchess of Windsor as saying that the Grenvilles were an ideally suited couple. Elsa Maxwell, smarting still because she hadn't been asked to Edith Bleeker's party and had missed out on what might have been the newspaper scoop of her career, belittled the duchess's statement in her society column as "extremely odd," since, as she wrote, "everybody who is anybody knew that Billy and Ann Grenville both had detectives spying on each other for months."

"ONE OF US MUST go to the hospital before the funeral, or it will appear to the press that we do not believe her story," said Alice Grenville, at the same time going over the list of pallbearers with her daughters. She crossed off one of the names on the list. "I don't want Neddie Pavenstedt to be a pallbearer."

"Mère, he was Billy's roommate at Groton, and at Harvard, and he's number-two man at Father's bank," said Cordelia.

"And he had an affair with Billy's wife," answered Alice. The daughters, stunned, looked at their mother.

"How do you know that, Mère?" asked Cordelia.

"I know," said Alice. "Which one of you is going to the hospital?"

"I won't go," said Felicity. "I don't like her. I never did like her. And I was the only one in the family, except you, Mère, who made my position perfectly clear to Billy."

"Grace?"

"I won't go either. I hated the manner in which she did me out of the breeding farm. Billy was so embarrassed that day."

"Rosamond?"

"I don't live in this country. I scarcely know her, Mère."

"I suppose it's me, Mère," said Cordelia.

"Do you mind?"

"She'll ask about you. She was always afraid of you. What will I tell her?" asked Cordelia.

"Perhaps we should think about having some of these flowers sent to the children's wards at the hospitals," replied Alice. "They are now going up the stairs, there are so many. The scent is overpowering. I hate stock. Why do they always put stock in funeral bouquets?"

"MÈRE HEARD FROM the President and Mrs. Eisenhower," said Cordelia, making conversation, aghast at the haggard sight of her sister-in-law in the hospital bed. "And Governor Milbank came to call. And the letters, and telegrams, and flowers are arriving by the hundreds each day. Billy's secretary is there at Mère's house, trying to keep track of everything, and the bank has been marvelous sending secretaries to help. There is simply no room for any more flowers, and Mère has sent them over to the children's wards at New York Hospital. The staff is devastated. Poor Cahill has had to take to his bed. He's old, you know."

"Where is my mail?" asked Ann.

"What mail?" replied Cordelia.

"My condolence notes. I am, after all, his widow, and all that I am hearing is about the hundreds of messages arriving each day at his mother's house, for his mother. What about me? It was an accident. They have caught the prowler. Is no one sorry for me?"

Cordelia, embarrassed, crimsoned.

"Are there any telephone messages for me?" asked Ann.

"A Mr. Claud Mertens called from Detroit," replied Cordelia.

Ann lay motionless in the bed. No muscle moved to indicate that she had heard the name that Cordelia told her.

"He said he was your father," Cordelia went on.

"My father is dead," said Ann, shaking her head in a dismissive way.

"A Mr. Billy Bob Veblen, from Pittsburg, Kansas."

"I never heard of him," said Ann.

"He said that—"

"Kooks," interrupted Ann, and then repeated the word again, although it was a word she had never used before. "Kooks. There's a certain kind of person who's attracted to the negative glamour of, uh"—she paused for the word—"this kind of tragic situation. Did Bertie Lightfoot call?"

"No, Babette Van Degan did," said Cordelia.

"Oh, Babette," said Ann. It was the first name that interested her. She thought of Babette warmly and remembered the friendship they had once shared. "I would like to see Babette."

"I will call and tell her," said Cordelia, getting up from a chair, ready to leave.

"Is there a policeman outside my door?" asked Ann.

"Yes," replied Cordelia.

"Are there press outside the hospital?"

"Yes."

"What will you say to them?"

"I don't know."

"Tell me about your mother."

"Mère? What do you want to know?"

"I have not heard from her."

"There are the preparations for the funeral. She is involved in those. It will be enormous, they say."

"Will she and I be in the same car at the funeral?" asked Ann.

Cordelia, stunned, stared at the woman on the bed. "You certainly don't plan on attending the funeral, Ann?"

"Why not?"

"My mother has gone all the way to the President of the United States to get the police to back off questioning you, Ann, until a suitable story is worked out. She has your Dr. Skinner telling the police that you are so hysterical with grief he has had to put you under sedation, so that they cannot question you. If you are well enough to attend the funeral, they will say you are certainly well enough to face the police."

Ann covered her face with her hands and started to weep uncontrollably, great heaving sobs. Miss Toomey, who had vacated the room on Cordelia's arrival, instantly returned. Cordelia quietly picked up her bag and gloves and walked out.

Charles, her mother's chauffeur, held open the rear door of her mother's Packard limousine, as Cordelia made her way through the reporters who waited outside the hospital.

"She's been having a terrible time, poor thing," said Cordelia to the reporters who questioned her. Inside the closed door, she looked out at them staring in at her, flashing pictures of her. What, she wondered, has this woman done to our lives? We have become the kind of people you read about in tabloids. And then the thought came to Cordelia that she dared not speak aloud, even to her sisters: If only Ann would commit suicide. It would make everything so much better. It would be over.

ANN WAS distressed to find that the pallbearers who would be carrying Billy's casket had already been picked without her approval. She felt the feeling that she most hated, that she was being left out by not being allowed to attend the funeral. But she insisted on playing a part, and her instructions were relayed to the family by Dr. Skinner. She wanted a particular hymn sung that she said had been Billy's favorite hymn from his days at Groton, and she wanted the flowers that covered the casket to be flowers from her. A great blanket of red and orange carnations, the colors of the Grenville stables, arrived at Alice Grenville's house on the morning of the funeral to displace the spray of white orchids provided by Alice and her daughters. In gold paper letters pasted on a cut ribbon and bow was the message: "To Fad, I love you always, Mud." Dr. Skinner explained to the family that Fad and Mud were nicknames for Father and Mother that Billy and Ann gave to each other after they became parents. Alice Grenville looked straight ahead. The sisters looked at each other but said nothing. Not one of them could ever remember having heard Ann call Billy Fad or Billy call Ann Mud.

The flags of the Brook Club, the Union Club, the Knickerbocker Club, and the Racquet Club flew at half-mast on the day of Billy Grenville's funeral. As the long black cars of the funeral cortege pulled up to the doors of St. James' Church, where the Grenville family had worshiped for fifty years, the occupants were astonished to see that thousands of people lined Madison Avenue to stare at the procession.

"Look, there's Edith Bleeker's entire staff," said Felicity to her sisters, looking out the window of her limousine.

"They say every servant on the Upper East Side got the morning off," said Felicity's husband.

"One of the policemen outside the house said it's the biggest funeral in New York since Babe Ruth's," said Grace.

"Poor Billy, wouldn't he have hated it," said Cordelia.

"Listen to this from this morning's *Times*," said Felicity's husband, reading. " 'Not in this century have circumstances combined to produce so sensational a shooting—a tragedy involving people of great wealth, the meteoric career of a poor girl carried to the heights of fame, and elements of mystery that will persist until a grand jury weighs all explanations.' "

"Put that paper away, Dexter," said Felicity.

"Look at Mère," said Cordelia.

A hush fell over the crowd as Alice Grenville, erect and dignified in black mourning veils, emerged from the first limousine, assisted by her chauffeur. She stopped to speak to Billy's great friend Alfred Twombley, who was a pallbearer, and then ascended the steps of the church with her granddaughter, Diantha, on one side of her and her grandson, William Grenville, on the other.

In a pew behind the family—bereft, forlorn, only she knowing the extent of her grief—sat Esme Bland, just returned from vacation, tanned still amid the white faces of November.

Later, after the Reverend Dr. Kinsolving's eulogy, after the hymns and prayers, after the filing-out while the organ played "The Battle Hymn of the Republic," in the Grenville family plot in Woodlawn Cemetery, close by the graves of Vanderbilts and Whitneys and other great families of the city of New York, the body of William Grenville, Junior, was laid to rest in a grave marked by chrysanthemums and carnations.

✛   ✛   ✛

EVEN SEDATED, Ann noticed things. She noticed that the paper around the yellow roses Babette Van Degan brought her had been squeezed tight from nervous fingers. She noticed, beneath Babette's Sen-Sen—scented breath, the whiff of gulped gin and knew it had been downed for courage in this encounter. Is this how people are going to react to me from now on? she wondered, observing the only visitor outside of Cordelia and Dr. Skinner and Sam Rosenthal allowed to visit her closely watched room.

Babette occupied herself filling a vase with water in the bathroom and then jammed the dozen and a half roses into the vase in an untidy arrangement, cutting her finger on a thorn in the process.

"Shit," she cried out in exaggerated pain and wrapped toilet paper around the bleeding finger. The moment relaxed the two old friends, and Babette dropped her huge mink coat on a chair and dragged another chair up to the side of the bed, and they began to talk. Other than what she had read in the few newspapers she was allowed to see, Ann had heard nothing about the funeral the day before.

"There wasn't an empty seat. Even the choir loft was full, and there were so many flowers there wasn't enough room on the main altar."

"What flowers were on the casket?" asked Ann, fearful that hers might not have been used.

"Awful. Red and orange carnations. Like something you'd put on a horse after a race," answered Babette. "Afterward everyone who wasn't going to Kitty Miller's lunch for the Duchess of Windsor made a beeline for the bars at the Westbury and the Carlyle. Only the family went to the cemetery."

"Was Simonetta d'Este there?"

"Simonetta d'Este's in Italy."

"Italy? How long has she been in Italy?"

"A couple of weeks. Fydor Cassati told me."

If Simonetta d'Este had been in Italy on Saturday night, who had Billy been talking to on the telephone during Edith Bleeker's party? Ann wondered. If she hadn't flared out, as she had, she might not have set in motion the terrible events that followed.

"Babette, tell me something."

"If I can."

"What are people saying about me?"

"They're saying you fought with Billy at Edith Bleeker's."

"Anything else?"

"They're saying at El Morocco that Billy cut you out of his will," said Babette.

"Who's saying that?" snapped Ann.

"They."

"Who's they?"

"The ladies'-room attendant."

"You believe me, don't you, Babette, about the prowler?"

Babette looked at Ann. "Sure, kid," she answered.

"I don't know which I'm more afraid of, Babette, the police or my mother-in-law."

"CAN YOUR life bear close scrutiny, Ann?" asked Sam Rosenthal.

"What do you mean?" asked Ann from her hospital bed, knowing full well what he meant.

"Just what you think I mean," said Sam. She was beginning to see the rough side of him that she had heard about. "Are there infidelities?"

"I don't think I need to answer that," she said with indignation, as if she were in a situation in which she was in charge.

"Please know I am undeterred by your arrogance and haughtiness, Mrs. Grenville." His assumption of her full name was not lost on her. "Nor will the district attorney be, should he put you on the stand."

She turned her head away, terrified. Tears sprang into her eyes. She was overwhelmed with fear at the thought of the police or a trial.

When Sam Rosenthal continued, his voice was more gentle. "You must remember that I am on your side, and it is my job to prepare you for the worst, Mrs. Grenville."

She nodded her head. "Call me Ann again," she said.

"Can your life bear close scrutiny, Ann?" he repeated.

"Whose life can bear close scrutiny?" she answered in a conciliatory tone.

"I'm only interested in yours at the moment."

"Have you, uh, have you heard things about me?"

"Yes."

"From whom?"

"From several of Mrs. Bleeker's guests."

"That's not true. Mrs. Bleeker's guests were unanimous in describing my husband and me as an ideally suited couple. I read that in the paper."

"That's so."

"Then what are you talking about?"

"That is what they said to Inspector Pennell and Detective Kramer, who questioned them. However, several of those same people, anonymously to be sure, wrote letters to Inspector Pennell, saying they had been pressured to make the statements that they had made."

It occurred to Ann as she looked around the flowerless room that she should ask to have pictures of her children brought to her. She poured herself a glass of water from a carafe on the hospital bed table and sipped it as she watched a barge on the East River outside her window. She speculated who had written the anonymous letters. Kay Kay Somerset, she imagined. Basil Plant. Names went through her mind.

Finally she spoke. "Did you say the letters were anonymous?"

"Yes. They won't hold up in court, but there is information
in those letters that could be tracked down."

"What sort of information?"

"Names of men who have been your lovers."

"What men?"

"Ali Khan. Viscount Kingswood. Edward Pavenstedt."

Ann continued to look out the window. She was relieved
that Billy Bob Veblen's name did not mar the magnificence
of the list.

"Imagine the headlines," she said simply, still not looking
at him.

"Is that all you have to say?"

"Are we talking adultery, Sam?"

"We are."

"What about Simonetta d'Este? Or that little mouse Esme
Bland? Or a certain Miss Winifred Plegg, also known as Boot-
sie, who runs an establishment catering to bizarre tastes on
West End Avenue and Ninety-first Street?"

"Have you been there, Ann?"

"I only go to the West Side on my way to Europe," she
answered.

Sam Rosenthal picked up his hat and put on his overcoat.

"Sam," she said. "It's very silly for the police to investigate
the marital lives of my husband and myself. In the marital
lives of anyone we know on the North Shore, they would find
reasons for murder."

"Don't try to impress me with how swell you are. I'm interested in the other part of your life, the part you outgrew, the
part people say you never talk about. You got any dark secrets
there, Ann?"

"No," she answered.

WITH THE unexpected entrance of Alice Grenville, all activity ceased. Tall, erect, her hat covered with veils of mourning, she stood in command of the room, an in-person reminder of the tragedy that still absorbed the city. Miss Toomey, wordlessly, abandoned her task of changing pillowcases and retreated to the hallway outside.

Ann, unprepared, looked like a ghost. She was thin and drawn, even plain in her appearance, and her hair, often described as her crowning glory, looked, to Alice Grenville, lank and even dyed. Alice wondered, as she often had, what her daughter-in-law's age was. Older certainly than Billy, although she claimed to be younger. Of that Alice was certain, but this was not the time for age speculation.

"How are you feeling, Ann?" Alice asked finally. She made no attempt to sit down. It was to be a standing visit.

"Oh, Mère," said Ann. Her eyes, which looked as if she had wept for a week, filled with tears. More than any person, Ann Grenville feared her mother-in-law. "Oh, Mère, I am so sorry. I have dreaded this moment, having to face up to you. I know how you loved him, your only son, and you must believe me that I loved him, too. It was an accident, Mère, I swear to you, what happened was an accident. It's true what they said, we had argued at Edith's, but every couple argues. There was a prowler, Mère. And we had guns. It was Billy who insisted we go to bed with guns in our rooms. He even said to me, 'If you hear anything, shoot first and ask questions later.' Let me tell you exactly what happened."

Alice Grenville raised the veils from her face, unpinned and removed her hat, and placed it and her bag at the foot of Ann's bed.

"I know how it happened," she said, "but I have chosen to believe your story. I will stand behind you from this day until the day I die, as will my daughters. You will be welcome in my home and theirs. We are prepared to accept this tragedy as the accident you say it is."

Ann, speechless, stared at Alice.

"Why? Are you wondering why, Ann? I do not want you

to go on trial for murdering my son. I do not want the filthy laundry of your marriage to come out in public. I want the headlines of this scandal to stop. And most of all, I do not want my already deeply scarred grandchildren to bear the further shame of growing up with a mother in prison."

"Mère," Ann whispered.

"My son's will has not been read yet, but there is speculation at every party in the city, and I believe it to be true, from Mr. Mendenhall at the bank, that my son cut you out of his will before he died. If this is true, I am prepared, from my own money, to settle on you what you would have received from him before he cut you out."

"I don't care about the money," said Ann.

"Of course you care about the money," replied Alice impatiently. "If there's one thing you've always been eminently practical about, Ann, it's money. I always felt your love for my son began on the moment you walked into my house the first time and saw the kind of life your handsome ensign came from."

Receiving absolution, Ann was in no position to reply to the taunt. Remembering back, she knew it was true.

"There are conditions to all this," said Alice.

"Conditions?"

"Things I want in return."

"Like what?"

"That you never, ever, for as long as you live, talk to a reporter, or a writer, or even a friend about what happened in Oyster Bay last Saturday night."

"I agree to that," whispered Ann.

"You must go to the grave with your story."

"I wish you believed my story, Mère."

"I do."

"No, I mean in your heart."

"I am trying."

"Have I ever lied to you?" asked Ann.

"Yes, you have," replied Alice, calmly meeting her gaze, without challenge in it, so certain was she of her position.

"When?" asked Ann. "Give me an instance."

"You told me your father was dead. There's an instance. You told me that on the first day we met, and you repeated it to me on your wedding day, and you have said it again several times over the years."

"My father is dead."

"According to this morning's papers," said Alice, opening her black bag and taking from it an envelope full of newspaper clippings, which she handed to Ann, "your father is very much alive and is a streetcar conductor in Detroit."

A deep hot flush of crimson burst through the pasty paleness of Ann's face. She dreaded exposure of her shabby origins, and there it was, for all to see, in every edition of every tabloid: the ramshackle farmhouse; the idiosyncrasies of her mother's curious personality; her father identified as a streetcar conductor.

"Is it for his occupation or his existence that you blush, Ann?" asked Alice.

Outside, on the East River, a tugboat passed, the same as any of a dozen tugboats that had passed in the last few hours. Ann watched it with a complete absorption that suggested a fear of dealing with the moment she was living.

"I don't like speaking to the back of your head," snapped Alice.

"Will you take your bag and hat off the foot of my bed? I don't like things on the foot of my bed," replied Ann.

Alice moved them to the window ledge.

"Would you like to sit down?" asked Ann.

"No, thank you."

"How are the children?"

"They're fine."

"Are they in school?"

"I haven't sent them back yet, no," replied Alice.

"They can't miss school."

"Surely you read the papers, Ann."

"I'm talking about my children."

"So am I," said Alice quietly. "The situation is all over the newspapers still and probably will be until you appear before the grand jury. It is the principal subject of conversation in every house on the Upper East Side. I have talked with the headmaster of Buckley and the headmistress at Spence, and they both agree that it would be terribly difficult at school for the children at this time. I have hired a tutor, who is working in conjunction with their teachers, and they are studying at home until after things die down."

"Don't you think I should have been consulted about these decisions?" asked Ann. A mild form of panic made itself felt beneath her worn-off sedation. She wondered if Alice was thinking of taking her children away from her.

Alice chose not to continue the conversation, although it occurred to her to say that this difficult woman might have thought of that before she killed her children's father.

"Cordelia and I took them to a film yesterday," she said instead.

"I want to see them," said Ann.

"But you will, when this is over," replied Alice.

"That's not what I mean. I want to see them here. I want them to come and visit me. I want them to hear from their mother what happened."

"I don't think that's wise, Ann," said Alice. "There are reporters camped out downstairs."

"I want my children brought here tomorrow," said Ann in the chilling tone Alice had often heard Ann use to Billy.

"Do you not wonder why it is you are here in this hospital overlooking the East River in Manhattan rather than in the Nassau County Hospital in Mineola, where you would have been in the jurisdiction of the police who are investigating your husband's killing? Or do you just accept this as your due?"

Ann's heart began to beat very fast. Feelings of fear rushed through her as she remembered the police questioning her on the night of the shooting before the doctor mercifully gave her the shot that sedated her for so many hours.

"Yes, of course, I will have the children brought here to-morrow," said Alice. She picked up her hat again and put it on, pinning it with two pearl-topped pins, noticing as she did so that there were no mirrors in the room. As she let the black mourning veil fall over her face, as a reminder of the circumstance in which they found themselves, she said, in a duplication of her daughter-in-law's chilling tone, "And, please, don't ever again, ever, and I repeat the word once more, ever, speak to me in that tone of voice. You need me more than I need you, Ann, although I wouldn't have thought I needed to point that out to you."

"Mère, I'm sorry," said Ann in a voice filled with alarm. She reached out and touched her mother-in-law's arm, but Alice moved past her bed to the door, opened it without looking back, and left the room.

AN ARRANGEMENT of birds of paradise in a clear glass bowl, left behind by a departed patient, filled the center of the round maple coffee table in the tenth-floor waiting room.

"Don't you loathe birds of paradise?" asked Cordelia when her mother, walking slowly, joined her. Alice Grenville glanced at the flamboyant flowers, which were just past their prime. They reminded her of the woman she had just left.

Alice looked down at her shoes and didn't answer. Her left hand brushed off the right sleeve of her black coat, which had just touched Ann. "I hate her," she said in a voice so low that only her daughter could hear.

"Are you all right, Mère?"

"Yes," she answered. "Let's go."

When the doors of the elevator opened, Cordelia and her mother entered and rode down to the street floor in silence, aware that the elevator operator and a nurse and two visitors were looking at them. When the doors opened on the ground floor, the other occupants of the car stood back in deference, or curiosity, and allowed them to exit first.

Cordelia took her mother's arm and steered her toward the entrance, where the car would be waiting. Outside the hospital on East End Avenue a crowd of reporters and photographers awaiting them became instantly alert. Cordelia held her hand in front of her mother's face to shield her from the flashbulbs popping and the reporters who started shouting questions at her, the pack moving in closer on the two women.

Charles, the chauffeur, made his way through the crowd to assist Cordelia in getting Alice into the car. Suddenly Alice Grenville stopped and brushed away her daughter's protective hand. She turned at the door of the car and faced directly the onslaught that was pressing in on her. She lifted her veil and did not flinch as the flashbulbs and newsreel cameras recorded the scene. There was about her presence a grace of carriage and aristocratic bearing that kept the crowd from jostling her and moving in any closer.

"How is she, Mrs. Grenville?" shouted one of the reporters.

"I grieve for my son," she said, "but I also grieve for my daughter-in-law. I am very fond of her. My son's death was an unfortunate accident. I have never thought otherwise. I am fed up with the scandalous rumors and innuendos that have plagued his death. It is time that you knew the truth. The police were convinced from the beginning that it was an accident, and they still believe that, because there is no reason for them to believe otherwise."

Alice Grenville appeared very old as she dropped the veil over her face again, signaling the completion of her statement. With the help of Cordelia and Charles, she entered her car.

"You understand the consequences of this, Mère?" said Cordelia.

"Certainly I do. We are bound to her forever."

"And how do you feel about that?"

"It is a very steep price to pay."

The limousine turned right on Eighty-sixth Street and made its way toward Fifth Avenue as the two women sat in silence in the darkening November afternoon.

FELICITY WAS less compliant than her sisters concerning their mother's decision. "We are more than bound to her; we are chained to her. A divorce would have been too scandalous, so she remained married to Billy. Now a murder trial would be too scandalous, so we remain sistered to her for all time. I am sick of that woman in our lives. I hate her."

No one answered Felicity. They allowed her to rant and rave. She voiced what the rest of them thought but did not speak. Then her mother spoke what were to be the last words on the subject.

"We must behave as if we believe her. All of us. That goes for you too, Felicity. To whoever speaks to us about it. Even our best friends. What happened to Billy was an accident, and our heart grieves for his widow."

"You are asking too much of us, Mère," said Felicity.

"I am not doing this for her, Felicity. I am doing it for Billy's children. My grandchildren. They will already have enough to grow up with, having a slain father. We cannot allow that their mother be in prison as well. Remember the children."

"Yes, Mère."

"If your father were alive, he would have arrived at this same conclusion."

"Yes, Mère."

⁂

When Inspector Pennell and Detective Kramer left Alice Grenville's house just off Fifth Avenue, the same group of reporters that had dogged their footsteps since the night of the shooting converged on them before they could get to the police car that was parked in front of the house. Among themselves the reporters made no secret of the fact that they felt Inspector Pennell behaved with obsequious deference to the powerful people connected with the Grenville case.

"What about this report that Mrs. Grenville made a mysterious telephone call after her husband was shot but before the police were notified?" asked the Hearst reporter.

"I don't know where you guys pick up all this stuff," replied Detective Kramer.

The reporters ignored Detective Kramer. "What about it, Inspector Pennell?"

Reporters made Inspector Pennell nervous. Out on the North Shore, when he said, "No comment," they would back off. In the city, where he was not on his home ground, they persisted when he ignored them.

"It seems to me ridiculous on the face of it," replied Inspector Pennell, trying to push his way through to the car.

"Check the telephone records and it won't look so ridiculous," said the Hearst reporter.

"Naturally, we'll check it," said Pennell.

"How about the telephone call that was made to Mr. Grenville during Mrs. Bleeker's party? Would you care to comment on that? Who was that from?"

"I have no information on that," said the inspector.

"When do you plan to question Mrs. Grenville?"

"We would prefer that the questioning take place either at headquarters or in some other suitable place rather than at the hospital, where there are so many people around. It's cold, gentlemen, and I would like to get into my car."

"The night watchman says Mrs. Grenville didn't scream for help until twenty minutes after the shots."

"I don't think that is significant," answered Pennell.

"Oh, no? Wouldn't that be when she was making the mysterious telephone call?"

"No one knows exactly what time the shooting took place. The watchman is probably very confused as to details now. It will be up to the grand jury to attack the watchman's statement, if they want to. Now please, enough. I have an appointment to get to."

Looking straight ahead, they drove off while the reporters continued to shout questions at them. At Fifth Avenue, they turned left and drove on in silence for a block.

"Jesus Christ," said Inspector Pennell.

"THERE ARE rumors everywhere that my son disinherited his wife," said Alice Grenville.

"She will not be destitute, Mrs. Grenville," said Mr. Mendenhall from the bank. The tone of his voice told her that he, and the bank, felt very little sympathy for the killer of her son.

"Why did Billy cut her out of his will?" asked Alice.

"He did not, in fact, cut her out. What he did was decrease her portion of his estate. He built up the children's shares and cut down hers. He was planning to divorce her."

"Still . . ."

"But the house in Oyster Bay is in her name. She insisted on that when he bought it, and Billy gave it to her. The same with the house in New York. That's in her name, too."

"She was always clever, Ann."

"Don't forget her jewels. She's supposed to have one of the best jewel collections in the city. And paintings."

Alice nodded, aware of the jewels and paintings.

"And her portfolio," added Mr. Mendenhall.

"What portfolio?"

"From time to time Billy gave her money, rather sizable amounts, and she has an aptitude for investment."

"I knew none of this."

"She has a friend called Babette Van Degan."

"Yes, yes, Mrs. Van Degan. Used to be married to Dickie Van Degan." Cut from the same piece of cloth, those two, she thought.

"Babette Van Degan is one of the shrewdest investors on the stock market," said Mr. Mendenhall, removing his pince-nez and massaging their resting place on either side of his nose. "She received a five-million-dollar divorce settlement from Dickie Van Degan when they divorced, and she has been able to turn that into about thirty million."

"My word."

"And Babette Van Degan has been helping your daughter-in-law invest."

Alice stood up and walked around the little sitting room off her bedroom where she dealt with her correspondence and business affairs. She was deep in thought. She looked for a moment into the fireplace, where a small fire laid by Cahill to take the chill off the late-fall day was burning down. She walked over to the window, lifted back the glazed-chintz curtain, and looked down on her bare garden below, her terrace stripped of furniture, her shrubs wrapped in burlap for the coming winter. Finally she turned back to the financial adviser who had acted in her behalf, and her children's, since her husband's death.

"I'm going to take care of her. I want her to have what she would have gotten from Billy if he hadn't changed his will."

"That is overly generous, Mrs. Grenville," said Mr. Mendenhall, who did not approve of remuneration for a woman who had brought so much grief to a family he had known for thirty years.

"I don't want her going to the newspapers, or around New York, saying that her husband's rich family refuses to take care of her. There has been enough about this family in the newspapers."

"I see your point."

"However, there will be conditions. She will have only the income from what she would have inherited, and that income will come monthly from me, signed by me, and is subject to stop at any time that certain requests I have made of her are not met."

IN THE GERMAN consulate on East Forty-second Street a hastily called meeting was taking place. The prowler arrested by the Oyster Bay police had been discovered to be a German.

"What information do you have on him?" asked Dolf von Hoffman, the German consul.

"His name is Horst Berger. Twenty-two years old. An immigrant from Berlin. Entered the United States two years ago. Has been in and out of trouble ever since. His father is a bricklayer, which is also his profession, although he does not work at it. He was arrested a year ago for robbing a market in Mineola. According to his sister, he is a bad sort." The undersecretary looked up from his clipboard.

"That is all you have?"

"Yes, sir."

"What I want to know is, was he on the grounds of the Grenville estate at the time of the killing?"

"He claims not to have been, although he admits to having been there on another occasion, the night before, when he broke into the cabana of the pool house."

"He took what?"

"Food, nothing of consequence."

"Was he armed?"

"He had a shotgun he had stolen from a house in Mineola."

"Is he represented by a lawyer?" asked the consul.

"No, sir."

"We must get a lawyer for him."

"Why would we want to be drawn into this thing?"

"These Grenvilles are rich and powerful people. I have seen them at the track and the opera. Whatever they think of their daughter-in-law, which is not much, I understand, they are not going to let her go to jail. She said she heard a prowler. They might force Horst Berger to say he was there, even if he wasn't, in order to make her story believable. I know people like this. They are not above handing money around to the police to work things out in their favor."

"There is an attorney called Strasser who represented him when he broke into the market in Mineola."

"Engage him. Pay him whatever he asks."

"WHO'S HE?" asked Third.

"Is he a detective?" asked Diantha.

"No, no, he's not a detective, children," said Ann. She had not known her children would walk into her hospital room unannounced. She had always been successful in keeping the separate elements of her complicated life compartmentalized, and when one converged upon another, unexpectedly, she was thrown into confusion. "This is, uh, Mr. Mertens, from Kansas. These are my children, Diantha and Third." She did not say to the children that Mr. Mertens from Kansas was their grandfather.

Claud Mertens had a hard weathered face and the stance of a person uncomfortable with his surroundings. Shaving with nervous fingers in strange surroundings had left several unsightly nicks on his chin, and his round silver-rimmed glasses magnified the confusion in his eyes over his role in his daughter's drama. Instinctively he knew, in front of these aristocratic little children, that his peaked baseball cap was wrong; he pulled it off and stuffed it into the pocket of the suit he had bought the day before.

"Third?" asked Claud Mertens, covering the awkward moment, as if it were a name he had never heard of before, which he had not.

"He's named after his father, who was a junior, you see. His name is William Grenville the Third, but we call him Third, you know, as a nickname."

"Pleased to make your acquaintance, Third, Diantha," said their grandfather.

"How do you do?" each child replied, perfectly mannered.

"We saw the detective," said Diantha.

"He asked us lots of questions," said Third. "He wanted to know if you and Daddy had fights, but we said no."

"Grand'mère told us to say no," said Diantha.

"Children, Mr. Mertens is going to have to leave in just a minute. I'd like you to wait outside, and as soon as he goes, you can come in, and the three of us will have a lovely visit."

"We brought you flowers," said Third, holding up a basket of carefully arranged carnations he carried on his arm. It looked to Ann as if their grandmother had sent them off with a basket someone had sent to her.

"She's a real Mertens all right, that Diantha," said Claud Mertens, after the children left the hospital room. His eyes were brimming over with tears.

It was true what he said, she realized, but Ann Grenville had long since forgotten that *she* was a Mertens. "She resembles her grandmother Grenville," she corrected her father. "Her height. The dark-brown velvet color of her eyes."

"I always think of that last time, Urse, when you were eight, when we had supper that night at Crowell's in Pittsburg, and you had the cheese delight and a chocolate milkshake, and—"

"I was as old that night as my son is today," she said, interrupting him. "Too much time has gone by. Too much has happened. It's too late for us. You've got to understand that. I've lived a lifetime without you. I can't take you back into my life now. I can't cope with any more than I already have to cope with."

"There's something I've got to tell you, Urse. It's important to me that you know. I didn't abandon you. I didn't. It was your mother who told you that. I swear to God I didn't. I tried to find you."

"All those Christmases. All those birthdays. Never a word," said Ann, looking out the window at the East River.

"But I sent you five dollars every birthday, every Christmas, even when I couldn't afford it," Claud Mertens said, standing by her bed in the same position Alice Grenville had stood the day before. Ann turned and looked at him. She remembered the five dollars. She had always assumed it was something her mother had managed to eke out of her small wages. "You must have gotten it, Urse, but I never heard back, and then you were gone from Pittsburg, and then you were gone from Kansas City, and I didn't know where to send it anymore."

"I'm sorry," said Ann.

"You know something, Urse? Somebody told me you'd changed your name to Arden and gone into the show business, like you always wanted to when you was a little girl. You know what I thought? I thought that actress Eve Arden, I thought that was you, and I was proud of you that you done so good."

"Oh, Daddy," she whispered, crying softly now.

"When I first read about it in the papers, Urse, I didn't even know it was you. Then Ken Simons from Pittsburg called me. Do you remember Ken? From the paper? He's the one who told me that Mrs. William Grenville was you. Pretty soon the phone started ringing off the hook, and all these reporters from everywhere were trying to question me to find out about you. That's how I got your number and your mother-in-law's number."

"Listen," she said.

"I'm sorry if I told them you was forty instead of thirty-two, Urse, but I was confused."

"Listen," she said. "It's okay. When this is all over, after the grand jury, if everything goes okay, I'll look you up. I'll find you, and we'll try to catch up, but not now. Please, please, Daddy. Not now. I can't handle any more."

HORST BERGER hoped Mr. Strasser would not make him go through the story again. He had spent most of the day with three detectives walking over the grounds of the Grenville estate in Oyster Bay, climbing the tree, walking across the roof of the house. He knew Mr. Strasser, who had been sent by the German consulate to represent him, did not believe his story.

"Let me understand you, Horst," said Mr. Strasser, speaking patiently. He noticed that the thin shifty young man rarely looked at him in the eye, fixing his stare instead on a color photograph of President Eisenhower in Western attire on the cover of the most recent copy of *Life* magazine that Inspector Pennell had left behind when he allowed his office to be used for this interview. In the magazine, both knew, was a ten-page article entitled "The Shooting of the Century" about the case that was the subject of this visit.

"Is my picture in there?" asked Horst.

"No," replied Mr. Strasser.

"They took my picture today, many times," said Horst.

"I want to get back to the night of the shooting, Horst," said Strasser, the first tone of impatience in his voice. "You said you waited for hours outside the Grenville house when you believed it was unoccupied, when they were at the party."

"I didn't know the cook and the kids were in there," said Horst.

"And you only tried to break into the house after Mr. and Mrs. Grenville returned home? That doesn't make sense, Horst."

"I saw the lights go on and off in the different rooms after they got back, and then waited about half an hour when it was quiet in the house before climbing up the tree and onto the roof," answered Horst.

"Now, you say that you climbed the tree with a loaded shotgun in one hand?" asked the lawyer.

"Yes, sir."

"And you were on the roof when you heard the shots from within the house?"

"Yes, sir."

"After you heard the shots, how did you get off the roof?"

"I jumped to the ground."

"Still carrying the shotgun?"

"Yes, sir."

"Are you aware, Horst, that it is twenty feet from the roof to the ground?"

"No, sir."

"You jumped, carrying a loaded shotgun, in the dark, from the roof to the ground twenty feet below?"

"Yes, sir."

"Why is it I don't believe you, Horst?"

"The truth."

"Horst."

"*Ja?*"

"Why did you say when you were first caught that you were not anywhere near the Grenville house that night?"

"I thought they would think I killed the man."

"Did they force you to change your story, Horst?"

"No, it is like I say."

"I want you to look at me straight in the eye, Horst, and answer a question," said Strasser.

Horst Berger looked at the lawyer and looked away again.

"In my eye, Horst."

"*Ja.*"

"Is someone from the Grenville family paying you to say you were on the roof of the house on Saturday night?"

The young German immigrant concurrently shook his head in denial and reddened.

    ✸   ✸   ✸

"You see, I knew he was unhappy. He didn't have to tell me in those words, but I am his mother. I know. I have always been able to understand more from the tone of someone's voice than from the words that are spoken, because we are trained from birth to say words that camouflage our feelings, but there is no way to hide the secrets of the tone of voice."

"Yes, ma'am."

"It haunts me now that I did not say to him, 'Come to me, talk to me, whatever it is, it's all right.' I would never have said to him, 'I told you so,' never, it wasn't in my nature to do that, but I understood his terrible pride. I understood that he didn't want me to know that the marriage had failed because he had gone so far out on a limb on a marriage that he knew was such a source of unhappiness for us."

"Yes, ma'am."

More and more pictures of Billy Grenville began to appear in his mother's room. When Alice wasn't meeting with Sam Rosenthal or Dr. Skinner or Mr. Mendenhall or Inspector Pennell, she poured through old scrapbooks and photograph albums and found pictures from the many stages of his life that reminded her of pleasant events and happy times and had them put in silver frames, on her bedside table and her writing table and her dressing table and the table by her chaise where she lay to rest each afternoon. Wherever she looked there were pictures of Billy.

"Look how handsome he was there," she said to Lyd, her personal maid. "That was the day of the Groton–St. Mark's game when he made a field goal. He said it was the happiest day of his life, and, oh, Lyd, if you could have seen Mr. Grenville, he was bursting, absolutely bursting, with fatherly pride. I know he wanted to hug Billy, and I think Billy even wanted to be hugged by his father, but you know how they were, all the Grenville men, they just shook hands instead, and Mr. Grenville said, 'I'm so proud of you, son,' and Billy answered, 'Thank you, Father,' and I think it was the closest moment they ever had together. Oh, Lyd, why did this have to happen? Why? Why?"

She was crying now, the sobs coming out of her in great heaving gasps. "I have led a good life," she said. "I believe in God. I honor Him in my prayers every day. I attend church regularly. I attend to my duties as a mother, and to my obligations as a woman of wealth. Why? Why has this happened to me?"

In secret Alice wished Ann had the decency to commit suicide, to swallow the pills or slit the wrists that would end her existence. She saw her daughter-in-law as a lowly cockroach, scurrying here, scurrying there, fighting for her existence, as if she mattered. At first she could not understand the feelings that were overwhelming her. She dared not confess them to anyone, not even Cordelia. They were all-consuming within her, hot and unpleasant, rage and anger and hate, all directed at Ann, for taking away the life of the son she loved so much. She hated this chorus girl who had undulated her way into Billy's existence. She wished that in the beginning she had acted on her instincts about the woman, instead of going against her feelings, and capitulating, because she could not bear to disappoint Billy. Oh, how she regretted that. Cut off from his family, and his money, the marriage would not have outlasted the war, and the wretched girl could have been paid off and gone her way. Instead she usurped Billy, took over his life, ran it, used it, all to advance herself. Alice understood that it was a marriage cemented only by sexual pleasure.

Awakening, she looked at the clock on her bedside table.

She felt a longing for her son and a sense of the great void his loss was in her life. It was five-thirty in the morning. Soon there would be stirring in the kitchen and servants' quarters in the house, and she knew that she would have to act quickly to do what she had to do before anyone ran into her. She got up from her bed, put on her slippers and her wrapper, and quietly opened the door to her bedroom and peered out into the hall. There was no one about. She walked out to the third-floor landing and looked down the several flights of stairs to the marble-floored main hallway below. No one. Quickly and quietly, pulling her wrapper around her for warmth, she walked down the three flights of red-carpeted stairway. Above, the twelve Caesars looked down upon her. She would meet their eyes on the way back up and think they were nodding in approval at what she was doing. The Caesars knew a thing or two about retribution.

It seemed odd to her to be operating in stealth in her own home where she had lived for forty years. At the bottom of the stairs she walked across the hall beneath the chandelier and opened a door to a secondary hall leading to the back rooms and the garden. Stored there in open disarray was sporting gear for all seasons: walking sticks, velvet riding hats, umbrellas, ice skates, raincoats, gloves, and dog leashes. Chinese export bowls held car keys and spare house keys and dark glasses. On a marble-topped table, where she knew it would be, was a riding crop. It had been William's. Then it had been Billy's. Various grandchildren now used it when they came into the city and wanted to ride in Central Park. She picked it up and felt the leather strength of it. Below her on the kitchen floor she heard the first sound of stirring. Quickly she returned up the three flights of stairs, one hand on the banister, the other holding the leather riding crop close to her side to escape detection if old Lyd should make an early appearance.

The activity heightened the adrenaline within her, but the rage she felt had not abated. She locked the door of the bedroom behind her. She stripped back the blankets and blanket cover on her bed. She placed in vertical position a long pillow. In her mind's eye, she conjured up the image of her daughter-in-law, Ann.

"Murderess!" she hissed at the pillow, repeating the word over and over. She raised the riding crop and began to beat the pillow. She beat it and beat it and beat it until exhaustion overtook her. The linen pillowcase was in tatters. Feathers from the down pillow rose in fright into the air, making Alice think of life leaving a body.

After several minutes of resting on her chaise to collect herself and calm her racing heartbeat, she rallied again, feeling tired but strangely tranquil for the exertion she had put herself through. She hid away the mutilated pillow in the back of a closet and the riding crop in the back of her lingerie drawer, ready for another day, unlocked her door, and returned to her bed, pulling the covers up over her. It was thus that Lydia found her when she arrived with her tray of hot water and quartered lemons a few minutes later.

"Good morning, Mrs. Grenville," said Lyd. "Did you rest well? You look better this morning."

Sipping her hot lemon juice, Alice Grenville watched the woman who had waited on her for a quarter of a century perform the tasks of morning: draw back the curtains, pick up the clothes of the night before, arrange the newspapers, draw the bath. She felt overcome with affection for her.

"Are you comfortable up there where you are, Lyd?" she suddenly asked.

"I'm comfortable, ma'am," replied Lyd.

"It's been years since I've been up on that floor. I can't remember which room you have."

"All the way at the end of the hall."

"Does it look out on the park?"

"The other end of the hall. I look out on Mrs. Vanderbilt's house."

"Do you share it?"

"Not since Mae died, ma'am. I have it alone."

"And the bathroom. It's right next to you, isn't it?"

"Yes, ma'am."

"And whom do you share it with?"

"Kathleen and Mary and Bridgit and Maeve."

"Do you know what I think?"

"No, ma'am."

"I think you ought to move down to the fifth floor, where the children's bedrooms used to be. Take one of those and have your own bath. Would you like that?"

"Oh, yes, ma'am."

"I'll have a television set put in there if there isn't one already."

"Thank you, ma'am."

"Mr. Grenville always wanted this house to go to Billy when I died. Now I don't know what will happen."

"You don't have to worry about it now, Mrs. Grenville."

"I wonder what they must think upstairs."

"Who, ma'am?"

"Fourteen of them up on that floor with only two bathrooms, and only me living in the rest of this enormous house."

"Your bath is ready, Mrs. Grenville."

"I'M HERE TO see my client," said the lawyer to the desk sergeant in the Mineola jail.

"Your client?"

"Horst Berger."

"Oh, yes, you are Mr. Strasser," said the sergeant, going through some papers on his desk.

"That's correct."

"I have a message here for you, Mr. Strasser."

"Is it from the German consulate?"

"No, sir."

"From whom?"

"From Horst Berger."

"That's who I've driven out from the city to see."

"He says to tell you he don't want a lawyer."

"This is ridiculous."

"I'm just readin' you the message as it was given to me."

"I would like to see Mr. Berger."

"It says here he don't wish to see you."

"Do you know what I think, Sergeant?"

"No."

"I think someone's paying this kid to say he was where he wasn't in order to back up this Mrs. Grenville's story."

THIS TIME Chief of Detectives Stanley Pennell was not caught unaware when stopped by the reporters in front of the television news cameras. He was, in fact, prepared and almost rehearsed.

"Our most searching investigation into the married life of this couple has revealed what is apparently a well-balanced marriage between two well-balanced people," he said. "They had their minor disagreements, as all married couples do, but they were well adjusted and happy despite all rumors, published and otherwise, to the contrary."

The reporters were disgruntled with his answer. Between them they thought of Inspector Pennell as a toady to the rich of the North Shore.

"Why did she make a telephone call to some unknown person after the shooting before she called the police?" asked the Hearst reporter, not for the first time.

"There was no call made by Mrs. Grenville after the shooting to anyone except the operator to ask for the police," replied Pennell. "I would like to set that rumor to rest. Oyster Bay does not have the dial system, and therefore every call must be placed with the operator on duty. The telephone company has no record of any such call."

"We've all heard of telephone records being suppressed before, Inspector Pennell," said O'Brien from the *Daily Mirror*.

Stanley Pennell ignored the reporter and continued with his statement. "I have found nothing in all of this investigation to indicate that the shooting of William Grenville was other than purely accidental."

THE STRAIN had told upon her. She needed no mirror to remind her that youth had left her forever. That she was not three years younger than her late husband, as had always been supposed, by her own admission, but five years older had been made much of in the press, because of her father's unfortunate interview with a reporter who had managed to track him down in a suburb of Detroit. The eight forgotten years, and more, had found themselves on her face in the twenty-two days since the night of the killing.

She dressed in silence in the black of widowhood, stopping only to gulp black coffee and inhale deeply on a Camel cigarette that rested in the saucer. She brushed her hair and powdered her face without meeting her own eye in the mirror provided by Miss Toomey. Finally she put on her black broadtail coat and wide-brimmed black hat, to which a black veil had been attached, to drop when the time came. She was ready for the ordeal ahead.

"I've put your tranquilizers in your gold pillbox inside your bag, Mrs. Grenville," said Miss Toomey.

"Thank you."

"Here's your black gloves. It's bitter cold out there today."

"Thank you."

"And your black glasses."

"Thank you."

"Dr. Skinner's going to wheel you down in the wheelchair, and Mr. Rosenthal is already downstairs, and the two gentlemen will take you from the wheelchair to the car at the hospital entrance."

"Did my mother-in-law send her car?"

"No, ma'am, it's Lee, your own chauffeur, in your Rover. I heard Mr. Rosenthal say that would look better to the reporters than a great limousine."

"Thank you for everything, Miss Toomey. I would like you to take this," said Ann, opening the black bag and taking out an envelope.

"It's not necessary, Mrs. Grenville."

"Please."

"I'll pack up all your things, and the pictures of the children, and have them sent over to your house."

"Thank you." Ann wanted to tell this good woman that she was frightened to go to Mineola to face the grand jury, but Sam Rosenthal, who knew about such things, had told her not to confide in other people about anything because they might sell her story to the press.

"Good luck, Mrs. Grenville."

"MRS. GRENVILLE was greatly concerned with the prowler that night," said Kay Kay Somerset on the stand. "As was Mr. Grenville. They talked of nothing else."

"You know of no argument that took place between Mr. and Mrs. Grenville at Mrs. Bleeker's house?" asked the district attorney.

"Argument? There was no argument that I know of," said Kay Kay.

"Are you aware that Mr. Grenville received a telephone call that night?"

"I'm not aware of that."

"Did Mrs. Grenville throw a drink at Mr. Grenville and break some of Mrs. Bleeker's china?"

"Goodness, no. I certainly would have known about *that* if it had happened. I don't know how these stories get started. Billy and Ann, Mr. and Mrs. Grenville rather, were as they always were that night, divine."

"Thank you, Miss Somerset. That will be all. Will you call the telephone operator, Mrs. Gaedgens, please. And have the cook, Anna Gorman, standing by."

Sam Rosenthal walked back and forth between the courtroom and an office that had been made available for Ann to wait in away from the reporters and photographers.

"There's a discrepancy between the time the guard said he heard the shots and the time the telephone operator said she got your call for help," reported Rosenthal.

Ann, pale, sat there knitting with a madness of speed, like a contestant in a knitting race. Both she and Sam knew they were talking about the time during which she had called Sam that night, but neither of them said it.

"It was the night Daylight Savings ended, did you know that?" asked Sam. "So everyone's fucked up about the time."

"Spring forward. Fall back," mumbled Ann to herself.

"What?"

"Nothing."

The door to the hallway was ajar. Ann looked up from her knitting as Horst Berger, the prowler of the North Shore, walked past accompanied by two uniformed guards. For an instant their eyes met. Each recognized the other from photographs in the newspapers. He, she knew, was her salvation. One of the guards roughly pulled him on.

She heard the clang of a cell door swinging closed, and the sound of the key in the lock, loud and metallic. Her body stiffened as a shiver ran through it. When she raised her eyes, she saw that Sam Rosenthal was looking at her, as if testing her reaction to the sound of what might have been her own fate. A blush flushed her cheeks.

"It's warm in here," she said, opening her broadtail coat.

"Steam heat," answered Sam in agreement.

"They're ready for you, Mrs. Grenville," said a police officer.

HER APPEARANCE before the grand jury was brief. Escorted to the stand by Sam Rosenthal, who stayed by her while she swore on a Bible to tell the truth, the whole truth, and nothing but the truth, she spoke barely above a whisper throughout the proceedings. Both the judge and the district attorney deferred to her importance with unfailing courtesy.

"I am sorry to have to put you through this, Mrs. Grenville," said the district attorney, "but would you recount for us, to the best of your ability, step by step, exactly what took place on the night of October thirty-first at your estate in Oyster Bay."

It was a story from which Ann Grenville had never veered, from the night of the shooting, and was never to veer, not for the rest of her life. She recounted her devotion to her husband. She told of her deep fear of the prowler and the decision of her husband to take guns to bed that night for protection of themselves and their children. She was awakened, she said, by a sound. She rose from her bed. She picked up her gun, a double-barreled shotgun that her husband had had specially made for her. She opened the door of her bedroom. There she saw the figure of a man in the dark hallway that separated the bedrooms of her husband and herself. She fired her gun twice. Almost instantly, she said, crying hysterically now on the stand, she realized the man she had mistaken for the prowler was her husband. At that point she collapsed in grief.

The eighteen-man jury hung on every word, completely fascinated by the former show girl turned society woman. Several of the jurors wept with her. Their verdict was swift. Ann Grenville was found blameless in the shooting death of her husband. It was termed a tragic accident. There were to be no criminal proceedings brought against her. There was to be no trial. Her ordeal was over.

Driving back from Mineola to New York City that night, Ann returned to her house for the first time since the shooting.

"MRS. GRENVILLE BLAMELESS!" screamed the headlines.

Sighs of relief were audible from Maine to Southampton. The sighs were not for the good fortune of Mrs. Grenville. The sighs were for the private, privileged, Protestant existences which Mrs. Grenville's damnable deed had almost laid open for the world to see. They had closed ranks and protected her, an outsider in their midst, but what they were protecting really was themselves. Now they could return to governing, to banking, to business, to sport, and to pleasure knowing that their superiority, although cracked a bit, remained undaunted.

"Thank God for Alice Grenville," men said at the Brook Club, the Knickerbocker Club, the Union Club, and the Racquet Club. "She did the right thing." They were gentlemen in high places, and they looked after one another like the old schoolmates they once were.

PART
FOUR

f the Duchess of Windsor should come," she said to her maid, "or Mrs. Bleeker, be sure to let me know, and I'll see them right away ahead of the others."

It was the day Ann Grenville had decreed she would accept her condolences. Declared blameless by the grand jury, she believed her acquittal and felt the suspicions of others would be allayed by it. The speculation of the press as to her culpability in the tragedy was at an end, and she was ready to begin her life again. She saw herself as a tragic figure, a participant in a ghastly accident, and she saw no reason why others would not accept the court's validation of her situation. Through Cordelia she let it be known that she would like to see her friends on an early December afternoon. It had distressed her, during her hospitalization, to hear of the many condolence messages that had been sent to her mother-in-law and sisters-in-law, messages she felt should have been sent to her.

She examined her house, from which she had been absent a month. She puffed up needlepoint cushions and arranged them in exact positions. She filled jade boxes with cigarettes. She lessened flower arrangements so as to diminish any appearance of festivity or party-giving. It was her intention to receive her callers upstairs in her bedroom one or two at a time while the others mingled in the living room with tea or drinks waiting their turn.

Sheets from Paris, sprayed with flowers and butterflies, scalloped and monogrammed, adorned her bed. Dressed in a satin-and-lace nightgown with matching negligee, she arranged herself on a chaise longue by the window so that when her guests entered they would find her reclining gracefully against the velvet cushions.

Her doorbell rang below. She speculated who it would be. The duchess, she thought. Or Edith Bleeker. Or both together probably. It rang again. Petal Wilson, she thought. Jeanne Twombley. Even Kay Kay Somerset. Or Eve Soby, if she wasn't tight already. From beneath her counterpane she produced her compact and applied powder again to her face and expressed satisfaction with her choice of a pale lipstick. There was a tap on her door.

"Come in," she said in a quiet voice.

"You have a visitor, ma'am," said the maid.

"Thank you, Mary," said Ann. "Send her in."

In came Babette Van Degan.

"Oh, Babette," said Ann. It was not who she was expecting. "Who else is here?"

"Honey, there's nobody here but us Cinderellas," said Babette.

Later, after Babette, she lay motionless on her chaise longue, beginning to realize that she had been ignored. Partially smoked cigarettes were ground into a Lowestoft plate by her side. Her eyes were red from crying. On a table next to her was a bowl of ice and half a dozen linen napkins, four of them soaked, that she used to keep her lids from swelling. Even Bertie Lightfoot, she thought bitterly, had not come.

At a sound in the street she peered out through her drawn curtains. Outside gold chairs and round tables were being delivered to a neighbor's house for a large party. She stared. A florist's truck pulled up. From behind her curtains she counted the number of pink-and-red rose centerpieces and estimated there would be forty-eight for dinner. Feeling rejected, although she did not know her neighbors, she wondered if she would ever again be asked anywhere.

In the shock of the happening, and the aftermath in the hospital and the court, she had buried deep within her all feelings of loss, grief, responsibility—perhaps, or perhaps not, to be dealt with at a later time. Now she experienced the sense of the void of his presence in her life. It was the hour that Billy usually came home after having stopped at one of his clubs to have a drink or play backgammon or talk horses with Alfred Twombley or Piggy French. He would open the door and call out, "I'm home," and the children would scream, "Daddy, Daddy, Daddy," and madly running footsteps would be heard racing down the several flights of stairs from the nursery to the living room. At that moment her longing for the man she had killed was overwhelming.

HER VERMEIL clock, which had once been given to the Empress Elizabeth of Austria by the mad King Ludwig of Bavaria, struck three. She was exhausted, but sleep eluded her again. She twisted and turned, trapped by her own thoughts, her vitality ebbing away in the darkness of the room she had once shared with her husband.

She could summon up no other picture of him than how he had looked dead, his face still so handsome, his head partially blown away. When that face crept into her dreams, as it began to do, she awakened from her pill-induced sleep, her satin-and-lace nightgown drenched with wet sweat, her moist hair clinging soggily to her face and forehead. She lay there in a state of near paralysis for several minutes until her heart calmed. Then she reached for the Porthault towel that she now took to bed with her each night, dried her face and armpits in the darkness, and took two more of the turquoise-and-scarlet capsules that were always at hand.

"Everybody dropped her like a hot potato. Most people wouldn't have her in the house."

Kay Kay Somerset

"Was there any mail, Myrna?" Ann asked her secretary.

"Only bills, which I have taken up to the office, a letter from the headmistress of Spence, which I did not open and left on your desk, an invitation to—"

"To what?" asked Ann, too quickly, she realized.

"To the showing of the Mainbocher collection."

"Oh."

"And the new edition of the Social Register, which I put on the telephone table in the sitting room."

"Thank you." She had forgotten about the Social Register. She wondered if they had dropped her name. Poor Babette made it for the two years she was married to Dickie Van Degan and then was never listed again. And Patsy French was dropped when Piggy named the groom at their stable as correspondent in their divorce. And Bratsie Bleeker's Mexican movie star disappeared from the pages in the edition following his demise. She did not want it to be apparent to her secretary that the matter was of any consequence to her, so she continued to read the latest issue of *Harper's Bazaar* until Myrna left the room to attend to a household matter.

When she was alone, she leaped to her feet and darted to the telephone table in her sitting room, where the latest edition of the Social Register had been placed next to her Louis Vuitton address book. She positioned herself in such a way that if Myrna English appeared in the doorway she would not be able to see what Ann was reading.

From years of practice she opened the book instantly to the G's, even to the Gr's. She turned two pages to the correct page. There, of course, was Alice, Mrs. William Grenville, Senior, in all her social perfection. Ann hardly dared to lower her eyes to the next name, fearing in her heart that it would be Diantha and Third, without her.

But it was there. Mrs. William Grenville, Junior, her address, her telephone number, her clubs, her children, all in their proper place. An immense feeling of relief passed through her. She felt that her own position in New York was inviolate, that she was not simply an appendage to her deceased husband.

She looked at a photograph of Billy in a silver frame on her desk, looked away, looked back again. She did not care to meet its eye. Abruptly she placed it face down on the table. It remained so for several days. The maid dared not move it. One day it was gone.

THE VELVET ropes were not put up to bar her way into the smart clubs and restaurants where she had become a fixture in the decade of her social success, but the attitudes of the proprietors and captains and maître d's who bowed her in were different. They remained courteous as always, but were less effusive in their welcomes. There were those, they knew, who did not wish to dine in proximity to the woman who had killed one of their own. For the first time Ann Grenville sometimes reached into her purse and rewarded her greeters with cash, in the manner of rich out-of-towners trying to establish credentials in fashionable watering holes.

She walked into "21" at the height of the lunch hour, without a reservation, in the company of a Spanish couple who were visiting New York. For a moment there was silence throughout the chattering crowd; not a person did not turn to look at her. On her face she fixed an expression of nonchalance as Mac Kriendler led her across the first section of the room to the table where members of the Grenville family were used to being seated. All her life she had craved to be the center of attention, and, in disgrace, she had succeeded.

Piggy French watched her entrance and turned quickly back to engage himself in conversation with his luncheon companions, hunching himself over his martini as if to make himself invisible.

"Hello, Piggy," cried out Ann, passing his table, in her

exaggerated society-woman voice, as if the circumstances of their friendship were unchanged.

Piggy French looked up as if he had not been aware of her and only half rose from his chair, saying as he did, "Oh, hello," not calling her by name.

Ann stopped and kissed him, first on one cheek and then on the other, in the fashion of their group, giving the impression of great friendship and the continuation of her husband's lifelong affection. She looked him in the eye and held his gaze with almost a defiance. She had learned to tell what the other person felt about her by reading the look in their eyes. Piggy mumbled something in reply and did not introduce her to his guests. Ann walked on to her table and reseated the Spaniards, who had already seated themselves.

"I wasn't a bit pleased to be kissed by her," said Piggy to his guests when conversation resumed.

"She was found to be blameless, though, wasn't she?" asked Taytsie Davis.

"Thanks to Billy's mother," said Piggy. "Alice Grenville is a saint. She loathed Ann and stood by her."

"Who are those people with her?" asked Taytsie.

"Foreigners. They're the only ones who see her."

"However you look at it, she's ruined," said the fascinated Taytsie, unable to take her eyes off Ann's table.

Ann remembered every slight, every averted eye, and stored this away in the recesses of her mind, to be dealt with later, when her life began again. This was not life that she was in. This was an interim period, a limbo, between what was and what would be.

"She was a woman who took advantage of every opportunity that life offered her, and the prowler offered her the opportunity of widowhood."

Tucky Bainbridge

Key figures in Alice Grenville's life let it be known to friends, who passed it on to acquaintances, that she wished not to have the tragedy mentioned to her. True to her word, she stood behind her daughter-in-law, appearing with her in public on occasion to give the show of unity in her family. Although people in their world were tolerant of Ann in the presence of the beloved Alice, they remained hostile to her when Ann, alone, tried to brazen out her situation in New York.

Leaving the opera with her one night, Alice told Charles that she had decided to go straight home rather than on to dinner in a restaurant, as had been planned. When he had closed the window that separated the chauffeur from the passengers, she sat in silence for a while looking out at the New York night while Ann talked on about someone she had seen in the box next to theirs.

"Yes, yes, you saw her, Mère, wearing that same dress Cordelia wore to the Pells last week. She's married to a Cypriot violinist and lives in Paris. The story is that she once—"

"I think you must give some thought to leaving the city, Ann," interrupted Alice, who had not been listening.

"What do you mean, leave the city?" asked Ann.

"Just that," replied Alice. "Move away."

As she always did when she felt trapped or nervous, Ann concentrated on a different activity. She opened her gold-and-diamod minaudier and took out her compact. Staring at herself in the compact mirror, she applied scarlet lipstick over and over to her lower lip.

"Your makeup is absolutely fine, Ann," said Alice.

"I was thinking of going to Palm Beach for a few weeks," said Ann, continuing her application.

"When you have completed your ministrations, I will continue this conversation," said Alice, looking out the window at Park Avenue.

The word "ministrations," pronounced in four syllables, signaled to Ann that her mother-in-law was not to be deterred. She put her compact back in her minaudier, clicked it shut, breathed deeply, and stared straight ahead. The two women sat in silence for a block.

"I think you should move to a different place," Alice began. "And I don't mean going to Palm Beach for two weeks. I think you should consider leaving the city, perhaps even leaving the country."

"Never," answered Ann, aghast at the suggestion.

"You must be aware that things have changed for you here."

"What about Newport?"

"I've decided against opening the house in Newport this year."

"I sense a beat missing in this story," said Ann.

"They have turned you down for membership at Bailey's Beach, Ann. Not your children. Just you. It would be an impossible situation there."

Ann, stung, wanted to retreat to her compact again, but dared not.

"Let us overlook sensibilities for a moment," said Alice, "and deal in realities. You are being dropped, right and left. Can't you feel it yourself?"

"I suppose you've heard from Felicity that Edith Bleeker cut me dead at Piping Rock last weekend. She must have loved running to you with that one."

Alive Grenville did not answer. The Packard drew up in front of Ann's house. Ann looked out at her black front door, expensively glossed, and saw the ending of her life in that perfect house that she had created and where she had reigned.

"Have you seen the new edition of the Social Register?" she asked, as if she were playing a trump card. "I have not been dropped by it."

"That's so."

"You've seen it?"

Alice Grenville smiled sadly. "If you were not listed, Ann, I would have withdrawn my name and the names of my four daughters."

"It was a deal then?" asked Ann.

"It was a deal."

Ann's heart sank. She knew it was true. Charles stood outside in the cold night waiting to open the door. She motioned out the window that she was ready.

"One more thing, Ann," said Alice, putting her hand on the sleeve of Ann's fur. "I would like to bring up my grandchildren."

Ann turned to her mother-in-law, flushed with anger. "I knew this was what was on your mind. I knew it from the day you came to visit me at Doctors Hospital. Never will you take my children from me. Never!"

Outside the car Charles heard the raised harsh voice and did not open the car door.

"I will send them to spend vacations with you. You may visit them anytime when you return to this country, but I would like to take over their education and upbringing."

"I repeat, never."

"Wherever you go, for the rest of your life, people are going to point at you and say, 'That's the woman who shot her husband.' Do you think that's fair to your children?"

"I think I know what's best for my children," snapped Ann.

"Diantha and Third have been deeply wounded by this terrible tragedy. Can't you see yourself how silent they've become? It is a wound that cannot begin to heal until the notoriety dies down."

"I will hire lawyers and go to the press before I allow you to take my children, Alice," said Ann, leaning forward to her mother-in-law. She had never called her by her first name before. It was not spoken with affection, and the time for calling her Mère was at an end.

"Let me remind you that we made a deal in the hospital that you would never talk to the press as long as you lived," said Alice.

"And let me remind you," said Ann, pointing her finger toward her mother-in-law's face, "that the deal we made referred to my not talking to the press, or anyone else, about the night of the accident in Oyster Bay. It had nothing to do about not talking to the press about your taking my children away from me."

"Don't point your finger at me."

"Have you picked a place for me?"

"The sneer in your voice is not necessary."

Ann tapped on the window for Charles to open the door. As she left the car, she turned back to Alice Grenville. "If Billy had accidentally shot me, everything would have gone on as normal."

"Billy Grenville would be alive today if he hadn't married that actress."

Sass Buffington

More than ten years in their midst had not made her one of them. The doors that counted on the Upper East Side, the North Shore, Newport, and Southampton were slammed in her face. The kind of people who were willing to see her were not the kind of people she was willing to see. In that world, once you were mixed up in a scandal that knocked the lid off their kind of life, it was inevitable that you would be dropped.

She felt rage at the lot that life had dealt her and refused to reason that it was she, not life, who had fired the shots that blew off her husband's head. There were those who believed that it was an accident, as she steadfastly maintained, but even those knew that she was capable of doing what the others believed she had done.

With no other options than what her mother-in-law suggested, she sold her house in New York and left the country. The house in Oyster Bay, with no buyers interested, was closed up. At the end of their school term, her children followed her to Switzerland.

ALTHOUGH THE Europeans were more tolerant of the position Ann Grenville found herself in than the Americans she knew, everyone felt she returned far too quickly to her old life in the International Set playgrounds. As if frightened she would be forgotten, she did not retire for a year or two of obligatory mourning and reflection, or even motherhood, in a quiet country atmosphere, but plunged back into the set that got on airplanes to go to parties. Wherever she went, it was at the height of the season. She told new acquaintances she felt banished, dramatizing her plight. They, mostly Europeans, accepted that what had happened was an accident, or else that it was passion, and, for them, a crime of passion was an excusable act.

Kay Kay Somerset, who no longer spoke to her, saw her at the Givenchy collection in Paris, sitting on a gilt chair in the front row checking off numbers on her program as models in evening dress paraded in front of her, as if she were anticipating a gala season ahead. Worse, under the circumstances, she continued to shoot and traveled with four gun cases to shooting weekends at country estates in Austria, France, and Spain.

It was in the bar of the Palace Hotel in St. Moritz, at the height of the season, that I heard her, in quite a loud voice, cast aspersions on my nature. I won't say the word she used. It pains me. Not that it's not true; it is. Of course, she was drunk at the time, or well on her way to being.

Outside it was nearly dark. The bar was mobbed. Late diners were still in après-ski dress, preparatory to going to their rooms to dress for dinner. Early diners were already in evening clothes. Every seat was taken. I, a celebrity now and in great social demand after the enormous international success of my book *Candles at Lunch,* made into an equally successful film with Audrey Hepburn and Cary Grant, was seated on a bar stool in conversation with the always entertaining Madame Badrutt, the then wife of the fashionable innkeeper who owned the Palace Hotel and kept the riffraff out. A Europeanized American who spoke English with a foreigner's intonations, Madame Badrutt, formerly of the San Fernando Valley, gave me a short précis of each guest whose looks interested me and brought many of them forward to meet me. "This is Mr. Basil Plant," she said to a very old woman emblazoned with diamonds. She was a countess, or a viscountess, or a duchess, or something, but she, an admirer of mine, told me to call her Kitty.

"Kitty knew Proust," said Madame Badrutt.

"Why, Kitty!" I cried, clapping my hands in delight. "How simply marvelous. Tell me everything. What was he like?"

"Ghastly!" exclaimed the old lady.

There were shrieks of laughter. The bar was in full cocktail swing.

"Of course, even in this swell group, the American murderess stands out in the pecking order," said Madame Badrutt.

"Who?" I asked.

"Mrs. Grenville," she said.

"Where?" I asked, fascinated, pushing my mimosa to the bartender to be refilled.

When the crowd broke, I saw her across the room in a corner. Her shoulder caressed the arm of the man with whom she was seated.

"Let's have another one of these," said Ann, pushing her empty glass ahead of her. He pushed his glass forward and signaled to the waiter.

"Who's the man?" I asked Madame Badrutt.

"Count Zeilern," she said. "No money. Fair title. Likes rich women."

Mrs. Grenville whipped out her lipstick and gave herself bright new lips. Her companion turned his attention back to her and whispered something in her ear. She looked at him. Her lovely mouth, long unkissed, yearned, not for love, but for promiscuity. When he, reading her signal, leaned forward to kiss her, she joined in the kiss. His whiskeyed tongue intoxicated her, and her eyes closed in public passion. Rarely am I shocked. In my mind I was figuring the time difference to New York and wondering if Jeanne Twombley or Petal Wilson would be at home, knowing it was the sort of story they would love and a pay-back, to boot, for all the juicy tales they had whispered in my willing ears.

As she opened her eyes from her lovemaking, she caught sight of me across the room staring at her. We had not seen each other since she had snubbed me, once again, at Edith Bleeker's party on the night of the tragedy. Her back became intimidatingly rigid. She was thinking, I knew, that Basil Plant was a bearer of tales.

That is when I heard her, in quite a loud voice, cast aspersions on my nature. Others heard it too and turned to me for my reaction. The dynamics of our acquaintance had changed. I excused myself from the woman who had found Proust ghastly, and from Madame Badrutt, rose from my bar stool, and walked across the crowded room to where Ann Grenville sat with her German. His mouth, I noticed, bore the stains of her lipstick. Ignoring him, I stared down at Ann Grenville, who had always resisted my attempts at friendship, and she, knowing she had made a mistake, gazed back insolently at me.

Suddenly I raised my hands, as if I were positioning a shot gun, one hand on the imaginary barrel and the other on the imaginary trigger, and aimed the imaginary shotgun straight at her head.

"Billy, is that you?" I called out. My high-trebled voice reverberated through the Palace bar. Silence screamed. Waiting for my moment, like the actor I always wanted to be, I then cried out the word, *"Bang!"* and pulled the imaginary trigger, allowing my body to react to the imaginary force of the imaginary shot. And then I repeated again, *"Bang!"* as if firing for the second time, again allowing my body to react to the imaginary force of the imaginary shot. Then I lowered the imaginary shotgun, my eyes never leaving hers. I watched a look of shame and humiliation replace the look of arrogance and insolence that had adorned her beautiful face only a moment before.

"When I write this up in my mosaic, Bang-Bang, I'll send you an advance copy."

Then I turned and walked out of the bar, secure in the feeling that I had done the right thing. Within minutes the story spread throughout the hotel. That night the dinner parties at the Palace Grill, or at the Chesa Viglia, talked of nothing else. The next day the skiers and the group who arrived by funicular to lunch at the Corviglia Club at the top of the mountain had embellishments on the story. "Is that you, Billy?" people were saying over and over, followed by a reenactment of my bang-bang performance, followed by help-less laughter. People claimed to have been eyewitnesses to the event who had not witnessed it at all but could not bear to be left out.

Next morning Mrs. Grenville left for Paris with instruc-tions that her luggage, twenty-eight pieces and four gun cases, be packed for her and sent on to the Ritz Hotel. Count Zeilern did not accompany her. The name Bang-Bang did.

"DON'T YOU FIND this odd?"

"What?"

"I mean, look here." I was sitting in an upstairs office of the Mineola Police Station, after hours, reading the state-ments of the guests at Edith Bleeker's party on the night that Ann Grenville shot and killed her husband. "The Duchess of Windsor, from her suite in the Waldorf Towers, described the Grenvilles to Inspector Pennell as an ideally suited couple."

"What's odd about that?" asked Detective Meehan, look-ing toward the door, nervous that he had allowed himself to be conned by me into opening what was supposed to be a closed file on the Grenville shooting. In the old you-scratchmy-back-I'll-scratch-yours theory, I had agreed to read the short stories of Margaret Mary Meehan, the detective's daughter, a sophomore at New Rochelle, and tell her, honestly, whether or not I thought she should pursue a literary career or go into nursing as her father wanted.

"Nothing, in itself. But look, on this page Brenda Frazier, in her New York apartment, described the Grenvilles to the inspector as an ideally suited couple. And here Mrs. Phipps, at her house in Westbury, described the Grenvilles as an ideally suited couple. And so did old Edith Bleeker. In fact, thirty-three of the fifty-eight people who attended the same party the Grenvilles attended on the night of the shooting described the Grenvilles to the police as an ideally suited couple. That's what strikes me as odd."

"I'm not following you." Detective Meehan was being, I felt, deliberately obtuse, but I chose to treat him as a confrere.

"Those words, 'an ideally suited couple,' are not four words that spring to the forefront of your mind, at least most people's minds, when asked to describe a couple, especially a couple who were most definitely *not* ideally suited."

"Are you building to a point?" asked Detective Meehan, gathering up the report and returning it to the file.

"I am. Yes. Closing the ranks, it's called. Bringing the stagecoaches in closer. Keeping the outsiders out. There must have been behind-the-scenes phone calls. Tell them, somebody must have said, when they question you, that Billy and Ann were an ideally suited couple, and the guests were, at least thirty-three out of fifty-eight of them, sufficiently uncreative as to repeat the exact words. That's the point I'm building to."

"You better clear out of here now."

"About that prowler."

"Another time. You better get out of here now."

"She traveled from country to country, made a gaffe, and moved on."

Eve Soby

She was a good traveler, kept track of an enormous quantity of luggage, gun cases, and fur coats, and intimidated customs officials into speeding her through. People thought it odd that she continued to shoot, after she had shot and killed, but she enjoyed her reputation as a huntress, and continue to shoot she did at shooting parties across the Continent.

In Austria she insisted that her host, Prince Windisch-Graetz, dismiss his gamekeeper for making improper advances toward her, when the truth of the matter was, as old Prince Windisch-Graetz and every other guest at the shooting party knew, that it was Mrs. Grenville who had made the improper advances toward the gameskeeper. Mrs. Grenville left. The gameskeeper remained.

In Spain the Duke of Lerma introduced her to the Marquis de Fuego as America's most famous instant widow, and she did not take offense. When, a few weeks later, their affair having expired, the Marquis de Fuego walked out on her, down the stairs of his hunting lodge, she toppled over a marble bust, narrowly missing him.

In Marrakesh she was asked to leave the Villa Naylor by the Countess de Guigne for luring young Moroccan boys over the wall at night.

During her brief friendship with Chiquita McFadden, before she slept with Chiquita's husband and ruined it, Ann and Chiquita traveled together in India, on safari, visiting various maharajas and maharanees along the way. Dressed in a pink mohair coat, a chiffon scarf over her head, pearls at her neck and wrist, she was not an inconspicuous figure when she rendezvoused with her lover at the gates of the pink palace in Jaipur.

"Who *are* all these people?" she asked the wife of an American film star at a cocktail party in Gstaad. She knew perfectly well who they all were. They were the second echelon of society in the resort and climbers from the third. She realized she had been recategorized in the social structure.

"Why doesn't she marry again?" she heard someone say about her at one of her own parties.

"Who would want her?" was the reply. "She gives it away so freely."

"Please remember that this is my party and I'm paying for it," said Ann, flushing with anger, pointing her finger.

"How could I forget, Mrs. Grenville?" said Count Stamirsky. "If you weren't paying, you wouldn't have been invited."

"She made herself available to too many men for the kind of man she wanted to marry to feel he had to marry her. And the shooting was always with her."

Alfred Twombley

"That woman is in town. Will you be a darling, Bertie, and come to dinner?" said Alice Grenville to Bertie Lightfoot.

Every time Ann returned to the country, whether by ship or air, Alice Grenville sent the car to meet her. There were always flowers waiting for her at the apartment on upper Fifth Avenue that she took after she sold her house, and an invitation to dinner. It was part of a ritual that was to continue always. At least once a year, never more than twice, each of Billy's sisters had Ann to a party. One often heard, in the drawing rooms of the city, "Yes, I saw Ann last night at Cordelia and Jack's" or "Ann was at Felicity and Dexter's anniversary dance last week." Her inclusion was often noted in the society columns, and the impression was given, as it was meant to be given, that the Grenville family, in all its various branches, remained on friendly terms with their widowed in-law.

Behind the scenes it was different. Disapprovingly, Alice Grenville saw her daughter-in-law going about with too many men, flaunting the independence of widowhood.

"I thought you would take a house somewhere and start a new life. I never imagined you would live in hotels and wander from resort to resort with the seasons. What kind of way is that to bring up your children?"

They were more comfortable with each other on the telephone. When they met in person, there was always another person there, usually one of the sisters, and they talked of inconsequential things—clothes, parties, plays they had seen, books they had read. On the telephone, however, Alice said what was on her mind.

" 'Unseemly' is such an old-fashioned word, but unseemly is exactly what it is."

"It suits you, however."

"They say you are often drunk or drugged."

"Who are 'they'?"

"What difference does that make, Ann? It is what is being said about you."

"And where there is smoke, there is fire. Is that what you're going to say next?"

"You are not a beloved figure, Ann, or a tragic one either. You are a mess. An embarrassing mess. Dinner is at eight promptly."

Ann would have liked not to go, but she did. Alice would have liked not to have her, but she did. "Do you know my daughter-in-law?" she asked new friends, taking Ann about her drawing room, and the friends marveled at the solidarity of the family and the goodness of Alice.

Ann was not pleased to see that her mother-in-law had seated her next to Bertie Lightfoot at the table. If it had been in any other dining room in New York, she would have switched her place card, not to improve her position, as she had in the past, but to remove herself from Bertie, for whom she felt bitterness for not having rallied to her side in the months following the tragedy.

"You're looking marvelous, Ann," said Bertie, knowing her to be unembarrassed by praise of her looks and appearance. He took the tactic of compliments to override the awkwardness between them.

She chose not to answer him. She could tell that he was nervous and as displeased as herself to be so seated at Alice's table. On the other side of her was the Spanish Ambassador to the United Nations, and she conversed with him in Spanish, about Madrid, the Prado, Horcher's restaurant, and the marvelous towels at the Ritz Hotel. After two courses, the lady on the other side of him, Alice's old friend Beth Leary, usurped the ambassador, with a withering look at Ann, and when he turned his head toward her, to answer her questions about the possible restoration of the monarchy after the death of Franco, she found herself excluded.

"Are you planning on keeping the house in Oyster Bay?" asked Bertie, making a second attempt at conversation.

"It is not a house in great demand on the real estate market," she replied coldly, without looking at him.

"You are living in Switzerland?" he asked.

"I will be taking a house in Sardinia for the summer and will probably go to Ireland in the fall." She looked straight ahead. She wondered if he had heard from Basil Plant about what had happened in Switzerland.

"Why did I think you were in Switzerland?" he asked.

"The children are in school there. I go there several times a year to be with them."

"How is Dolly?"

"She prefers to be called Diantha," said Ann, spacing her words, letting him know that he was intruding.

"Look here, Ann," he said. "I don't know why you're taking this position with me. Alice thought that—"

"Oh, Alice thought, did she?" interrupted Ann. "You've moved up in the world to become Alice's confidant now, have you? It's called 'taking advantage of a situation.' "

"Please, Ann."

"You should have written me, Bertie, or telephoned me, at the time of the accident, or come to see me," she said. Her words were very precise and she was very angry, although she kept her voice down and did not call attention to herself.

"I wanted to write, but I didn't know what to say," said Bertie. "It was so awful."

"Bullshit, Bertie. You've never been at a loss for words about anything. If you think I'm not going to remind you that

I came to your aid when you were in trouble and had no one else in New York to turn to, you're quite wrong, because I am going to remind you of exactly that."

"I know, Ann. I know you did," he replied quickly, panicked that others would pick up on the conversation.

"I was eight months pregnant at the time, Bertie."

"I know."

"I could have made you the laughingstock of New York if I had told that story," she said, her fury building quietly.

"Please, Ann."

"All tied up and fat and naked, amid the carnage of smashed antiquities. You don't think that would have gotten a laugh in these very circles and dining rooms where you take your position as the number-one escort of New York so seriously?"

"Please, Ann."

"I never told one soul that story, not even my husband, and you couldn't find the time or take the trouble to write me or call me because you didn't know what to say? You, who have something to say about everything?"

"I'm sorry, Ann," he said, crushed by the scene. "I'm deeply sorry for you, for Billy, for the children, for the terrible tragedy that's happened."

"Too late, Miss Lightfoot," she said, meeting his gaze, knowing she had gone too far once more, mocking him at a gender level, finishing forevermore the possibility of resurrecting a friendship that she had once cared about.

THE DOGWOOD was fading and the daffodils already withered. I forgot to look at spring this year, thought Ann.

She was alone in the house in Oyster Bay, without servants, without children. There was no one to observe her. She walked through the rooms of her house deciding if she could be there, or if the terrible event had darkened the premises for habitation. The furniture was covered with cretonne. Rugs were rolled up. She felt no ghostly reverberations. There, on that slipper chair, she thought, had been the gun. She walked toward her bedroom door, melding into an image of herself in her blue nightgown, black brassiere, and blue bedjacket. She opened the door, expecting him to be there to relive the scene with her so that she could know and quiet her demons.

"Who's there?" cried Ralph Wiggins. "Oh, my God, it's you, Mrs. Grenville."

She walked past him, out to the courtyard, and got into the Rover. When she reached New York, she made plans to return to Europe. Her publicized past lingered with her, as much a part of her as a hump on her back.

"There are some people they widen the ranks for; she was not one of them."

Kay Kay Somerset

Ann had always liked Rosie Fairholm. She was one of the few, she used to say, out of that inner-circle group, who was nice to her, not because she was Billy's wife, but because she was Ann. But Rosie Fairholm cut her dead at Harry's Bar in Venice. She heard Rosie say, to one of the Van Degan brothers, "You simply have to draw the line somewhere. I mean, she did kill him."

Slowly Ann began to pass from the center of things. She was heard of as being in Marbella with a handsome French boy, but out of season. Someone saw her in Ireland at the rented castle of a Hollywood film director. There was a story about a problem in Tahiti on somebody's yacht, and the threat of lawsuits for damages done. Brookie Herbert said she was at the *feria* in Seville with her two children quietly following her with brand-new cameras. But she no longer belonged anywhere. She was no longer a part of a group. She was at a side table watching the dinner party in the center of the room. She was a rich nomad, wandering from place to place, creating incidents and moving on. Banished from her land, the heights that had been her aspiration had crashed down on her like an avalanche.

There were always young men in tow, but she clung to her distinguished name as if it were a title.

PACO CAME and went. Pablo came and went. Each complained Ann was ungenerous with him on his departure. And then there was Paul. Paul was English, twenty-two years old, handsome, like all of them, but, as Ann was the first to say about him, different from all of them. He worked. He was the bartender at the Gringo Club in Sardinia, outside of Porto Cervo, where, that season, late-nighters ended up their late nights, after the dinners and dances on the Costa Esmeralda. He spent his days, when he wasn't at the beach, where he turned very brown, and swam very well, writing a screenplay on a battered Olivetti about a Cambridge drop-out who worked as a bartender at the Gringo Club in Sardinia at the height of the season.

It was, for Ann Grenville, lust at first sight. The group she arrived with, some second-rate titles she had met at a second-rate party on the same night the Aga Khan was entertaining the first-rate titles at a first-rate party, became bored and tired and cranky that the first-rate crowd hadn't shown up at the Gringo and wanted not to mix with the third-rate crowd who were already there.

"Let's go, Ann," said Jaime Carrera, whose well-trimmed goatee did not totally disguise his unfortunate chin. She had seated herself at the bar, on a stool, and pushed her glass toward the handsome bartender for a refill.

"But we just got here," she answered.

"It's a dog's dinner tonight," Jaime said, contemptuously, about the crowd. Ann, once so particular about being in the right place at the right time with the right people, yearned less those days about social perfection, knowing it had escaped from her grasp forever that night in Oyster Bay.

"I'm staying," she replied.

"Lucille's got a crowd at her house. We thought we'd go there," he insisted.

"You go on," said Ann.

"How will you get back to Cervo?" he asked.

The bartender handed Ann a freshened drink. For the first time he met the eyes of the beautiful woman who had been staring at him for the last fifteen minutes.

"Do you have a car, bartender?" she asked him.

"I do," he answered. She liked the sound of his voice. It was not too eager.

"That's how I'll get back to Cervo, Jaime," she said to her escort, gesturing her blonde head toward the bartender. "Anyway, I can't stand Lucille."

"Don't mix with the help, Ann," said Jaime.

"*Buenas noches*, Jaime," she replied, dismissing him.

She did not look after him as he left. Instead she lit a cigarette and further examined the face and figure of the young man behind the bar.

"You don't look like a bartender," she said.

"So they tell me," he answered.

"Let me guess. You're really a painter."

"Guess again."

"A writer. You're here writing the great English novel."

"The great English screenplay," he corrected her.

"Ah, movies. You see, I wasn't that far off. You be good to me, and I'll introduce you to my friend David Ladera. You know who that is, don't you?"

"Of course. He directed *Candles at Lunch*."

"By that little shit Basil Plant."

"You don't like Basil, I take it."

"Don't tell me you know Basil?"

"Everyone knows Basil."

She opened her purse and took out some cash. "Turn this into pesos, will you, and put it all in that jukebox, and let's you and me dance for a bit."

"It's a hot night to dance in here."

"Take off your shirt if you're hot," she answered.

"You don't mean that," he said, smiling at her.

"Oh, yes, I do," she replied. "Here, I'll unbutton it for you."

"Let me get somebody to take over back here," he said, stripped to the waist. "José."

"You know who that is, don't you?" whispered José to him when he asked José to take over the bar duties.

"No."

"She's the rich American lady who shot her husband."

"I HAVE TO GO," he whispered. Although shades and curtains and draperies kept the bedroom of this rented villa in darkness from outside, he knew that dawn must be breaking.

"No, no, don't go," she whispered back, looking down on his young and handsome face. The bed they shared was lit by a lamp covered with the head scarf she had worn when he drove her home from the Gringo Club several hours earlier. He reminded her of Billy, not the Billy she had killed, but the Billy of the beginning, the beautiful Billy, when life seemed so full of love and hope.

"I have to. I have to work."

"You just got home from work."

"My other work. I write for three hours every morning."

"Just put your head down there again," she whispered. "I love the way you do that. It looks so nice, watching the top of your head do that. Oh, my darling bartender, you have what is known as a magical tongue. Now, swing around here, the rest of you, but don't stop what you're doing. I want to return the favor."

"I can't come another time."

"At your age, of course you can."

"I can't."

"Try."

In the building frenzy of rekindled passion, neither heard the door of the bedroom open, nor noticed the child, Third, who stood there.

"I don't even know your name," she said, lifting her head from its sexual duties and then returning to them when she finished speaking.

"Paul," he answered, lifting his head from his.

"Paul what?"

"Cooper."

"As in Duff and Diana?"

"I can't talk and fuck at the same time, and you're getting me very close to blast-off time."

"My darling bartender."

Later, finished, he pulled on his trousers, put his feet into loafers without socks, and stuck his shirt into his belt. Dressed, ready to leave, he stood at the foot of her bed and looked down on her.

"Was this a one-night stand, or did you have something more affairlike in mind?" he asked.

No, she thought to herself, he isn't a bit like Billy Grenville. Beneath his youth and beauty, there was a wantonness, without refinement, that matched her own. Lying nude, she looked back at him; her magnificent breasts, she knew, were at their most appealing angle. She smiled.

"How much do you earn at the Gringo Club?" she asked.

"Why?"

"I'll triple it, whatever it is. You move in here, write your movies, teach my kids how to swim and sail, and spend your nights doing what we just did all night."

"Will I get to meet David Ladera?"

"He's in Ireland."

"When I finish my screenplay, can we go to Ireland and show it to him?"

"Yes."

"You're quite a lady, Mrs. Grenville."

"How did you know my name?"

"You're pretty famous, Mrs. Grenville."

"It's Ann."

"Ann."

"Write well."

"Did you know your bedroom door was open all the time?" he asked.

PAUL WAS unlike Paco and unlike Pablo. He seemed to want nothing from her. In Milan she had some suits made for him, and shoes, and shirts, but they were not things that he had asked for. They were things that she wanted him to have. When the season was over in Sardinia, and they went on to the next place, after the children returned to school in Switzerland, she wanted him to look presentable, so that their situation, which was obvious to most of the people in their set in Porto Cervo, would not be so obvious when they checked into the Ritz in Paris in the fall.

Diantha and Third had reluctantly come to accept him in their lives, although at first they were resistant to him in a way that Ann could not understand. Diantha was now fourteen. Third twelve. Sometimes she wondered about the open bedroom door and wondered if one or the other had come in that night and seen what was going on, but she did not pursue the subject with them. She was, she knew, afraid of her children in a way. When they looked at her sometimes, they looked with the look of Grenvilles, not the look of Mertenses, and she reexperienced each time the feelings of her first visit with Billy's family when he had brought her to the great New York house to meet his mother and sisters for tea. She had always meant to sit down with her children and explain to them the circumstances of the night of the shooting, but she never had, other than repeating to them over and over in the hospital that it had been an accident. She would have been satisfied with that if she had not made the discovery that the acoustics of the house in Oyster Bay made everything that was said in her bedroom audible to the bedroom upstairs at the far end of the house where her children slept.

Within a week of moving into the villa, Paul had won over Diantha and Third. He loved to swim and sail and water-ski, and he had infinite patience in teaching them sports. They seemed to him like wounded birds, spending most of their time together, and not mixing with the other English-speaking young people on the island that their mother would round up for them to befriend. Paul came to realize that other children, hearing from their parents of the shooting, invariably brought up the story, and each time Diantha and Third suffered and did not wish to see the child again. When Paul was around, the children got along with their mother, and the strained silences that often existed between Ann and her children disappeared. He possessed an almost childlike understanding of children, and the weeks passed in a vacation atmosphere.

One day, returning from a sailing trip, Paul rushed up the steps to the house with the children to discover that his Olivetti typewriter and reams of paper had been moved from the place on the terrace where he had left them before going to the beach. Seated on the terrace next to Ann, who was dressed in a silk dress and pearls, rather than her customary trousers or shorts and shirt, was a distinguished older woman, also dressed in silk and wearing pearls, as well as a younger woman, similarly attired.

"Grand'mère!" shrieked the children, who ran up the steps and threw themselves into the arms of their grandmother and their Aunt Felicity.

"Isn't this a surprise?" said Alice Grenville to the children. "Felicity and I have been staying in the South of France with friends, and, on a whim, we decided to fly over and spend a few days at the hotel so we could see you."

Ann, as surprised by the visit as her children, looked on at the affection displayed between Alice and Diantha and Third. Never did her children run to her in that way.

When Paul reached the top of the steps to the terrace, wearing only a pair of cut-off shorts, the conversation stopped. He looked to Ann almost young enough to be her son, and she cringed that she had told him only a few hours before, during a sexual climax, that she loved him. Felicity, with a trace of a smile on her face, took in the sight of the nearly naked young man who had joined the group and looked from him to her sister-in-law and back again. Alice, who noticed everything, saw a look on her daughter-in-law's face that signaled a warning to the young man.

"Oh, Mère, and Felicity, this is the children's tutor," she said after a moment of silence. "Mr. Paul Cooper. This is my mother-in-law, Mrs. Grenville, and my sister-in-law, Mrs. Ashcomb."

"Tutor? I didn't know you children had a tutor," said Alice. "What are you studying?"

"Mostly sports," answered Ann, before her children could reply. "Mr. Cooper has been teaching them how to sail and water-ski. Mr. Cooper went to Cambridge and is going to be a writer." She knew she was talking too quickly. She could never cope when her worlds overlapped. "Paul," she said, in the voice she used when she talked to her help, "would you get ice and some white wine. Then you may have the evening off. We'll be dining with Mrs. Grenville at her hotel."

"Yes, Mrs. Grenville," answered Paul.

IN SEPTEMBER Diantha and Third went back to school. Ann took them to Switzerland. Paul stayed behind to close up the rented house in Porto Cervo. By that time he had finished the screenplay and it was time for Ann to deliver on her promise to introduce him to David Ladera and ask him to read his screenplay. Ann spent several days in Paris ordering clothes for the winter and then went on to Ireland, where she arrived at David Ladera's Georgian house several days ahead of Paul. He was due to arrive in time for dinner, and a car had been dispatched to the airport in Dublin to bring him back to Roscommon.

There had been a change in their relationship since the visit of Alice and Felicity. For the first time since they had been together, he felt like a hustler. There had been no fight afterward. He had not called her on the way she had treated him. He wanted so much to meet and possibly work for the famous director that he put aside his feelings and went along as if nothing had changed.

But it had. The sexual part of their lives, so fulfilling in the beginning, had become strained. She, fearing to lose him, put more and more demands on him, barking out sexual orders. Often she could not reach her satisfaction, as he could, and she blamed him for selfishness in the sexual act.

She looked forward to the sojourn in Ireland with mixed feelings. She had read his screenplay and thought it was good. It occurred to her that if Ladera liked his work and hired him, Paul might leave her, not needing her anymore. On the other hand, she thought that his gratitude to her for arranging the meeting might be so overwhelming that they could return to the bliss of the first weeks of their meeting.

Sardinia was shrouded with fog on the morning that Paul was to leave, and the plane for Milan was hours late in taking off. When finally he arrived in Milan, he had missed the plane for London, and when he finally got to London, he had missed the plane for Dublin. When he got to Dublin, the driver who was sent to meet him had returned to Roscommon, and he had to hire a car to make the hour-and-a-half drive through a strange countryside. He drove through the gates of the Ladera house at two in the morning.

David Ladera, who had started in Hollywood and had achieved an international reputation, both as a film director and as a womanizer, was going up the stairs to bed as Paul entered the front door. "There are sandwiches out in the dining room, and several bottles of wine," he called down. "I'm sorry I can't stay down to greet you, but I've had too much to drink. You and I will talk in the morning."

"Thank you, sir," replied Paul at the bottom of the stairs.

"Your room is next to Ann's down that corridor and to the left, and the bathroom that you will use is outside your door, turn left, turn right, and it's the second door. 'Night."

Paul had not eaten for hours and went into the dining room. He poured himself a glass of red wine and drank it down and ate several chicken sandwiches and drank another glass of wine. He was weary from the long day. Carrying the bottle of red wine with him, he took his bag upstairs. A butler, in a robe and slippers, appeared to show him the way and help him and told him again the directions to the bathroom.

"Would you like me to unpack for you, sir?" asked the butler.

"Oh, no, thank you very much," he replied. "I'm going straight to sleep. I'm exhausted. I'll unpack in the morning." He pulled off his clothes down to his shirt and shorts and flopped on the bed. Within seconds he was asleep.

The door to the adjoining bedroom opened, and Ann entered, dressed in a satin-and-lace nightgown and matching negligee. Her perfume preceded her. She was dressed for reunion and seduction. It surprised her to see that he was asleep. She went to his bed and sat down on the mattress beside him and began to shake him.

"Paulie, Paulie, wake up," she said. Paul hated to be called Paulie. "Wake up."

"Hi," he answered sleepily.

"You were just going to go to sleep and not bother to say hello to me?" she asked.

"It was a terrible day, Annie. The plane was late leaving Sardinia, and I missed my connection in Milan, and then I missed my connection in London, and the driver left before I got to Dublin, and I had to find my own way here in the dark in a rented car, and I caved in."

"You weren't going to come in and say hello to me?" she asked again.

"I thought you'd be asleep," he answered.

"You knew I wouldn't be asleep. You knew I'd be waiting for you."

"I saw Ladera. He said we'd talk in the morning."

"Mr. Ladera," she corrected him.

"Mr. Ladera, I mean."

Her hands began to rub the inside of his thighs, starting at his knees and working upward. Eyes closed still in near sleep, he shifted position. She slid her fingers under his shorts and began to massage his flaccid penis.

"Come on, Annie. I don't feel like it. It's been a terrible day. I'm tired and dirty and I need a bath and I need some sleep. Let's wait till tomorrow."

"I like the smell of a man's sweat," she answered, oblivious of his protestations. She unbuttoned his shirt and began to kiss his chest, at the same time pulling down his undershorts.

"How about that I don't feel like doing this?" he asked angrily.

"Well, start to feel like it," she answered in the same tone of voice. She could hear herself speak as she had sometimes spoken to Billy Grenville.

"What the hell am I? Your wind-up dildo?" He sat up in the bed and picked up the red wine from the bedside table and drank it from the bottle, gulp after gulp.

"You drink too much," she said.

He looked at her. She saw in his eyes the look of Billy

Grenville in the final months of their marriage. He placed
the bottle back on the table, turned away from her, and
started to go back to sleep, lying on his stomach.

He could hear her get off the bed. He assumed that she was
returning to her adjoining room. He could not see that she
was removing the belt from the trousers that he had dropped
on the floor. With all her strength she whipped the leather
belt, straplike, across his exposed buttocks.

Paul leaped from the bed. He saw on her face the look of a
woman who could kill.

"You want to get fucked that bad, cunt?" he lashed out at
her, hate in his voice. He grabbed her, forced her against the
side of the bed, and pushed his now erect penis into her,
ripping her nightgown. In four brutal thrusts, the act was
complete. Shamed, he withdrew from her. In silence, they
retreated to their separate beds.

PAUL AWAKENED earlier than he had intended, considering
the lateness of the hour that he had finally closed his eyes for
rest. He had, furthermore, a red-wine hangover. His tongue
was dry. His breath was foul, even to him. His head throbbed.
His stomach, he knew, was about to erupt. He remembered
being told on his arrival the night before that the bathroom
for this room was down the hall to the left, and then turn
down a corridor to the left, or maybe the right, and it was the
first door, or maybe the second.

He knew he was going to be sick. He sat up in the bed.
The Irish linens were wet and wrinkled from sweat and angry
sleep. Goose feathers rose from the pillows. Around him, he
was aware, were bits and pieces of paper, ripped or cut, like
large confetti, but he did not linger to examine them. His eye
spied a basin and pitcher for morning ablutions, and he bolted
from the bed toward them. Naked, he vomited, poured cold
water over his head, and vomited again, sometimes missing

the flowered basin. He pulled on a robe. He now had to get down the hall to the bathroom for further relief.

At the door, when he opened it, was the butler from the night before, holding a cup of tea on a small silver tray. The cord from his robe was missing, and he held the robe together with one hand, while covering his mouth with the other.

"Which way is the bathroom?" he asked.

The butler directed him to the left and then to the right and to the second door.

"I'm afraid I've made rather a mess in there," Paul said as he retreated down the hall to the bathroom. When he returned some minutes later, the offending basin had been removed, and in the center of the room was his traveling bag, with his clothes in it, neatly packed. Laid out for him was a clean shirt, tie, undershorts, socks, flannels, and jacket.

"The car is ready, sir," said the butler.

"For what?" asked Paul.

"Mrs. Grenville has informed me that your plans have changed and that you will be leaving," he answered.

"Oh," said Paul.

"The train for Dublin leaves at nine-oh-five from Roscommon, which is about a twenty-five-minute drive from here," continued the butler, carrying out his orders in the domestic drama without wishing to play a part in it.

"Where is Mrs. Grenville?" he asked.

"She is sleeping, sir, and asked not to be disturbed."

"And Mr. Ladera? He was to meet with me this morning to discuss my screenplay."

"Mr. Ladera has gone hunting, sir."

"And will be back when?"

"For tea."

The realization came to Paul Cooper that he had been dismissed, like one of the maids that Ann hired and fired in such quick succession.

"I'll carry your bag down, sir, and cook will pack some biscuits for you to eat in the car."

"Thank you," said Paul. He sat back on the edge of the bed to pull on his socks. Around him he became aware again of pieces of paper strewn on the bed, thousands of pieces. He picked up a handful of them. It was a moment before he realized that they were his screenplay, ripped in spite for services not satisfactorily performed.

When Diantha and Third returned to the United States, during vacations, they always stayed with their grandmother if their mother remained behind in Europe. They looked like Grenvilles; Alice was pleased about that. They spoke French as well as they spoke English, but they had become strangers in the land of their birth, and the friends they had left behind had found new friends to replace them. Nearly everyone remarked on how quiet they were. Their grandmother and their aunts, with cousins in tow, took them to films and plays, and arranged for them to attend dances and parties in New York and Newport for teen-agers home from boarding schools for the holidays.

They felt, in New York and on the North Shore, that people, outside the family, meeting them, always reacted to their name and the turbulent history of their parents. "Yes, yes, I'm the one who was in the house on the night my mother killed my father," screamed Third at a young girl who had asked him if he was related to the Grenvilles who used to live in Oyster Bay, and pink cheeks of embarrassment followed.

He did not do well in school and had to repeat a year. He said he had no wish to go to college. Asked what he wanted to do in life, he invariably replied that he wanted to become a carpenter. Ann scoffed at the notion, but his grandmother, as a gift, put in a woodworking shop in the basement of her house, and Third spent more and more time there, working on boxes and miniature furniture.

Throughout their adolescence both Diantha and Third saw doctors, in Switzerland when they were there, in New York when they were there. The person with whom they never discussed what they were feeling was their mother. As they grew older and more independent, they spent less and less time where she was. She wondered often what they had heard that night their father died. Anna Gorman, the cook, who had been with them on the night their father died, had sworn to the police and the grand jury that she had heard nothing. Ann did not allow herself to think that Anna Gorman had been paid off for her silence. She knew only that Anna was no longer in her employ when she returned from the hospital. Once she tried to find her. Anna Gorman had retired at an early age and lived in a sunny apartment in Queens, but Ann could not bring herself to enter the apartment when she got there.

Third did not live to take his mother dancing, as she always promised him he would. People said about Third Grenville that his leap was incredibly considerate. He landed on no one. He damaged nothing. In the early morning he walked out the window of the room his father had grown up in on the fifth floor of his grandmother's house off Fifth Avenue.

"I INTEND TO sell the house, and I intend to sell everything in it, right down to the glasses in the cupboards," said Alice Grenville to Cordelia.

"But why?"

"I want to move to a hotel. I want to entertain in restaurants. I want to change my entire way of life."

☙ ☙ ☙

No LONGER attractive, Ann avoided her reflection in shop windows to keep the knowledge from herself. Her skin was pulled tightly on her thin face, the tiny scars visible where her earlobes had been made smaller, and other scars below where the skin had been tightened. The harsh lights of her dressing-table mirror were changed to pink, and in her boudoir she saw herself as she once was. She imagined herself still a seductress. Man-hungry, she prowled parties for prey. Boys came, boys went. Terminating before she was terminated, she imagined herself in charge of her romantic life.

"I HATE THAT coat," said Ann. "You look like Ann Sheridan in *They Drive by Night.*"

"All your references are before my time," replied Diantha.

"It's the belt that's so awful, and the way you have the collar turned up in the back," Ann went on.

"I'll take it off," said Diantha, unbelting the coat, letting it slide off her shoulders, placing it on the foot of her mother's bed.

"Please don't place it on the foot of my bed. I can't bear to have anything on the foot of my bed."

"Aren't we off to a nice start," said Diantha. She sat awkwardly whenever she was with her mother, which was not often, her feet circled around the rungs of the French chair.

"You look mussed. Those ink-stained fingers. When did you wash your hair last?"

"Stop it! I'm only here because you called me and said that you were in trouble. This is not a social call. Now what's the matter? I have a date, and I can't stay long."

"Please God, not that assistant political science professor from NYU, with the hairy hands. I thought you were over your despising-the-rich period."

"No, Mother. I'm going to Grand'mère's for dinner," replied Diantha.

"Oh." Outside, on Fifth Avenue, a siren screamed. Ann disguised the shiver that passed through her. She had never told anyone that every time she heard a siren she shivered with fear that they—the police, the law—were coming to take her away.

Diantha watched her mother. "Why were you so hysterical on the telephone?"

"The maid's gone."

"So what else is new? Did she quit, or did you fire her?"

"Quit."

"What did you do this time? Accuse her of stealing? Or did she iron creases into your sheets, and you told her how stupid she was? I don't even know their names anymore, Mother, they come and go so quick in this house."

"Will you call the agency tomorrow and get me someone else?"

"Will I call the agency and get you someone else? No. Did it ever occur to you that it's you, not the maids, and the cooks, and the chauffeurs, and the nannies?"

"I'm sick."

"I won't do it. Get that Prince Tchelitchew you're always talking about. Let him hire you a new maid."

"His great-grandfather killed Rasputin."

"At least you have something in common."

Diantha stood up. "I'm sorry I said that, Mother. It was uncalled for. It just came out."

Her mother turned her head away.

"I don't suppose there's anything in that pharmacy by the side of your bed so simple as an aspirin?" asked Diantha. A memory of times past struck both of them at the same time, and they looked at each other.

"There's a Percodan, but it seems a shame to waste that on pain."

"I don't want a Percodan."

"Your hair's too short."

"I like it like that."

"Are you a dyke?"

"I might have known I could count on you to reduce my life to a four-letter word, Mother," said Diantha, letting comtempt pour over the word "Mother."

"You are, aren't you?" asked Ann. "It's what I always suspected. Back at Château Brillantmont, that Greek girl in your class, what was her name, the one who didn't shave her armpits in Sardinia that summer. Oh, I know all about her. I asked Ari and Stavros who she was. Not even one of the good Greeks. Salad oil, or something like that. I mean, they roared with laughter about her family."

"The next time you have one of your emergencies, don't call me. I don't want to hear from you again. I like living in Seattle. I like running a bookstore. I like never having anyone say to me, 'Aren't you the one whose mother killed your father?' No one ever heard of us out in Seattle, and if people mispronounce my name and call me Granville, I never even correct them, because I know it's me they're responding to, not the name of my illustrious family."

"You can't go back."

"Oh, yes I can. That's why I'm having my farewell dinner with Grand'mère."

"I won't leave you my money if you go. It won't be easy for you."

"That's what it's all about with you, isn't it, Mother, the money? You know, I don't care about your money, but one of the things Grand'mère had me do while I was here was see old Mr. Mendenhall down at the bank, and you don't have any say over your money. It's only on loan to you for as long as you live. It's not yours to give. My father saw to that. He was willing to have it taxed doubly and triply in order not to give you any rights over the disposition of it."

"Is that what Mr. Mendenhall told you?"

"I'm going to be the richest one of anybody. I'm going to have your money, and Third's money, and Granny's money, when she dies. I'm going to be worth millions. I'm going to be one of the richest girls of my generation."

"I never saw this side to you before, Diantha."

"I may have my father's looks, but I'm as tough as my mother when pushed to the edge, and you have pushed me to the edge. Don't you think at some point in our lives, you owed us an explanation, Third and me, about what happened? Not your story, your famous story from which you never veered, not for your whole life, but what happened, what really happened that night? I was eleven years old, remember. I wasn't any babe in arms. We heard you fighting with Daddy that night. Do you ever think about it? Do you ever dream about it? Do you ever run it over in your mind and relive those minutes when you picked up the shotgun and killed him?"

"Is that what you've always thought about me?"

"Always."

"And Third, too?"

"And Third, too."

"Why didn't Third ever say anything to me?"

"He did. He jumped out a window. That was his statement to you. He sent you a Mother's Day card. It was Mother's Day, you know, the day he jumped. I often wondered if you had noticed."

"Dear God."

"You never talked to us about anything. You had a mother and a father and aunts and a life in Kansas, and you never told us a word about that part of your life, and we were your children. We wouldn't have snubbed you. You never talked about your past for all the years we lived in your houses and hotel suites as your children. All we ever heard about was Jaime, and Pablo, and Paul, and Vere, and Gianni, and Gunther, and—"

"Don't leave me, Diantha. I'm afraid to be alone. Jaime's gone. Jaime left me. He opened up my purse and took all the money out and called me some terrible names and left. He said I was old."

"I have to go. I can't be late for my grandmother. Goodbye, Mother."

PART
FIVE

or several long moments I stood there staring after the retreating figure of Ann Grenville. Was this, I wondered, the point of my trip? Nowadays, with all the legal technicalities available to criminal offenders, the guilty walk among us, exonerated, and a few I could mention are lionized as social catches by some of the same people who slammed their doors in the face of Ann Grenville nearly three decades ago.

My story began to form. I am the receptacle of other people's secrets and have long understood there is no point in having a secret if you make a secret of it. Yes, she warned me off her, but I sensed that in time, the next day, or the next, she would return to her post by the ship's rail to stare at the coastline. She had started to talk, and then withdrew, but she would come again, and I would be there.

IT WAS HER Fracas perfume I smelled before I realized she was standing beside me, her elbows leaning on the rail. She made no sign of greeting.

"Do you suppose that's Seattle we're passing?" she asked.

"Yes," I replied.

"My daughter, Diantha, lives there. She runs a bookshop, of all things. I once longed for her to be a figure in social life, but she, wise girl, wanted no part of it. We are—what is the right word to use?—estranged."

"How many children do you have?" I asked, knowing perfectly well how many children she had.

She hesitated a moment, eyeing me deeply. "Why is it I never trusted you, Basil?"

"Too much alike, maybe," I offered for an explanation.

"I think I recognize in you the things I dislike about myself," she said.

"That's what I mean," I answered.

"I had two children, and one of them is dead, as you probably know."

"Yes, yes, I had heard."

"It's hard when people ask how many children I have. I never know whether to say 'Two, and one is dead,' or just 'One.' If I say 'One,' I feel guilty about poor Third, but when I say 'Two, and one is dead,' I have to explain."

"I'm sorry."

"I am, too. I was a lousy mother. In many ways I was frightened of my kids when they were little. They were so incredibly upper class. They were Grenvilles, and I was always an outsider with the Grenvilles."

"I'm sure your kids didn't feel that."

"That's what my daughter told me the last time I saw her."

"Was it an illness?"

"No."

"An accident?"

"No. It was a suicide. I spent several years saying it was an accident, that his jump out the fifth-floor window of his grandmother's house was a fall. But it wasn't. Heirs to ten million dollars don't wash their own windows, especially at five o'clock in the morning, in a house filled with servants. But that is what I insisted happened, and if I was able to convince people of that, then I believed it was so."

"Perhaps it was so," I said.

She shook her head slowly. "There was a note, written on a Mother's Day card. Did I tell you it was Mother's Day when he jumped?"

I was moved by her admission. "Terrible things have happened to you," I said.

"Sometimes I think I make terrible things happen," she replied quietly.

"Ann," I said, matching her quietness, my business unfinished. "Esme Bland told Jeanne Twombley you were married before Billy married you, and you'd never gotten a divorce."

What was it I read on her face at that moment? Shock? Fear? Or relief? "Perhaps that's why Esme Bland is in the loony bin today," she answered, as if it were an answer.

"Is it true, Ann?" I persisted, but she had turned away.

I longed for a drink. Cruise festivities were in high gear in the public rooms of the old ship. I pretended I did not see Mr. Shortell from Tacoma waving to me to join his table of merrymakers in party hats. In my stateroom were dozens of the miniature bottles of Scotch whiskey that I had taken to stuffing my pockets with in recent years, for bathroom gulps during editorial meetings, and I repaired there. One. Two. Three. I gulped them down and reached for one of the lined yellow tablets by my bunk and took a sharpened soft-lead pencil from a drawer and began to write in my neat precise hand.

The telephone rang. It was long after midnight. I knew before I picked up the telephone that it was going to be her. "Hello?"

"Basil?"

"Hi."

"It's Ann Grenville."

"I know."

"There's something that's bothering me that I've got to get off my chest," she said.

"What's that?"

"Are you writing down everything I was saying to you?"

"Of course not," I replied, rising from my bunk, letting go of both tablet and pencil.

"This is my life. These are my secrets. It would be very

painful for me," she said, discounting my reply. "I'll sue you if you betray me."

"I'm not," I repeated.

"Basil?"

"Yes?"

"I don't want to walk into that bar alone with all those people in funny hats," she said.

"Want me to walk in with you?" I asked.

"Yes."

"Five minutes?"

"Yes."

You see, at some subliminal level of her, she was setting it up for me to do what she said she did not want me to do. That was the night I decided to write her story.

She did not want the solitude of the deck. She wanted to be where the crowd was, but not part of the crowd. There was but one table left in the noisy bar, and we made our way to it. I ordered a bottle of wine, and for a moment or two we watched the revelers on the dance floor.

"I always wanted to dance with you," I confessed to her.

"Now's not your chance," she replied, but she was pleased to have been asked.

"Once I saw you dancing at the Stork Club, and you sang the lyrics of the song into the ear of the man you were dancing with, and I thought to myself, 'This is the reason I came to New York, to see people like this.' "

"That was probably Billy," she answered, smiling. "He used to love it when I did that."

The wine came. I poured for us both. She drank a glass in a few swallows, and I poured her another.

"I couldn't sleep," she said finally. She did not raise her voice to combat the din of the room. Instead she turned her head and leaned toward me, her chin on her hand, so that she talked directly into my ear. "You're the first person who ever said that to me, what you said about Esme Bland."

"Was it true?"

"Do many people know that? Is it a thing that's said about me, that I was married before Billy Grenville and not divorced?"

"I don't think so. No one believed Esme," I said.

"She's in the bins, Esme," said Ann.

"So you said."

"Funny that she would have known."

"Is it true?"

"Billy bought an airplane a week before he died. The plant where they built the plane was in the very same little town in southwest Kansas where I was born and where I fled from when I was seventeen and had returned to only once, when I went home to bury my mother. It was just a coincidence. I didn't know until the night he died that that was where he'd gone to buy the plane."

"And that's where Billy found out?"

"He said at the factory that he thought his wife was from that town, but no one remembered me, which is the way I always wanted it. But one of the men at the aircraft plant called Billy later at the motel where he was staying and they went out for dinner in a Chinese restaurant, and he told Billy that if his wife's name was Urse Mertens, he was married to me."

I reached for the bottle of wine. She placed her fingers over the glass to tell me that she cared for no more, but I poured anyway, over her fingers, between her fingers, filling her glass again, and all the time she went on talking, so absorbed was she in releasing her secrets, even licking her wine-coated fingers before drying them on a cocktail napkin, as if she had not noticed.

"His name was Veblen. Billy Bob Veblen. I was only married to him for two days, and he went off to join the Marines. Then I left Kansas City for New York to do an audition for George White's Scandals, which I didn't get, but I never went back. I changed my name and started a career in clubs. I always intended to get a divorce one day, but I didn't do anything about it, and then I met Billy Grenville, and everything happened so quickly."

"I always heard you met and married in ten days," I said, but she seemed not to have heard me and proceeded with her story at her own pace as the noise level in the ship's bar grew louder and louder.

"There's no way to describe to you what it was like, the romance, the glamour of it, being pursued by a young man like Billy Grenville. It was like being in the midst of a drama, and nothing, absolutely nothing, was going to mar that chance for me, to make a marriage like that. The reason he fell so madly in love with me—and make no mistake about that, he did fall madly in love with me, in a way that he could never have fallen madly in love with any of the ladies of his own circle—was that I saved him from what he most deeply feared about himself."

"What was that?" I asked.

"You of all people ought to be able to figure that one out, Basil. It happened in a lot of those families. And he wasn't going to let me go. His family hated me. Oh, they were polite and courteous, as they always are, even to this day, but I was not what they had in mind for their darling Junior, which is what they called him in those days. When they saw he was determined, his mother tried to talk him into waiting until after the war, but if we had done that, it never would have happened. I knew I could only marry him if it happened quickly. One more obstacle besides the fact that I was a show girl, like having to get a divorce first, or even being divorced, and I would have lost him, and I took the chance."

"Go on," I urged quietly, as she seemed to falter.

"I used to live in horror that what happened would happen, that Billy would someday find out, but when it didn't, I gradually forgot about it, that first marriage, and as the years went by it became to me like a thing that never happened. And then about six months before the acc—before Billy was killed, I saw my first husband in the coffee shop of the Astor

Hotel and pretended I didn't know who he was. It was like an omen of what was going to happen."

"What was he doing there?"

"He was on a convention for the aircraft plant where Billy later bought his plane," she said. "It was all in the works, I guess. I'll say this for Billy. He was always a gentleman. He asked me for a divorce on the way to Edith Bleeker's party that night, and I turned him down flat, saying he knew my price, which was exactly half of all his money, knowing he'd never agree to that. I still thought I had the upper hand. It wasn't until we got home from Edith's party, where I had made an ass out of myself over a phone call Billy got, that he told me he'd met my first husband and that I was still married to him when we were married. He called me Mrs. Veblen. It was like the bottom fell out of my life. It meant that he didn't even have to leave me with sufficient financial provision. I panicked, you see. I totally panicked. The only thing I could think of was the newspapers saying that I was a bigamist. He went in to take a shower, and I went down to the gun room and got the gun. There was that prowler, you remember. Fortuituous, that prowler. Billy had said, about the prowler, that we would shoot first and ask questions later. I screamed, as if the prowler were in the house, and Billy came charging in and I fired twice and killed him. I didn't know what I'd done until after I'd done it, and then it was too late."

She pulled back from me, reached in her bag, and got out a cigarette. While I reached for a match, she lit her own cigarette, inhaled deeply, and exhaled as she quietly said, "People say I got away with it. Ha. Do you call this getting away with it? Sometimes I wonder if prison wouldn't have been better."

I didn't answer, nor did she expect me to. "It was madness what I did," she went on. "I thought his family would turn on me, publicly disavow me. I thought the shooting would be proof positive to them that I was everything they ever thought I was, and worse.

"But no. They publicly embraced me, for all the world to see. They stood by me. They said they believed me. They said they grieved for me.

"And they did. Publicly. Privately was something else. But you see, Basil, Alice Grenville didn't do it for me. She did it for my children. For the Grenville name.

"And what I have come to realize over the years is that Billy would have done the same thing. He would never have denounced me as a bigamist at the time of our marriage. Whatever else he was, he was a gentleman, and he wouldn't have done that to his children. He would have let me divorce him on ordinary grounds and probably have taken good care of me. It's what I think about."

She began to look about for her bag and cigarettes and made preparations for leaving. "I used to fear my past coming out, the secrets of my humble origins, about which I was then ashamed, but am no longer. Then all my secrets came out, after the shooting, and it didn't matter anymore." She stood up. "Be kind to me, Basil," she said and walked out.

When I awakened the next morning, late and hungover, I noticed a note had been slipped under my door. It said simply, "Dear Basil: By the time you receive this, I will have disembarked. I am flying from Fairbanks directly back to New York. Love, Ann Grenville."

INSIDE THE house in Oyster Bay, the real estate woman, Mrs. Pratt, was showing the house to one of the new buyers, a priest named Father Kiley. "It is no more than a meter," she said. She meant the distance between what had once been the bedrooms of Billy and Ann Grenville. She meant that however long a meter was, it was too short a distance not to be able to distinguish that the figure one shot at was one's husband. She meant that it was unlikely, at such a short distance, to mistake one's naked husband for a prowler. But she said none of these things, only that it was no more than a meter between their two rooms. To this small group of priests who would soon be occupying the country home that had once been called the Playhouse, its murderous history that had frightened off potential purchasers for years was the thing that had made it financially feasible for them.

Outside, Ann Grenville, there for a last look at the closed-up structure, said to the young priest, Father Hodiac, who walked about the untended grounds with her, "I've always had a passion for this house. I've always felt about it as a lover feels." Tears welled up in her eyes but did not fall. "I came here one night to a dance, and I said to Billy Grenville, 'This is the house where we must live.' It wasn't even for sale, but we bought it anyway, as if it were meant for us to have it. A pity you never saw my garden. We loved it here, all of us. Odd that it should have been the scene where everything ended."

She walked away from him. Her hands were in the pockets of her coat. She was having, Father Hodiac supposed, a private moment about her smashed life, and he did not follow her. Instead he sat on a wooden garden bench in the chilled comfort of the October sun and surveyed the overgrown flower beds of the Grenvilles' Playhouse. In time she sat beside him on the bench.

"Nice," he said.

"What?"

"These garden benches."

"I bought those in England. They used to be at Kingswood Castle, near Salisbury. You can have them."

"Oh, no, no, Mrs. Grenville."

"What in the world am I going to do with them?"

"They're beautiful."

"I'd like you to have them."

"It's odd about you, Mrs. Grenville," said Father Hodiac.

"What's odd?"

"You're much nicer than people say you are. If I had only hearsay to go on, I wouldn't have thought much of you."

"Perhaps you've caught me in a rare tender moment, Father Hodiac."

"Perhaps not."

"I tend to wear out my welcomes."

Through the woods came the sound of horses' hooves and laughter. They turned to look as two riders in tweed jackets, jodhpurs, and velvet riding hats cantered along a bridle path onto the grounds of the Grenville property.

"Those people are coming on your land," said Father Hodiac.

"People on horseback are allowed to ride across all the estates," she answered. "Some kind of North Shore communal courtesy borrowed from the English." She turned back, faced away from them. They, unaware they were being observed, rode closer to the house than they would have if it had been occupied.

"Oh, God, it's the Twombleys," said Ann.

"Who?" asked the priest.

"Alfred and Jeanne Twombley."

"Horseracing?"

She seemed to draw herself into her coat and sink down in the wooden bench as if she wanted them to ride by without seeing her.

"Ann," cried the woman, reining in her horse. "Is that you? Alfred, look, it's Ann Grenville."

"Ann," said Alfred Twombley.

Ann rose from the bench and walked across the lawn toward them. As she did, her stance and gait changed, and in a few steps across the hard ground her enormous style returned to her.

"Hello," she said to them.

"It's been years," said Jeanne.

"Forever," she answered.

"We were so sorry about Third."

"He was lovely, Third," answered Ann.

"Are you going to open the house again?" asked Alfred.

"I've sold it. I've just come to look at it for the last time," she answered.

"Not developers, I hope."

"Priests," she answered.

"Priests?"

"They're turning the music room into a chapel. Now your maids can walk through the woods to Mass, Alfred, and you won't have to get up and drive them into St. Gertrude's in Bayville every Sunday. It used to drive Billy mad, having to get up on Sundays and drive them over to St. Gertrude's, especially after a late night."

The mention of Billy's name in the conversation seemed to remind them of their relationship to each other, and a moment of silence ensued. Alfred turned back to his horse and got on.

"We're riding over to the Ebury's for tea," he said.

"Ann," said Jeanne Twombley suddenly. "Why don't you come with us? Neddie and Petal are going to be there, and then we're going to have dinner on trays back at our house. It's been so long, Ann. Come."

"Yes, do, Ann," said Alfred.

"I can't," Ann answered.

"Why?"

"I have to get back to the city. I have an engagement for dinner. Prince Tchelitchew. In fact, I should go. There's a four fifty-nine from Syosset."

They said their goodbyes.

"Could you drive me into the station, Father Hodiac?" she asked the young priest. "Or, if it's inconvenient, I could call a cab." She seemed in a hurry to be gone.

♣   ♣   ♣

I<small>N</small> S<small>YOSSET</small> she sat in the front seat of the young priest's old Oldsmobile. When her train pulled into the station, she watched it from the car but made no attempt to get out to catch it.

"You're going to miss your train," he said to her.

"It doesn't matter," she answered. "I don't have any place to go, Father. I haven't had any place to go in a long time."

"What you said to the Twombleys. About a dinner engagement, with the prince."

"I didn't want them to think I was up for grabs on a Saturday night."

"Oh, Mrs. Grenville."

"Don't feel sorry for me. Tell me I'm a silly ass with a lot of false pride, but don't feel sorry for me."

"Okay. You're a silly ass with a lot of false pride."

"And don't get too familiar either," she said and smiled at the same time. In the dark October afternoon he thought he saw the trace of a tear in her eye. "There's not another train for fifty-five minutes," she said.

"I'll wait with you."

"Are you hungry?"

"Sure."

"There's a coffee shop over on Main Street. I'll buy you the blue plate special."

T<small>HE</small> W<small>AITRESS</small> spilled the coffee into Ann Grenville's saucer. From a dispenser on the vinyl table Ann took a handful of paper napkins and dried out her saucer and the bottom of her cup and went on talking to the priest. "I acquired the look of belonging, and the manner of belonging, but I always felt like an outsider here on the North Shore. My life was a life of appearance. If I could make you believe what I was acting out, then I would have succeeded. No matter how many diamonds I put on my fingers or wrists, no matter how many Balenciaga dresses I hung in my closet, no matter how many signed French pieces I had in my various drawing rooms, no matter how many Impressionist paintings I had on my walls, I still felt I was going through life on a scholarship. Do you know anything about photography, Father?"

"A bit. Why?"

"I used to be pretty good at taking pictures. Someday I'll show you all my scrapbooks. I'm thinking of going into the business."

"What business?"

"Photography. Taking pictures professionally. There's a course they give in the extension program at NYU, and I signed up for that."

"You did?"

"Something to do. Not under my own name, of course. Ann Arden, I'm going to call myself. That's what I used to call myself before I married Billy Grenville. I've got a man coming to see me about turning Diantha's room—Diantha is my daughter—into a darkroom."

"I'd like to see that."

"If you come to town on priestly duties, give me a ring."

"I will."

"What kind of Catholic do you think I'd be, Father?"

"Are you thinking about that, too?"

"I don't know."

"We should talk. How's your week?"

"Wednesday afternoon there's an auction of French furniture from Madam Balsan's estate at Parke-Bernet. That's my week."

She began to gather up her things from the orange Naugahyde booth where they were sitting. "I think I hear my train."

"Are you going to be all right, Mrs. Grenville?"

"Yes, I'm going to be fine."

"I'll call you when I'm in town."

"Yes, do, Father. I'll take you to the Côte Basque for lunch.

You'll like that. And don't forget about that outdoor furniture. It's yours. Goodbye."

She was gone.

MRS. GRENVILLE rarely missed an afternoon at the auctions. Although shunned by people she once knew, she found herself always welcome at Parke-Bernet, where, on even the most crowded days, a seat was found for her. Mrs. Grenville was a bidder and a buyer, and her knowledge of French furniture of the eighteenth century was respected by the authorities of the auction house. She enjoyed the afternoons there more than sitting in a movie house because she liked to watch the people and feel a part of the excitement. She understood how to bid. While less experienced buyers held up paddles with numbers on them, she simply nodded her head, almost imperceptibly, when the auctioneer looked at her.

"Sold to Mrs. Grenville," said the auctioneer.

People turned around to look at her. She rose to leave.

"Nicely priced, that pair of *bergères*," said Mr. Crocus of Parke-Bernet, catching up with her at the entrance of the room. Mr. Crocus admired Mrs. Grenville.

"I need another gilt *bergère* chair like I need a hole in the head," replied Ann. They looked at each other quickly, in embarrassment, at her using the expression "hole in the head." "I'll have to do a bit of rearranging of furniture at home to make room. Perhaps you'd let me keep all this here for a bit until I decide where to put everything."

"Of course," said Mr. Crocus.

At the entrance on Madison Avenue she ran into Prince Tchelitchew, who was coming in as she was leaving. He kissed her hand.

"I'd hoped to get here," he said, "but I was detained at Petal Wilson's lunch."

"It's all right," replied Ann. She seemed muted, and he had expected anger.

"How was the auction?"

"Another auction."

"What did you buy?"

"Some things I don't need and don't have room for."

"You seem down."

"No, I'm fine."

"Shall I put you in a taxi?"

"I think I'll walk."

"Awfully cold."

"I don't mind."

"Shall I walk with you?"

"If you like."

She pulled her sable coat around her and started up Madison Avenue. After nine blocks they turned west toward Fifth Avenue.

"Isn't that the house where you used to live?" he asked suddenly.

"No," she said. "I never lived in that house."

"Why did I think that?"

"My mother-in-law lived in that house for fifty years. My husband grew up in that house. My son jumped out the window of that house. But, no, I never lived there."

"What is it now?"

"Something religious, I believe. If Billy hadn't died, we were supposed to have moved in there after his mother died. It was what his father wanted. It's a bad-luck house."

"Beautiful chandelier," he said, looking up into the windows of the vast gray stone house.

"Once that chandelier fell on the day before a ball and killed the man who was cleaning it, and the ball went on the next night, and no one mentioned that a man was killed."

"Dear."

"People say I'm tough, I know. But my mother-in-law's

tougher. I don't get away with it, though, and she does. People think of her as a saint."

"Do you still see her?"

"Sometimes. Rarely now. For years, when I was living abroad, she would give a dinner for me every time I came back to visit New York, but that petered out."

"Here you are home."

"Thank you, Alexis. I'd ask you in, but I'm tired."

"Are you all right, Ann?"

"Yes, yes, I'm fine."

Inside she went through her mail on the hall table. In a manila envelope delivered by messenger was an advance copy of *Monsieur*, an elegant magazine with a literary following, containing a chapter from Basil Plant's long-awaited novel, intended to prove to his detractors that his writing career was neither blocked nor finished. An interior warning let her know that the contents of the magazine pertained to her. She could see Basil Plant's face on the ship to Alaska listening to her, studying her, writing in his mind as she knew he had been writing. Without removing her heavy sable coat, she walked into her overcrowded drawing room that she would have to rearrange to accommodate her afternoon's acquisitions, switched on a lamp, sat down in the center of a white damask sofa, and began to read the chapter called "Annie Get Your Gun."

SHE WAS STILL in her sable coat when she finished reading Basil Plant's story an hour later. For a long time she simply sat on her white damask sofa in her overcrowded drawing room, lit by a single lamp, and looked off into space. She had for years given the impression that she was impervious to the slights and barbs of others, because she thought that one day it would end, that her atonement would be recognized. But that was not to be. Basil's piece brought up the old story again, for a new generation to gloat over, like a wound that would never heal. Basil Plant had called her what no one had ever called her in print before. He had called her a murderess.

An immense weariness came over her. Rising, she looked at herself in a gilt mirror over the mantelpiece. In the semi-darkened room, she saw herself as she had once looked in her glamorous heyday as Mrs. William Grenville, Junior, and, face to face with herself, made her decision. For weeks she had been only going through the motions of life; death had been lingering in the outskirts of her mind. She was tired of running away and had run out of places to run away to. She took a bottle of vodka from her long-unused liquor cabinet. In the kitchen she put ice in a glass and more ice in a silver bowl.

Upstairs, she drew a bath and filled her tub with scented oil. She bathed with purpose and did not linger in the warm comforts of her sunken tub. She put fresh linen sheets on her bed. She wound her vermeil clock. From a drawer she took a satin-and-lace nightgown made for her in Paris, and a negligee to match, and put them on. She sat at her makeup table and made up her face and perfumed her body. She was glad that she had had her hair and nails done that day. She took off her sapphire and diamond rings and watched them reflected doubly in the mirrored top of her dressing table. She wanted those to be for Diantha.

A longing for her daughter overcame her. They had not spoken, nor been in contact, for several years. She worried how Basil Plant's story would affect Diantha, even in the faraway life she had picked for herself. She picked up the receiver and dialed her daughter in Seattle. The telephone rang and rang without a reply. She wondered if it was still the right number that she had. Then it was picked up.

"Miss Grenville's residence."

"Is she there?"

"This is the answering service. She's not here."

"Do you know where I can reach her?"

"No."

"Is she in Seattle, or is she traveling?"

"I don't know. Would you like to leave a message?"

"Tell her her mother called."

"Does she have a number where she can reach you?"

"Just give her the message. Thank you."

She hung up the telephone and then picked it up again and dialed the private number of her mother-in-law. On the day Alice Grenville realized people were deferring to her in bridge, because she was old, she had ceased to play except with her nurses, although it was one of the few things left that she enjoyed. Shortly thereafter, she had withdrawn to her apartment high in the Waldorf Towers and did not venture forth again. In time she stopped receiving and maintained contact only on the telephone. Only nurses, maids, daughters, and an occasional grandchild glimpsed her in her decline. Bertie Lightfoot, encountering old friends in restaurants or at parties, always said, "Phone Alice, and tell her about the party. She loves to hear everything. She's sharp as a tack still. It's just physically she's so unwell."

"Hello?" It was the voice of a very old woman.

"Alice?"

"Yes, who is it? Speak up."

"It's Ann."

"Oh, Ann. What is it?"

"I'm trying to locate Diantha. I wondered if you knew where she was."

"She lives in Seattle."

"I know, but she's not there, and I thought she might have been in touch with you. You see, I haven't seen her in quite a while, and I would like to talk to her."

"Is something the matter?"

"I need to talk to her."

"I'm playing bridge, Ann. Couldn't you call tomorrow?"

"Goodbye, Mère."

She had not called her mother-in-law Mère for many years, and Alice listened.

"I'm sorry," said Ann, very quietly.

"About what?" asked Alice.

Ann's answer could scarcely be heard. "About Billy," she said.

"You'll have to talk louder, Ann. You know I have trouble hearing. What are you sorry about?"

"I'm sorry that I disturbed your bridge game."

She sat down at her ormolu escritoire and began to write a letter to her daughter. "I want to set the record straight," she wrote, offering her estranged child the explanation she had never given her. From the bathroom cabinet she took a vial of Seconal pills and began, slowly, to swallow them with the iced vodka as she wrote.

She remembered that in her closet, hidden behind racks of clothes and furs, was the Salvador Dali portrait, and she wanted to look at it. The pills were starting to work, and she knew that she had to act quickly. She pulled the picture out and looked at it. The slash where she had once attacked it with a knife had been repaired, she could not remember how. She looked at the face of the beautiful young woman in whom the artist had seen evil. She wondered why she had not destroyed the picture. Weakened by her intake of pills, she had to return to her bed before she could replace the picture in its hiding place.

On her bed she picked up her telephone once more and dialed the number of her house in Oyster Bay. The telephone was immediately answered.

"Hello?"

"May I speak with Father Hodiac, please."

"This is Father Hodiac."

"This is Ann Grenville, Father."

"Oh, Mrs. Grenville." His voice sounded glad to hear her. "Has the man come to see you about your darkroom yet?"

"The darkroom? I don't understand."

"For your photography."

"Oh, no, not yet."

"Are you all right, Mrs. Grenville?"

"Yes." Her voice was weak. "Father?"

"Yes?"

"I'm not a Catholic."

"I know."

"Can you pray for someone who's not a Catholic?"

"Of course."

"Pray for me, Father."

"Of course."

"Do you like the house?"

"Oh, yes."

"Once I went upstairs in that house, after my husband's death, and I was standing in the bedroom where my children had slept when they were little. From downstairs, way on the other side of the house, in the rooms where my husband and I slept, I could hear people talking as clearly as if they were in the room next to me. Through some acoustical fluke in the architecture, their voices carried up through the walls. That was how I realized that my children had heard their father and me fight on the night that he was killed. It has always haunted me. If you should ever meet my daughter, Diantha, will you tell her that, Father? Will you tell her I'm sorry? Will you tell her I love her."

"Mrs. Grenville, are you all right?"

"Promise, Father."

"I promise."

"I have to go, Father."

As she lay there dying, her hair, makeup, dress, nails, all perfectly attended to, she wondered if anyone would come to her funeral. She wondered if Alice Grenville would bury her next to Billy and Third in the family plot. She even wondered about God, if there really was more afterward, if you really did meet up with those who had gone before. She looked forward to the possibility of encountering Billy Grenville.

❧   ❧   ❧

THE OBITUARY said Ann Grenville had been found dead in her duplex apartment on upper Fifth Avenue. It said she was the widow of sportsman William Grenville, Junior, the mother of Diantha Grenville, the daughter-in-law of Alice Grenville, the philanthropist. It said she had a history of heart ailments. It said she was fifty-two years old. It said she had been cleared in 1955 of slaying her husband.

A LOT OF PEOPLE didn't see the obituary, and by the time the word was out, most of the ones who might have come had gone to the country for the weekend. The service took place at St. James' Episcopal Church, on Madison Avenue and Seventy-first Street, with not a single photographer or reporter in sight and barely thirty people in attendance. The thing that was on each person's mind was the other funeral of twenty years before, the companion piece to this, when one thousand people had crowded into the same church, with thousands more lined up outside to watch, and the flags of the Brook Club, the Union Club, the Knickerbocker Club, and the Racquet Club had flown at half-mast, in tribute. No flags flew today.

One who did see the obituary was Babette Van Degan. She became aware of the slow thump of her heartbeat against her ample breast. Tears welled in her eyes. If Ann Grenville had been hovering about, as some think the dead do, watching the reactions to her demise, she would have been surprised to see that Babette Van Degan, who had not figured importantly in the events of her life for many years, exhibited a remorse, in the privacy of her boudoir, greater than that of any of the principal players in her story. But then, for someone who created the role she played in life, as Ann Grenville had created her role, she very often misjudged the effects of her spectacular performance.

"They could have held this at the side altar," whispered Babette to the man beside her, Bertie Lightfoot, as they waited in a pew midway in the nearly empty church for the service to begin. "Surprised to see you here, Bertie," she added when he did not reply.

"I'm only here because of dear Alice," whispered Bertie Lightfoot in his precise and slightly sibilant voice, feeling it necessary to declare what branch of the grand Grenville family he was allied with. "Alice is my friend."

Babette looked sideways at Bertie Lightfoot and decided not to say what it was on her mind to say. Instead she took in his exquisitely groomed self and leaned closer toward him, squinting her eyes, knowing how uncomfortable it made him, and decided his eyes had been "done" and his reddish-tinged hair touched up.

"I didn't know Ann had a history of heart ailments," whispered Bertie in a conciliatory manner, anxious to have Babette's scrutiny of him terminated.

"She wasn't fifty-two either, darling, as you perfectly well know," answered Babette, pulling the voluminous folds of her mink coat around her. She was glad the weather had turned autumnal and brisk. She was sick to death of Indian summer. She felt less obese when she could lose herself in her furs.

"You mean she didn't have a history of heart ailments?" whispered Bertie again, a bit of excitement in his whisper, as it began to dawn on him what might have happened.

"Shhhh," said Babette, tapping the forefinger of her gloved hand against her lips, smearing it with lipstick the way she smeared her coffee cups with lipstick. "Your eyebrows are hitting what used to be your hairline."

"You don't mean . . . ?"

"There's your friend Alice coming in."

"She's such a wonderful woman," said Bertie. Whenever people mentioned Alice Grenville's name, they invariably said about her that she was a wonderful woman. Everyone knew what she had done for her daughter-in-law.

"Did you ever stop to think how many caskets she's followed down this aisle?" asked Babette.

Bertie Lightfoot looked back to where the eight pallbearers were lining up, four to a side, by the rose-covered casket in the rear of the church, and then back at Babette Van Degan again, questions churning within him.

Alice Grenville moved slowly down the aisle to the front pew of the church where she had worshiped most of her life. Tall, slender, erect of carriage, her only concession to her advanced years was the ivory-handled ebony cane that she carried. Black-veiled, formidable still, she evoked feelings of awe from the scattered assemblage. She stared straight ahead, but it was not lost on her how few were there, or even that Babette Van Degan, a name from the past, had grown enormously fat.

Beside Alice, but not assisting her as one assists the elderly, walked and sat her granddaughter Diantha Grenville. Hatless, plainly dressed, only just returned to New York for the occasion at hand, she was unmistakably her parents' daughter, although she possessed neither the beauty of Ann Grenville nor the aristocratic elegance of Billy Grenville. Like her grandmother, she was there to do her duty.

Old Dr. Kinsolving, who had performed at Grenville baptisms, weddings, and funerals for nearly forty years, was gone, of course, long since dead, and a new minister, without connections to the family, went about the religious duties: a few psalms; a hymn, some prayers for the dead; no personal words of farewell; the amenities observed, nothing more.

Alice Grenville looked up at the rose window that she had given in memory of the three William Grenvilles who had gone before her, her husband William, her son Billy, and her grandson Third. The late-morning sun shone through its stained glass, and rose and violet rays fell on her and Diantha, missing the casket of Ann Grenville.

Her doctor had forbidden her to make the long journey to Woodlawn Cemetery, but Alice overruled his decision, as she knew she was going to when she agreed to comply with it, and accompanied the small cortege to watch her daughter-in-law be buried in the Grenville plot, between her husband and her son. Never could it be said of Alice Grenville that she had failed to honor her beloved son's widow.

AFTERWARD, for the reception, the receiving of the loyal who had attended the service and journeyed to Woodlawn Cemetery, Diantha volunteered to take over the hostess obligations at her mother's apartment on Fifth Avenue, freeing her grandmother to return to her own home, her duties completed. Ann Grenville's apartment was shortly to be sold and its contents to be auctioned. James Crocus, of the Parke-Bernet auctioneer firm, was already at work—sorting, cataloguing, appraising—but he remained upstairs throughout.

Some of the guests knew each other. Some of them didn't. A few came out of curiosity, attracted by the negative glamour of Ann Grenville's story. There was Babette Van Degan, of course, and Bertie Lightfoot, and Kay Kay Somerset, and Prince Tchelitchew, who had been friends of Ann's at different points in her life. There was a Brazilian woman whose name none of them seemed to know. There was a crisp and tweedy Miss Petrie, who had once been a social secretary for Ann. And a few others. And me, Basil Plant, who looked and felt awkward, as if I should not have been there.

The entrance hall had a black-and-white marble floor and a graceful winding stairway. To the right was the drawing room where they gathered. It was a high-ceilinged gilt-and-white room, but dark. Antique furniture, in far too great abundance, filled it in multiple groupings in the French manner. She always had far too much furniture, far too many dresses, far too many fur coats, far too many pairs of shoes. It was one of the things about her that gave her away. Of course, there were very good pictures in gilt frames lit from above, and collections of jade and porcelain and Fabergé eggs. A cheerless fire beneath an elaborate mantelpiece did not draw the group to it. Among the disparate company there was a low-spirited intimacy, for the common bond of the occasion, that would evaporate at the completion of the rite.

"It was good of you to come," said Diantha, repeating the same words to each, but she remained a hostess on the outskirts of the gathering. Bottles and glasses crowded an ornate table, and she indicated self-service, with a wave of her hand, when the single servant, a butler from a catering agency, was hard pressed in pouring and passing and replenishing. No frou-frou about her, I noticed. She picked up a bellows and began to puff at the dying fire, coaxing it back, until the firelight danced on her face.

"Hello, Mrs. Van Degan," she said.

"Oh, Dolly, it's been so many years," said Babette.

"I'm not called Dolly anymore. It's Diantha. I always hated the name Dolly. I think my mother used to think that Dolly Grenville would look good in the society columns when I was a debutante, but I never became a debutante and my name never appears in columns."

"Where is it you live?" asked Babette.

"Seattle," replied Diantha.

"And what's that like?"

"Quite nice."

"Far from the madding crowd, I suppose?"

"The very point." She smiled for the first time. Her looks grew on you as she talked, I noticed, watching the exchange. There was a shyness about her that was appealing.

"You sounded like your mother when you said that," said Babette. Diantha rose from her kneeling position by the fire, placed her fingertips on the mantelpiece between delicate pieces of china on teakwood stands, and stared into the re-newed fire. It occurred to me that she was not, perhaps, pleased with the comparison to her mother.

The Brazilian lady approached to speak to Diantha. Turn-ing too abruptly to acknowledge her, she knocked over a piece of china, and it crashed to the hearth, smashing. People rushed forward to assist. "It doesn't matter," said Diantha, meaning it, waving away their concern for smashed porcelain. She is nothing like her mother, I thought. For her mother it would have been a tragic experience.

Some of the people she remembered, like Bertie Lightfoot, who had decorated all their houses. Others she didn't, like Kay Kay Somerset, except by name. A few she had never known, like Prince Tchelitchew, who had entered her moth-er's life after her own defection from it.

"You're meant to take anything you want to take," said Diantha, waving around the room, indicating other rooms, and upstairs, with her expressive hands. "As a memento, if you desire, of Mother. It is what she would have wanted."

"Except the Balenciaga dresses," piped in the crisp and tweedy Miss Petrie, a model of efficiency. She put her clip-board bearing lists and check marks and Polaroid photographs of paintings on one of a pair of glass-topped tables skirted in heavy velvet and covered with small objects of great value, each with its individual history. "The Balenciaga dresses are earmarked for the Fashion Institute."

"Except the Balenciaga dresses," repeated Diantha, not caring, but remembering other instructions. "And, oh yes, certain of the paintings. The Modigliani, the two Vuillards, the Fantan La Tour, the Manet of the prunes, the Cézanne drawings, and the Bonnard of the two women. They are going to the Metropolitan Museum. Other than that." She shrugged, or shuddered faintly, as she indicated her mother's possessions.

Racks of dresses and shoes and furs were out on display in

the dining room, and the table was laden with pieces of silver. Babette Van Degan, the richest by far of the assembled group, took a sable coat. Bertie Lightfoot could not decide between two Fabergé eggs and was told he could take both. Kay Kay Somerset, who loathed Ann Grenville but liked to go to funerals, took the small vermeil clock that King Ludwig had given to the Empress Elizabeth. The Brazilian lady picked a pair of Georgian candlesticks, and Prince Tchelitchew decided upon, of all things, the Salvador Dali portrait of Ann that had so enraged her she had gone to court over it.

During the rummage-sale atmosphere, I sought out Miss Petrie. "There's that lovely little jade Chinese clock. Would you like that?" she asked, trying to be helpful.

"No, no, thank you," I said.

"There's the Allejo Vidal-Quadras drawings of her. And the René Bouché portrait's lovely, in the white evening dress."

"There's something I must know, Miss Petrie," I said.

"Luggage!" she cried, clapping her hands as if the solution had been found. "She had all the good kind of Vuitton, before the wrong sort of people took it up. Masses of it."

"Do you happen to know if she received a manila envelope I mailed her?"

"A manila envelope?"

"With a magazine inside."

"What magazine?"

"*Monsieur.*"

"I don't recall seeing it. Why?"

"Would you tell me something, Miss Petrie?" I looked around to make sure no one was listening.

"If I can."

"Did Mrs. Grenville commit suicide?"

"No." She clipped the word and closed her eyes, signifying a termination to the way the conversation had turned.

"It's vital that I know."

"The medical examiner's report isn't in yet."

"Did she leave a note?"

"Mrs. Grenville had a history of heart ailments."

"So I read."

A burst of thunder and the sound of rain against the curtained windows ended our conversation. People started to leave. When the door opened, fat round raindrops plopped on the sidewalk noisily.

"How about that photograph of Mrs. Grenville on safari in India, with the ten-foot tiger she shot?" suggested Miss Petrie, wanting to be rid of me. "She was so proud of that."

"No, thank you."

"There must be something, Mr. Plant."

"An umbrella," I answered.

"An umbrella?" repeated Miss Petrie.

"Yes," I said. "That's all I want."

My choice resulted in a single moment of intimacy, only a look, between myself and Diantha, as if she understood that, like her, I didn't want anything either in this stage set of props and dressing.

"Goodbye," I said to her.

She, not knowing me, made a vague gesture of farewell.

Upstairs, in a drawer of the escritoire that had once belonged to Marie Antoinette, James Crocus, the man from Parke-Bernet, found an advance copy of *Monsieur*. In the magazine was an unsealed envelope containing a letter on pale-blue stationery written in the hand he had come to recognize as Ann Grenville's. "Dear Diantha," the letter began. "I would like to set the record straight."

Propriety did not allow James Crocus to peer further, but, in replacing the pale-blue pages with shaking fingers in their matching envelope, he could not help but read these words: "When last we met, you said to me, 'Don't you think at some point in our lives you owed us an explanation, Third and me, about what happened, what really happened, that night?' Now Mr. Basil Plant has taken it upon himself to tell, not

only you, but anyone with the price of a magazine what I
promised your grandmother I would never tell. . . ."

YESTERDAY EVENING, dining at Le Cirque, at a less good
table than I used to receive, I looked up from the desultory
chatter of my companion, the former wife of a television
personality, whom, in truth, I would not have had time for
in the days when I was riding high, and peered straight into
the relentless stare of Diantha Grenville. My face, already
flushed from red wine, pinkened in distress, and our eyes
locked for what seemed an eternity, every eon of which I
hated. It was she, finally, who broke the look, and when her
eyes discharged mine I saw in them the disdain of the two
Mrs. Grenvilles, her grandmother Alice and her mother Ann.
  Don't you think it's odd how, in death, people beatify for
sainthood the most unlikely prospects? Bratsie Bleeker, for
instance. Everyone knows that Bratsie was shot because he
was screwing the wife of the foreman on his mother's plantation, but to have listened to Edith Bleeker, in the years after
Bratsie's elimination, you would have thought that Bratsie
died helping the Boat People. Such is the strange command-
ing power of death. It's the same thing with Diantha Grenville. She couldn't stand her mother. Everyone knows that.
They didn't even speak for the last two years. But once her
mother died, that all changed. She lives, they say, in rooms
as overcrowded as her mother's, with all that French furniture
that once belonged to famous ladies that her mother collected
for so many years, and that Diantha always laughed at. Diantha tried to see me several times, but there was no point to
that. Once I did see her, face to face, on Ninth Street, in the
Village. I screamed at her, "Stop following me!" How was I
to know her psychiatrist was in the same building that my
psychiatrist was in?

No. No. No. I am not responsible for what happened to Ann Grenville. I don't care what that priest said that she telephoned at the last minute. Imagine Ann Grenville asking someone to pray for her! So likely. That's the trouble with those Catholic priests. They always think everyone wants to convert. Her trouble was that she had all those face lifts, and the wrinkles were still coming, and there were no longer men in attendance as there had been all her life, and without a man around, she couldn't function. "I always like to see a man's shoes in my closet." That was one of her lines.

There was nothing in my story that she had not told me herself, or that I had not heard firsthand from someone in her life. At least, almost all of it. I wanted not to let go of my theory. I didn't want it to turn out to be an accident, like she said, in that story she stuck to, like Bette Davis in *The Letter*.

Last night I dreamed of Alice Grenville. Her face was covered with mourning veils, but I was able to see through them to her. She was trying to tell me something, but I could not understand what it was that she was trying to tell me, except that she was, slowly, shaking her head, as if telling me that I had intruded into places where I did not belong. She was, I suppose, still protecting her daughter-in-law, from outsiders, like me, as if, finally, she, and the rest of them, had accepted Ann as one of them.